Titles by Nora Roberts

HOT ICE
SACRED SINS
BRAZEN VIRTUE
SWEET REVENGE
PUBLIC SECRETS
GENUINE LIES
CARNAL INNOCENCE
DIVINE EVIL
HONEST ILLUSIONS
PRIVATE SCANDALS
BORN IN FIRE
BORN IN ICE
BORN IN SHAME
HIDDEN RICHES
TRUE BETRAYALS
DARING TO DREAM
HOLDING THE DREAM
FINDING THE DREAM
MONTANA SKY
SEA SWEPT
RISING TIDES
INNER HARBOR
SANCTUARY
HOMEPORT
THE REEF

ONCE UPON A CASTLE
(anthology with Jill Gregory, Ruth Ryan Langan, and Marianne Willman)

FROM THE HEART *(anthology)*

SILENT NIGHT
(anthology with Susan Plunkett, Dee Holmes, and Claire Cross)

Titles written as J. D. Robb

NAKED IN DEATH
GLORY IN DEATH
IMMORTAL IN DEATH
RAPTURE IN DEATH
CEREMONY IN DEATH
VENGEANCE IN DEATH
HOLIDAY IN DEATH
CONSPIRACY IN DEATH

CONSPIRACY IN DEATH

J. D. Robb

BERKLEY BOOKS, NEW YORK

CONSPIRACY IN DEATH

A Berkley Book / published by arrangement with
the author

PRINTING HISTORY
Berkley edition / April 1999

The Penguin Putnam Inc. World Wide Web site address is
http://www.penguinputnam.com

ISBN: 0-425-16813-1

BERKLEY®
Berkley Books are published by The Berkley Publishing Group,
a division of Penguin Putnam Inc.,
375 Hudson Street, New York, New York 10014.
BERKLEY and the "B" logo
are trademarks belonging to Penguin Putnam Inc.

PRINTED IN THE UNITED STATES OF AMERICA

10 9 8 7 6 5 4 3 2 1

All men think all men mortal but themselves.

—Edward Young

Let us hob-and-nob with Death.

—Tennyson

CONSPIRACY
IN
DEATH

prologue

In my hands is power. The power to heal or to destroy. To grant life or to cause death. I revere this gift, have honed it over time to an art as magnificent and awesome as any painting in the Louvre.

I am art, I am science. In all the ways that matter, I am God.

God must be ruthless and far-sighted. God studies his creations and selects. The best of these creations must be cherished, protected, sustained. Greatness rewards perfection.

Yet even the flawed have purpose.

A wise God experiments, considers, uses what comes into His hands and forges wonders. Yes, often without mercy, often with a violence the ordinary condemn.

We who hold power cannot be distracted by the condemnations of the ordinary, by the petty and pitiful laws of simple men. They are blind, their minds are closed with fear—fear of pain, fear of death. They are too limited to comprehend that death can be conquered.

I have nearly done so.

If my work was discovered, they, with their foolish laws and attitudes, would damn me.

When my work is complete, they will worship me.

chapter one

For some, death wasn't the enemy. Life was a much less merciful opponent. For the ghosts who drifted through the nights like shadows, the funky-junkies with their pale pink eyes, the chemi-heads with their jittery hands, life was simply a mindless trip that circled from one fix to the next with the arcs between a misery.

The trip itself was most often full of pain and despair, and occasionally terror.

For the poor and displaced in the bowels of New York City in the icy dawn of 2059, the pain, the despair, the terror were constant companions. For the mental defectives and physically flawed who slipped through society's cracks, the city was simply another kind of prison.

There were social programs, of course. It was, after all, an enlightened time. So the politicians claimed, with the Liberal Party shouting for elaborate new shelters, educational and medical facilities, training and rehabilitation centers, without actually detailing a plan for how such programs would be funded. The Conservative Party gleefully cut the budgets of what programs were already in place, then made staunch speeches on the quality of life and family.

Still, shelters were available for those who qualified and could stomach the thin and sticky hand of charity. Training and assistance programs were offered for those who could keep sane long enough to wind their way through the endless tangled miles of bureaucratic red tape that all too often strangled the intended recipients before saving them.

And as always, children went hungry, women sold their bodies, and men killed for a handful of credits.

However enlightened the times, human nature remained as predictable as death.

For the sidewalk sleepers, January in New York brought vicious nights with a cold that could rarely be fought back with a bottle of brew or a few scavenged illegals. Some gave in and shuffled into the shelters to snore on lumpy cots under thin blankets or eat the watery soup and tasteless soy loaves served by bright-eyed sociology students. Others held out, too lost or too stubborn to give up their square of turf.

And many slipped from life to death during those bitter nights.

The city had killed them, but no one called it homicide.

As Lieutenant Eve Dallas drove downtown in the shivering dawn, she tapped her fingers restlessly on the wheel. The routine death of a sidewalk sleeper in the Bowery shouldn't have been her problem. It was a matter for what the department often called Homicide-Lite—the stiff scoopers who patrolled known areas of homeless villages to separate living from dead and take the used-up bodies to the morgue for examination, identification, and disposal.

It was a mundane and ugly little job most usually done by those who either still had hopes of joining the more elite Homicide unit or those who had given up on such a miracle. Homicide was called to the scene only when the death was clearly suspicious or violent.

And, Eve thought, if she hadn't been on top of the rotation for such calls on this miserable morning, she'd still be in her nice warm bed with her nice warm husband.

"Probably some jittery rookie hoping for a serial killer," she muttered.

Beside her, Peabody yawned hugely. "I'm really just extra weight here." From under her ruler-straight dark bangs, she sent Eve a hopeful look. "You could just drop me off at the closest transpo stop and I can be back home and in bed in ten minutes."

"If I suffer, you suffer."

"That makes me feel so . . . loved, Dallas."

Eve snorted and shot Peabody a grin. No one, she thought, was sturdier, no one was more dependable, than her aide. Even with the rudely early call, Peabody was pressed and polished in her winter-weight uniform, the buttons gleaming, the hard black cop shoes shined. In her square face framed by her dark bowl-cut hair, her eyes might have been a little sleepy, but they would see what Eve needed her to see.

"Didn't you have some big deal last night?" Peabody asked her.

"Yeah, in East Washington. Roarke had this dinner/dance thing for some fancy charity. Save the moles or something. Enough food to feed every sidewalk sleeper on the Lower East Side for a year."

"Gee, that's tough on you. I bet you had to get all dressed up in some beautiful gown, shuttle down on Roarke's private transpo, and choke down champagne."

Eve only lifted a brow at Peabody's dust-dry tone. "Yeah, that's about it." They both knew the glamorous side of Eve's life since Roarke had come into it was both a puzzlement and a frustration to her. "And then I had to dance with Roarke. A lot."

"Was he wearing a tux?" Peabody had seen Roarke in a tux. The image of it was etched in her mind like acid on glass.

"Oh yeah." Until, Eve mused, they'd gotten home and she'd ripped it off of him. He looked every bit as good out of a tux as in one.

"Man." Peabody closed her eyes, indulged herself with

a visualization technique she'd learned at her Free-Ager parents' knees. "Man," she repeated.

"You know, a lot of women would get pissed off at having their husband star in their aide's purient little fantasies."

"But you're bigger than that, Lieutenant. I like that about you."

Eve grunted, rolled her stiff shoulders. It was her own fault that lust had gotten the better of her and she'd only managed three hours of sleep. Duty was duty, and she was on it.

Now she scanned the crumbling buildings, the littered streets. The scars, the warts, the tumors that sliced or bulged over concrete and steel.

Steam whooshed up from a grate, shot out from the busy half-life of movement and commerce under the streets. Driving through it was like slicing through fog on a dirty river.

Her home, since Roarke, was a world apart from this. She lived with polished wood, gleaming crystal, the scent of candles and hothouse flowers. Of wealth.

But she knew what it was to come from such places as this. Knew how much the same they were—city by city— in smells, in routines, in hopelessness.

The streets were nearly empty. Few of the residents of this nasty little sector ventured out early. The dealers and street whores would have finished the night's business, would have crawled back into their flops before sunrise. Merchants brave enough to run the shops and stores had yet to uncode their riot bars from the doors and windows. Glide-cart vendors desperate enough to hawk this turf would carry hand zappers and work in pairs.

She spotted the black and white patrol car, scowled at the half-assed job the officers on scene had done with securing the area.

"Why the hell didn't they finish running the sensors, for Christ's sake? Get me out of bed at five in the damn morning, and they don't even have the scene secured? No wonder they're scoopers. Idiots."

Peabody said nothing as Eve braked hard behind the black and white and slammed out of the vehicle. The idiots, she thought with some sympathy, were in for an expert dressing down.

By the time Peabody climbed out of the car, Eve had already crossed the sidewalk, with long, purposeful strides, heading for the two uniforms who huddled miserably in the wind.

She watched the two officers' shoulders snap straight. The lieutenant had that effect on other cops, Peabody mused as she retrieved the field kit from the vehicle. She brought you to attention.

It wasn't just the way she looked, Peabody decided, with that long, rangy body, the simple and often disordered cap of brown hair that showed hints of blonde, hints of red, hints, Peabody thought, of everything. There were the eyes, all cop, and the color of good Irish whiskey, the little dent in the firm chin below a full mouth that could go hard as stone.

Peabody found it a strong and arresting face, partially, she decided, because Eve had no vanity whatsoever.

Although the way she looked might gain a uniform's attention, it was what she so clearly was that had them snapping straight.

She was the best damn cop Peabody had ever known. Pure cop, the kind you'd go through a door with without hesitation. The kind you knew would stand for the dead and for the living.

And the kind, Peabody mused as she walked close enough to hear the end of Eve's blistering lecture, who kicked whatever ass needed kicking.

"Now to review," Eve said coolly. "You call in a homicide, you drag my butt out of bed, you damn well have the scene secured and have your report ready for me when I get here. You don't stand here like a couple of morons sucking your thumbs. You're cops, for God's sake. Act like cops."

"Yes, sir, Lieutenant." This came in a wavery voice from the youngest of the team. He was hardly more than a boy, and the only reason Eve had pulled her verbal punch. His partner, however, wasn't a rookie, and she earned one of Eve's frigid stares.

"Yes, sir," she said between her teeth. And the lively resentment in the tone had Eve angling her head.

"Do you have a problem, Officer . . . Bowers?"

"No, sir."

Her face was the color of aged cherry wood, with her eyes a striking contrast of pale, pale blue. She kept her dark hair short under her regulation cap. There was a button missing on her standard-issue coat and her shoes were dull and scuffed. Eve could have poked her about it but decided being stuck in a miserable job was some excuse not to buff up for the day.

"Good." Eve merely nodded, but the warning in her eyes was clear. She shifted her gaze to the partner and felt a little stir of sympathy. He was pale as a sheet, shaky, and so fresh from the academy she could all but smell it on him.

"Officer Trueheart, my aide will show you the proper way to secure a scene. See that you pay attention."

"Yes, sir."

"Peabody." At the single word, her field kit was in her hand. "Show me what we've got here, Bowers."

"Indigent. Male Caucasian. Goes by the name of Snooks. This is his crib."

She gestured to a rather cleverly rigged shelter comprised of a packing crate cheerfully painted with stars and flowers and topped by the dented lid of an old recycling bin. There was a moth-eaten blanket across the entrance and a hand-drawn sign that simply said Snooks strung over it.

"He inside?"

"Yeah, part of the beat is to give a quick eye check on the cribs looking for stiffs to scoop. Snooks is pretty stiff," she said at what Eve realized after a moment was an attempt at humor.

"I bet. My, what a pleasant aroma," she muttered as

she moved closer and the wind could no longer blow the stench aside.

"That's what tipped me. It always stinks. All these people smell like sweat and garbage and worse, but a stiff has another layer."

Eve knew the layer all too well. Sweet, sickly. And here, sneaking under the miasma of urine and sour flesh was the smell of death, and she noted with a faint frown, the bright metallic hint of blood.

"Somebody stick him?" She nearly sighed as she opened her kit to take out the can of Seal-It. "What the hell for? These sleepers don't have anything worth stealing."

For the first time, Bowers allowed a thin smile to curve her lips. But her eyes were cold and hard, with bitterness riding in them. "Somebody stole something from him, all right." Pleased with herself, she stepped back. She hoped to God the tight-assed lieutenant got a nice hard shock at what she'd see behind the tattered curtain.

"You call the ME?" Eve asked as she clear-coated her hands and boots.

"First on scene's discretion," Bowers said primly, with the malice still bright in her eyes. "I opted to leave that decision to Homicide."

"For God's sake, is he dead or not?" Disgusted, Eve moved forward, bending a bit to sweep back the curtain.

It was always a shock, not the hard one Bowers had hoped for. Eve had seen too much too often for that. But what one human could do to another was never routine for her. And the pity that stirred underneath and through the cop was something the woman beside her would never feel and never understand.

"Poor bastard," she said quietly and crouched to do a visual exam.

Bowers had been right about one thing. Snooks was very, very dead. He was hardly more than a sack of bones and wild, straggly hair. Both his eyes and his mouth gaped, and she could see he hadn't kept more than half of his teeth. His type rarely took advantage of the health and dental programs.

His eyes had already filmed over and were a dull mud brown. She judged him to be somewhere around the century mark, and even without murder, he'd never have attained the average twenty more years decent nutrition and medical science could have given him.

She noted, too, that his boots, while cracked and scarred, had plenty of wear left in them, as did the blanket that had been tossed to the side of the box. He had some trinkets as well. A wide-eyed doll's head, a penlight in the shape of a frog, a broken cup he'd filled with carefully made paper flowers. And the walls were covered with more paper shapes. Trees, dogs, angels, and his favored stars and flowers.

She could see no signs of struggle, no fresh bruising or superfluous cuts. Whoever had killed the old man had done so efficiently.

No, she thought, studying the fist-sized hole in his chest. Surgically. Whoever had taken Snook's heart had very likely used a laser scalpel.

"You got your homicide, Bowers."

Eve eased back, let the curtain fall. She felt her blood rise and her fist clench when she saw the self-satisfied smirk on the uniform's face.

"Okay, Bowers, we don't like each other. Just one of those things. But you'd be smart to remember I can make it a hell of a lot harder on you than you can on me." She took a step closer, bumping the toe of her boots to the toe of Bowers's shoes. Just to be sure her point was taken. "So be smart, Bowers, and wipe that fucking sneer off your face and keep out of my way."

The sneer dropped away, but Bowers's eyes shot out little bullet points of animosity. "It's against departmental code for a superior officer to use offensive language to a uniform."

"No kidding? Well, you be sure to put that in your report, Bowers. And you have that report done, in triplicate, and on my desk by oh ten hundred. Stand back,'' she added, very quietly now.

It took ten humming seconds with their eyes warring before Bowers dropped her gaze and shifted aside.

Dismissing her, Eve turned her back and pulled out her communicator. ''Dallas, Lieutenant Eve. I've got a homicide.''

Now why, Eve wondered, as she hunkered inside the crate to examine the body, *would someone steal a so obviously used-up heart?* She remembered that for a period after the Urban Wars, stolen organs had been a prize commodity on the black market. Very often, dealers hadn't been patient enough to wait until a donor was actually dead to make the transfer, but that had been decades ago, before man-made organs had been fully perfected.

Organ donating and brokering were still popular. And she thought there was something about organ building as well, though she paid little attention to medical news and reports.

She distrusted doctors.

Some of the very rich didn't care for the idea of a manufactured implant, she assumed. A human heart or kidney from a young accident victim could command top prices, but it had to be in prime condition. Nothing about Snooks was prime.

She wrinkled her nose against the stench, but leaned closer. When a woman detested hospitals and health centers as much as she did, the faintly sick smell of antiseptic sent the nostrils quivering.

She caught it here, just a trace, then frowning, sat back on her heels.

Her prelim exam told her the victim had died at 0:2:10, given the outside temperature through the night. She'd need the blood work and tox reports to know if there'd been drugs in his system, but she could already see that he'd been a brew guzzler.

The typical brown refillable bottle used to transport home brew was tucked in the corner, nearly empty. She found a small, almost pitiful stash of illegals. One thin, hand-rolled joint of Zoner, a couple of pink capsules that were probably Jags, and a small, filthy bag of white powder she assumed after a sniff was Grin laced with a whiff of Zeus.

There were telltale spiderwebs of broken blood vessels over his dented face, obvious signs of malnutrition, and the scabs of what was likely some unattractive skin disease. The man had been a guzzler, smoked, ate garbage, and had been nearly ready to die in his sleep.

Why kill him?

"Sir?" Eve didn't glance back as Peabody drew back the curtain. "ME's on scene."

"Why take his heart?" Eve muttered. "Why surgically remove it? If it was a straight murder, wouldn't they have roughed him up, kicked him around? If they were into mutilation, why didn't they mutilate? This is textbook work."

Peabody scanned the body, grimaced. "I haven't seen any heart ops, but I'll take your word on that."

"Look at the wound," Eve said impatiently. "He should have bled out, shouldn't he? A fist-sized hole in the chest, for Christ's sake. But they—whatever it is—clamped, closed off, the bleeders, just like they would in surgery. This one didn't want the mess, didn't see the point in it. No, he's proud of his work," she added, crab walking back through the opening, then standing to take a deep gulp of the much fresher air outside.

"He's skilled. Had to have had some training. And I don't think one person could have managed this alone. You send the scoopers out to canvass for witnesses?"

"Yeah." Peabody scanned the deserted street, the broken windows, the huddle of boxes and crates deep in the alleyway across the street. "Good luck to them."

"Lieutenant."

"Morris." Eve lifted a brow as she noted she'd hooked the top medical examiner for an on-scene. "I didn't expect to get the cream on a sidewalk sleeper."

Pleased, he smiled, and his lively eyes danced. He wore

his hair slicked back and braided with a siren red ski cap
snugged over it. His long, matching coat flapped madly
in the breeze. Morris, Eve knew, was quite the snazzy
dresser.

"I was available, and your sleeper sounded quite interesting. No heart?"

"Well, I didn't find one."

He chuckled and approached the crate. "Let's have a
look-see."

She shivered, envying him his long, obviously warm
coat. She had one—Roarke had given her a beauty for
Christmas—but she resisted wearing it on the job. No way
in hell was she going to get blood and assorted body fluids
all over that fabulous bronze-colored cashmere.

And she thought as she crouched down yet again, she
was pretty sure her new gloves were cozily tucked in the
pockets of that terrific coat. Which was why her hands
were currently freezing.

She stuffed them in the pockets of her leather jacket,
hunched her shoulders against the bite of the wind, and
watched Morris do his job.

"Beautiful work," Morris breathed. "Absolutely beautiful."

"He had training, right?"

"Oh yes." Affixing microgoggles over his eyes, Morris
peered into the open chest. "Yes indeed, he did. This is
hardly his first surgery. Top of the line tools as well. No
homemade scalpel, no clumsy rib spreaders. Our killer is
one mag surgeon. Damn if I don't envy his hands."

"Some cults like to use body parts in their ceremo-
nies," Eve said half to herself. "But they generally hack
and mutilate when they kill. And they like rituals, ambi-
ance. We've got none of that here."

"Doesn't look like a religious thing. It looks like a
medical one."

"Yeah." That corroborated her thoughts. "One person
pull this off?"

"Doubt it." Morris pulled out his bottom lip, let it snap
back. "To perform a procedure this slick under these dif-

ficult conditions he'd need a very skilled assistant.''

''Any idea why they'd take his heart if it wasn't to worship the demon of the week?''

''Not a clue,'' Morris said cheerfully and gestured for her to back up. When they were outside again, he blew out a breath. ''I'm surprised the old man didn't die of asphyxiation in all that stink. But from a visual exam, my guess would be that heart would have very few miles left on it. Got your prints and DNA sample for IDing?''

''Already sealed and ready for the lab.''

''Then we'll bag him, take him in.''

Eve nodded. ''You curious enough to bump him up to the top of your stack of bodies?''

''As a matter of fact, I am.'' He smiled, gestured to his team. ''You should wear a hat, Dallas. It's fucking freezing out here.''

She sneered, but she'd have given a month's pay for a hot cup of coffee. Leaving Morris to his work, she turned to meet Bowers and Trueheart.

Bowers clenched her teeth. She was cold, hungry, and she bitterly resented the chummy consult she'd witnessed between Eve and the chief medical examiner.

Probably fucking him, Bowers thought. She knew Eve Dallas, knew her type. Damn right she did. A woman like her only moved up the ranks because she spread her legs while she made the climb. The only reason Bowers hadn't moved up herself was because she refused to do it on her back.

That's the way the game's played, that's how. And her heart began to pound in her chest, the blood to thunder in her head. But she'd get her own, one day.

Whore, bitch. The words echoed in her brain, nearly trembled off her tongue. But she sucked them in. She was, she reminded herself, still in control.

The hate Eve read in Bowers's pale eyes was a puzzle. It was much too vicious, she decided, to be the result of a simple and deserved dressing down by a superior officer. It gave her an odd urge to brace for attack, to slide a hand down to her weapon. Instead, she lifted her eyebrows, waited a beat. "Your report, Officer?"

"Nobody saw anything, nobody knows anything," Bowers snapped. "That's the way it is with these people. They stay in their holes."

Though Eve had her eyes on Bowers, she caught the slight movement from the rookie. Following instinct, she dug in her pocket and pulled out some loose credits. "Get me some coffee, Officer Bowers."

Disdain turned so quickly to insulted shock, Eve had to work hard to hold off a grin. "Get you coffee?"

"That's right. I want coffee." She grabbed Bowers's hand, dumped the credits into it. "So does my aide. You know the neighborhood. Run over to the nearest 24/7 and get me some coffee."

"Trueheart's lowest rank."

"Was I talking to Trueheart, Peabody?" Eve said pleasantly.

"No, Lieutenant. I believe you were addressing Officer Bowers." As Peabody didn't like the woman's looks, either, she smiled. "I take cream and sugar. The lieutenant goes for black. I believe there's a 24/7 one block over. Shouldn't take you long."

Bowers stood another moment, then turned on her heel and stalked off. Her muttered "Bitch" came clearly on the cold wind.

"Golly, Peabody, Bowers just called you a bitch."

"I really think she meant you, sir."

"Yeah." Eve's grin was fierce. "You're probably right. So, Trueheart, spill it."

"Sir?" His already pale face whitened even more at being directly addressed.

"What do you think? What do you know?"

"I don't—"

When he glanced nervously at Bowers's stiff and re-treating back, Eve stepped into his line of vision. Her eyes were cool and commanding. "Forget her. You're dealing with me now. I want your report on the canvass."

"I . . ." His Adam's apple bobbed. "No one in the immediate area admits to having witnessed any disturbance in the vicinity or any visitors to the victim's crib during the time in question.''

''And?''

''It's just that—I was going to tell Bowers,'' he continued in a rush, ''but she cut me off.''

''Tell me,'' Eve suggested.

''It's about the Gimp? He had his crib on this side, just down from Snooks, as long as I've had the beat. It's only a couple of months, but—''

''You patrol this area yesterday?'' Eve interrupted.

''Yes, sir.''

''And there was a crib by Snooks's?''

''Yes, sir, like always. Now he's got it on the other side of the street, way at the end of the alley.''

''Did you question him?''

''No, sir. He's zoned. We couldn't roust him, and Bowers said it wasn't worth the trouble, anyway, because he's a stone drunk.''

Eve studied him thoughtfully. His color was back, pumped into his cheeks from nerves and the slap of the wind. But he had good eyes, she decided. Clear and sharp. ''How long have you been out of the academy, Trueheart?''

''Three months, sir.''

''Then you can be forgiven for not being able to recognize an asshole in uniform.'' She cocked her head when a flash of humor trembled on his mouth. ''But I have a feeling you'll learn. Call for a wagon and have your pal the Gimp taken down to the tank at Central. I want to talk to him when he's sobered up. He knows you?''

''Yes, sir.''

''Then you stay with him, and bring him up when he's coherent. I want you to stand in on the interview.''

''You want me to—'' Trueheart's eyes went huge and bright. ''I'm assigned to Lite—Bowers is my trainer.''

''Is that how you want it, Officer?''

He hesitated, blew out a quiet breath. ''No, sir, Lieutenant, it's not.''

"Then why aren't you following my orders?" She turned away to harass the crime scene team and left him grinning after her.

"That was really sweet," Peabody said when they were back in their vehicle with cups of hot, horrible coffee.

"Don't start, Peabody."

"Come on, Dallas. You gave the guy a nice break."

"He gave us a potential witness and it was another way to burn that idiot Bowers's ass." She smiled thinly. "Next chance you get, Peabody, do a run on her. I like to know everything I can about people who want to rip the skin off my face."

"I'll take care of it when we're back at Central. You want hard copy?"

"Yeah. Run Trueheart, too, just for form."

"Wouldn't mind running him." Peabody wiggled her eyebrows. "He's very cute."

Eve slanted her a look. "You're pathetic, and you're too old for him."

"I can't have more than a couple, maybe three years on him," Peabody said with a hint of insult. "And some guys prefer a more experienced woman."

"I thought you were still tight with Charles."

"We date," Peabody lifted her shoulders, still uncomfortable discussing this particular man with Eve. "But we're not exclusive."

Tough to be exclusive with a licensed companion, Eve thought but held her tongue. Snapping out her opinion of Peabody developing a relationship with Charles Monroe had come much too close to breaking the bond between them a few weeks before.

"You're okay with that?" she said instead.

"That's the way we both want it. We like each other, Dallas. We have a good time together. I wish you—" She broke off, firmly shut her mouth.

"I didn't say anything."

"You're thinking pretty damn loud."

Eve set her teeth. They were not, she promised herself, going back there. "What I'm thinking," she said evenly, "is about getting some breakfast before we start on the paperwork."

Deliberately, Peabody rolled the stiffness out of her shoulders. "That works for me. Especially if you're buying."

"I bought last time."

"I don't think so, but I can check my records." More cheerful, Peabody pulled out her electronic memo book and made Eve laugh.

chapter two

The best that could be said about the slop served at Cop Central's Eatery was that it filled the hole serious hunger could dig. Between bites of what was supposed to be a spinach omelette, Peabody accessed data on her palm PC.

"Ellen Bowers," she reported. "No middle initial. Graduated from the academy, New York branch, in '46."

"I was there in '46," Eve mused. "She'd have been right ahead of me. I don't remember her."

"I can't get her academy records without authorization."

"Don't bother with that." Scowling, Eve hacked at the cardboard disguised as a pancake on her plate. "She's been on the force a dozen years and she's scooping stiffs downtown? Wonder who else she pissed off."

"Assigned to the one sixty-two for the last two years, spent another couple at the four-seven. Before that, assigned to Traffic. Man, she's bounced all over, Dallas. Did time in Cop Central in Records, another stint at the two-eight—that's Park Patrol, mostly on-foot stuff."

Since even the small lake of syrup Eve had used to drown the pancake didn't soften it, she gave up and switched to gut-burning coffee. "Sounds like our friend's had trouble finding her niche or the department's been shuffling her.''

"Authorization's required to access transfer documents and/or personal progress reports."

Eve considered, then shook her head. "No, it feels sticky, and we're probably done with her, in any case."

"I've got that she's single. Never married, no kids. She's thirty-five, parents live in Queens, three sibs. Two brothers and one sister. And, we have my personal take," Peabody added as she set the PPC aside. "I hope we're done with her, because she'd really, really like to hurt you."

Eve only smiled. "That's gotta be frustrating for her, doesn't it? Do you have a personal take on why?"

"Not a clue except you're you and she's not." Uneasy, Peabody moved her shoulders. "I'd pay attention, though. She looked like the kind who'd come at you from behind."

"We're not likely to run into each other on a regular basis." Eve filed the matter, dismissed it. "Eat up. I want to go see if this sleeper of Trueheart's knows anything."

She decided to use an interview room, knowing the stark formality of that often loosened tongues. One look at the Gimp warned her that while he might be coherent now, thanks to a hefty dose of Sober-Up, his skinny body still jittered and his nervous eyes jumped.

A quick spin through the decontamination tank had likely chased off any parasites and had laid a thin layer of faux citrus over the stink of him.

An addict, Eve thought, with an assortment of vices that had certainly fried a good portion of his brain cells.

She brought him water, knowing most brew hounds suffered from dry mouth after decon. "How old are you, Gimp?"

"Dunno, maybe fifty."

He looked to be a very ill-preserved eighty, but she thought he was probably close to the mark. "You got another name?"

He shrugged. They'd taken away his clothes and disposed of them. The gray smock and drawstring pants hung on him and were nearly the same color as his skin. "Dunno. I'm Gimp."

"Okay. You know Officer Trueheart here, right?"

"Yeah, yeah." Suddenly, the beaten face glowed with a smile as pure as a baby's. "Hi! You slipped me some credits, said I should get some soup."

Trueheart flushed painfully, shifted on his regulation shoes. "I guess you bought brew with it."

"Dunno." The smile faded as his busy eyes landed on Eve again. "Who are you? How come I have to be here? I didn't do nothing. Somebody's gonna take my stuff if I don't watch out."

"Don't worry about your stuff, Gimp. We'll take care of it. I'm Dallas." She kept her voice low and easy, her face bland. Too much cop, she thought, would just spook him. "I just want to talk to you. You want something to eat?"

"Dunno. Maybe."

"We'll get you something hot after we talk. I'm going to turn on the recorder, so we get it all straight."

"I didn't do nothing."

"Nobody thinks you did. Engage recorder," she ordered. "Interview with witness known as the Gimp regarding case number 28913-H. Interviewer Dallas, Lieutenant Eve. Also attending, Peabody, Officer Delia, and Trueheart, Officer . . . ?" She glanced over.

"Troy." He flushed again.

"Troy Trueheart?" Eve said with her tongue in her cheek. "Okay." Then she pinned her gaze on the pitiful man across from her. "Subject witness is not under suspicion for any wrongdoing. This investigator appreciates his cooperation. Do you understand that, Gimp?"

"Yeah, guess. What?"

She didn't sigh, but was momentarily afraid the detestable Bowers was right about him. "You're not here because you're in trouble. I appreciate you talking to me. I hear you moved your crib last night."

He wet his cracked lips, drank. "Dunno."

"You used to have it across the street, near Snooks. You know Snooks, don't you, Gimp?"

"Maybe." His hand shook, slopping water on the table. "He draws pictures. Nice pictures. I traded him some Zoner for a pretty one of a tree. He makes flowers, too. Nice."

"I saw his flowers. They're pretty. He was kind of a friend of yours?"

"Yeah." His eyes filled and tears spilled over the red rims. "Maybe. Dunno."

"Somebody hurt him, Gimp. Did you know that?"

Now he shrugged, a hard jerk of the shoulder, and began to look around the room. Tears were still rolling down his cheeks, but his eyes were glazed with confusion. "How come I have to be in here? I don't like being inside. I want my stuff. Somebody's for sure gonna steal my stuff."

"Did you see who hurt him?"

"Can I keep these clothes?" Cocking his head, he began to finger the sleeve of the smock. "Am I gonna keep 'em?"

"Yeah, you can keep them." Narrowing her eyes, she went with her gut. "How come you didn't take his boots, Gimp? He was dead, and they were good boots."

"I don't steal from Snooks," he said with some dignity. "Not even when he's dead. You don't steal from your bud, no way, no how. How come you think they done that to him?" Looking genuinely puzzled, he leaned forward. "How come you think they put that big hole in him?"

"I don't know." Eve leaned forward, too, as if they were having a quiet, personal conversation. "I keep wondering about that. Was anybody mad at him?"

"Snooks? He don't hurt nobody. We just mind our own, that's what. You can panhandle some if the beat droids don't look your way. We got no fucking beggar's license, but you can shake some credits loose if the droids aren't around. And Snooks he sells his paper flowers sometimes, and we get some brew or some smoke and mind our own. No call to put a big hole in him, was there?''

"No, it was a bad thing they did to him. You saw them last night?"

"Dunno. Dunno what I saw. Hey!" He beamed that smile at Trueheart again. "Maybe you give me some credits again, all right? For some soup."

Trueheart shot a glance at Eve, got her nod. "Sure, Gimp. I'll give you some before you go. You just have to talk to the lieutenant for awhile more."

"You liked old Snooks, right?"

"I liked him fine." Trueheart smiled and, taking the cue from Eve, sat. "He drew nice pictures. He gave me one of his paper flowers."

"He'd only give them to people he liked," Gimp said brightly. "He liked you. Said so. Didn't like that other one and me neither. She's got mean eyes. Like to kick you in the teeth if she could." His head bobbed up and down like a doll's. "What you doing going around with her?"

"She's not here now," Trueheart said gently. "The lieutenant is. Her eyes aren't mean."

Gimp pouted, studied Eve's face. "Maybe not. Cop's though. Cop's eyes. Cops, cops, cops." He giggled, guzzled water, eyed Peabody. "Cops, cops, cops." He all but sang it.

"I feel really bad about old Snooks," Trueheart continued. "I bet he'd want you to tell Lieutenant Dallas what happened. He'd want it to be you who tells, because you were buds."

Gimp paused, pulled on his earlobe. "You think?"

"I do. Why don't you tell her what you saw last night?"

"Dunno what I saw." Head cocked again, Gimp began to tap the sides of his fists on the table. "People coming around. Don't see people coming around at night that way. Driving a big black car. Big fucker! Shined in the dark. They don't say nothing."

Eve held up a finger, indicating to Trueheart she was taking over again. "How many people, Gimp?"

"Two. Wore long black coats. Looked warm. Had masks on so all you can see over it's the eyes. I think, *Hey! It ain't fucking Halloween.*" He broke himself up, laughing delightedly. "It ain't fucking Halloween," he repeated, snorting, "but they got masks on and they carrying bags like for trick or treat."

"What did the bags look like?"

"One has a nice big black one, shines, too. And the other has something else, it's white and it makes sloshy noises when he walks with it. They go right into Snooks's crib like they was invited or something. I don't hear nothing but the wind, maybe I go to sleep."

"Did they see you?" Eve asked him.

"Dunno. They got warm coats and good shoes, big car. You don't go thinking they gonna put a big hole in Snooks?" He leaned toward her again, his homely face earnest, tears trembling again. "If you think that, you'd try to stop them maybe, or go run for the beat droid, 'cause you're buds."

He was crying now. Eve leaned over, laid a hand over his, despite the scabs that covered it. "You didn't know. It's not your fault. It's their fault. What else did you see?"

"Dunno." His eyes and nose dripped like faucets. "Sleep maybe. Then maybe I woke up and looked out. No car now. Was there a car there? Dunno. It's getting light out, and I go over to see Snooks. He'll know maybe if there was a big black car. And I see him, see that big hole in him, and the blood. His mouth's wide open and his eyes, too. They put a big hole in him, and maybe they want to put one in me so I can't be there. Can't do that, no way, no how. So I have to get my stuff away from there. All my stuff right away from there. So that's what I do, you bet, and then I drink all the rest of the brew I got and go back to sleep. I didn't help old Snooks."

"You're helping him now." Eve leaned back. "Let's talk about the two people in the long coats some more."

•　•　•

She worked him another hour, tugging him back when he wandered too far for too long. Though she didn't slide any more information out of him, Eve didn't consider the hour wasted. He would know her now if she had to hunt him up again. He'd remember her well enough, and remember the meeting hadn't been unpleasant. Particularly since she ordered him in a hot meal and gave him fifty credits she knew he'd spend on brew and illegals.

He should have been in Psych, she thought, or in a halfway house. But he wouldn't have stuck. She'd long ago accepted that you couldn't save everyone.

"You did a good job with him, Trueheart."

He blushed again, and while she found the trait a bit endearing, she hoped he learned to control it. The other cops would eat him alive before the bad guys had a chance for a nibble.

"Thank you, sir. I appreciate you giving me a chance to help with him."

"You found him," Eve said simply. "I figure you've got plans for yourself out of Homicide-Lite."

This time he squared his shoulders. "I want a detective shield, when I've earned it."

It was rare to find a uniform rookie without that particular aspiration, but she nodded. "You can start earning it by sticking. I could and would be willing to put in a plug for your transfer—see that you got another beat and another trainer. But I'm going to ask you to stay where you are. You've got good eyes, Trueheart, and I'd like you to use them on your beat until we close this case."

He was so overwhelmed with the offer and the request, his eyes nearly popped out of his head. "I'll stick."

"Good. Bowers is going to give you grief over this."

He grimaced. "I'm getting used to it."

It was an opening to ask him more, to pump him for some details on Bowers. She let it pass, not wanting to put a rookie in the position of ratting on his own trainer. "Fine, then. Go back to your station and write your report. If you come across anything you think might apply to this case, get in touch with either me or Peabody."

She headed to her office, already issuing orders to Peabody to have the interview disc duped. "And let's get the rundown on known dealers in that area. We can't absolutely rule out the illegals connection. I can't think of a chemi-dealer who offs his deadbeat clients by surgically removing vital organs, but stranger things have happened. We'll run known cults, too," she continued as Peabody input the orders into her memo pad. "It feels wrong, but we'll give it some attention."

"I can contact Isis," Peabody suggested, referring to a Wiccan they had dealt with on another case. "She might know if any of the black magic cults have a routine like this."

Eve grunted, nodded, and caught the glide with Peabody beside her. "Yeah, use the connection. Let's get that angle eliminated."

She glanced toward the window wall where the glass tubes she avoided like poison carried cops, clerks, and civilians up and down the outside of the building. Beyond them she saw a pair of air support units scream off to the west, blasting between an advertising blimp and a commuter tram.

Inside, the pulse of the building was fast and strong. Voices, rushing feet, a crowd of bodies with jobs to do. It was a rhythm she understood. She glanced at her wrist unit, oddly pleased to see it was barely nine. She'd been on duty four hours, and the day was just getting started.

"And let's see if we can get a real ID on the victim," she continued when they stepped off the glide. "We got his prints and DNA sample. If Morris is into the postmortem, he should at least have an approximate age."

"I'll get right on it." Peabody swung left, heading through the bullpen as Eve turned into her office. It was small, but she preferred it that way. The single window was narrow, letting in little light and entirely too much noise from air traffic. But the AutoChef worked and was stocked with Roarke's impeccable coffee.

She ordered a mug, then sighed as the rich, strong scent of it tickled her system. Sitting down, she engaged her tele-link with the intention of harassing Morris.

"I know he's doing a PM," she said to the assistant who tried to block her. "I have some information for him concerning the body. Put me through."

She leaned back in her chair, indulged herself with coffee, drummed her fingers against the mug, and waited.

"Dallas." Morris's face swam on-screen. "You know how I hate being interrupted when I've got my hands in someone's brains."

"I have a witness who puts two people on the scene. Big shiny car, nice shiny shoes. One carried a leather bag, the other a white bag that made—I quote—sloshy noises. Ring any bells?"

"I hear a ding," Morris said, frowning now. "Your witness see what happened?"

"No, he's a brewhead, slept through most of it. They were gone when he woke up, but according to the time line, he discovered the body. Would that sloshy bag be what I think it would be?"

"Could be an organ transport sack. This is neat, professional work here, Dallas. First-rate major organ removal. I've got some of the blood work back. Your victim was given a nice, comfy dose of anesthesia. He never felt a thing. But if what's left in him is any indication, the heart was next to worthless. His liver's shot, his kidneys are a mess. His lungs are the color of a coal mine. This is not someone who bothered with anticancer vaccines or regular medical treatments. His body's full of disease. I'd have given him six months, tops, before he'd have kicked from natural causes."

"So they took a worthless heart," Eve mused. "Maybe they figure on passing it off as a good one."

"If it's like the rest of him, a first-year med student would spot the condition."

"They wanted it. It's too damn much trouble to go through just to kill some sidewalk sleeper."

Possibilities circled in her mind. Revenge, some weird cult, a black-market scam. Kicks, entertainment. Practice.

"You said it was first-rate work. How many surgeons in the city could handle it?"

"I'm a dead doctor," Morris said with a ghost of a smile. "Live ones don't run in the same circles. Snazziest private hospital in New York would be the Drake Center. I'd start there."

"Thanks, Morris. I can use the final reports as soon as you can manage it."

"Then let me get back to my brain." With that, he ended transmission.

Eve turned to her computer, eyes narrowed. It was making a suspicious buzzing noise, one she'd reported twice to the jokers in maintenance. She leaned toward it, teeth bared in threat.

"Computer, you sack of shit, search for data on the Drake Center, medical facility, New York City."

Working. . . .

It hiccupped, whined, and the screen flashed into an alarming red that seared the eyes.

"Default to blue screen, damn it."

Internal error. Blue screen is unavailable. Continue search?

"I hate you." But she adjusted her eyes. "Continue search."

Searching. . . . The Drake Center of Medicine, located Second Avenue, New York City, established 2023 in honor of Walter C. Drake, credited with the discovery of anticancer vaccine. This is a private facility, which includes hospital and health care clinics, rated Class A by the American Medical Association, teaching and training facilities also rated Class A, as well as research and development laboratories with Class A ratings. Do you wish list of board members on all facilities?

"Yes, on screen and hard copy."

Working. . . . Internal error.

There was a distinct increase in the buzzing noise, and the screen began to shimmer.

Please repeat command.

"I'm going to eat those maintenance assholes for lunch."

Command does not compute. Do you wish to order lunch?

"Ha ha. No. List board members on all facilities of the Drake Center of Medicine."

Working. . . . Health Center Board: Colin Cagney, Lucille Mendez, Tia Wo, Michael Waverly, Charlotte Mira . . .

"Dr. Mira," Eve murmured. It was a good connection. The doctor was one of the top criminal profilers in the city and affiliated with the New York Police and Security Department. She was also a personal friend.

Eve drummed her fingers, listening to the names of the board of the teaching facilities. One or two vaguely rang a bell, but the ringing became louder when the computer reached the board of the research and development arm.

Carlotta Zemway, Roarke—

"Hold it, hold it." Her drumming fingers curled into fists. "Roarke? Damn it, damn it, damn it, can't he stay out of anything?"

Please rephrase question.

"Shut the hell up." Eve pressed her fingers to her eyes; sighed. "Continue list," she ordered as her stomach continued to sink. "Print out, then disengage."

Internal error. Unable to comply with multiple commands at this time.

She didn't scream, but she wanted to.

After a frustrating twenty minutes of waiting for the data to dribble out, she swung through the detectives' bullpen and around to the stingy area where aides and adjutants were penned in cubicles the size of a drying tube.

"Peabody, I have to head out."

"I've got data incoming. Do you want me to transfer it to my portable unit?"

"No, you stay here, finish the runs. I shouldn't be more than a couple of hours. When you're done with this, I want you to go find a hammer."

Peabody had taken out her memo book, nearly plugged in the order, when she stopped, frowned up at Eve. "Sir? A hammer?"

"That's right. A really big, heavy hammer. Then you take it into my office and beat that fucking useless excuse for a data spitter on my desk to dust."

"Ah." Because she was a wise woman, Peabody cleared her throat rather than loosen the chuckle. "As an alternate to that action, Lieutenant, I could call maintenance."

"Fine, you do that, and you tell them that at the very first opportunity, I'm coming down there and killing all of them. Mass murder. And after they're all dead, I'm going to kick the bodies around, dance on top of them, and sing a happy song. No jury will convict me."

Because the idea of Eve singing and dancing anywhere made her lips twitch, Peabody bit the inside of her cheek. "I'll inform them of your dissatisfaction with their work."

"You do that, Peabody." Turning on her heel, Eve shrugged into her jacket and stalked out.

It would have been more logical for her to hunt up Mira first. As a psychiatrist, a medical doctor, a criminologist, Mira would be a valuable source on the case. But Eve drove uptown to the shimmering spear of a building that was Roarke's New York headquarters.

There were other buildings in other cities, on and off planet. Her husband had his clever fingers in too many pies to count. Rich pies, she knew, complicated pies. And at one time, very questionable pies.

She supposed it was inevitable that his name would pop up in connection with so many of her cases. But she didn't have to like it.

She slipped her vehicle into the space Roarke had reserved for her in the multilevel garage. The first time she'd come there, not quite a year before, she hadn't had such privileges. Nor had her voice and palm prints been programmed onto the security system of the private elevator. Before, she had entered the main lobby with its acres of tiles, its banks of flowers, its moving map and screens, and had been escorted to his offices to interrogate him over a murder.

Now the computerized voice greeted her by name, wished her well, and told her as she stepped in that Roarke would be informed of her visit.

Eve jammed her hands in her pockets, paced the car on its smooth ride to the top of the spear. She imagined he was in the middle of some megadeal or complex negotiation to buy a medium-sized planet or financially strapped country. Well, he was just going to have to hold off on making his next million until she had some answers.

When the doors whispered open, Roarke's assistant was waiting with a polite smile. As always, she was perfectly groomed, her snow-white hair sleekly styled. "Lieutenant, how nice to see you again. Roarke's in a meeting. He asked if you'd mind waiting in his office just a few moments."

"Sure, fine, okay."

"Can I get you anything while you're waiting?" She led Eve through the glass breezeway where New York rushed by some sixty stories below. "If you haven't had lunch, I can shift Roarke's next appointment to accommodate you."

The quiet deference always made her feel stupid—a flaw, Eve thought, in herself. "No, this shouldn't take long. Thanks."

"Just let me know if I can do anything for you." Discreetly, she closed the doors and left Eve alone.

The office was huge, of course. Roarke liked his space. The sea of windows were tinted to cut the glare and offer a staggering view of the city. He also liked height—a fondness that Eve didn't share. So she didn't wander over to the window but paced the ocean of plush carpet instead.

The trinkets in the room were clever and unique. The furnishings sleek and comfortable, in rich shades of topaz and emerald. She knew the ebony slab of desk was just one more power center for a man who exuded power like breath.

Efficiency, elegance, power. He never lacked for any of them.

And when, ten minutes later, he came in through a side door, it was so easy to see why.

He could still stop her heart. Just the look of him: that glorious face, as perfectly sculpted as a Renaissance statue, was highlighted by eyes impossibly blue and a mouth designed to make a woman crave it on hers; his black hair fell nearly to his shoulders, adding just a touch of the rogue; and she knew just how strong and sleek that body was, now elegantly clad in a tailored black suit.

"Lieutenant." Ireland whispered, silky and romantic, in his voice. "An unexpected pleasure."

She wasn't aware she was frowning or that she often did when swamped with the heady combination of love and lust he caused in her. "I need to talk to you."

His brow lifted as he crossed to her. "About?"

"Murder."

"Ah." He had already taken her hands in his, was already leaning down for a long, slow kiss of greeting. "Am I under arrest?"

"Your name popped up during a data search. What are you doing on the board of the Drake Center's R and D unit?"

"Being an upstanding citizen. Being married to a cop does that to a man." He ran his hands up her arms to her shoulders, felt the tension there, and sighed. "Eve, I'm on all sorts of tedious boards and committees. Who's dead?"

"A sidewalk sleeper named Snooks."

"I don't believe we were acquainted. Sit down; tell me what this has to do with me being on the board of the Drake Center."

"Possibly nothing, but I have to start somewhere." Still, she didn't sit but roamed the room.

Roarke watched her, the restless, nervous energy that seemed to spark visibly around her. And knowing her, he understood all that energy was already focused on finding justice for the dead.

It was only one of the reasons she fascinated him.

"The victim's heart had been surgically removed while he was in his crib down in the Bowery," she told him. "The ME claims the procedure required a top-flight surgeon, and the Drake was my first pass."

"Good choice. It's the best in the city, and likely the best on the East Coast." Considering, Roarke leaned back against his desk. "They took his heart?"

"That's right. He was a brewhead, an addict. His body was worn down. Morris says the heart was no good anyway. The guy would've been dead in six months." She stopped pacing and faced him, tucking her thumbs in his front pockets. "What do you know about organ trading on the black market?"

"It wasn't something I dabbled in, even in my more . . . flexible days," he added with a faint smile. "But the advances in man-made organs, the supply still available from accidental deaths, the strides in health care and organ building all have cut the market for street organs down to nothing. That area peaked about thirty years ago.''

"How much for a heart off the street?" she demanded.

"I really don't know." His brow winged up, and a smile ghosted around that sexy poet's mouth. "Do you want me to find out?"

"I can find out myself." She began to pace again. "What do you do on that board?"

"I'm an adviser. My own R and D department has a medical arm that cooperates and assists Drake's. We have a contract with the center. We supply medical equipment, machines, computers." He smiled again. "Artificial organs. Drake's R and D deals primarily with pharmaceuticals, prostheses, chemicals. We both manufacture replacement organs."

"You make hearts?"

"Among other things. We don't deal in live tissue."

"Who's the best surgeon on staff?"

"Colin Cagney is the chief of staff. You've met him," Roarke added.

She only grunted. How could she remember all the people she'd met in some social arena since Roarke came into her life? "Wonder if he makes—what did they call them—home calls?"

"House calls," Roarke corrected with a hint of a smile. "I can't quite see the distinguished Dr. Cagney performing illegal surgery in a sidewalk sleeper's crib."

"Maybe I'll have a different vision once I meet him again." She let out a deep sigh and tunneled her fingers through her hair. "Sorry to interrupt your day."

"Interrupt it a bit longer," he suggested and indulged himself by crossing to her and rubbing his thumb over her full bottom lip. "Have lunch with me."

"Can't. I've got more legwork." But the light friction on her lip made it curve. "So, what were you buying?"

"Australia," he said then laughed when she gaped at him. "Just a small piece of it." Delighted with her reaction, he yanked her close for a quick, hard kiss. "Christ, I adore you, Eve."

"Yeah, well. Good." It continually left her hot and loose to hear it. To know it. "I gotta go."

"Would you like me to see what I can find out about organ research at Drake?"

"That's my job, and I know how to do it. It'd be really nice if you didn't get mixed up in this one. Just . . . go buy the rest of Australia or something. I'll see you at home."

"Lieutenant?" He turned to his desk, opened a drawer. Knowing how she worked, he tossed her an energy bar. "Your lunch, I imagine."

It made her grin as she tucked it in her pocket. "Thanks."

When she closed the door behind her, he glanced at his wrist unit. Twenty minutes before his next meeting, Roarke calculated. Time enough.

He took a seat at his computer, smiled a little as he thought of his wife, then called up data on the Drake Center.

chapter three

Eve discovered it was just as well she hadn't gone after Mira first. The doctor was out. She shot off a quick E-mail requesting a case consult the following day, then headed down to Drake.

It was one of those block-stretching buildings she'd seen hundreds of times and never paid attention to. Before Roarke, that is. Since then, he had dragged, strong-armed, or carried her into their emergency treatment centers a number of times. When, she thought now, she'd have been perfectly fine with a first aid kit and a nap.

She hated hospitals. The fact that she was going into this one as a cop and not a patient didn't seem to make a difference.

The original building was an old and distinguished brownstone that had been lovingly, and she imagined expensively, preserved. Structures sheer and white speared up from it, out from it, joined together by the shimmering tubes of breezeways, the circling ring of glides that glinted silver.

There were juts of white that formed what she supposed might be restaurants, gift shops, or other areas where staff or visitors or patients might be allowed to gather and enjoy the view. And delude themselves that they weren't in a structure full of the sick and suffering.

Because her vehicle's computer was more reliable than her office unit, she was able to access some general data. The Drake Center was more of a city within a city than a health center. It contained training facilities, teaching facilities, labs, trauma units, surgeries, patient rooms and suites, a variety of staff lounges, and visitor waiting areas as one would expect from a medical center.

But in addition, it held a dozen restaurants—two of which were rated five star—fifteen chapels, an elegant little hotel for the family and friends of patients who wished to remain close by, a small, exclusive shopping arcade, three theaters, and five full-service salons.

There were numerous roving maps and information centers to assist visitors in finding their way to their sector of choice. Trams ran from key parking areas to various entryways, and the slick glass tubes sparkled in the thin winter sunlight as they slid up and down the sides of the mammoth white structure like water.

Impatient, and because it was the section she knew best, Eve pulled her car into the ER lot, twisted it into a street-level space, then snarled at the meter that demanded to know the extent of the injuries she suffered.

This is an emergency only parking area. Your injuries or illness must be verified in order for your vehicle to remain in this parking area. Please state the nature and extent of your injuries or illness and step forward to be scanned.

"I've got terminal annoyance," she shot back and shoved her badge into the view screen. "Police business. Deal with it."

While the meter squawked, she turned away to stride across the lot toward the hated glass double doors.

The ER was full of wailing, sobbing, and complaining. Patients in different stages of distress huddled in chairs, filled out the forms on the porta-screens, or waited glassy-eyed for their turn.

An orderly was busy mopping up blood or God knew what, keeping the steel gray floor sanitized. Nurses moved briskly in pale blue uniforms. Occasionally doctors zipped through with their long, flapping lab coats and were careful not to make eye contact with the suffering.

Eve located the first map and asked for the surgical wing. The quickest route was the underground tram, so she joined a moaning patient strapped to a gurney, two exhausted looking interns, and a couple who sat close together whispering about someone named Joe and his chances with his new liver.

When she reached the right wing, she took the glide up a level.

The main floor here was quiet as a cathedral and nearly as ornate with its soaring mosaic ceilings and sumptuous tableaus of flowers and blooming shrubbery. There were several seating areas, all with communications centers. Guide droids stood by in pleasant pastel jumpsuits to lend assistance when necessary.

It cost dearly to be opened by a laser scalpel, to have internal organs repaired or replaced in a private facility. The Drake Center had provided a proper welcome area for those who could afford its services.

Eve chose one of a half-dozen reception consoles at random and flashed her badge at the clerk to insure no evasions. "I need to speak with Dr. Colin Cagney."

"One moment, please, while I locate the doctor." The clerk wore a stone gray suit and precisely knotted tie. Efficiently, he ran a location search on his board, then offered Eve a polite smile. "Dr. Cagney is on the tenth floor. That's the Consultation Level. He is currently with a patient."

"Is there a private waiting area on that level?"

"There are six private waiting areas on ten. Let me see if one is available for you." He called up another board, sent lights blinking red or green. "Waiting Area Three is available. I'll be happy to reserve it for you here."

"Fine. Tell Dr. Cagney I'm waiting to speak with him, and I'm pressed for time."

"Of course. Take any elevator in bank six, Lieutenant. Good health."

"Right," she muttered. Anyone that incessantly polite made her shudder. Whatever training they gave their non-medical staff must have included personality draining, she decided. Edgy, she rode the car up and searched out the right waiting room.

It was a small, tastefully decorated room with a mood screen set to soft, shifting colors. The first thing she did was turn it off. Ignoring the low sofa and two deep chairs, she roamed the room.

She wanted out. The best substitute was a window overlooking Second Avenue.

There, at least, both street and traffic were predictably snarled and nasty. She watched a medi-copter zoom in and circle on its trajectory to one of the pads. She counted two more, an ambu-jet, and five street ambulances before the door opened behind her.

"Lieutenant." The doctor had a dazzling smile, his teeth as white and straight as a Navy band. He flashed it as he crossed the room.

It suited, Eve thought, the smooth, pampered face, the patient, intelligent gray eyes under dramatically black brows. His hair was a gleaming white blazed on the left side with a sweeping strip of black.

He didn't wear a lab coat but a beautifully cut suit the same slate gray as his eyes. His hand, when he took hers, was soft as a child's and firm as a rock.

"Dr. Cagney."

"I hoped you'd remember to call me Colin." The smile spread again as he squeezed and released her hand. "We've met a few times at various functions. But I imagine between your business and Roarke's, you meet seas of people."

"True enough, but I remember you." She had, as soon as she'd seen him. His wasn't a face that slipped the mind. Sharp cheekbones, square jaw, high forehead. And the coloring left an impression. Pale gold skin against black and white. "I appreciate you agreeing to speak with me."

"Happy to do so." He gestured toward the chair. "But I hope you haven't come seeking my professional services. You're not ill?"

"No, I'm fine. It's my profession that brings me to you." Though she'd rather have remained on her feet, she sat. "I'm working on a case. A sidewalk sleeper was murdered early this morning. By someone with excellent surgical skills."

His eyebrows drew together as he shook his head. "I don't understand."

"His heart was removed and taken from the scene. A witness described one of the suspects carrying what you call an organ sack."

"My God." He folded his hands on his knee. Concern flitted along with confusion in his eyes. "I'm appalled to hear it, but I still don't understand. You're telling me his heart was surgically removed and transported?"

"Exactly. He was anesthetized and murdered in his own crib. Two people were seen entering, one carried what sounds very much like a doctor's bag, the other the transfer sack. The operation was performed by someone very skilled. The bleeders, I think you call them, were clamped off and sealed, the incision was precise. It was not done by an amateur."

"For what purpose?" Cagney murmured. "I haven't heard about organ theft, not of this nature, for years. A sidewalk sleeper? Have you determined his state of health before this was done?"

"The ME says he'd have died in his sleep in a matter of months. We don't believe they took a prime heart out of him."

With a heavy sigh, he sat back. "I imagine you see all manner of what men do to men in your line of work, Lieutenant. I've pieced back bodies that have been torn, broken, hacked. On one level, we get used to it. We must. But on another, it never fails to shock and to disappoint. Men continually find new ways to kill men."

"And always will," Eve agreed. "But instinct tells me this man's death was incidental. They got what they wanted from him. I have to ask, Dr. Cagney, where you were this morning between one and three A.M.?"

He blinked, and his well-formed mouth fell open before he recovered. "I see." He spoke slowly, sitting up again. "I would have been at home, sleeping with my wife. I've no way to prove that, however." His voice had cooled, his eyes chilled. "Do I require a lawyer, Lieutenant?"

"That's up to you," she said evenly. "But I see no reason for one at this time. I will need to speak with your wife at some point."

Mouth grim now, he nodded. "Understood."

"Each of our professions runs on routines that are often unpleasant. This is mine. I need a list of the top surgeons in the city, starting with those who specialize in organ transplants."

He rose at that, paced to the window. "Doctors stand for each other, Lieutenant. There's pride and loyalty involved here."

"Cops stand for each other. And when one of them is found to be dirty, it smears us all. I can go through other channels to get the list I need," she added, rising, "but I'd appreciate your cooperation. A man's been murdered. Someone decided he shouldn't be allowed to finish out his time. That pisses me off, Dr. Cagney."

His shoulders moved as he sighed. "I'll send you a list, Lieutenant," he said without turning around. "You'll have it by the end of the day."

"Thanks."

She drove back to Cop Central, remembering her energy bar as she swung into the garage. She ate it on the way up to her office, chewing nutrients and chewing over her impressions of Cagney.

He had a face a patient would trust, even fear a bit, she imagined. You would tend to believe his word—medically—was law. She intended to do a run on him, but calculated him in his mid to late sixties. That meant he'd been a doctor for more than half of his life so far.

He could kill. She learned that anyone could under the right circumstances. But could he kill so cold-bloodedly? Would he protect, under the guise of professional loyalty, someone else who had?

She wasn't sure of the answers.

The light on her computer was blinking green, indicating a new input of data. Peabody, she thought, had been hard at work. After stripping off her jacket, she called it up. It only took five frustrating minutes of grinding noises before the data popped.

Victim identified as Samuel Michael Petrinsky, born 5-6-1961, Madison, Wisconsin. ID number 12176-VSE-12. Parents deceased. No known siblings. Marital status: divorced June 2023. Former spouse Cheryl Petrinsky Sylva, age 92. Three children from marriage: Samuel, James, Lucy. Data available on request in cross file.

No known employment in last thirty years.

What happened to you, Sam? she wondered. Why'd you leave the wife and kids and come to New York to fry your mind and wreck your body on brew and smoke?

"Hell of a way to end up," she muttered, then asked for the cross-reference on his children. She would have to notify next of kin.

You have performed an illegal function. Please delete request and enter your ID number immediately or all unsaved data will be destroyed.

"You son of a bitch." Furious, Eve leaped to her feet and punched the side of her computer with a bunched fist. Even as the pain sang in her knuckles, she prepared to punch it again.

"A problem with your equipment, Lieutenant?"

She hissed, set her teeth, and straightened. It was rare for Commander Whitney to visit her office. And not too happy a moment to have him do so when she was beating up departmental property.

"Respectfully, sir, this unit sucks."

It might have been a smile that flitted into his dark eyes, but she couldn't be sure.

"I suggest you contact maintenance, Dallas."

"Maintenance, Commander, is full of morons."

"And the budget is full of holes." He stepped in, shut the door at his back, which made Eve's stomach jitter uneasily. He glanced around, then shook his head. "Your rank entitles you to an office, Dallas. Not a dungeon."

"This suits me, sir."

"So you always say. Is that AutoChef stocked with your coffee or the department's?"

"Mine, sir. Would you like some?"

"I certainly would."

She turned to order him a cup. The closed door meant he wanted privacy. The request for coffee indicated he wanted to put her at ease.

The combination made Eve nervous. But her hand was steady as she offered him the cup, and her eyes stayed level on his.

His face was wide, tended to be hard. He was a big man with wide shoulders, wide hands, and very often, fatigue darkening his eyes. "You caught a homicide early this morning," he began, pausing long enough to sip and appreciate the genuine coffee from genuine beans Roarke's money could buy.

"Yes, sir. The victim has just been identified. I'll be notifying next of kin." She shot her computer a vicious look. "When I can drag the data out of that heap. I'll have an updated report for you by end of day."

"I have a report from the first officer on-scene on my desk now. Along with a complaint. You and Bowers appear to have bumped heads."

"I came down on her. She deserved it."

"She's filed a complaint that you used abusive and inappropriate language." When Eve rolled her eyes, he did smile. "You and I both know that kind of a complaint is no more than a nuisance and generally makes the complainant look like a soggy-spined fool. However . . ." His smile faded. "She also claims that she observed your work on-scene as sloppy and careless. That you misused her trainee and threatened her with physical harm."

Eve felt the blood begin to sizzle hot under her skin. "Peabody recorded the on-scene investigation. I'll have a copy of it on your desk immediately."

"I'll need that to dismiss the complaint officially. Unofficially, I'm fully aware it's bullshit."

There were two chairs. Because both of them were battered and creaky, Whitney gave them a dubious look before settling into one. "I'd like to hear your take on this before I act."

"My investigation will stand, and so will my report."

He laced his fingers, kept the expression on his wide face bland. "Dallas," was all he said and had her blowing out a huff of breath.

"I handled it. I don't believe in running to a superior officer or filing papers over a minor incident between cops." When he only continued to stare, she jammed her hands in her pockets. "The ranking officer on-scene had not secured the area properly upon my arrival. She was appropriately chastised about the lack of proper procedure. Officer Bowers displayed a marked tendency toward insubordination, which was dealt with, again in my opinion, appropriately. On his own, her trainee indicated to me that on previous scans of the area, there had been another crib beside the victim's, which had, since the day before, been moved. He had reported same to his trainer and his observation had been dismissed. This observation, when followed up on, netted a witness. I invited the trainee, Officer Trueheart, to join in the interview of this witness, who was known to him. Trueheart, as will be stated in my report, shows excellent potential."

She paused in her flat recitation, and heat flashed in her eyes for the first time. "I deny all charges but the last. I might very well have threatened Officer Bowers with physical harm and will ask my aide for verification. My regret, at this time, is that I did not follow through with any threat I may have made and knock her on her fat ass. Sir.''

Whitney lifted his brows but managed to conceal amusement. It was a rare thing for his lieutenant to add personal temper to a verbal report. "Had you followed through, Lieutenant, we'd have a nice little mess on our hands. I assume, knowing exactly how thorough you are, that you or your aide has done a run on Officer Bowers. At least a minimal run, and are therefore aware of her record of transfer. She is what we call a problem child. The department tends to move their problem children from area to area.''

He paused a moment, rubbed a hand over the back of his neck as if to ease some ache. "Bowers is also a champion filer. Nothing she likes better than to file complaints. She's taken a strong dislike to you, Dallas, and off the record, I'm warning you that she's likely to make trouble for you, however she can.''

"She doesn't worry me.''

"I came down here to tell you that she should. Her type feeds on trouble, on causing trouble for other cops. And she's aiming for you. She copied Chief Tibble and her department representative on this complaint. Get the on-scene record, and your report, and a carefully worded response to this complaint on my desk before end of day. Use Peabody,'' he added with a slight smile, "on the last. She'll have a cooler head.''

"Sir.'' Resentment shimmered in her voice, in her eyes, but she held her tongue.

"Lieutenant Dallas, I've never had a better cop under my command than you, and my personal response to the complaint will say so. Cops like Bowers rarely go the distance. She's stumbling her way out of the department, Dallas. This is only a hitch in your stride. Take it seriously, but don't give it more of your time and energy than necessary.''

"Spending more than five minutes of my time and energy on it when I've got a case to close seems excessive. But thank you for your support.''

He nodded, rose. ''Damn good coffee,'' he said wistfully and set aside the empty cup. ''By end of shift, Dallas,'' he added as he walked out.

''Yes, sir.''

She didn't kick the desk. She thought about it, but her knuckles were still stinging from bashing them against another inanimate object. Rather than risk hurting herself again, she called Peabody in to deal with the machine and access the contact numbers for Snooks's next of kin.

She managed to reach the daughter who, though she hadn't seen her father in nearly thirty years, wept bitterly.

It did nothing to soothe Eve's mood. The closest she came to cheerful was watching Peabody's reaction to the complaint filed by Bowers.

''That flat-faced, piss-for-brains bitch!'' Red-faced, hands fisted on her hips, Peabody went into full rant. ''I ought to go dig her out of whatever hole she's in and kick her ugly butt. She's a fucking liar, and worse, she's a lousy cop. Where the hell does she get off filing some whiny, trumped-up complaint against you? What house was she out of?''

Peabody whipped out her memo book and began to call it up. ''I'll go down there right now and show her just what a complaint feels like when it belts you between the eyes.''

''Whitney said you'd be a cool head,'' Eve said with a grin. ''I'm so glad to see the commander knows his troops this well.'' Then she laughed because Peabody's eyes were all but bulging out of her head. ''Take a couple of breaths, Peabody, before something explodes in your brain. We'll handle this in an appropriate manner through the proper channels.''

''*Then* we'll flatten the bitch, right?''

''You're supposed to be a good influence.'' With a shake of her head, Eve sat down. ''I need you to copy the on-scene record to Whitney and to write your own report. Keep it straight and simple, Peabody. Just the facts. We'll write them independently. I'll compose a response to the complaint, and when you have that cool head Whitney believes in, you can go over it for me.''

"I don't know how you can take this so calmly."

"I'm not," Eve muttered. "Believe me. Let's get to work here."

She got it done, keeping her tone coolly professional throughout. During the final pass of her response, the list she requested from Cagney came through. Ignoring the headache beginning to blaze a trail behind her eyes, she copied all discs pertaining to the case, made what she considered a rational, reasonable call to maintenance—she only called them morons twice—then took everything with her. It was end of shift, and by God, she was going home on time for a change, even if she did intend to work once she got there.

But her temper began to simmer and spike as she drove. Her hands clenched and unclenched on the wheel. She'd worked hard to become a good cop. She'd trained and studied and observed and was willing to work until she dropped to stay a good cop.

Her badge didn't simply define what she did but who she was. And in some ways, Eve knew, that badge, what it meant, had saved her.

The first years of her life were either gone or a blur of pain and misery and abuse. But she'd survived them, survived the father who had beaten her, raped her, who had damaged her so badly that when she was found broken and bleeding in an alley, she hadn't even remembered her name.

So she'd become Eve Dallas, a name given to her by a social worker and one she had fought to make mean something. Being a cop meant she wasn't helpless any longer. More, it meant she was able to stand for those who were helpless.

Every time she stood over a body, she remembered what it was like to be a victim. Every time she closed a case, it was a victory for the dead, and for a young girl without a name.

Now some stiff scooper with an attitude had attempted to put a smear on her badge. For some cops, it would be an annoyance, an irritation. For Eve, it was a deep, personal insult.

A physical woman, she tried to amuse herself by imagining what it would feel like to take Bowers on in a good sweaty match of hand-to-hand. The satisfying sound of bone against bone, the sweet scent of first blood.

All the image managed to do was infuriate her. Her hands were tied in that arena. A superior officer couldn't go around whipping on a uniform, no matter how much she deserved it.

So she drove through the gates and up the gracious sweep of private road to the stunning house of stone and glass that was Roarke's. She left her car in front, hoping, really hoping, that tight-assed Summerset said something snotty about it.

She barely felt the cold as she jogged up the steps and opened the tall front door. There she waited, one beat, two. It normally took Roarke's butler no longer to slide into the foyer and insult her. Today, she wanted him to, craved it.

When the house remained silent, she snarled in frustration. The day, she thought, was going just perfectly. She couldn't even take a swing at her worst enemy to release some steam.

She really, really wanted to hit something.

She stripped off her leather jacket, deliberately tossed it over the carved newel post. But still, he didn't materialize.

Bastard, she thought in disgust and stalked upstairs. What the hell was she supposed to do with this barely controlled fury bubbling inside her if she couldn't hammer Summerset? She didn't want a round with the sparring droid, damn it. She wanted human contact. Good, violent human contact.

She stepped into the bedroom, intending to sulk in a

hot shower before going to work. And there was Roarke. She eyed him narrowly. Obviously, he'd just come in himself and was just hanging his suit jacket in the closet.

He turned, angled his head. The glittering eyes, flushed face, and aggressive stance told him just what kind of mood she was in. He closed the closet door and smiled. "Hello, darling, and how was your day?"

"It sucked. Where's Summerset?"

Roarke arched a brow as he crossed the room. He could all but see waves of temper and frustration pumping off of her. "He has the evening off."

"Great, fine." She swung away. "The one time I actually want the son of a bitch, he's not here."

Roarke's eyebrow stayed lifted as he slanted a look toward the fat gray cat curled on the bed. They shared a brief, silent stare, and Galahad, preferring to avoid violence, leaped to the floor and slinked out the door.

Cautious himself, Roarke ran his tongue around his teeth. "Something I can do for you?"

She whipped her head around, scowled at him. "I like your face, so I don't want to break it."

"Lucky me," Roarke murmured. He watched for a moment as she paced, prowled, kicked halfheartedly at the sofa in the seating area. And muttered to herself. "That's a lot of energy you've got going on in there, Lieutenant. I think I can help you with that."

"If you tell me to take a goddamn soother, I'm going to—" It was as far as she got before her breath whooshed out and she found herself tackled onto the bed. "Don't mess with me, ace." She shifted, bucked. "I'm in a pisser of a mood."

"So I see." He barely blocked her elbow, managed to cuff her wrists with one hand, and used his weight to keep her pinned. "Let's just put all that to good use, shall we?"

"When I want sex, I'll let you know," she said between her teeth.

"Okay." Even as she hissed at him, he lowered his head and bit her lightly on the throat. "While I'm waiting,

I'll just amuse myself a bit. You have a . . . ripe taste when you're mad.''

"Damn it, Roarke.'' But his tongue was doing incredible things to the side of her neck, and the juices stirred by anger began to swim in a different direction. "Cut it out,'' she muttered, but when his free hand closed over her breast, her body arched toward him.

"Nearly done.'' His mouth skimmed her jaw, then crushed onto hers in the fierce and feral kiss her mood seemed to demand. He tasted temper, the edge of violence, the whip of passion. His body tightened, his own needs flashed. But when he eased back, he gave her a bland smile. "Well, if you'd rather be alone—''

She broke his loosened hold on her hands and grabbed him by the front of his shirt. "Too late, pal. Now I want sex.''

Grinning, he let her shove him onto his back. She straddled him, planted her hands on his chest. "And I'm feeling mean,'' she warned him.

"Well, I did say for better or worse.'' He reached up, releasing her weapon harness before he began to unbutton her blouse.

"I said *mean*.'' Her breath was already coming short as her fingers curled into the black silk of his shirt. "How much did this thing cost?''

"I have no idea.''

"Just as well,'' she decided and tore it open. Before he could decide whether to laugh or curse, she pounced, her teeth digging into his shoulder. "It's going to be rough.'' Empowered by the taste of flesh, she fisted her hands in his hair. "And it's going to be fast.''

Her mouth dived to his, taking greedily, driving the kiss toward violence. Glorying in it. She clawed at him, ripping at his clothes as they rolled over the bed.

Wrestling now, hands grappling to take, mouths ravenous. Frantic groans, quick shudders came from both of them as weaknesses were sought out and exploited. They knew each other's bodies and those weaknesses well.

All the frustrated energy peaked into hunger, a need to

take and take quickly, to take all. His teeth on her naked
breast, his hands bruising her flesh in their rush to possess,
only heightened the appetites. Her own breath was in rags
and her mind in tatters as she arched up, pressed sex to
sex.

There was a feral sound in her throat as he yanked her
up to her knees, as their bodies met, torso to torso, and
mouth plundered mouth.

"Now, damn it." Her nails bit into his back, scraped,
slid off skin gone damp with sweat. Desire, of the darkest
and most dangerous hue was swirling inside her. She saw
something of the same mirrored in Roarke's brilliant blue
eyes as they dragged each other down again.

She rose over him, lowered onto him in two agile mo-
tions, and arched her back with a moan, as pleasure lanced
through her.

Then it was all speed again. Speed, motion, still more
greed. *More and more* was all she could think as he
pounded into her, harder, faster. The orgasm had claws.

He watched her give herself to it, to him, her body
bowed back now, gleaming with sweat, her eyes dark and
blind to everything but what they brought to each other.

And when she shuddered, when she screamed, he
yanked her down, shoving her onto her back. And dragging her hips high, thrusting deep, deeper, drove them
both over.

chapter four

Lazily, Roarke nuzzled Eve's throat. He loved the dark, rich taste that good, healthy sex brought to her skin. "Feel better now?"

She managed something between a grunt and a moan and made his lips curve. In a slow roll, smooth with practice, he reversed their positions, stroked her back, and waited.

Her ears were still ringing, her body so limp she didn't think she could fight off a toddler with a water laser. The hands gliding up and down her back were lulling her gently toward sleep. She was teetering on the edge of it when Galahad, deciding all was clear, padded back into the room to leap cheerfully on her naked ass.

"Jesus!" Her jerk of protest caused him to dig for balance with his sharp little claws. She yelped, swatted, bounced, then crawled off Roarke to safety. When she twisted to check for blood, she caught Roarke's grin and saw the cat now purring maniacally under his long, clever fingers.

There was nothing to do but scowl at both of them. "I guess the two of you think that was funny."

"We each like to welcome you home in our own way."

Even as her lip curled, he was sitting up, taking her face in his hands. Within that frame, her cheeks were flushed, her mouth sulky, her eyes sleepy. "You look very attractively . . . used, Lieutenant." His mouth cruised over hers, nibbled, and nearly made her forget she was annoyed with him. "Why don't we have a shower, then, over dinner, you can tell me what's upset you."

"I'm not hungry." She muttered it. Now that the temper had flashed, she wanted to brood.

"I am." He simply pulled her off the bed with him.

He let her sulk, let himself speculate, until they were down in the kitchen. Knowing Eve, he decided whatever had put her blood on boil was job-related. She would tell him, he thought as he chose stuffed shells for both of them from the menu of the AutoChef. Sharing her burdens wasn't a natural act for her, but she would tell him.

He poured wine, then sat across from her at the cozy eating area tucked under the window. "Did you identify your sidewalk sleeper?"

"Yeah." She ran a fingertip up the stem of the wineglass, then shrugged. "He was one of those post–Urban War dropouts. It's unlikely anyone will be able to say why he traded an ordinary life for a miserable one."

"Maybe his ordinary one was miserable enough."

"Yeah, maybe." She shrugged it off. Had to. "We'll release his body to his daughter when we're done with it."

"It makes you sad," Roarke murmured and had her gaze lifting to his.

"It can't get inside you."

"It makes you sad," he repeated. "And the way you channel that is to find who killed him."

"That's my job." She picked up her fork, stabbed one of the shells on her plate without interest. "If more people would do their jobs instead of screwing with people doing theirs, we'd be a hell of a lot better off."

Ah, he thought. "So, who screwed with you, Lieutenant?"

She started to shrug again, wanted to act as if it didn't matter a damn. But it came bubbling up her throat and out before she could stop it. "Fucking stiff scooper. Hated me on sight, who knows why."

"And assuming a stiff scooper is what its colorful name indicates, does he have a name?"

"She. Half-ass Bowers from the one-six-two filed a complaint against me after I gave her a wrist slap for sloppy work. Over ten years on the force, I've never had an official complaint on my record. Goddamn it." She snatched up her wine, gulped.

It wasn't the temper that had him laying a hand over hers but the sheer unhappiness crowded with it in her eyes. "Is it serious?"

"It's bullshit," she tossed back, "but it's there."

Roarke turned her hand, palm up, to his, squeezed once. "Tell me about it."

It spewed out of her with considerably less restraint than the formal oral report she'd given Whitney. But as she snapped the words out, she began to eat without realizing it.

"So," he said when she'd run down. "Basically, you pissed off a troublemaker who retaliated by filing a whiny complaint—something she appears to have a habit of doing—and your commanding officer is officially and personally in your corner."

"Yeah, but . . ." She closed her mouth, simmered in silence for a moment because he'd encapsulized it all so neatly. "It's not as simple as you make it sound."

It wouldn't be, Roarke mused, *not for Eve.* "Maybe not, but the fact is, if anyone put your record against hers, she'd just look like more of an idiot than she does now."

That cheered her a little. "She put a smear on my record," Eve continued. "The goons in IAB love to look at smears, and I had to take time away from a case to answer her stupid accusation. Otherwise, I'd have been able to run data scans on the surgeons Cagney sent me. She doesn't give a damn about the case. She just wanted to take a shot at me because I dressed her down and sent her off for coffee. She's got no business on the force.''

"Very likely she's never made the mistake of going after a cop quite so clean and well-respected as you.'' He watched her brows draw together at his comment, smiled a little as she squirmed.

"I want to go stomp on her face.''

"Of course,'' Roarke said lightly. "Or you wouldn't be the woman I adore.'' He picked up her hand, kissed her fingers, and was pleased to see a reluctant smile soften her lips. "Want to go find her and beat her up? I'll hold your coat.''

This time she laughed. "You just want to watch two women fight. Why do guys get off on that?''

Eyes deeply blue and amused, Roarke sipped his wine. "The constant hope that during the battle clothes will be ripped away. We're so easily entertained.''

"You're telling me.'' She glanced down with some surprise at her empty plate. She supposed she'd been hungry after all. Sex, food, and a sympathetic ear. Just more of the wonders, she thought, of marriage. "Thanks. Looks like I do feel better.''

Because he'd put the meal together, she thought it only fair she deal with the dishes. She carried them to the dishwasher, dumped them in, and considered the job done.

Roarke didn't bother to mention she'd put the plates in backwards and had neglected to give the machine any orders. The kitchen wasn't Eve's turf, he thought. And Summerset would deal with it.

"Let's go up to my office. I have something for you.''

Wary suspicion narrowed her eyes. "I told you after Christmas, no more presents.''

"I like giving you presents,'' he said and opted for the elevator rather than the stairs. He trailed a fingertip down the sleeve of the cashmere sweater he'd given her. "I like seeing them on you. But this isn't that kind of present.''

"I've got work. Time to make up.''

"Mmm-hmm.''

She shifted her stance as the elevator glided from vertical to horizontal mode. "It's not a trip or anything? I can't take off after I lost all those days due to injury last fall."

The hand he'd laid lightly on her shoulder flexed into a fist before he could control it. She'd been badly hurt a few months earlier, and he didn't care to be reminded of it. "No, it's not a trip." Though he intended to drag her away for at least a couple of days to the tropics as soon as their schedules allowed.

She relaxed at the beach, he thought, the way she seemed to nowhere else.

"Okay, then what? Because I really have to put in a couple of hours."

"Get us some coffee, will you?" He said it carelessly as he stepped out into his office. And made her grind her teeth. She had to remind herself that he'd let her vent her frustrations, that he'd listened to her side of things. And he'd offered to hold her coat.

But her teeth were still clamped together in annoyance when she set the coffee on his console.

He gave her an absent hum of thanks and was already fiddling with controls. He could have just used voice command, she knew, but he often liked to work his machines—toys, she often thought—manually. Keeping those clever, one-time thief's fingers nimble, she mused now.

His home office suited him as much as his plush headquarters did. The sleek console with colorful controls and lights was an excellent frame for him when he slid into the deep U to work.

In addition to the jazzy technology, the faxes and communications, the holo options and screens, there was an elegance to the room, the kind that seemed to walk hand in hand with him whether he was in a boardroom or an alley.

The gorgeous tiles of the floor, the expansive windows clear-treated for privacy, the scattering of art and artifact, the streamlined machines and cabinets that would offer exclusive food or drink at the most careless command.

It was, she thought, occasionally disconcerting to look

at him in here, while he worked. To see over and over again how gorgeous he was and know he belonged to her. It tended to weaken her at the oddest moments. Because it weakened her now, she made her voice cold and sharp.

"Want dessert, too?"

"Maybe later." His gaze glanced over her face before he nodded to the opposing wall. "On screens."

"What?"

"Your list of surgeons, along with personal and professional data."

She whirled around, then back so quickly she would have knocked his coffee onto his controls if he hadn't snatched it out of the way in time. "Careful, darling."

"Damn it, Roarke. *Damn it!* I told you specifically to stay out of this."

"Did you?" In direct contrast to hers, his voice was mild and amused. "It would appear I disobeyed."

"This is my job, and I know how to do it. I don't want you running names and accessing data."

"I see. Well." He passed his hand over something and the screens across the room went blank. "All gone," he said cheerfully and watched, with delight, as her mouth dropped open. "I'll just catch up on my reading while you spend the next hour or so accessing the data I already had for you. That makes sense."

She could think of nothing to say that wouldn't sound idiotic, so she merely made frustrated sounds. It would indeed take her an hour, minimum, and in all likelihood, she wouldn't be able to go as deep as he had. "You think you're so damn smart."

"Aren't I?"

She managed to choke back a laugh and folded her arms. "Bring it back. You *can* bring it back."

"Of course, but now it'll cost you." He angled his head, crooked a finger.

Pride fought with expediency. As always, the job won, but she kept a scowl on her face as she skirted the console and joined him behind it. "What?" she demanded, then swore when he yanked her onto his lap. "I'm not playing any of your perverted games, pal."

"And I had such hopes." He passed a hand over the controls again, and the data popped back on the screens. "There are seven surgeons in the city who meet the requirements of your case."

"How do you know the requirements? I didn't get that specific when I saw you today." She turned her head until they were nose to nose. "Did you poke into my case files?"

"I'm not going to answer that without counsel present. Your witness indicated two people," he continued while she studied him with narrowed eyes. "I'm assuming you're not ruling out women."

"Do I poke into your files?" she demanded, jabbing a finger into his shoulder to emphasize each word. "Do I go sneaking around into your stock options or whatever?"

She couldn't access his files with a homemade boomer, but he only smiled. "My life's an open book for you, darling." Since it was there, he caught her bottom lip between his teeth and tugged gently. "Would you like to see the video record of my last board meeting?"

She would have told him to bite her, but he already had. "Never mind." She turned around again and tried not to be overly pleased when his arms came cozily around her. Still, she leaned back against him and settled in. "Tia Wo, general surgeon with specialty in organ transplant and repair, private practice, affiliated with Drake, East Side Surgery, and the Nordick Clinic, Chicago."

Eve read the initial data thoughtfully. "Description and visual on-screen. She's six foot," Eve noted, "and hefty. Easy for a brewhead to mistake her for a man in the dark, especially if she was wearing a long coat. What do we know about Dr. Wo?"

Responding to her voice command, the computer began to list details while Eve studied the image of an unsmiling woman of fifty-eight with straight, dark hair; cool, blue eyes; and a sharply pointed chin.

Her education had been excellent, her training superior. And her nearly thirty years as an organ plucker had earned her a dazzling annual salary, which she supplemented by endorsing the products of NewLife Organ Replacement, Inc. A manufacturing firm that, Eve noted with barely a sigh, was owned and operated by Roarke Enterprises.

She'd been twice divorced, once from a man, once from a woman, and had held single status for the last six years. She had no children, no criminal record, and only three malpractice suits pending.

"Do you know her?" Eve asked.

"Hmm. Very slightly. Cold, ambitious, very focused. She's reputed to have the hands of a god and the mind of a machine. As you see, she was president of the American Medical Association five years ago. She is a powerful woman in her field."

"She looks like she'd enjoy cutting people open," Eve murmured.

"So I'd imagine. Why else do it?"

She jerked a shoulder and requested the rest of the names. She studied them in turn: data, faces.

"How many of these people do you know?"

"All of them," Roarke told her. "In a disconnected, social way for the most part. Fortunately, I've never required their professional services."

And his instincts, Eve thought, were as sharp as his health. "Who's the most powerful here?"

"Power, that would be Cagney, Wo, Waverly."

"Michael Waverly," she murmured, calling back his data. "Forty-eight, single, chief of surgery at Drake and current president of the AMA." She studied the elegant face, the intense green eyes, and the golden mane of hair.

"Who's the most arrogant?" she asked Roarke.

"I believe that's a requirement of all surgeons, but if I had to choose degrees, I'd go for Wo again, certainly Waverly, and toss in Hans Vanderhaven—head of research at Drake, another organ plucker affiliated with the top three health centers in the country, with solid connections abroad. He's about sixty-five and on his forth marriage. Each successive wife goes down a decade in age. This one's a former body sculpting model and barely old enough to vote."

"I wasn't asking for gossip," Eve said, rather primly, then caved. "What else?"

"His former wives hate his guts. The last one tried to perform a little impromptu surgery on him with a nail file when she discovered him playing doctor with the model. The AMA's Morals Board wagged their finger at him over it, and did little else."

"Those are the ones I'll look at first," she decided. "What was done to Snooks took arrogance and power as well as skill."

"You're going to run into a lot of walls on this one, Eve. They'll close ranks on you."

"I've got murder one, with body mutilation and organ theft backing it." She dragged her hands through her hair. "When the heat's turned up high enough, people roll over. If one of these slicers knows something, I'll get it out of them."

"If you want a more personal look, we can attend the Drake Center's fund-raiser fashion show and dinner dance at the end of the week."

She winced. She'd rather have gone bare-knuckled with a Zeus addict. "Fashion show." She suppressed a shudder. "Whoopee. Yeah, we'll do that, but I should put in for distress pay."

"Leonardo's one of the designers," he told her. "Mavis will be there."

The thought of her free-wheeling, uniquely stylish friend at a stuffy medical fund-raiser perked Eve up. "Wait until they get a load of her."

If it hadn't been for the Bowers situation, the following day Eve would have opted to work in her home office on a computer that didn't give her grief. But as a matter of pride, she wanted to be visible at Cop Central when the buzz started.

She spent the morning in court giving testimony on a case she'd closed some months before and arrived at Central just after one. Her first move was to hunt up Peabody. Rather than go straight to her office and put out a call on her communicator, Eve walked through the detective's bullpen.

"Hey, Dallas." Baxter, one of the detectives who most enjoyed razzing her, sent her a wink and a grin. "Hope you kick her ass."

It was, Eve knew, a show of support. Though it cheered her, she shrugged and kept moving. A few other comments were tossed out from desks and cubicles, all running on the same theme. The first order of business when a finger was pointed at one of their own was to break the finger.

"Dallas." Ian McNab, an up-and-coming detective assigned to the Electronic Detective Division, loitered outside Peabody's cubicle. He was pretty as a picture with his long golden hair braided back, six silver dangles in his left ear, and a cheerful smile on his face. Eve had worked with him on a couple of cases and knew under the pretty-boy exterior and chatterbox mouth hid a quick brain and steady instincts.

"Things slow in EDD, McNab?"

"Never." He flashed his grin. "I just did a search and run for one of your boys here, thought I'd harass Peabody before I headed back to where real cops work."

"Would you get this pimple off my butt, Lieutenant?" Peabody complained, and she did indeed look harassed.

"I haven't touched her butt. Yet." McNab smiled. Irritating Peabody was one of his favorite pastimes. "Thought maybe you could use a little E-work on this problem you've got."

Well able to read between the lines, Eve lifted a brow. He was offering to bypass channels and dig into Bowers. "I'm handling it, thanks. I need Peabody, McNab. Shoo."

"Your call." He glanced back into the cubicle, leered. "Catch you later, She-Body." Even as she hissed at him, he swaggered away, whistling.

"Jerk," was all Peabody could say as she got to her feet. "My reports are filed, Lieutenant. The ME's findings came in an hour ago and are waiting for you."

"Shoot everything pertaining to the current homicide down to Dr. Mira. Her office is squeezing me in on a quick consult. Add this," she said, passing Peabody a disc. "It's a list of the top surgeons in the city. Clean up as much of the paperwork as you can in the next couple of hours. We're going back to the scene."

"Yes, sir. Are you okay?"

"I haven't got time to worry about idiots." Eve turned and headed for her office.

And there she found a message from the idiots in maintenance telling her there was nothing wrong with her equipment. She was reduced to scowling as she engaged her tele-link to contact Feeney in EDD.

His comfortably rumpled face filled her screen and helped her ignore the whiny buzz on audio.

"Dallas, what is this pile of shit? Who the hell is Bowers? And why are you letting her live?"

She had to smile. There was no one more reliable than Feeney. "I don't have time to waste on her. I've got a dead sidewalk sleeper missing his heart."

"Missing his heart?" Feeney's ragged, rust-colored eyebrows shot up. "Why didn't I hear that?"

"Must be slipping," she said easily. "And it's more fun to gossip about cops squaring off against each other than one more dead sleeper. But this one's interesting. Let me give you the rundown."

She told him, in that quick, formal shorthand cops use like a second language. Feeney nodded, pursed his lips, shook his head, grunted. "Life just gets sicker," he said when she'd finished. "What do you need?"

"Can you do a quick like-crimes check for me?"

"City, national, international, interplanetary?"

She tried a winning smile. "All? As much as you can by end of shift?"

His habitually morose face only drooped a bit more.

"You never ask for the little things, kid. Yeah, we'll get on it."

"Appreciate it. I'd hit IRCCA myself," she continued, referring to one of Feeney's loves, the International Resource Center on Criminal Activity, "but my equipment's acting up again."

"Wouldn't if you'd treat it with some respect."

"Easy for you to say when EDD gets all the prime stuff. I'm going to be in the field later. If you get any hits, get in touch."

"If there's anything to hit, I'll have it. Later," he said and disconnected.

She took the time to study Morris's final report, found no surprises or new data. So Snooks could go home to Wisconsin, she thought, with the daughter he hadn't seen in thirty years. Was it sadder, she wondered, that he'd chosen to live the last part of his life without anyone, cut off from family, cut off from his past?

Though it hadn't been a matter of choice, she'd done the same. But that break, that amputation from what had been, had made her who she was. Had it done the same for him, in the most pathetic of ways?

Shaking it off, she coaxed her machine—by ramming it twice with her fist—to spill out the list of dealers and chemi-heads from the area surrounding the crime scene. And a single name made her smile, thin and sharp.

Good old Ledo, she mused, and sat back in her chair. She had thought the long-time dealer of smoke and Jazz had been a guest of the state. Apparently, he'd been kicked three months before.

It wouldn't be hard to track Ledo down, she decided, and to coax him—in the same manner she'd used with her equipment if necessary—to chat.

But Mira came first. Gathering up what she would need for both interviews, Eve started out of her office. She tagged Peabody en route and ordered her aide to meet her in the garage at the vehicle in one hour.

• • •

Mira's office might have been a clearinghouse for emotional and mental problems. It might have been a center for the dissemination, examination, and analysis of the criminal mind, but it was always soothing, elegant, and classy.

Eve had never worked out how it could be both. Or how the doctor herself could work day after day with the worst that society spat out and still maintain her calm, unruffled poise.

Eve considered her the only genuine and complete lady she knew.

She was a trim woman with sable-colored hair waving back from a quietly lovely face. She favored slim, softly colored suits and such classic ornamentations as a single strand of pearls.

She wore one today, with discreet pearl drops at her ears, to accessorize a collarless suit in pale pine green. As usual, she gestured Eve to one of her scoop-shaped chairs and ordered tea from her AutoChef.

"How are you, Eve?"

"Okay." Eve always had to remember to change gears when meeting with Mira. The atmosphere, the woman, the attitude didn't allow her to dive straight into business. The little things mattered to Mira. And, over time, Mira had come to matter to Eve. She accepted the tea she would pretend to drink. "Ah, how was your vacation?"

Mira smiled, pleased Eve remembered she'd been away for a few days, and had thought to ask. "It was marvelous. Nothing revitalizes body and soul quite so much as a week at a spa. I was rubbed, scrubbed, polished, and pampered." She laughed and sipped her tea. "You'd have hated every minute of it."

Mira crossed her legs, balancing her delicate cup and saucer one-handed with a casual grace Eve decided some women were simply born with. The feminine floral china always made her feel clumsy.

"Eve, I've heard about this difficulty you're having with one of the uniforms. I'm sorry for it."

"It doesn't amount to anything," Eve said, then

breathed a sigh. This was, after all, Mira. "It pissed me off. She's a sloppy cop with an attitude, and now she's put a blotch on my record."

"I know how much that record means to you." Mira leaned forward, touched her hand to Eve's. "You should know that the higher you rise and the more your reputation shines, the more a certain type of person will want to tarnish it. This won't. I can't say much, as it's privileged, but I will tell you that this particular officer has a reputation for frivolous complaints and is not taken seriously in most cases."

Eve's gaze sharpened. "You've tested her?"

Inclining her head, Mira lifted a brow. "I can't comment on that." But she made certain Eve knew the answer was affirmative. "I simply want, as a friend and a colleague, to offer you my complete support. Now . . ." She sat back again, sipped her tea again. "On to your case."

Eve brooded for a minute before reminding herself that her personal business couldn't interfere with the job. "The killer has to be trained, and highly skilled, in laser surgery and organ removal."

"Yes, I read Dr. Morris's conclusions and agree. This doesn't, however, mean you're looking for a member of the medical community." She held up a finger before Eve could protest. "He could be retired or he could have, as many, many surgeons do, burnt out. Quite obviously he's lost his way, or he would never have violated the most sacred of oaths and taken a life. Whether or not he's licensed and practicing, I can't tell you."

"But you agree that if not now, at one time he was."

"Yes. Undoubtedly, based on your findings at scene and Morris's postmortem, you're looking for someone with specific skills that require years of training and practice."

Considering, Eve angled her head. "And what would you say about the type of person who could coldly and skillfully murder an essentially dying man for an essentially worthless organ, then save the next patient under his care on the table in the operating room?"

"I would say it's a possible type of megalomania. The God complex many doctors possess. And very often need to possess," she added, "in order to have the courage, even the arrogance to cut into the human body."

"Those who do, enjoy it."

"Enjoy?" Mira made a humming sound. "Perhaps. I know you don't care for doctors, but most have a vocation, a great need to heal. In any highly skilled profession there are those who are . . . brusque," she said. "Those who forget humility." She smiled a little. "It isn't your humility that makes you an excellent cop but your innate belief in your own talent for the job."

"Okay." Accepting that, Eve sat back, nodded.

"However, it's also your compassion that keeps you from forgetting why the job matters. Others in your field and in mine lose that."

"With cops who do, the job becomes routine, with maybe a little power tweaked in," Eve commented. "With doctors, you'd have to add money."

"Money's a motivator," Mira agreed. "But it takes years for a doctor to pay back the financial investment in his education and training. There are other, more immediate compensations. Saving lives is a powerful thing, Eve, having the talent, the skill to do so is for some a kind of burst of light. How can they be like others when they've put their hands into a human body and healed it?"

She paused, sipped contemplatively at her tea. "And for some among that personality type," she continued in her soft, soothing voice, "there can and often is the defense of emotional distance. This is not a human under my scalpel, but a patient, a case."

"Cops do the same."

Mira looked straight into Eve's eyes. "Not all cops. And the ones who don't, who can't, might suffer, but they make much more of a difference. In this investigation, I think we can agree straight off on some basic points. You are not looking for someone with a personal grudge against the victim. He is not driven by rage or violence. He is controlled, purposeful, organized, and detached."

"Wouldn't any surgeon have to be?" Eve asked.

"Yes. He performed an operation, successfully, for his purpose. He cares about his work, demonstrated by the time and effort he took in the operation. Organ removal and transplant is well out of my field, but I am aware that when the donor's life is not a concern, such a procedure doesn't require this kind of meticulous care. The careful incision, the sealing of the wound. He's proud of what he is, very likely past the point of arrogance. He is not afraid of consequences, in my opinion, because he doesn't believe there will be any. He is above that."

"He doesn't fear being caught?"

"No, he doesn't. Or he feels protected in the event his actions are discovered. I would conclude that he is successful—whether he is now actively practicing or not—secure, devoted to his task, and very likely enjoys some prominence in his circle."

Mira sipped her tea again, frowned. "I should say *they*. Your report stated there were two involved. I would think it would be standard practice to bring an anesthesiologist or trained assistant to handle that end of the procedure, or a second surgeon with some knowledge of anesthesia to assist."

"They didn't have to worry about the patient surviving, Eve pointed out. "But I'd think he wouldn't settle for anyone but the best. And it would have to be someone he trusted."

"Or controlled. Someone he knew was loyal to the purpose."

Eve lifted her cup, then had to control a wince when she remembered it wasn't coffee. "What's the purpose?"

"As to the motive behind taking the heart, I only see two avenues. One is profit, which seems very narrow, given Dr. Morris's evaluation of the victim's overall health. The second would be experimentation."

"What kind of experiments?"

Mira lifted a hand, waved it vaguely. "I don't know, but I'll tell you, as a doctor myself, the possibility frightens me. During the height of the Urban Wars, illegal experimentation on the dead and dying was quietly accepted. It wasn't the first time in history atrocities were commonplace, but one always hopes it would be the last. The justification then was that so much could be learned, other lives saved, but there is no justification.''

She set her tea aside, folded her hands on her lap. "I'm praying, Eve, that this is an isolated incident. Because if it's not, what you're dealing with is more dangerous than murder. You could be dealing with a mission, cloaked under a veil of the greater good.''

"Sacrifice the few to save the many?'' Eve shook her head slowly. "It's a stand that's been taken before. It always crumbles.''

"Yes.'' There was something of pity and something of fear in Mira's quiet eyes. "But never soon enough.''

chapter five

Most people were creatures of habit. Eve figured a second rate chemi-dealer who enjoyed gobbling up his own products would follow the rule. If memory served, Ledo liked to spend his worthless days fleecing suckers at Compu-Pool or Sexcapades at a nasty little joint called Game-town.

She didn't think a few years in a cage would have changed his recreational choices.

In the bowels of downtown, the buildings were slicked with filth, the streets scattered with it. After a recycling crew had been attacked, their bones broken and their truck destroyed, the union had crossed this four-block section off the list. There wasn't a city employee who ventured into what was known as the Square without combat gear and stunners. It was in their contract.

Eve wore a riot vest under her jacket and had ordered Peabody to do the same. It wouldn't keep them from getting their throats slit, but it would stop a knife to the heart.

"Put your stunner on wide range," Eve ordered, and though Peabody exhaled sharply, she said nothing.

Her run on cults that linked any knowns to the type of murder they were investigating had turned up nothing.

She'd been relieved. Having dealt with that kind of terror and butchery once, Peabody knew she'd live happily never having to deal with it again.

But as they drove into the Square, she thought she'd take a few bloodthirsty Satan worshipers over the residents of this sector any day of the week.

The streets weren't empty, but they were quiet. Action here waited for dark. The few who loitered in doorways or roamed the sidewalks did so with their eyes sharp and moving, their hands in pockets that held a weapon of choice.

Midway down a block, a Rapid Cab rested on its roof like an upturned turtle. Its windows were smashed, its tires stripped, and several interesting sexual suggestions had already been spray painted over its sides.

"Driver must have been brain damaged to bring a fare down here," Eve muttered as she swung around the abandoned cab.

"What does that make us?" Peabody asked.

"Tough-ass cops." Eve grinned and noted that while the graffiti looked very fresh, there were no signs of blood.

Eve spotted two beat droids in full riot gear making their pass in an armored black and white. She flagged them, holding her badge to the window.

"The driver make it out?"

"We were in the vicinity and dispersed the crowd." The droid in the passenger's seat smiled just a little. Occasionally some E-man programmed a beat droid with a sense of humor. "We secured the driver and transported him to the edge of the sector."

"Cab's a dead loss," she commented, then forgot it. "You know Ledo?"

"Sir." The droid nodded. "Convicted illegals manufacturer and distributor." That faint smile again. "Rehabilitated."

"Yeah, right. He's a pillar of the community now. He still hang down in Gametown?"

"It is his known area of amusement."

"I'm leaving my car here. I want it in one piece when I get back." She activated all antitheft and vandalism alarms and deterrents, then stepped out and chose her mark.

He was lanky, mean-eyed, and sipping mechanically from a brown brew bottle as he leaned against a scarred steel wall decorated with various suggestions on sexual activities that ran along the same lines as those decorating the overturned cab. Several were misspelled, but the visual aids weren't bad.

As Peabody fought to keep her heart from blocking her throat, Eve strode up to him, leaned into his face. "You see that car?"

His mouth turned up in a sneer. "Looks like a cop-bitch car to me."

"That's right." She caught his free hand by the wrist, twisting it hard before he could reach into his pocket. "And if I come back and see that anybody's messed with it, this cop-bitch is going to kick your balls into your throat, then tie them around your neck and choke you with them. You got that?"

He wasn't sneering now. Color had flooded into his cheeks, rage shined in his eyes. But he nodded.

"Good." She released him, stepped back, then turned and walked away without looking back.

"Jesus, Dallas, Jesus. Why did you do that?"

"Because now he's got an investment in making sure we've got transpo when we leave. That type doesn't mess with cops. He just thinks mean thoughts. Usually," Eve added with a wicked grin as they started down the dirty metal stairs to the underground.

"That's a joke, right? Ha ha?" Peabody's fingers twitched over the weapon strapped to her side.

"Watch your back," Eve said mildly as they plunged into the gloomy, urine-colored light of New York's underbelly.

Slime, Eve mused, had to breed somewhere. This was ripe ground for it. Below the streets, out of the air, into the deep, dank world of unlicensed whores and doomed addicts.

Every few years, the mayor's office made noises about cleaning up the underground. Every few years, the talk channels on-screen debated and condemned. Occasionally, a quick, half-assed police and security sweep was employed, a handful of losers picked up and tossed in cages, some of the worst of the joints shut down for a day or two.

She'd been on one of those sweeps during her days in uniform, and she hadn't forgotten the bowel-loosening terror, the screams, the flash of blades or stink of home-made boomers.

She hadn't forgotten that Feeney had been her trainer then as she was Peabody's now. And he'd gotten her through it whole.

Now she kept her pace brisk while her gaze scanned side to side.

Music echoed: harsh, clashing sounds that battered the walls and the closed doors of the clubs. The tunnels weren't heated, not any longer, and her breath whooshed out in white puffs and vanished into the yellow light.

A used-up whore in a ragged peacoat completed financial transactions with a used-up john. Both eyed her, then Peabody's uniform before slinking away to get to the heart of the deal.

Someone had built a barrel fire in one of the spit-narrow alleyways. Men huddled around it, exchanging credits for little packs of illegals. All movement stopped when she came to the head of the alley, but she kept walking by.

She could have risked broken bones and blood, called for backup, rousted them. And they or others like them would have been dealing death over the smelly fire by nightfall.

She'd learned to accept that not everything could be changed, not everything could be fixed.

She followed the snake of the tunnel, then paused to study the flashing lights of Gametown. The murky reds and blues didn't look celebrational, pumping against the sickly yellow overheads. Somehow they looked both sly and hopeless to her, like the aging whore she'd just passed in the tunnels.

And they reminded her of another garish light, pulsing red against the dirty window of the last dirty room she'd shared with her father. Before he'd raped her that final time.

Before she'd killed him and left that beaten young girl behind.

"Sir?"

"I don't remember her," Eve murmured as the memories threatened to wash over and drown her.

"Who? Lieutenant? Dallas?" Uneasy with the blank look in Eve's eyes, Peabody tried to look everywhere at once. "Who do you see?"

"Nobody." She snapped back, infuriated that her stomach muscles quivered with the memory flash. It happened now and again. Something would trigger those memories and the fear and guilt that swam with them. "Nobody," she said again. "We go in together. You stay with me, follow my moves. If things get sticky, don't worry about procedure. Play dirty."

"Oh, you bet." Swallowing hard, Peabody stepped up to the door, then through, shoulder to shoulder with Eve.

There were games and plenty of them. Blasts, screams, moans, laughter poured out of machines. There were two holo-fields on this level, with one in use as a skinny kid with vacant eyes paid his shot to do battle with his choice of Roman gladiator, Urban War terrorist, or spine cracker. Eve didn't bother to watch the first round.

For live entertainment, there was a wrestling pit where two women with enormous man-made breasts shiny with oil grunted and slithered to the cheers of the crowd.

The walls were alive with screens that flashed action from dozens of sporting events, on and off planet. Bets were laid. Money lost. Fists flew.

She ignored them as well, working her way through the areas, beyond privacy tubes where patrons drank and played their games of chance or skill in greedy solitude, past the bar where others sat sulkily, and into the next area where music played low and dark in an edgy backdrop to more games.

A dozen pool tables were lined up like coffins, the border lights flickering as balls clicked or bumped. Half the tables were empty, but for those in use, the stakes were serious.

A black man with his shining bald head decorated with a gold tattoo of a coiled snake matched his skill against one of the house droids. She was tall, beefy, dressed in a pair of neon green swatches that covered tits and crotch. A knife with a pencil-slim blade was strapped, unsheathed, at her hip.

Eve spotted Ledo at the back table, playing what appeared to be round the clock with three other men. From the smug smile on Ledo's face and the dark expression on the others, it was a safe bet who was winning.

She passed the droid first, watched her finger her sticker in warning or out of habit as the snake tattoo muttered something about cop cunts.

Eve might have made an issue of it, but that would have given Ledo a chance to rabbit. She didn't want to have to hunt him down a second time.

Conversation dropped off table by table, with the murmured suggestions running from vile to annoyed. In the same kind of second-nature gesture as the droid, Eve flicked open her jacket, danced her fingers over her weapon.

Ledo leaned over the table, his custom-designed cue with its silver tip poised against the humming five ball. The challenge light beeped against the left bank. If his aim was true and he popped that, then sank the ball, he'd be up another fifty credits.

He wasn't drunk yet, or smoke hazed. He never touched his products during a match. He was as straight as he ever was, his bony body poised, his pale straw hair slicked back from a milk-white face. Only his eyes had color, and they were a chocolate brown going pink at the rims. He was a few slippery steps away from becoming one of the funky-junkies he served.

If he kept up the habit, his eyes wouldn't stay sharp enough to play the ball.

Eve let him take his shot. His hands were trembling lightly, but he'd adjusted the weight of his cue to compensate. He popped the light, ringing the score bell, then the ball rolled across the table and dropped cleanly into the pocket.

Though he was smart enough not to cheer, the wide grin split his face as he straightened. Then his gaze landed on Eve. He didn't place her right away, but he recognized cop.

"Hey, Ledo. We need to chat."

"I ain't done nothing. I got a game going here."

"Looks like it's time out." She stepped forward, then shifted her gaze slowly to the bulk of muscle that moved into her path.

He had skin the color of copper, and his chest was wide as Utah. A little frisson of anticipation snuck up her spine as she lifted her gaze to his face.

Both eyebrows were pierced and sported gold hoops. His eyeteeth were silver and filed to points that glinted as his lips peeled back. He had a foot on her in height, likely a hundred pounds in weight.

Her first thought was: Good, he's perfect. And she smiled at him.

"Get out of my face." She said it quietly, almost pleasantly.

"We got a game going here." His voice rumbled like thunder over a canyon. "I'm into this fuckface for five hundred. Game's not over until I get my chance to win it back."

"As soon as the fuckface and I have a chat, you can get back to your game."

She wasn't worried about Ledo running now. Not since the two other players had flanked him and were holding his spindly arms. But the slab of meat blocking her gave her a light body shove and showed his fangs again.

"We don't want cops in here." He shoved her again.
"We *eat* cops in here."

"Well, in that case . . ." She took a step back, watched
his eyes glint in triumph. Then, quick as a snake, she
snatched up Ledo's prized cue, rammed the point end into
the copper-colored gut. And when he grunted, bent forward, she swung it like a pinch hitter in the bottom of the
ninth.

It made a satisfactory cracking sound when it connected
with the side of his head. He stumbled once, shook his
head violently, then with blood in his eye, came at her.

She shot her knee into his balls, watched his face go
from gleaming copper to pasty gray as he dropped.

Stepping out of the way, Eve scanned the room. "Now,
anybody else want to try to eat this cop?"

"You broke my cue!" Close to tears, Ledo lunged forward and grabbed for his baby. The handle jerked up and
caught Eve on the cheekbone. She saw stars, but she
didn't blink.

"Ledo, you asshole," she began.

"Hold it." The man who walked in looked like one of
the ladder-climbing execs that raced along the streets
overhead and several blocks north. He was slim and stylish and clean.

The thin layer of scum that coated everything else
didn't seem to touch him.

With one hand restraining Ledo, Eve turned, yanked
out her badge. "At the moment," she said evenly, "I've
got no problem with you. Do you want that to change?"

"Not at all . . ." He flicked his silvery blue eyes at her
badge, over her face, let them pass over Peabody, who
stood at alert. "Lieutenant," he finished. "I'm afraid we
rarely have any of New York's finest visit the establish-
ment. My customers were taken by surprise."

He dropped his gaze to the man who still moaned on
the floor. "In a number of ways," he added. "I'm Carmine, and this is my place. What can I do for you?"

"Not a thing, Carmine. I just want to chat with one of
your . . . customers."

"I'm sure you'd like to have somewhere quiet to chat. Why don't I show you to one of our privacy rooms?"

"That'll be just dandy, Carmine. Peabody?" Eve wrenched the cue out of Ledo's grip and passed it over. "My aide's going to be walking right behind you, Ledo. If you don't keep up, she's likely to stumble and that precious stick of yours might get rammed right up your butt."

"I didn't do nothing," Ledo claimed in something close to a wail, but he kept pace with Eve as she followed Carmine through a curtained area to a line of doors.

Carmine opened one, gestured. "Anything else I can do for you, Lieutenant?"

"Just keep your customers chilled, Carmine. Neither one of us wants NYPSD to order a sweep on this place."

He acknowledged the warning with a nod, then left them alone as Eve tossed the whining Ledo into the room. "You stand, Peabody. You're cleared to use your weapon if anyone blinks at you."

"Yes, sir." Peabody shifted her grip on the cue, set her free hand on her stunner, and put her back to the wall.

Satisfied, Eve stepped inside, closed the door. As amenities went, it was a zero, with its narrow cot, smudged view screen, and sticky floor. But it was private.

"Well, Ledo." Eve fingered the raw bruise on her cheekbone—not because it stung, though it did. She used the gesture to make Ledo tremble in fear of retribution. "Been awhile."

"I've been clean," he said quickly, and she laughed, keeping the sound low and sharp.

"Don't insult my intelligence. You wouldn't be clean after six days in a decontamination chamber. You know what this does?" She tapped a finger on her facial bruise. "This assaulting an officer deal gives me the right to search you right now, to haul your skinny butt into Central, and to get a warrant to go through your flop."

"Hey, Dallas, hey." He held up both hands, palms up. "It was an accident."

"Maybe I'll let it go at that, Ledo. Maybe I will—if

you convince me you're in a cooperative mood."

"Damn straight, Dallas. What d'ya want? Some Jazz, Go Smoke, Ecstasy?" He started to dig in his pockets. "No charge, none whatsoever for you. I don't got it now, I'll get it."

Her eyes turned to bright gold slits. "You take anything out of your pockets but your ugly fingers, Ledo, you're even more stupid than I figured. And I figured you for a brain the size of a walnut."

His hands froze, his thin face went blank. Then he tried a manly chuckle, lifting his empty hands clear. "Like you said, Dallas, been a while. I guess maybe I forgot how you stand on shit. No harm, right?"

She said nothing, simply stared him down until the sweat popped out on his upper lip. She'd see he was back in a cage, she mused, at the first opportunity. But for now, she had bigger fish on the line.

"You—you want info? I ain't your weasel. Never was any cop's weasel, but I'm willing to trade info."

"Trade?" she said, coldly.

"Give." Even his tiny brain began to click in. "You ask, I know, I tell. How's that?"

"That's not bad. Snooks."

"The old man with the flowers?" Ledo shrugged what there was of his shoulders. "Somebody sliced him open, I hear. Took pieces of him. I don't touch that stuff."

"You deal to him."

Ledo did his best to look cagey. "Maybe we had some business, off and on."

"How'd he pay?"

"He'd beg off some credits, or sell some of his flowers and shit. He had the means when he needed a hit of something—which was mostly."

"He ever stiff you or any other dealers?"

"No. You don't give sleepers nothing unless they pay up first. Can't trust 'em. But Snooks, he was okay. No harm. He just minded his own. Nobody was doing for him that I ever heard. Good customer, no hassle."

"You work the area where he camped regularly?"

"Gotta make a living, Dallas." When she pinned him with her stare again, he realized his mistake. "Yeah, I deal there. It's mostly my turf. Couple others slide in and out, but we don't get in each other's way. Free enterprise."

"Did you see anybody who didn't look like they belonged down there lately, anybody asking about Snooks or those like him?"

"Like the suit?"

Eve felt her blood jump, but only leaned back casually against the wall. "What suit?"

"Guy came down one night, duded top to bottom. Frigid threads, man. Looked me up." More comfortable now, Ledo sat on the narrow bed, crossed one stick leg over the other. "Figured at first he didn't want to buy his stuff in his own neighborhood, you know. So he comes slumming. But he wasn't looking for hits."

Eve waited while Ledo entertained himself by picking at his cuticles. "What was he looking for?"

"Snooks, I figure. Dude said what he looked like, but I can't say that meant dick to me. Mostly the sleepers look alike. But he said how this one drew stuff and made flowers, so I copped to Snooks on that."

"And you told him where Snooks kept his crib."

"Sure, why not?" He started to smile, then his tiny little brain began the arduous process of deduction. "Man, shit, the suit cut Snooks open? Why'd he do that for? Look, look, Dallas, I'm clean here. Dude asks where the sleeper flops, I tell him. I mean, why not, right? I don't know how he's got in mind to go killing anybody."

Sweat was popping again as he jumped to his feet. "You can't bounce it back on me. I just talked to the bastard is all."

"What did he look like?"

"I don't know. Good." In plea or frustration, Ledo threw out his arms. "A dude. A suit. Clean and shiny."

"Age, race, height, weight," Eve said flatly.

"Man, man." Grabbing hanks of his hair, Ledo began to pace the tiny room. "I don't pay attention. It was a couple, three nights ago. A white dude?'' He posed it as a question, tossing Eve a hopeful look. She only watched him. "I think he was, maybe white. I was looking at his coat, you know. Long, black coat. Looked real warm and soft.''

Moron, was all Eve could think. "When you talked to him, did you have to look up, or down, or straight on?''

"Ah . . . up!'' He beamed like a child acing a spelling quiz. "Yeah, he was a tall dude. I don't get his face, Dallas. Man, it was dark and we weren't standing in no light or nothing. He had his hat on, his coat all buttoned. It was cold as a dead whore out there.''

"You never saw him before? He hasn't come around since?''

"No, just that one time. A couple—no three nights back. Just the once.'' Ledo swiped the back of his hand over his mouth. "I didn't do nothing.''

"You ought to get that tattooed on your forehead, Ledo, then you wouldn't have to say it every five minutes. I'm done for now, but I want to be able to find you, real easy, if I need to talk to you again. If I have to hunt you up, it's going to piss me off.''

"I'll be around.'' His relief was so great, his eyes went shiny with tears. "Everybody knows where to find me.''

He started to dash out, then froze like an icicle when Eve clamped a hand on his arm. "If you see the suit again, Ledo, or one like him, you get in touch. You don't say anything to put the suit off, then you get your ass on your 'link and call me.'' She bared her teeth in a smile that made his bowels loosen. "Everybody knows where to find me, too.''

He opened his mouth, then decided that cold look in her eyes meant he shouldn't attempt to negotiate weasel pay. He bobbed his head three times and sprang through the door when she opened it.

The muscles in Peabody's gut didn't unknot until they were back in their vehicle and three blocks east. "Well, that was fun,'' she said in a bright voice. "Next, let's find some sharks and go swimming.''

"You held, Peabody."

The muscles that had just loosened quivered with pleasure. From Eve, it was the staunchest of cop compliments. "I was scared right down to the toes."

"That's because you're not stupid. If you were stupid, you wouldn't be riding with me. Now we know they wanted Snooks in particular," Eve mused. "Not just any sleeper, not just any heart. Him. His. What made him so damn special? Pull up his data again, read it off."

Eve listened to the facts, the steps of a man's life, from birth to waste, and shook her head. "There has to be something there. They didn't pull him out of a damn hat. A family thing maybe . . ." She let the theory wind through her mind. "One of his kids or grandkids, pissed off about the way he dropped out, left them flat. The heart. Could be symbolic."

"You broke my heart, I'm taking yours?"

"Something like that." Families, all those degrees of love and hate that brewed in them, confused and baffled her. "We'll dig into the family, run with this idea for a bit, mostly just to close it off."

She pulled back up at the scene, scanning the area first. The police sensors were still in place, everything secure. Apparently, there was no one in this neighborhood with the skill or knowledge to bypass them to get to whatever was left in Snooks's crib.

She spotted the pair of glide-cart vendors on the corner, huddling unhappily in the smoke pouring off the grill. Business was not brisk.

A couple of panhandlers wandered aimlessly. Their beggars' licenses hung in clear view around their scrawny necks. And, Eve thought, they were likely forged. Across the street, the homeless and the mad crowded around a barrel fire that appeared to let off more stink than warmth.

"Talk to the vendors," Eve ordered Peabody. "They see more than most. We could get lucky. I want another look at his crib."

"Ah, I bet they'd talk looser if I were to buy a soy-dog."

Eve arched a brow as they climbed out of opposite doors. "You must be desperate if you're willing to risk putting anything that comes from this neighborhood in your mouth."

"Pretty desperate," Peabody agreed and squared her shoulders, strode purposefully toward the grill.

Eve felt eyes on her as she uncoded the sensors long enough to pass through. The eyes burned into her back: anger, resentment, confusion, misery. She could feel all of it, every degree of despair and hope that slithered its way across the littered street to crawl over her skin.

She struggled not to think of it.

Pulling back the ratty blanket, she ducked inside the crib, hissed once through her teeth at the lingering stench of waste and death.

Who were you, Snooks? What were you?

She picked up a small bouquet of paper flowers, coated now with the thin layer of dust the crime team sweepers had left behind. They'd have sucked up hair, fibers, fluids, the dead cells the body sloughs off routinely. There would have been grime and muck and dirt to sift through. A scene as nasty as this one would take time. Separating, analyzing, identifying.

But she didn't think the findings there would lead her to the answers she needed.

"You were careful," she murmured to the killer. "You were neat. You didn't leave any of yourself here. Or so you thought."

Both victim and killer always left something. An imprint, an echo. She knew how to look and listen for it.

They'd come in their fancy car, in the dead of night, in the dead of winter. Dressed warmly, dressed well. They hadn't crept in, hadn't attempted to blend.

Arrogance.

They hadn't rushed, hadn't worried.

Confidence.

Disgust. They would have felt it, mildly, as they drew the curtain back and the smell hit them. But doctors would be used to unpleasant odors, she imagined.

They wore masks. Surgical masks. And their hands would have been encased in gloves or Seal-It. For protection, for routine, for caution.

They'd used antiseptic. Sterilizing? Routine, she mused, just routine as it wouldn't have mattered if the patient had suffered from any contamination.

They would have needed light. Something stronger and cleaner than the wavering glow from the candle stub or battery flash Snooks kept on one of his lopsided shelves.

In the doctor's bag, she imagined. A high-powered minilamp. Microgoggles. Laser scalpel, and other tools of the trade.

Did he wake up then? she wondered. *Did he surface from sleep for just a moment when the light flashed? Did he have time to think, wonder, fear before the pressure syringe punched flesh and sent him under?*

Then it was all business. But that she couldn't imagine. She knew nothing about the routine of doctors opening bodies. But she thought it would be just that. More routine.

Working quickly, competently, saying little.

How did it feel to hold a man's heart in your hands?

Was that routine as well, or did it shoot a thrill of power, of accomplishment, of glory through the mind? She thought it would. Even if it was only for an instant, he or she felt like a god.

A god proud enough to take the time, to use his talents to do the job well.

And that's what they had left behind, she thought. *Pride, arrogance, and cool blood.*

Her eyes were still narrowed in concentration when her communicator sounded. Laying the paper flowers aside, she reached for it.

"Dallas."

Feeney's mournful face swam on the miniscreen. "I found another one, Dallas. You better come in and have a look."

chapter six

"Erin Spindler," Feeney began, nodding toward the image on the view screen in one of the smaller conference rooms at Cop Central. "Mixed race female, age seventy-eight, licensed companion, retired. Last few years, she ran a small stable of LCs. All street workers. Got slapped regularly with citations. Let some of her ponies' licenses lapse or didn't bother with the regulation health checks. She got roused for running scams on johns a few times but slithered clear."

Eve studied the image. A sharp, thin face, skin faded to yellow paste, eyes hard. Mouth flat with a downward, dissatisfied droop. "What section did she work?"

"Lower East Side. Started out uptown. Looks like she had some class if you go back fifty years. Started using, started sliding." He moved his shoulders. "Had a taste for Jazz, and that doesn't come cheap uptown. She went from appointment book whore to pickup by the time she hit forty."

"When was she murdered?"

"Six weeks ago. One of the LCs found her in her flop down on Twelfth."

"Was her heart taken?"

"Nope. Kidneys." Feeney turned and brought straight data on-screen. "Her building didn't have any security, so there's no record of who went in and out. Investigator's report is inconclusive as to whether she let the killer in or he bypassed her locks. No sign of struggle, no sexual assault, no apparent robbery. Victim was found in bed, minus the kidneys. Postmortem puts her dead for twelve hours before discovery."

"What's the status of the case?"

"Open." Feeney paused. "And inactive."

"What the hell do you mean, *inactive*?"

"Thought that would get you." His mouth thinned as he brought up more data. "The primary—some dickhead named Rosswell attached to the one sixty-second—concluded the victim was killed by an irate john. It's his decision that the nature of the case is unclosable and not worth the department's time or efforts."

"The one six-two? Same house as Bowers. Do they breed morons down there? Peabody," she snapped, but her aide already had her 'link out.

"Yes sir, contacting Rosswell at the one six-two. I assume you'll want him here as soon as possible for a consult."

"I want his sorry ass in my office within the hour. Good tag, Feeney, thanks. You get any others?"

"This was the only local that fit like crimes. I figured you'd want to move on it right away. I've got McNab running the rest."

"Let him know I want a call if anything pops. Can you feed this data into my office and home units?"

"Already done." With the faintest of grins, Feeney tugged on his ear. "I haven't had much fun lately. Mind if I watch you ream Rosswell?"

"Not a bit. In fact, why don't you help me?"

He let out a sigh. "I was hoping you'd say that."

"We'll do it in here. Peabody?"

"Rosswell will report in one hour, Lieutenant." Struggling not to look smug, she pocketed her 'link. "I believe we could say he's terrified of you."

Eve's smile was slow and grim. "He should be. I'll be in my office; tag me when he gets here."

Her 'link was ringing when she walked in. She answered absently as she hunted through her drawers for anything that might resemble food.

"Hello, Lieutenant."

She blinked at the screen, then dropped into her chair to continue the search when she saw it was Roarke. "Somebody's been stealing my candy again," she complained.

"There's no trusting cops." When she only snorted, his eyes narrowed. "Come closer."

"Hmm." Damn it, she wanted her candy bar. "What?"

"Where did you get that?"

"Get what? Aha! Didn't find this one, did you, you thieving bastard." In triumph she plucked a Gooybar from under a stack of yellow sheets.

"Eve, how did you bruise your face?"

"My what?" She was already ripping it open, taking a bite. "Oh, this?" It was the annoyance, barely audible under that musical voice, that made her smile. "Playing pool with the guys. Got a little rough for a minute. Now there are a couple of cues that won't ever be quite the same."

Roarke ordered himself to relax the hands he'd fisted. He hated seeing marks on her. "You never mentioned you liked the game. We'll have to have a match."

"Anytime, pal. Anywhere."

"Not tonight, I'm afraid. I'll be late."

"Oh." It still jolted her that he so routinely let her know his whereabouts. "Got an appointment?"

"I'm already there. I'm in New L.A.—a little problem that required immediate personal attention. But I will be home tonight."

She said nothing, knowing he'd wanted to assure her she wouldn't be sleeping alone, where the nightmares would chase her. "Um, how's the weather?"

"It's lovely. Sunny and seventy." He smiled at her. "I'll pretend not to enjoy it since you're not with me."

"Do that. See you later."

"Stay out of pool halls, Lieutenant."

"Yeah." She watched the screen go blank and wished she didn't have this vague dissatisfaction that he wouldn't be there when she went home. In less than a year, she'd gotten much too used to him being there.

Annoyed with herself, she engaged her computer. Her mood was distracted enough that she didn't bother to smack it when it buzzed at her.

She called up the files from Snooks and Spindler, ordered both images on, split screen.

Used up, she thought. Self-abuse, neglect. It was there on both faces. But Snooks, well, there was a kind of pitiful sweetness in his face. As for Spindler, there was nothing sweet about her. There was some twenty years between them in age. Different sex, different races, different backgrounds.

"Display crime scene photos, Spindler," she ordered.

The room was a flop, small, crowded, with a single window the width of a spread hand in one wall. But, Eve noted, it was clean. Tidy.

Spindler lay on the bed, on faded sheets that were stained with blood. Her eyes were closed, her mouth lax. She was nude, and her body was no pretty picture. Eve could see that what appeared to be a nightgown was neatly folded and laid on the table beside the bed.

She might have been sleeping if not for the blood that stained the sheets.

They'd drugged her, Eve decided, then undressed her. Folded the gown. Tidy, organized, precise.

How had they chosen this one? she wondered. *And why?*

In the next shot, the crime scene team had turned the body. Dignity, modesty were cast aside as the camera zoomed in. Scrawny legs on a scrawny body. Sagging breasts, wrinkled skin. Spindler hadn't put her profits into body maintenance, which was probably wise, Eve mused, as her investment would have been cut short.

"Close-up of injury," she ordered, and the picture

shifted. They had opened her, the slices narrower than Eve had imagined. Nearly delicate. And though no one had bothered to close her back up, they had used what she now knew was surgical freeze-coat to stop the flow of blood.

Routine again, she concluded. Pride. Didn't surgeons often allow an underling to close for them? The big, important work had already been done, so why not let someone less prominent do a little sewing?

She would ask someone, but she thought she'd seen that on-screen in videos.

"Computer, analyze surgical procedure on both subjects. Run probability scan thereafter. What probability percentage that both procedures were performed by the same person?"

Working . . . analysis will require approximately ten minutes.

"Fine." She rose, walked to her window to watch the air traffic sputter. The sky had gone the color of bruises. She could see one of the minicopters wavering as it tried to compensate for a gust of wind.

It would snow or sleet before the end of shift, she thought. The drive home would be hideous.

She thought of Roarke, three thousand miles away, with palm trees and blue skies.

She thought of those nameless lost souls struggling to find a little heat around an ugly fire in a rusted barrel and where they would be tonight when the snows came and the wind howled down the streets like a mad thing.

Absently, she pressed her fingers to the window, felt the chill on her skin.

And it came to her, sharp as a slap, a memory long buried with other memories of the girl she had been. Thin, hollow-eyed, and trapped in one of the endless horrid rooms where the windows were cracked and the heat broken so that the wind screamed and screamed against the damaged glass and shook the walls and burst over her skin like fists of ice.

Cold, so cold. So hungry. So afraid. Sitting in the dark, alone in the dark. All the while knowing he would come back. He always came back. And when he did, he might not be drunk enough to just fall on the bed and leave her be.

He might not leave her huddled behind the single ratty chair that smelled of smoke and sweat where she tried to hide from him and the brittle cold.

She fell asleep shivering, watching her breath form and fade in the dark.

But when he got home, he wasn't drunk enough, and she couldn't hide from him or the bitterness.

"Chicago." The word burst out of her, like a poison that burned the throat, and she came back to herself with both hands fisted hard against her heart.

And she was shivering, shivering again as she had in that freezing room during another winter.

Where had that come from? she asked herself as she fought to even her breathing, to swallow back the sickness that had gushed into her throat. How did she know it was Chicago? Why was she so sure?

And what did it matter? Furious now, she rapped one of her fists lightly, rhythmically against the window. It was done, it was over.

It had to be over.

Analysis complete. . . . Beginning probability ratio . . .

She closed her eyes a moment, rubbed her hands hard over her dry lips. This, she reminded herself, was what mattered. What she was now, what she did now. The job, the justice, the answers.

But her head was throbbing when she turned back to her computer, sat in her chair.

Probability ratio complete. Probability that the proce-
dures on both subjects were done by the same person
is 97.8%.

"Okay," Eve said softly. "Okay. He did them both.
Now, how many more?"

Insufficient data to compute . . .

"I wasn't asking you, asshole." She spoke absently,
then, leaning forward, forgot her queasy stomach, her aching head as she began to pick her way through data.

She'd worked through the bulk of it when Peabody
knocked briskly and stuck her head in the door. "Rosswell's here."

"Great. Good."

There was a gleam in Eve's eyes as she rose that had
Peabody feeling a stir of pity for Rosswell, and—she was
human, after all—a ripple of anticipation for the show
about to start. She was careful to hide both reactions as
she followed Eve to the conference room.

Rosswell was fat and bald. A detective's salary would
have covered standard body maintenance if he was too
lazy or stupid to exercise. It would have covered elemen-
tary hair replacement treatment if he had any vanity. But
self-image couldn't compete with Rosswell's deep and
passionate love of gambling.

This love was very one-sided. Gambling didn't love
Rosswell back. It punished him, laughed at him. It beat
him over the head with his own inadequacies in the area.
But he couldn't stay away.

So he lived in little more than a flop a block from his
station house—and a two-minute walk from the nearest
gaming dive. When he was lucky enough to beat the odds,
his winnings were funneled back to cover previous losses.
He was constantly dodging and making deals with the
spine crackers.

Eve had some of these details from the data she'd just
scanned. What she saw waiting in the conference room

was a washed-up cop, one who'd lost his edge and was simply cruising his way toward his pension.

He didn't rise when she came in but continued to slouch at the conference table. To establish dominance, Eve merely stared at him silently until he flushed and got to his feet.

And Peabody was right, she noted. Under the show of carelessness, there was a glint of fear in his eyes.

"Lieutenant Dallas?"

"That's right, Rosswell." She invited him to sit by jabbing a finger at the chair. Once again, she said nothing. Silence had a way of scraping the nerves raw. And raw nerves had a way of stuttering out the truth.

"Ah . . ." His eyes, a cloudy hazel in a doughy face, shifted from her to Feeney to Peabody, then back. "What's this about, Lieutenant?"

"It's about half-assed police work." When he blinked, Eve sat on the edge of the table. It kept her head above him, forcing him to tip his back to look up at her. "The Spindler case—your case, Rosswell. Tell me about it."

"Spindler?" Face blank, he lifted his shoulders. "Jesus, Lieutenant, I got a lot of cases. Who remembers names?"

A good cop remembers, she thought. "Erin Spindler, retired LC. Maybe this'll jog your memory. She was missing some internal organs."

"Oh, sure." He brightened right up. "She bought it in bed. Kinda seems funny since she got bought there plenty." When no one cracked up at his irony, he cleared his throat. "It was pretty straight, Lieutenant. She ragged on her ponies and their johns all the time. Had a rep for it. Kept herself whacked on street Jazz most of the time. Nobody had a good word to say about her, I can tell you. Nobody shed a tear. Figures one of her girls or one of the customers got fed up and did her. What's the deal?" he asked, lifting his shoulders again. "No big loss to society."

"You're stupid, Rosswell, and while that annoys me, I have to figure maybe you were born stupid. But you've got a badge, so that means you can't be careless, and you sure as hell can't decide a case isn't worth your time. Your investigation in this matter was a joke, your report pathetic, and your conclusions asinine.''

"Hey, I did my job."

"The hell you did." Eve engaged the computer, shot an image on-screen. The neat slice in Spindler's flesh dominated. "You're telling me a street pony did that? Why the hell isn't she raking in seven figures a year at a health center? A john, maybe, but Spindler didn't work the johns. How did he get to her? Why? Why the hell did he take her kidneys?''

"I don't know what's in some lunatic killer's mind, for Christ's sake."

"That's why I'm going to see to it you're not working Homicide after today."

"Wait just a damn minute." He was on his feet, eyeball to eyeball with her. Peabody gave Feeney a quick glance to gauge his reaction and saw his thin, wicked grin. "You got no cause to go to my boss on this and make trouble for me. I followed the book on this case."

"Then your book's missing a few pages." Her voice was calm, deadly calm. "You didn't pursue organ replacement or disbursement centers. You didn't do a run on surgeons, you never attempted contact with black market sources on illegal organ transfer."

"Why the hell would I?" His toes bumped hers as he leaned forward. "Some sicko cut her open and took some souvenirs. Case closed. Who the hell gives a shit about some worn-out whore?"

"I do. And if you're not out of my face in five seconds, I'll write you up."

It took him three, with teeth grinding audibly, but he shifted away. "I did the job," he said, with the words bitten off sharp as darts. "You got no cause to poke into my caseload and give me grief."

"You did a crappy job, Rosswell. And when one of your cases crosses one of mine, and I see just how crappy a job you did, I've got plenty of cause. I've got a sidewalk sleeper missing a heart. My probability scan tells me the same one who opened him up did Spindler.''

"I heard you screwed up on that one." He smiled now, panicked enough to challenge her.

"Know Bowers, do you?" She smiled back, so fiercely he began to sweat again.

"She ain't no fan of yours."

"Now, that hurts, Rosswell. It really hurts my feelings. And when my feelings get hurt, I like to take it out on somebody." She leaned down. "Want it to be you?"

He licked his lips. If they'd been alone, he could have backed down easily. But there were two more cops in the room. Two more mouths that could flap. "If you lay hands on me, I'll file a complaint. Just like Bowers. Being Whitney's pet won't save you from an IAB investigation then."

Her hand curled into a fist. And, oh, she yearned to use it. But she only kept her eyes steady on his. "Hear that, Feeney? Rosswell here's going to tell teacher on me."

"I can see you're shaking in your boots over that, Dallas." Cheerfully, Feeney moved forward. "Let me punch this fat-assed fucker for you."

"That's real nice of you, Feeney, but let's try to handle this like mature adults first. Rosswell, you make me sick. Maybe you earned that badge years ago, but you don't deserve it now. You don't deserve to work the shit and piss detail on body removal. And that's just what it's going to say in *my* report. Meanwhile, you're relieved as primary on the Spindler case. You'll turn over all data and reports to my aide."

"I don't do that unless I get it straight from my boss." Saving face was paramount now, but even his valiant attempt to sound disdainful fell far short. "I don't work for you, Dallas, and your rank, your rep, and all your husband's money don't mean squat to me."

"So noted," Eve said levelly. "Peabody, contact Captain Desevres at the one six-two."

"Yes, sir."

She held her temper, but it cost her. The headache

turned up from simmer to boil, and the knots in her stomach grew teeth. It helped a little to watch Rosswell sweat while she meticulously outlined the details, tore his investigation into tattered shreds, and requested the transfer of the case, with all data and reports, to her.

Desevres asked for an hour to review the matter, but everyone knew that was for form's sake. Rosswell was out, and very likely soon to receive a much pithier dressing down from his own division head.

When she ended transmission, Eve gathered up files and discs. "You're dismissed, Detective."

His face bone white with fury and frustration, he got to his feet. "Bowers had it right. I hope she buries you."

Eve glanced in his direction. "Detective Rosswell, you are dismissed. Peabody, contact Morris at the ME's office. He needs to be made aware of this connecting homicide. Feeney, can we light a fire under McNab? See what he's come up with?"

The embarrassment of being ignored washed color, ugly and red, back into Rosswell's face. When the door slammed behind him, Feeney flashed Eve a grin.

"You sure are making lots of new friends these days."

"It's my sparkling personality and wit. They can't resist it. God, what an ass." But she sat, struggling to shrug off annoyance. "I'm going to check out the Canal Street Clinic. Spindler used it for her health checks over the last twelve years. Maybe Snooks hit it a couple times. It's a place to start. Peabody, you're with me."

She took the elevator straight down to the garage level and had just stepped through the doors when Feeney tagged her by communicator. "What have you got?"

"McNab hit on a chemi-head named Jasper Mott. Another heart theft, three months back."

"Three months? Who's the primary? What are the leads?"

"It wasn't NYPSD's deal, Dallas. It was Chicago."

"What?" The cold came shimmering back to her skin, the image of the long spider crack in window glass.

"Chicago," he repeated, eyes narrowing. "You okay?"

"Yeah, yeah." But she stared down the long tube of the garage to where Peabody waited patiently at their vehicle. "Can you get Peabody the name of the primary on it, the necessary data? I'll have her contact CPSD for the files and status."

"Sure, no problem. Maybe you should eat something, kid. You look sick."

"I'm fine. Tell McNab I said good work, and keep at it."

"Trouble, sir?"

"No." Eve crossed to her car, uncoded, and climbed in. "We got another one in Chicago. Feeney's going to send you the details. Put out a request to the primary and his division head for a copy of appropriate data. Copy to the commander. Do it by the book, but do it fast."

"Unlike some," Peabody said primly, "I know all the pages. How come a jerk like Rosswell makes detective?"

"Because life," Eve said with feeling, "often sucks."

Life definitely sucked for the patients at the Canal Street Clinic. The place was jammed with the suffering, the hopeless, and the dying.

A woman with a battered face breast-fed an infant while a toddler sat at her feet and wailed. Someone hacked wetly, monotonously. A half dozen street LCs sat glassy-eyed and bored, waiting for their regulation checkup to clear them for the night's work.

Eve waded her way through to the window where the nurse on duty manned a desk. "Enter your data on the proper form," she began, the edge of tedium flattening her voice. "Don't forget your medical card number, personal ID, and current address."

For an answer, Eve took out her badge and held it up to the reinforced glass. "Who's in charge?"

The nurse's eyes, gray and bored, flicked over the badge. "That would be Dr. Dimatto today. She's with a patient."

"Is there an office back there, a private room?"

"If you want to call it that." When Eve simply angled her head, the nurse, annoyed, released the coded lock on the door.

With obvious reluctance, she shuffled in the lead down a short hallway. As they slipped through the door, Peabody glanced over her shoulder. "I've never been in a place like this before."

"Consider yourself lucky." Eve had spent plenty of time in such places. A ward of the state didn't rate private health care or upscale clinics.

At the nurse's gesture, she stepped into a box-sized room the doctors on rotation used for an office. Two chairs, a desk barely bigger than a packing crate, and equipment, Eve mused, glancing at the computer system, even worse than what she was reduced to using at Central.

The office didn't boast a window, but someone had tried to brighten it up with a couple of art posters and a struggling green vine in a chipped pot.

And there, on a wall shelf, tucked between a teetering stack of medical discs and a model of the human body, was a small bouquet of paper flowers.

"Snooks," Eve murmured. "He used this place."

"Sir?"

"His flowers." Eve picked them from the shelf. "He liked someone here enough to give them, and someone cared enough to keep them. Peabody, we just got our connection."

She was still holding the flowers when the door burst open. The woman who strode in was young, tiny, with the white coat of her profession slung over a baggy sweater and faded jeans. Her hair was short and even more ragged that Eve's. Still, it's honeycomb color set off the pretty rose-and-cream face.

Her eyes were the color of storms, and her voice was just as threatening.

"You've got three minutes. I've got patients waiting, and a badge doesn't mean dick in here."

Eve arched a brow. The opening would have irritated

her under most circumstances, but she noted the shadows of fatigue under the gray eyes and the stiffness of posture that was a defense against it.

She'd worked until exhaustion often enough to recognize the signs and sympathize with them.

"We sure are popular these days, Peabody. Dallas," she said briefly. "Lieutenant, Eve. I need data on a couple of patients."

"Dimatto, Dr. Louise, and I don't give data out on patients. Not to cops, not to anyone. So if that's all—"

"Dead patients," Eve said as Louise spun toward the door again. "Murdered patients. I'm Homicide."

Turning back, Louise took a more careful look at Eve. She saw a lean body, a tough face, and tired eyes. "You're investigating a murder?"

"Murders. Two." Watching Louise, she held out the paper flowers. "Yours?"

"Yes. So . . ." She trailed off and concern washed over her face. "Oh, not Snooks! Who would kill Snooks? He couldn't have been more harmless."

"He was your patient?"

"He wasn't anyone's patient, really." She moved over to an ancient AutoChef and programmed coffee. "We take a medi-van out once a week, do on-site treatments." The machine made a hissing sound, and swearing, Louise yanked the door open. Inside was a puddle of what appeared to be some offensive body fluid. "Out of cups again," she muttered and left the door swinging open as she turned back. "They keep cutting our budget."

"Tell me about it," Eve said dryly.

With a half laugh, Louise ran her hands up over her face and into her hair. "I used to see Snooks around when it was my rotation on the medi-van. I bribed him into a street exam one night about a month ago. It cost me ten credits to find out he'd be dead of cancer in about six months without treatment. I tried to explain it all to him, but he just didn't care. He gave me the flowers and told me I was a nice girl."

She let out a long sigh. "I don't think anything was

wrong with his mind—though I couldn't bribe him into a psych. He just didn't give a damn.''

"You have the records of the exam.''

"I can dig them up, but what's the point? If he was murdered, cancer didn't get him.''

"I'd like them for my files,'' Eve said. "And any records you have on Erin Spindler. She got her health checks here.''

"Spindler?'' Louise shook her head. "I don't know if she was one of mine. But if you want patient records, Lieutenant, you're going to have to give me more data. How did they die?''

"During surgery, so to speak,'' Eve said, and told her.

After the first shock leaped into Louise's eyes, they went cool and flat. She waited, considered, then shook her head. "I don't know about Spindler, but I can tell you that there was nothing in Snooks worth harvesting, not even for black market use.''

"Somebody took his heart, and they did a superior job of it. Who's your top surgical consult?''

"We don't have outside consults,'' Louise said wearily. "I'm it. So if you want to take me in for interview or to charge me, you'll just have to wait until I finish with my patients.''

Eve nearly smiled. "I'm not charging you, Doctor, at this time. Unless you'd like to confess. To this.'' From her bag, Eve took two stills, one of each victim, offered them.

Lips pursed, Louise studied them, breathed out slow. "Someone has magic hands,'' she murmured. "I'm good, but I'm not even close to this level of skill. To manage this in a sleeper's crib, for God's sake. Under those conditions.'' She shook her head, handed the stills back. "I can hate what those hands did, Lieutenant, but I admire their ability.''

"Any opinion on whose hands they might be?''

"I don't mingle with the gods professionally, and that's what you're looking for here. One of the gods. I'll have

Jan get you what you need. I have to get back to my patients."

But she paused, studying the flowers again. Something came into her eyes that was more than fatigue. It might have been grief. "We've eradicated or learned to cure nearly every natural killer of human beings but one. Some suffer and die before their time anyway because they're too poor, too afraid, or too stubborn to seek help. But we keep chipping away at that. Eventually, we'll win."

She looked back over at Eve. "I believe that. We'll win on this front, but on yours, Lieutenant, there'll never be full victory. The natural predator of man will always be man. So I'll keep treating the bodies that others have sliced or hacked or pummelled, and you'll keep cleaning up the waste."

"I get my victories, Doctor. Every time I put a predator in a cage, I get my victory. And I'll get one for Snooks and Spindler. You can count on it."

"I don't count on anything anymore." Louise walked out to where the hurt and the hopeless waited.

I am . . . amused. Great work must be balanced by periods of rest and entertainment, after all. In the midst of mine, I find myself pitted against a woman with a reputation for tenacity. A clever woman, by all accounts, and a determined one with great skill in her chosen field.

But however tenacious, clever, and determined Eve Dallas might be, she remains a cop. I've dealt with cops before, and they are easily dispatched in one manner or another.

How absurd that those who impose laws—laws that change as easily and often as the wind—should believe they have any jurisdiction over me.

They choose to call what I do murder. The removal— the humane removal, I should add—of the damaged, the useless, the unproductive is no more murder than the removal of lice from a human body is murder. Indeed, the units I have selected are no less than vermin. Diseased and dying vermin at that.

Contagious, corrupted, and condemned by the very society whose laws would now avenge them. Where were the laws and the cries for justice when these pathetic creatures huddled in their boxes and laid in their own waste? While they lived, they were held in disgust, ignored, or vilified.

These vessels serve a much grander purpose dead than they ever could have achieved alive.

But if murder is their term, then I accept. As I accept the challenge of the dogged lieutenant. Let her poke and prod, calculate and deduce. I believe I will enjoy the bout.

And if she becomes a nuisance, if by some stroke of luck she stumbles too close to me and my work?

She'll be dealt with.

Even Lieutenant Dallas has her weaknesses.

chapter seven

McNab found another sidewalk sleeper dead in the alleyways of Paris. He'd been missing his liver, but his body had been so mutilated by the feral cats that roamed the slums that most of the physical evidence had been destroyed. Still, Eve put the name into her files.

She took them all home with her, opting to work there until Roarke got back from New L.A. Summerset didn't disappoint this time, but slipped into the foyer moments after she came through the door.

His dark eyes skimmed over her, his elegant nose wrinkled. "Since you're quite late, Lieutenant, and didn't see fit to notify me of your plans, I assume you've already had your evening meal."

She hadn't eaten since the chewy bar she'd scavenged, but only jerked her shoulders as she shrugged out of her jacket. "I don't need you to fix my dinner, ace."

"That's fortunate." He watched her sling her jacket over the newel post. An act they both knew she repeated because it annoyed his rigid sense of order. "Because I have no intention of doing so since you refuse to keep me informed of your schedule."

She cocked her head, giving his tall, skinny body the

same once-over he'd given hers. "That'll teach me."

"You have an aide, Lieutenant. It would be a simple matter to have her notify me of your plans so the household could maintain some order."

"Peabody's got better things to do, and so do I."

"Your job doesn't concern me," he said with a sneer. "This household does. I've added the AMA fund-raiser to your calendar. You will be expected to be ready and presentable . . ." He paused long enough to sniff at her scarred boots and wrinkled trousers. "If that's possible, by seven-thirty on Friday."

She took one meaningful step forward. "Keep your bony fingers out of my calendar."

"Roarke requested I make the notation and remind you of the engagement." Pleased, he smiled.

She decided she'd have a little chat with Roarke about foisting his personal Nazi on her. "And I'm telling you to keep out of my business."

"I take my orders from Roarke, not you."

"And I don't take them from either of you," she tossed back as she started upstairs. "So bite me."

They separated, both of them fairly well satisfied with the encounter.

She went straight to the AutoChef in her office kitchen and would have been mortified if she'd known Summerset had planted the thought of dinner in her mind, knowing she would remember to eat out of spite if nothing else. Otherwise, she would most likely have forgotten.

There was a beef and dumpling stew at the top of the menu, and since it was one of her personal favorites, she programmed a bowl. The minute the machine beeped its acceptance of her order, the cat was winding through her legs.

"I know damn well you've already had yours," she muttered. But as soon as she opened the door and the fragrant steam hit the air, Galahad sent up a screeching meow. As much in defense as affection, she spooned some into his dish. He pounced on it as if it were a lively mouse that might escape.

Eve carried the stew and coffee to her desk, eating absently as she engaged her machine and began to review data. She knew what her gut told her, what her instincts told her, but she would have to wait for the transfer of files and pictures to run a probability scan to verify her conclusions.

Her scan of Spindler's medical records from the Canal Street Clinic had stated that the patient had a kidney disorder, a result of some childhood infection. Her kidneys had been functional but damaged and had required regular treatment.

A bum heart, she mused, and faulty kidneys. She'd bet a month's pay when she got data on the hits in Chicago and Paris, those organs would prove to be damaged as well.

Specific, she thought. *Specific victims for specifically flawed parts.*

"You get around, don't you, Dr. Death?"

New York, Chicago, Paris. Where else had he been, and where would he go next?

He might not be based in New York after all, she speculated. He could be anywhere, traveling the world and its satellites for his pickings. But someone knew him, would recognize his work.

He was mature, she decided, adding her conclusions to Mira's profile. Educated and trained. It was likely he'd saved countless lives in his career. What had turned him to the taking of them?

Madness? No ordinary madness seemed to fit. Arrogance, yes. He had arrogance and pride and the hands of a god. His work was methodical, and he trolled the same types of areas of his cities to select his specimens.

Specimens, she thought, pursing her lips. Yes, she thought that was how he viewed them. Experiments then, but of what kind, for what purpose?

She'd have to start scraping into the Drake research department.

What link could she find between the health palace of Drake and the ghetto of the Canal Street Clinic? Somehow he'd seen the records, knew the patients. He knew their habits and their flaws.

It was the flaws he was after.

Brows knit, she ordered a search for articles and data on organ transplant and reconstruction.

An hour later, the words were blurring, her head was throbbing. Frustration had risen to top levels as she'd been forced to ask for definitions and explanations of hundreds of terms and phrases.

It would take her forever to access and dissect this medical bullshit, she thought. She needed an expert consultant, somebody who either knew this area already or who could study and relate it to her in layman's terms. In cop terms.

A glance at her wrist unit told her it was nearly midnight and too late to contact either Mira or Morris. These were the only medical types she trusted.

Hissing in impatience, she began to slog through yet another article, then her brain cleared with a jolt as she read a report from a newspaper article dated 2034.

NORDICK CLINIC FOR HEALTH
ANNOUNCES MEDICAL BREAKTHROUGH

After more than two decades of research and study on the construction of artificial organs, Dr. Westley Friend, chief of research for the Nordick Clinic, has announced the center's successful development and implantation of a heart, lung, and kidneys into Patient X. Nordick, along with the Drake Center in New York, has devoted nearly twenty years to research on developing organs that can be mass-produced to replace and outperform human tissue.

The article continued, detailing the impact on medicine and health. With the discovery of a material the body would easily accept, the medical community was dancing on the ceiling. Though it was rare with in vitro testing and repair for a child to be born with a heart defect, for example, some slipped through. An organ could be built using the patient's tissue, but that took time.

Now the flawed heart could be quickly removed and replaced with what Friend called a longevity replacement that would continue to perform long after the child had used up his one-hundred-twenty-year average life.

They could, the article continued, be recycled and implanted in other patients in the event of the death of the original owner.

Though research on the reconstructing of human organs was being discontinued at both centers, the work on artificial devices would move forward.

Reconstructing human organs had taken the back burner some twenty years ago, Eve thought. Had someone decided to move it back up again?

The Nordick Center in Chicago. The Drake in New York. One more link. "Computer, search and display data on Friend, Dr. Westley, attached to Nordick Clinic for Health, Chicago."

Working. . . . Friend, Dr. Westley, ID# 987-002-34RF, born Chicago, Illinois, December 15, 1992. Died, September 12, 2058. . . .

"Died? How?"

Death ruled self-termination. Subject injected fatal dose of barbiturates. He is survived by spouse, Ellen, son, Westley Jr., daughter, Clare. Grandchildren—

"Stop," Eve ordered. She would worry about personal details later. "Access all data on subject suicide."

Working. . . . Request denied. Data is sealed.

Sealed, my ass, Eve thought. She'd get around that in the morning. She rose to pace and think. She wanted to know all there was to know about Dr. Westley Friend, his work, and his associates.

Chicago, she thought again and shuddered. She might have to take a trip to Chicago. She'd been there before, she reminded herself. It never bothered her.

But she'd never remembered before.

She shook that off and went in to refill her coffee. She'd linked the two centers, the two cities. Would she find that there was a sister center in Paris as well? And maybe other cities, other places?

It made sense, didn't it? He'd find his specimen, take his sample, then wouldn't he want to work in worthy surroundings: top-notch labs—places where he would be known and not questioned?

Then she shook her head. How could he run experiments, do research, or whatever the hell he was doing in the lab of a reputable facility? There had to be paperwork, there would be staff. There had to be questions and procedures.

But he was taking the damn things, and he had a purpose.

She rubbed her tired eyes, gave in enough to sit down in her sleep chair. A five-minute break, she told herself, to give her brain a chance to play with this new information. Just five minutes, she thought again and closed her eyes.

She dropped into sleep like a stone into a pond.

And dreamed of Chicago.

The flight home from the coast had given Roarke time to deal with the last of his business matters. So he arrived home with his mind clear. He imagined he'd find Eve in her office. She tended to avoid their bed when he wasn't beside her.

He hated knowing nightmares chased her when business kept him from home. Over the last few months, he'd juggled whatever he could to keep his trips to a minimum. For her, he thought as he took off his coat. And for himself.

Now there was someone to come home to, someone who mattered. He hadn't been lonely before she'd come into his life, certainly hadn't felt unfulfilled. He'd been content, focused, and his business—the many arms and branches of it—had satisfied him.

Other women had entertained him.

Love changed a man, he decided as he walked to the in-home scanner. After love, everything else took second place.

"Where is Eve?" he asked.

Lieutenant Dallas is in her office.

"Naturally," Roarke murmured. She'd be working, he thought as he started up the stairs. Unless exhaustion had finally taken over and she'd curled into her sleep chair for one of her catnaps. He knew her so well and found an odd comfort in that. He knew this case would occupy her mind and her heart, all of her time and skills, until it was closed. Until she'd found justice, once again, for the dead.

He could distract her for short bursts of time, ease the tension. And he could—would—work with her. That, too, was a mutual benefit. He'd discovered he enjoyed the stages of police work, the puzzle slowly put together, piece by piece.

Perhaps it was because he'd lived on the other side of the law most of his life that he seemed to have a knack for it. It made him smile, a bit nostalgically, for the old days.

He would change nothing, nothing he had done, for every step of his life had brought him here. And had brought her to him.

He turned down a corridor, one of many in the enormous house that was filled with art and treasures he'd collected—by fair means or foul—over the years. Eve didn't fully understand his delight in material possessions, he decided. How the acquiring and owning of them, even the giving of them, put more distance between him and the boy from the Dublin alleys who'd had nothing but his wits and his guts to call his own.

He stepped to the doorway where the most precious of

treasures was curled, fully dressed, weapon still strapped
to her side, in the chair.

There were shadows under her eyes and the mark of
violence on her cheek. One concerned him nearly as much
as the other, and he had to remind himself yet again that
each was a sign of who and what she was.

The cat was sprawled over her lap and woke to stare
unblinkingly.

"Guarding her, are you? I'll take over now."

The smile that curved his lips as he started forward
faded as Eve began to moan. She thrashed once, a sob
catching in her throat.

He was across the room in two strides, gathering her
up as she struggled and struck out.

"Don't. Don't hurt me again."

Her voice was the thin, helpless voice of a child, and
it broke his heart.

"It's all right. No one's going to hurt you. You're
home. Eve, you're home. I'm here." It ripped at him that
a woman strong enough to face death day after day could
be so beaten down by dreams. He managed to shift her
until he could sit, draw her onto his lap, and rock.
"You're safe. You're safe with me."

She clawed her way out and to the surface. Her skin
was clammy and shivering, her breath a harsh burn in her
throat. And she smelled him, felt him, heard him. "I'm
all right. I'm okay."

The weakness, the fear snuck out of the dream with
her, and left her ashamed. But when she tried to draw
back, he wouldn't let her. He never did. "Just let me hold
you." He spoke quietly, stroking her back. "Hold me
back."

She did, curving herself into him, pressing her face to
his throat, holding on, holding until the shuddering
stopped. "I'm okay," she said again, and nearly meant it
this time. "It was nothing. Just a memory flash."

His hand paused, then slid up to soothe the muscles
gone to knots at the back of her neck. "A new one?"

When she merely jerked a shoulder, he eased her back to look at her face. "Tell me."

"Just another room, another night." She drew a deep breath, let it out slowly. "Chicago. I don't know how I'm so sure it was Chicago. It was so cold in the room, and the window was cracked. I was hiding behind a chair, but when he came home, he found me. And he raped me again. It's nothing I didn't already know."

"Knowing doesn't make it hurt less."

"I guess not. I have to move," she murmured and rose to pace off the shakiness. "We found another body in Chicago—same MO. I guess that put the memory at the top of my brain. I can handle it."

"Yes, you can and have." He rose as well, crossed to her to lay his hands on her shoulders. "But you won't handle it alone, not anymore."

It was another thing he wouldn't allow, and that made her—by turns—grateful and uneasy. "I'm not used to you. Every time I think I am, I'm not." But she laid her hands over his. "I'm glad you're here. I'm glad you're home."

"I bought you a present."

"Roarke."

The knee-jerk exasperation in her voice made him grin. "No, you'll like it." He kissed the shallow dent in her chin, then turned away to pick up the briefcase he'd dropped when he'd come into the room.

"I already need a warehouse for all the stuff you've bought me," she began. "You really need to develop a control button about this."

"Why? It gives me pleasure."

"Yeah, maybe, but it makes me . . ." She trailed off, baffled, when she saw what he took out of the briefcase. "What the hell is that?"

"I believe it's a cat." With a laugh, he held the doll out to her. "A toy. You don't have nearly enough toys, Lieutenant."

A chuckle tickled her throat. "It looks just like Gala-

had.'' She ran a finger down the wide, grinning face.
''Right down to the weird eyes.''

''I did have to ask them to fix that little detail. But
when I happened to see it, I didn't think we could do
without it.''

She was grinning now, stroking the soft, fat body. It
didn't occur to her that she'd never had a doll before—
but it had occurred to Roarke. ''It's really silly.''

''Now, is that any way to talk about our son?'' He
glanced back at Galahad who'd taken possession of the
chair again. His dual-colored eyes narrowed with suspicion before he shifted, lifted his tail in derision, and began
to wash. ''Sibling rivalry,'' Roarke murmured.

Eve set the doll in a prominent position on her desk.
''Let's see what they make of each other.''

''You need sleep,'' Roarke said when he saw her frown
at her computer. ''We'll deal with work in the morning.''

''Yeah, I guess you're right. All this medical stuff is
jumbled in my head. You know anything about NewLife
replacement organs?''

His brow lifted, but she was too distracted to notice.
''I might. We'll talk about it in the morning. Come to
bed.''

''I can't contact anyone until tomorrow, anyway.''
Burying impatience, she saved data, disengaged. ''I might
have to take some travel, go talk to other primaries in
person.''

He simply made agreeable noises and led her to the
door. If Chicago held bad memories for her, she wouldn't
be going alone.

She woke at first light, surprised by how deeply she'd
slept and how alert she was. Some time during the night,
she'd wrapped herself around Roarke, legs and arms
hooked as if binding him to her. It was so rare for her to
wake and not find him already up and starting his day that
she savored the sensation of warmth against warmth and
let herself drift.

His body was so hard, so smooth, so . . . tasty, she

thought, skimming her mouth over his shoulder. His face, relaxed in sleep, was heart stopping in its sheer male beauty. Strong bones, full, sculpted mouth, thick, dark lashes.

Studying him, she felt her blood begin to stir. A low, spreading neediness filled her belly, and her heart began to thud in anticipation and in the knowledge that she could have him, keep him, love him.

Her wedding ring glinted in the light pouring through the sky window over the bed as she slid a hand up his back, nuzzled his mouth with hers. His lips, already warmed, opened with hers for a slow, tangling dance of tongues.

Slow, easy, and no less arousing for its familiarity. The skim and slide of hands over curves, planes, angles well known, only added to the excitement that built, layer by layer, in the clear light of dawn. Even as his heart began to pound against hers, they kept the rhythm loose and lazy.

Her breath caught once, twice, as he cupped her, as he sent her up that long, long curve to a peak that shimmered like wine in sunlight. And his moan mixed with hers.

Every pulse in her body throbbed, every pore opened. The need to take him into her, to mate, was an ache in the heart as sweet as tears.

She arched to him, breathed his name, then sighed it as he slid into her. The ride was slow, slippery, a silky ebb and flow of breath and bodies. His mouth met hers again, with an endless tenderness that swamped her.

He felt her soar again, tighten around him, tremble. Lifting his head, he watched her in the harsh winter light. His heart stumbled, love destroyed him, as he watched the glow pleasure brought to her face, watched those golden brown eyes blur even as they stayed locked on his.

Here, he thought, they were both helpless. And bringing his mouth to hers again, he let himself go.

She felt limber, steady, and very close to cheerful as she showered. When she stepped out, she heard the muted sound of the morning news on-screen and imagined Roarke half listening to the headlines as he studied the stock reports and sipped his first cup of coffee.

It was so *married,* she thought with a quick snort and jumped into the drying tube. When she came out into the bedroom, it was exactly as she'd imagined. He was drinking coffee in the sitting area, scanning the financial data on the computer, while Nadine Furst gave Channel 75's take on the news of the day on the screen just over his shoulder.

When she moved by him to the closet, his eyes followed her. And he smiled. "You look rested, Lieutenant."

"I feel pretty good. I need to get a jump on the day, though."

"I thought we already did."

That made her toss a grin over her shoulder. "I should've said on the workday."

"I should be able to help you in that area as well." He watched her shrug on a plain white shirt, button it briskly. "Last weather update calls for high in the midteens. You won't be warm enough in that."

"I'll be inside mostly." She only rolled her eyes when he rose, crossed over, and selected a navy pullover in thin, warm wool. Handed it to her. "You're a nag, Roarke."

"What choice do I have?" When she dragged the sweater over her head, he shook his own and adjusted the collar of her shirt himself. "I'll order up breakfast."

"I'll catch something at Central," she began.

"I think you'll want to take time to have it here so we can discuss a couple of matters. You mentioned NewLife products last night."

"Yeah." She remembered only vaguely. She'd been tired and still a little shaken by the dream. "It's an angle I'll be looking into later. They're artificial replacements made from this longevity stuff discovered at the Nordick Clinic, but there may be a connection with the organ thefts I'm dealing with."

"If there is, we're both going to be very unhappy about it. I bought out NewLife about five years ago."

She stared. "Shit, Roarke."

"Yes, I thought you'd feel that way about it. Though I did tell you one of my companies manufactures artificial organs."

"And it just had to be NewLife."

"Apparently. Why don't we sit down? You can tell me how you worked your way around to NewLife, and I'll do what I can to get you all the data you need."

She told herself it was useless to be irritated, as she dragged both hands through her hair. It was certainly unfair to want to snarl at Roarke. So she snatched trousers out of the closet and jammed her legs in.

"Okay, I'm going to try to look at this as a good thing. I won't get any runaround or a bunch of company bullshit when I need information. But damn it." She yanked the trousers over her hips and snarled at him anyway. "Do you have to own everything?"

He considered a moment. "Yes," he said and smiled beautifully. "But that's really a different matter. Now I want some breakfast."

He ordered them both a plate of high-protein waffles, some fresh seasonal fruit, and more coffee. When he settled back into his chair, Eve was still standing. Still scowling.

"Why do you have to own everything?"

"Because, darling Eve, I can. Drink your coffee. You won't be so cross once you do."

"I'm not cross. What a stupid word that is, anyway." But she sat, picked up her cup. "It's a big business, artificial organs?"

"Yes, NewLife also manufactures limbs as well. It's all quite profitable. Do you want financial statements?"

"I might," she murmured. "Do you have doctors on the payroll, as consultants?"

"I believe so, though it's more of an engineering sort of thing." He moved his shoulders. "We have an ongoing R and D department, but the basic products were refined years before I took over the company. How does NewLife fit in with your investigation?"

"The process for mass-producing artificial organs was developed at the Nordick Center, in Chicago. They have connections to Drake. I have bodies in both cities. I've got another in Paris, and I need to see if there's another health center that connects to these two. NewLife was the product Westley Friend endorsed specifically."

"I don't have the information on Paris, but I can get it. Very quickly."

"Did you know Dr. Westley Friend?"

"Only slightly. He was on the board at NewLife during the takeover, but I never had cause to deal with him otherwise. Do you suspect him?"

"Hard to, since he self-terminated last fall."

"Ah."

"Yeah, ah. From what I can gather from the data I sifted through, he headed the team that developed the process for mass-producing organs. And at the time that was implemented, the research on reconstructing human organs was cut. Maybe someone decided to start it up again, in his own way."

"Hardly seems cost effective. Organ growing is time consuming and quite expensive. Reconstruction, from the little I know is not considered viable. We can manufacture a heart at somewhere around fifty dollars. Even adding overhead and profit, it can be sold for about twice that. You add the doctor's take, the health center's cut of the operation, and still you have yourself a new heart, one guaranteed for a century, for less than a thousand. It's an excellent deal."

"Cut out the manufacturer, deal with the subject's damaged organ, or a donor's, repair, reconstruct, and the medical end takes all the profit."

Roarke smiled a little. "Very good, Lieutenant. That's a clear view of business at work. And with that in mind, I believe you can feel safe that none of the major stockholders of NewLife would care for that scenario."

"Unless it's not about money," she said. "But we'll

start there. I need everything you can give me on the deal you made, who was involved on both sides. I want a list of personnel, concentrating on research and development. And any and all medical consultants.''

''I can get you that within the hour.''

She opened her mouth, waged a small personal war, and lost it. ''I could use any underground data you can get me on Friend. His suicide seems very timely and convenient.''

''I'll take care of it.''

''Yeah, thanks. In at least two of the cases, he went after flawed organs specifically. Snooks had a messed-up heart, Spindler dinky kidneys. I'm betting we'll find it's the same deal with the other two. There has to be a reason.''

Thoughtfully, Roarke sipped his coffee. ''If he's a doctor, practicing, why not confiscate damaged organs that are removed during a legitimate procedure?''

''I don't know.'' And it irritated her that her brain had been too mushy the night before to see that chink in her theory. ''I don't know how it works, but there'd have to be records, donor or next of kin permission, and the medical facility would have to endorse his experiments or research or whatever.''

She drummed her fingers on her knee a moment. ''You're on the board, right? What's Drake's policy on— what would you call it? High-risk or maybe radical experimentation?''

''It has a first-class research department and a very conservative policy. It would take a great deal of paperwork, debate, theorizing, justification—and that's before the lawyers come in to wrangle around, and the public relations people get into how to spin the program to the media.''

''So it's complicated.''

''Oh.'' He smiled at her over the rim of his cup. ''What isn't when it's run by committee? Politics, Eve, slows down even the slickest wheel.''

''Maybe he got turned down at some point—or knows

he would—so he's doing it on his own first." She pushed her plate away and rose. "I've got to get going."

"We have the Drake fund-raiser tonight."

Her eyes went grim. "I didn't forget."

"No, I see that." He took her hand, tugging her down for a kiss. "I'll be in touch."

He sipped his coffee as she left and knew this was one time she would be on time for a social event. For her, for both of them now, it was business.

chapter eight

As her plans had been to dive straight into work, Eve wasn't pleased to see IAB waiting in her office. She wouldn't have been pleased in any case.

"Get out of my chair, Webster."

He kept his seat, turned his head, and flashed her a smile. She'd known Don Webster since her early days at the academy. He'd been a full year ahead of her, but they'd bumped into each other from time to time.

It had taken her weeks to clue in to the fact that he'd gone out of his way to make certain they'd bumped into each other. She remembered now that she'd been a little flattered, a little annoyed, and then had dismissed him.

Her reasons for joining the academy hadn't been for socializing and sex but for training.

When they'd both been assigned to Cop Central, they'd bumped into each other some more.

And one night during her rookie year, after her first homicide, they'd had a drink and sex. She'd concluded that it had been no more than a distraction for both of them, and they'd remained marginally friendly.

Then Webster had shifted into Internal Affairs and their paths had rarely crossed.

"Hey, Dallas, looking good."

"Get out of my chair," she repeated and walked straight to the AutoChef for coffee.

He sighed, rose. "I was hoping we could keep this friendly."

"I never feel friendly when the rat squad's in my office."

He hadn't changed much, she noted. His face was keen and narrow, his eyes a cool and pleasant blue. He had a quick smile and plenty of charm that seemed to suit the wavy flow of dark brown hair. She remembered his body as being tough and disciplined, his humor as being sly.

He wore the boxy black suit that was IAB's unofficial uniform, but he individualized it with a tie of screaming colors and shapes.

She remembered, too, Webster had been a fashion hound as long as she'd known him.

He shrugged off the insult, then turned to close the door. "When the complaint came down, I asked to take it. I thought I could make it easier."

"I'm not a whole lot interested in easy. I don't have time for this, Webster. I've got a case to close."

"You're going to have to make time. The more you cooperate, the less time you'll have to make."

"You know that complaint's bullshit."

"Sure, I do." He smiled again and sent a single dimple winking in his left cheek. "The legend of your coffee's reached the lofty planes of IAB. How about it?"

She sipped, watching him over the rim. If, she thought, she had to deal with this nonsense, best to deal with it through the devil you know. She programmed another cup.

"You were a pretty good street cop, Webster. Why'd you transfer to IAB?"

"Two reasons. First, it's the most direct route to administration. I never wanted the streets, Dallas. I like the view from the tower."

Her brow lifted. She hadn't realized he had ambitions that pointed to chief or commissioner. Taking the coffee out, she handed it to him. "And reason number two?"

"Wrong cops piss me off." He sipped, closed his eyes in pleasure, sighed gustily. "It lives up to the hype." He opened his eyes again, studied her.

He'd had a mild thing for her for a dozen years, he thought now. It was just a little mortifying to know she'd never realized it. Then again, she'd always been too focused on the job to give men much attention.

Until Roarke, he mused.

"Hard to picture you as a married woman. It was always business for you. It was always the job."

"My personal life doesn't change that. It's still the job."

"Yeah, I figured." He shifted, straightening. "I didn't take this complaint just for old times' sake, Dallas."

"We didn't have enough old times to generate a sake."

He smiled again. "Maybe you didn't." He sipped more coffee. His eyes stayed on hers and sobered. "You're a good cop, Dallas."

He said it so simply it dulled the leading edge of her temper. She turned, stared out the window. "She smudged my record."

"Only on paper. I like you, Dallas, always did, so I'm stepping out of procedure here to tell you—to warn you—she wants your blood."

"What the hell for? Because I slapped her down over sloppy work?"

"It goes deeper. You don't even remember her, do you? From the academy."

"No."

"You can bet your excellent ass she remembers you. She graduated with me, we were on our way out when you were coming in. And you shone, Dallas, right from the start. Classes, simulations, endurance tests, combat training. Instructors were saying you were the best to ever come through the doors. People talked about you."

He smiled again when she glanced over her shoulder, her brows knit. "No, you wouldn't have heard," he said.

"Because you wouldn't have been listening. You concentrated on one thing: getting your badge."

He leaned a hip on her desk, savoring the coffee as he spoke. "Bowers used to bitch about you to the couple of friends she'd managed to make. Muttered that you were probably sleeping with half the instructors to get preferential treatment. I had my ear to the ground even then," he added.

"I don't remember her." Eve shrugged, but the idea of being gossiped about burned a hole in her gut.

"You wouldn't, but I can guarantee she remembered you. I'm going to stay outside of procedure and tell you that Bowers is a problem. She files complaints faster than a traffic droid writes citations. Most are dismissed, but every now and again, she finds a thread to tug and a cop's career unravels. Don't give her a thread, Dallas."

"What the hell am I supposed to do?" Eve demanded. "She fucked up, I pinned her for it. That's the whole deal here. I can't sit around worrying she's going to make life tough for me. I'm after somebody who's cutting people open and helping himself to their parts. He's going to keep doing it unless I find him, and I can't find him unless I can do my goddamn job."

"Then let's get this over with." He took a microrecorder out of his pocket, set it on her desk. "We do the interview—keep it clean and formal—it gets filed, and we forget this ever happened. Believe me, nobody in IAB wants to see you take heat for this. We all know Bowers."

"Then why the hell aren't you investigating her?" Eve muttered, then pursed her lips when Webster smiled, thin and sharp. "Well, maybe the rat squad has some uses, after all."

The experience left her feeling raw and irritated, but she told herself the matter was now closed. She put a call in to Paris first, and wound her way through red tape until she reached Detective Marie DuBois, primary on the like-crime case.

Since her French counterpart had little English and Eve

had no French, they worked through the translation program on their computers. Frustration began to build as twice her computer sent her questions to DuBois in Dutch.

"Hold on a minute, let me send for my aide," Eve requested.

DuBois blinked, frowned, shook her head. "Why," the computer animated voice demanded, "do you say I eat dirt for breakfast?"

Eve threw up her hands in disgust. Despite the barrier, her frustration and apology must have shown clearly enough. Marie laughed. "It is your equipment, yes?"

"Yes. Yes. Please, wait." Eve contacted Peabody, then cautiously tried again. "My equipment is a problem. Sorry."

"No need. Such problems are, for cops, universal. You are interested in the Leclerk case?"

"Very. I have two like crimes. Your data and your input on Leclerk would be very helpful."

Marie pursed her lips and humor danced in her eyes. "It says you would like to have sex with me. I don't think that is correct."

"Oh, for Christ's sake." Eve slammed a fist against the machine just as Peabody walked in.

"I take it that wasn't a love tap."

"This piece of shit just propositioned the French detective. What's wrong with my translation program?"

"Let me have a shot." Peabody came around the desk, began to fiddle as she studied the monitor. "She's very attractive. Let's not blame the computer for trying."

"Ha ha, Peabody. Fix the fucker."

"Sir. Run systems check, update and clean translation program. Reload."

Working. . . . .

"It should only take a minute. I've got a little French; I think I can explain what's going on."

With some fumbling, Peabody called out her schoolgirl French and made Marie smile.

"Oui, pas de quoi."
"She says, cool."

System fault repaired. Current program cleaned and re-loaded.

"Give it another shot," Peabody suggested. "No telling how long the repair will hold."

"Okay. I have two like crimes," Eve began again, and as quickly as possible outlined her situation and requests.

"I'll send you copies of my files, once I have clearance," Marie agreed. "I believe you'll see that, given the condition of the body at the time of discovery, the missing organ was not considered unusual. The cats," she added with a curl of her lip, "had dined well on him."

Eve thought of Galahad and his ravenous appetite, then quickly decided not to go there. "I think we'll find your victim fits into the profile. Have his medical records been checked?"

"There was no call. The Leclerk case is not a priority, I'm afraid. The evidence was compromised. But now I would like to see also your data on the like crimes."

"I can do that. Can you give me a list of the top medical care and research centers in Paris, particularly any center that has an extensive organ replacement facility?"

Marie's brow winged up. "Yes. This is where your investigation is leading?"

"It's an avenue. And you'll want to find out where Leclerk got his health checks. I'd like to know the condition of his liver before he lost it."

"I'll start on the paperwork, Lieutenant Dallas, and try to push it through so we both have what we need as soon as possible. It was determined that Leclerk was an isolated incident. If this is incorrect, the priority on the case will be changed."

"Compare the stills of the bodies. I think you'll want to bump up the priority. Thanks. I'll be in touch."

"You think this guy's cruising the world for samples?" Peabody asked when Eve disengaged.

"Specific parts of the world, specific victims, specific samples. I think he's very organized. Chicago's next."

Despite the fact that she could dispense with the translator, she had a great deal more trouble with Chicago than she'd had with Paris.

The investigating officer had retired less than a month after the onset of the case. When she asked to speak with the detective who'd taken over, she was put on hold and treated to a moronic advertisement for a CPDS fund-raiser.

Just about the time she decided her brain would explode from the tedium, a Detective Kimiki came on. "Yeah, what can I do for you, New York."

She explained the situation and her requests while Kimiki looked faintly bored. "Yeah, yeah, I know that case. Dead end. McRae got nowhere. Nowhere to go. We got it open and it's on his percentage record but it's been shifted down to unsolved."

"I've just told you I've got like crimes here, Kimiki, and a link. Your data is important to my case."

"Data's pretty thin, and I can tell you I'm not bouncing this to the top of my list. But you want it, I'll ask the boss if it can be transferred."

"Hate to see you work up such a sweat, Kimiki."

He merely smiled at the sarcasm. "Look, when McRae took early retirement, most of his opens got dumped on me. I pick and choose where I sweat. I'll get you the data when I can. Chicago out."

"Putz," Eve muttered, then rubbed at the tension building at the base of her neck. "Early retirement?" She glanced at Peabody. "Find out how early."

An hour later, Eve was pacing the corridors of the morgue, waiting to be cleared in to Morris. The minute the locks snicked open, she was through the doors and into the autopsy room.

The smell hit her first, hard, making her suck air between her teeth. The sweet, ripe stink of decomposing flesh blurred the air. She glanced briefly at the swollen mass on the table and grabbed an air mask.

"Jesus, Morris, how do you stand it?"

He continued to make his standard Y cut, his breath coming slow and even through his own mask. "Just another day in paradise, Dallas." The air filter gave his voice a mechanical edge, and behind the goggles, his eyes were big as a frog's. "This little lady was discovered last night after her neighbors finally decided to follow their noses. Been dead nearly a week. Looks like manual strangulation."

"Did she have a lover?"

"I believe the primary is currently trying to locate him. I can say, with relative certainty, she'll never have another."

"A laugh riot as always, Morris. Did you compare the Spindler data to Snooks?"

"I did. My report's not quite finished, but since you're here, I assume you want answers now. My opinion is the same hands were used on both."

"I've got that. Tell me why the Spindler case was closed."

"Sloppy work," he muttered, slipping his clear-sealed hands into the bloated body. "I didn't do the PM on her, or I'd have clicked to it right away when I saw your body. Of course, if I'd done the PM, I would have had different findings. The examiner who did the work has been reprimanded." He looked up from his own work and met Eve's eyes. "I don't believe she'll make a similar mistake again. Not to excuse her, but she claims the primary pushed her through, insisted he knew how it went down."

"However it happened, I need the full records."

Now Morris stopped and looked up. "Problem there. We can't seem to locate them."

"What do you mean?"

"I mean they're gone. All her records are gone. I wouldn't have known she came through here if you hadn't been able to access the primary's files. We've got nothing.''

"What does your examiner have to say about that?''

"She swears everything was filed properly.''

"Then she's either lying or stupid or they were wiped.''

"I don't see her as a liar. And she's a bit green at the edges, but not stupid. The records could have been inadvertently wiped, but the search and retrieve found nothing. Zip. We don't even have Spindler on the initial sign in.''

"Purposely wiped then? Why?'' She hissed through her breathing tube, jammed her hands in her pockets. "Who has access to the records?''

"All the first-level staff.'' For the first time, his concern began to show. "I've scheduled a meeting, and I'll have to implement an internal investigation. I trust my people, Dallas. I know who works for me.''

"How tight's the security on your equipment?''

"Obviously, not tight enough.''

"Somebody didn't want the connection made. Well, it's been made,'' she said half to herself as she paced. "That idiot from the one sixty-second is going to have a lot to answer for. I've got like cases, Morris, so far in Chicago and Paris. I'm afraid I'm going to find more.''

She paused, turned. "I've got a possibility, a strong one, of a connection with a couple of high-class health centers. I'm trying to slog through a bunch of medical articles and jargon. I need a consultant who knows that stuff.''

"If you're looking at me, I'd be happy to help you. But my field is a different channel. You want a straight—and smart—medical doctor.''

"Mira?''

"She's a medical doctor,'' Morris agreed, "but her field's also in a different channel. Still, between the two of us—''

"Wait. I think I might have someone.'' She turned back to him. "I'll try her first. Somebody's screwing with us, Morris. I want you to make disc copies for me of all the data you have on Snooks. Make one for yourself and put it someplace you consider safe.''

A smile ghosted around his mouth. ''I already have. Yours is on its way to your home via private courier. Call me paranoid.''

''No, I don't think so.'' She pulled off the mask and headed for the door. But some instinct had her looking back one more time. ''Morris, watch your ass.''

Peabody got up from her seat in the corridor. ''I finally accessed some data on McRae from Chicago. It's easier to get the scoop on a psycho than a cop.''

''Protect your own,'' Eve mumbled as she strode to the exit door. That was worrying her.

''Yeah, well, our colleague's barely thirty—only had eight years in. He retires on less than ten percent of his full pension. Another two years, he could've doubled that.''

''No disability, no mental fatigue, no admin request to resign?''

''None on record. What I can get.'' The wind slapped Peabody in the face with glee as she stepped outside. ''What I can get,'' she said again once she had her breath back, ''is he was a pretty solid cop, worked his way up the ranks, was in line for a standard promotion in less than a year. He had a good percentage rate on closing cases, no shadows on his record, and worked Homicide the last three years.''

''Got any personal data—spousal pressure might've pushed him out of the job, money problems, threat of divorce. Maybe he boozed or drugged or gambled.''

''It's tougher to get personal data. I have to do the standard request and have cause.''

''I'll get it,'' Eve said, slipping behind the wheel. She thought of Roarke and his skills. And his private office with the unregistered and illegal equipment. ''When I have it, you'd be better off not asking how I came by it.''

''Came by what?'' Peabody asked with an easy smile.

''Exactly. We're taking a little personal time now, Peabody. Call it in. I don't want our next stop on the log.''

"Great. Does that mean we're going to hunt up some men and have disgusting, impersonal sex?"

"Aren't you getting enough with Charles?"

Peabody hummed in her throat. "Well, I can say I'm feeling a little looser in certain areas these days. Dispatch," she said into her communicator. "Peabody, Officer Delia, requesting personal time on behalf of Dallas, Lieutenant Eve."

"Received and acknowledged. You are off log."

"Now, about those men," Peabody said comfortably. "Let's make them buy us lunch first."

"I'll buy you lunch, Peabody, but I'm not having sex with you. Now, get your mind off your stomach and your glands, and I'll update you."

By the time Eve pulled up in front of the Canal Street Clinic, Peabody's eyes were sober. "You think this goes deep, a lot deeper than a handful of dead street sleepers and LCs."

"I think we start making a safe copy of all reports and data, and we keep certain areas of investigation quiet."

She caught sight of a sleepy-eyed brewhead loitering in the doorway and jabbed a finger at him. "You have enough brain cells left to earn a twenty?"

"Yeah." His bloodshot eyes brightened. "For what?"

"My car's in the same shape it is now when I come out, you get twenty."

"Good deal." He hunkered down with his bottle and stared at her car like a cat at a mousehole.

"You could've just threatened to kick his balls into his throat like you did with the guy the other day," Peabody pointed out.

"No point in threatening the harmless." She breezed through the doors of the clinic, noted that the waiting area looked very much as it had on her previous visit, and walked straight to the check-in window.

"I need to speak with Dr. Dimatto."

Jan the nurse gave Eve a sulky look. "She's with a patient."

"I'll wait, same place as before. Tell her I won't take much of her time."

"Dr. Dimatto is very busy today."

"That's funny. So am I." Leaving it at that, Eve stood at the security door, lifted a brow and stared down the nurse.

She let loose the same gusty sigh as she had on Eve's first visit, shoved out of her chair with the same irritable shrug of motion. What, Eve wondered, made so many people resent doing their jobs?

When the locks opened, she stepped in, met Jan's eyes on level. "Gee, thanks. I can see by your cheerful attitude how much you love working with people." She could see by Jan's confused expression it would take a while for the sarcasm to sink in.

Eve went through and settled into the cramped little office to wait for Louise.

It took twenty minutes, and the doctor didn't look particularly pleased to see Eve again. "Let's make this fast. I've got a broken arm waiting to be set."

"Fine, I need you as an expert consultant on my case for the medical end of things. The hours suck, the pay's lousy. There may be some possibility of risk, and I'm very demanding of the people who work with me."

"When do I start?"

Eve smiled with such unexpected warmth and humor, Louise nearly goggled. "When's your next day off?"

"I don't get whole days, but I don't start my rotation tomorrow until two."

"That'll work. Be at my home office tomorrow, eight sharp. Peabody, give her the address."

"Oh, I know where you live, Lieutenant." It was Louise's turn to smile. "Everyone knows where Roarke lives."

"Then I'll see you at eight."

Satisfied, Eve headed back out. "I'm going to like working with her."

"Do you want me to put in the request and papers to add her as consult?"

"Not yet." Thinking of wiped records, of cops that didn't seem particularly interested in closing cases, she shook her head as she climbed back into her vehicle. "Let's keep this unofficial for awhile yet. Put us back on log."

Using her best pitiful look, Peabody said only, "Lunch?"

"Hell. All right, but I'm not buying anything in this neighborhood for internal consumption." A woman of her word, she headed uptown and stopped when she saw a fairly clean glide-cart.

She made do with a scoop of oil fries while Peabody feasted on a soy pocket and vegetable kabob.

Eve put her vehicle on auto, letting it drive aimlessly while she ate. And she thought. The city swirled around her, the bump and grind of street traffic, the endless drone of air commuters. Stores advertised their annual inventory clearance sales with the endless monologue from the blimps overhead or huge, splashy signs.

Bargain hunters braved the frigid temperatures and shivered on people glides as they went about their business. It was a bad time for pickpockets and scam artists. No one stood still long enough to be robbed or conned.

Still, she spotted a three-card monte game and more than one sneak thief on airskates.

If you wanted something badly enough, she mused, a little inconvenience wouldn't stop you.

Routine, she thought. It was all a routine, the grifters and the muggers and the purse grabbers had theirs. And the public knew they were there and simply hoped they could avoid contact.

And the sidewalk sleepers had theirs. They would shiver and suffer through the winter and hope to evade the lick of death that came with subzero temperatures while it lapped at their cribs.

No one paid much attention if they were successful or not. Is that what he'd counted on? That no one would pay much attention? Neither of her victims had had close family to ask questions and make demands. No friends, no lovers.

She hadn't heard a single report on the recent killing on any of the news and information channels. It didn't make interesting copy, she supposed. It didn't bump ratings.

And she smiled to herself, wondering how Nadine Furst would feel about the offer of a one-on-one exclusive. Munching on a fry, she put a call through to the reporter.

"Furst. Make it fast and make it good. I'm on air in ten."

"Want a one-on-one, Nadine?"

"Dallas." Nadine's foxy face glowed with a smile. "What do I have to do for it?"

"Just your job. I've got a homicide—sidewalk sleeper—"

"Hold it. No good. We did a feature last month on sleepers. They freeze, they get sliced. We do our public interest bit twice a year. It's too soon for another."

"This one got sliced—sliced open, then his heart was removed and taken from the scene."

"Well that's a happy thought. If you're working a cult angle, we did a feature in that area in October for Halloween. My producer's not going to go for another. Not for a sleeper. Now, a feature on you and Roarke, on what it's like inside your marriage, that I could run with."

"Inside my marriage is my business, Nadine. I've got a retired LC who ran ponies. She was sliced open a couple of months back. Somebody took her kidneys."

The slight irritation in Nadine's eyes cleared, and they sharpened. "Connected?"

"Do your job," Eve suggested. "Then call my office and ask me that question again."

She disengaged and shifted the car back to manual.

"That was pretty slick, Dallas."

"She'll dig up more in an hour than six research droids could in a week. Then she'll call and ask me for an official statement and interview. Being a cooperative kind of woman, I'll give it to her."

"You ought to make her jump through a few hoops, just to keep up tradition."

"Yeah, but I'll keep the hoops wide and I'll keep them low. Put us back on log, Peabody. We're going to check out Spindler's place, and I want it on record. If anybody has any doubt the connection's been made, I want them to know it has. I want them to start to sweat."

The crime scene had been cleared weeks before, but Eve wasn't looking for physical evidence. She wanted impressions, the lay of the land, and hopefully, a conversation or two.

Spindler had lived in one of the quick-fix buildings that had been tossed up to replace those that had crumbled or been destroyed around the time of the Urban Wars.

The plan had been for fast, temporary housing to be replaced by more solid and aesthetically pleasing structures within the decade, but several decades later, several of the ugly, sheer-sided metal buildings remained in place.

A street artist had had a marvelous time spray painting naked couples in various stages of copulation over the dull gray surface. Eve decided his style and perspective were excellent, as was his sense of place. This particular building housed the majority of street LCs in that area.

There was no outside security camera, no palm plate. If there had ever been such niceties in place, they had long ago been looted or vandalized.

She walked into a cramped, windowless foyer that held a line of scarred mailboxes and a single elevator that was padlocked.

"She had 4C," Peabody said, anticipating Eve, then looked at the stained stairwell with its swaybacked treads. "I guess we walk up."

"You'll work off your lunch."

Someone had turned their choice of music entertainment up to a scream. The nasty sound of it echoed down the staircase and deafened the ears on the first-floor landing. Still, it was better than the sounds of huffing and puffing they heard through one of the thin doors on the second floor. Some lucky LC was earning her fee, Eve imagined as she headed up.

"I guess we can deduce that soundproofing isn't one of the amenities of this charming little unit," Peabody commented.

"I doubt the tenants give a damn." Eve stopped in front of 4C, knocked. Street hookers worked twenty-four/seven, but usually in shifts. She thought someone would be around, and unemployed.

"I'm not working till sundown," came the response. "So blow off."

In answer, Eve held her badge up to the security peep. "Police. I want to talk to you."

"My license is up to date. You can't hassle me."

"Open the door, or you'll see just how fast I can hassle you."

There was a mutter, curse, the rattle of locks. The door opened a slit and a single bloodshot brown eye peered out. "What? I'm not on for hours, and I'm trying to get some sleep here."

From the look in that single eye, she'd been getting that sleep with a little chemical aid. "How long have you lived in this apartment?"

"A few weeks. So the fuck what?"

"Before that?"

"Across the hall. Look, I got my license, my health checks. I'm solid."

"Were you one of Spindler's?"

"Yeah." The door opened another fraction. The other eye and a hard mouth appeared. "So the fuck what?"

"You got a name?"

"Mandy. So the—"

"Yeah, I got that part. Open up, Mandy, I need to ask you some questions about your former boss."

"She's dead. Been dead. Those're the only answers I got." But she opened the door. Her hair was short and spiked. Easier, Eve imagined, for her to don one of the many wigs street LCs liked to play with. She was probably no more than thirty, but looked ten years older if you went by the face.

Whatever profit Mandy made obviously went into her body, which was lush and curved, with huge, uptilted breasts that strained against the thin material of a dingy pink robe.

It was, Eve decided, the right investment for a woman in her field. Johns rarely looked at the face.

Eve stepped inside and noted that the living area had been converted so that it accommodated both ends of the business. A curtain was drawn down the center, cutting the room in two. In one half were two beds on casters with rates and services clearly posted on a board between them.

The other half held a computer, a tele-link system, and a single chair.

"Did you take over Spindler's business?"

"Four of us got together to do it. We figured, hell, somebody's got to run the stables, and if it's us, we can cut back on street time." She smiled a little. "Be like, executives. Trolling for johns in the winter's murder."

"I just bet. Were you around the night Spindler was killed?"

"I figure I was around—in and out, you know, depending. I remember business was pretty good." She took the single chair, stretched out her legs. "Wasn't so freaking cold."

"You got your book handy?"

Mandy's eyes went sulky. "You got no need to poke into my books. I'm being straight."

"Then tell me what you know, where you were. You remember," Eve said before Mandy could deny it. "Even in this kind of flop, you don't get your boss carved open on a nightly basis."

"Sure I remember." She jerked a shoulder. "I was catching a break when Lida found her and went nutso. Jesus, she screamed like a virgin, you know? Came screaming and crying and beating on my door. Said how the old bitch was dead and there was blood, so I told her to shut the fuck up and call the cops if she wanted to. I went back to bed.''

"You didn't come in and check it out for yourself?''

"What for? If she was dead, fine and dandy. If she wasn't, who cares?''

"How long did you work for her?''

"Six years.'' Mandy yawned hugely. "Now I work for me.''

"You didn't like her.''

"I hated her guts. Look, like I said to the other cop, to know her was to hate her. I didn't see anything, didn't hear anything, and I wouldn't have cared if I did.''

"What cop did you talk to?''

"One of her kind.'' She jerked up her chin in Peabody's direction. "Then one of your kind. They didn't make a big deal out of it. Why should you?''

"You don't know my kind, Mandy. But I know yours.'' She stepped closer, leaned down. "Woman runs a stable, she keeps some cash around. She deals in cash, and she doesn't run out at night to make a deposit until the shift's over. She was dead before that, and I don't see anything on the report about any cash being found in this place.''

Mandy crossed her legs. "So, one of the cops helped himself. So the fuck what?''

"I think a cop's going to be smart enough not to take the whole stash. I don't think there was anything to take once they got here. Now, you either play straight with me, or I'll take you and your book into interview and sweat it out of you. I don't give a damn if you took her stash, but I can care about what happened in here that night.''

She waited a beat to make sure Mandy caught the full drift. "To review: Your pal came screaming to your door and told you what was up in here. Now, we both know you didn't turn around and go back to bed. So let's try that part again.''

Mandy studied Eve's face, measured. A woman in her profession who intended to survive until retirement learned to read faces and attitudes. This cop, she decided, would push until she got her answers. "Somebody was going to take the money, so I did. Lida and I split it. Who cares?"

"You went in and looked at her."

"I made sure she was dead. Didn't have to go past the bedroom door for that. Not with the blood and the smell."

"Okay, now tell me about the night before. You said you were in and out, busy night. You know the kind of johns that use this place. Did you see anybody who didn't fit?"

"Look, I'm not getting tangled up in some cop shit over that old bitch."

"You want to stay untangled, you tell me who and what you saw. Otherwise, you become a material witness, one who may have compromised the crime scene." A new and nastier drift, Eve mused, another pause to let it sink in thoroughly. "I can get an order for a truth test out of that, and some time for you in holding."

"Goddamn it." Mandy pushed out of the chair, walked over to a minifridge, and found a beer. "Look, I was busy, working my ass off. Maybe I saw a couple guys who looked out of place coming out of the building when I was bringing a john in. I just thought, *Fuck it, I got this half-wit to get off, and one of the other girls got these two dudes who looked like they had money enough to tip just fine.*"

"What did they look like?"

"Expensive coats. They were each carrying something, like bags. I figured they brought their own sex toys."

"Men? You're certain you saw two men?"

"Two of them." Her lips pursed briefly before she took another slug of beer. "I figured them for men, but I didn't get a good look because the half-wit was already drooling on me."

Eve nodded, sat on the corner of the desk. "Okay, Mandy, let's see if talking all this over again improves your memory."

chapter nine

Normally, Eve approached splashy social events like medicine. She avoided them whenever possible—which wasn't often enough now that she was married to Roarke—and when she couldn't wiggle out, she gritted her teeth, swallowed fast and hard, and tried to ignore the bad taste in her mouth.

But she was looking forward to the fund-raiser for the Drake Center.

This time, she approached the event like a job.

But she was going to miss the comforting weight of her weapon. There was no place to conceal it in the dress she wore. It had seemed appropriate to wear one of Leonardo's designs, as he would be one of the couturiers spotlighted in the fashion show.

She'd had a lot to choose from. Since Leonardo had come into Mavis's life—and therefore Eve's—her wardrobe had expanded dramatically from jeans, trousers, shirts, and one boxy gray suit to include what she considered enough fancy clothes to outfit a theater troupe.

She'd picked the dress out of the closet at random, because she liked the dark copper tone of it. A long, smooth column, it fell straight from its off-the-shoulder neckline to her ankles, which made her consider strapping her clutch piece to her calf.

In the end, she stuck it and her shield in the little evening bag she carried. Just, she told herself, in case.

Weapons seemed out of place in the glitter of the ballroom, in the sweeping sparkle of beautiful people dressed in shimmering clothes and draped with glinting gold and flashing stones. The air was rich with the fragrances of hothouse flowers, of perfumed flesh and hair. And music, a low, elegant throb, played discreetly.

Champagne and other fashionable, exotic drinks were served in crystal glasses by waiters in distinguished black uniforms. Conversation was a sophisticated murmur, punctuated by an occasionally muted laugh.

To Eve's eye, nothing could have looked more contrived, more staged, or more tedious. She was about to say just that to Roarke when there was a delighted squeal, a flurry of color and movement, and the sharp sound of crystal shattering on the floor.

Mavis Freestone waved a jubilant hand that was studded with rings on every finger, offered a giggling apology to the waiter she'd bumped, and dashed across the ballroom through the perfectly poised crowd on five-inch silver heels designed to show off toenails painted a blistering blue.

"Dallas!" She squealed again and all but launched herself into Eve's arms. "This is *so* mag! I didn't think you'd show. Wait till Leonardo sees you. He's back in the dressing area having a real case of nerves. I told him to take a chill pill or something or I swear he's just going to woof all over somebody. Hey, Roarke!"

Before Eve could speak, Mavis had leaped over to hug Roarke. "Man, do you two look frigid! Have you had a drink yet? The tornadoes are killers. I've had three."

"They seem to agree with you." Roarke couldn't help but grin. She was small as a fairy, lark happy, and well on her way to being completely drunk.

"Yeah, you bet. I've got some Sober-Up with me so I

can maintain while Leonardo's designs hit the ramp. But
for now . . ."

She started to snag another glass from a passing waiter,
nearly teetered over. Eve simply slid an arm around her
shoulders. "For now, let's check out the eats."

They made an interesting picture: Roarke, sexy and elegant in suave black tie; Eve, long and lanky in her copper
column; and Mavis, in a silver dress that looked wet to
the touch and faded into transparency a wink below her
crotch, while a temporary tattoo of a grinning lizard slithered up her right thigh. Her hair spilled over her shoulder
and was dyed the same eye-popping blue as her nails.

"We get real food after the show," Mavis commented,
but popped a canapé into her mouth.

"Why wait?" Amused by the brilliant shine in Mavis's
eyes, Eve nonethcless piled a plate with finger food, then
held it while her friend plowed through.

"Man, this stuff rocks." She swallowed. "What is it?"

"Fancy."

With a snorting laugh, Mavis pressed a hand to her
stomach. "I better watch it or I'll be the one woofing. I
guess I'll take my Sober-Up and go back to see if I can
hold Leonardo's hand. He gets so wired up before a show.
Really glad you guys are here. Most of these people are,
you know . . . drags."

"You get to go back and hang with Leonardo," Eve
said. "I have to stay out here and talk to the drags."

"We'll sit together at dinner, okay? And make fun of
them. I mean, some of these outfits!" With a shake of her
blue hair, she scampered off.

"We're releasing her recording and video later this
month," Roarke told Eve. "What is the world going to
make of Mavis Freestone?"

"They won't be able to resist her." Smiling now, she
looked up at Roarke. "So, introduce me to some of the
drags. I'm hoping to make somebody very nervous tonight."

Eve didn't think of the tedium now. Every new face
she met was a potential suspect. Some smiled, some nod-

ded, some lifted eyebrows when they learned she was a homicide cop.

She spotted Dr. Mira, Cagney, and with some surprise, Louise Dimatto. She'd save them for later, Eve decided, and held out her hand to formalize her introduction to Dr. Tia Wo.

"I've heard of you, Lieutenant."

"Really?"

"Yes, I never miss the local news. You've been featured quite a bit the last year or so—through your own exploits and your connection with Roarke."

Her voice was gravel rough but not unpleasant. She looked both stark and dignified in basic black. She wore no jewelry but for a small, gold pin, the ancient medical symbol of two snakes wound around a staff topped by wings.

"I never thought about police work being exploits."

Wo smiled, a kind of quick reflex that curved the lips up for a brief instant, left the eyes unwarmed, then settled down again. "No offense meant. I often consider the news the highest form of entertainment. More than books or videos, it shows people in their genuine form, reciting their own lines. And I'm quite fascinated with crime."

"Me, too." As openings went, it was perfect. "I have one you'd find interesting. I'm investigating a series of murders. The victims are sidewalk sleepers, addicts, street LCs."

"It's an unfortunate life for them."

"An unfortunate death for some. Each of these victims had an organ surgically removed. Quite skillfully removed, stolen from the unwilling donor."

Wo's eyes flickered, narrowed. "I've heard nothing of this."

"You will," Eve said easily. "I'm making connections right now, following leads. You specialize in organ transplants, Dr. Wo." She waited a bit while Wo's mouth opened and closed. "I wonder if you might have any theories, from a medical standpoint?"

"Oh, well." Her wide fingers lifted to toy with her pin.

Her nails were trimmed short, left unpainted. "The black market would be a possibility, though the easy availability of artificial organs has cut that venue down dramatically."

"These weren't healthy organs."

"Unhealthy? A madman," she said with a shake of her head. "I've never understood the mind. The body is basic, it is form and function, a machine that can be repaired, tuned, so to speak. But the mind, even when clinically or legally healthy, has so many avenues, so many quirks, so much potential for error. But you're right, it's quite fascinating."

Her eyes had shifted, making Eve smile to herself. *She wants to be gone,* Eve thought, *but hasn't quite worked out how to ditch me without insulting Roarke—and all his money.*

"My wife is a tenacious cop." Roarke slid a hand over Eve's shoulder. "She won't give up until she finds who and what she's looking for. I suppose you have a lot in common," he continued smoothly. "Cops and doctors. A demanding schedule and a singular purpose."

"Yes. Ah—" Wo signaled, lifting one finger.

Eve recognized Michael Waverly from his photo on his data sheet. He was the youngest on her list of surgeons, single, she recalled, and the current president of the AMA.

He was tall enough, she decided, to have had Ledo looking up at him. He was slickly attractive, at ease, and slightly less traditional than his colleagues. His gilded hair curled toward his shoulders, and he wore a black, collarless shirt with dull silver buttons with his formal tux.

His smile was a quick nova flash of power and charm.

"Tia." Despite her stiff posture, he kissed her on the cheek, then held out a hand to Roarke. "Nice to see you again. We at Drake very much appreciate your generosity."

"As long as it's put to good use, it's my pleasure. My wife," Roarke said, keeping a possessive hand on Eve's shoulder. He understood the look of pure male interest in Waverly's eyes as they settled on her face. And didn't particularly appreciate it. "Eve Dallas. Lieutenant Dallas."

"Lieutenant?" Waverly offered his hand and another potent smile. "Oh yes, I'm sure I knew that. I'm delighted to meet you. Can we assume the city's safe as you're free to join us tonight?"

"A cop never assumes, Doctor."

He laughed, giving her hand a friendly squeeze. "Has Tia confessed her secret fascination with crime? The only thing I've ever seen her read other than medical journals are murder mysteries."

"I was just telling her about one of mine. Of the nonfiction variety." She outlined the facts, watched a variety of expressions cross Waverly's face. Mild interest, surprise, puzzlement, and finally understanding.

"You believe it's a doctor—a surgeon. That's very difficult to accept."

"Why?"

"Dedicating yourself to years of training and practice to save lives only to take them for no apparent reason? I can't fathom it. It's baffling but intriguing. Do you have a suspect?"

"A number of them. But no prime, as yet. I'll be taking a close look at the top surgeons in the city at this point."

Waverly gave a short laugh. "That would include me and my friend here. How flattering, Tia, we're suspects in a murder investigation."

"Sometimes your humor falls very flat, Michael." With anger sparking in her eyes, Wo turned her back on them. "Excuse me."

"She takes things quite seriously," Waverly murmured. "Well, Lieutenant, aren't you going to ask me my whereabouts on the night in question?"

"I have more than one night in question," Eve said easily. "And that would be very helpful."

He blinked in surprise, and his smile didn't shine quite so brightly. "Well this hardly seems the time and place to discuss it."

"I'll schedule an interview as soon as possible."

"Will you?" His voice had dropped several degrees and bordered on cold. "You're straight to the point, I see, Lieutenant."

Eve decided she'd insulted him but hadn't unnerved him. He wasn't a man who expected to be questioned, she concluded. "I appreciate your cooperation. Roarke, we should say hello to Mira."

"Of course. Excuse us, Michael. That was smoothly done," he murmured in Eve's ear as they moved through the crowd.

"I've watched you cut somebody off at the knees politely often enough to get the hang of it."

"Thank you, darling. I'm so proud."

"Good. Find me another one."

Roarke scanned the crowd. "Hans Vanderhaven should suit your mood."

He steered her through the crowd toward a big man with a gleaming bald head and a natty white beard, standing beside a tiny woman with enormous breasts and a waterfall of gilt-edged red hair.

"That would be the doctor's newest wife," Roarke murmured in Eve's ear.

"Likes them young, doesn't he?"

"And built," Roarke agreed, moving forward before Eve could add a pithy comment to his observation. "Hans."

"Roarke." His voice was huge, barreling out and echoing through the room. Lively eyes the color of chestnuts landed on Eve, took her measure. "This must be your wife. Enchanted. You're with the police department?"

"That's right," She didn't much care for the way he took her hand, or the way those eager eyes played over her as he kissed her knuckles. But it didn't seem to bother the newest Mrs. Vanderhaven, who stood smiling inanely with a glass of champagne in one hand and a diamond the size of Pittsburgh on the other. "My wife Fawn, Roarke and . . ."

"Dallas, Eve Dallas."

"Oh." Fawn giggled, batted eyes of Easter egg blue.

"I've never talked to a policewoman before."

If Eve had anything to do with it, they weren't going to change that record by much. She merely smiled, giving Roarke a light but none-too-subtle elbow nudge. Understanding, he shifted toward Fawn and, recognizing type and priorities, began to compliment her on her dress.

Eve turned away from the giggle and gave her attention to Vanderhaven. "I noticed Dr. Wo had a pin like the one you're wearing."

He lifted a wide, capable hand to the gold pin on his lapel. "The caduceus. Our little medal of honor. I imagine those in your profession have their own symbols. Now, I don't imagine you asked Roarke to distract my delightful wife so we could discuss accessories."

"No. You're observant, Doctor."

His eyes sobered, his barrel voice lowered. "Colin told me you were investigating a homicide that involves organ theft. Is it true you believe a surgeon is involved?"

"That's right, a very skilled one." So there would be no dancing, no pleasantries. Vanderhaven might have been on her short list of suspects at the moment, but she could find room to be grateful. "I hope I can count on your cooperation. I'll be scheduling interviews over the next several days."

"It's insulting." He lifted a short, squat glass. From the color and scent, she took it to be whiskey, straight up, rather than one of the elegant party drinks. "Necessary from your viewpoint, I'm sure, but insulting. No surgeon, no doctor would have willfully, uselessly terminated a life as you described to Colin."

"It's only useless until we know his motive," Eve said evenly and watched Vanderhaven's lips tighten. "The murder was done, the organ taken, and according to several expert sources, the surgical procedure was performed by skilled hands. Do you have another theory?"

"A cult." He said it shortly, then took a sip of whiskey, took a deep breath. "You'll pardon me for being sensitive about this issue, but we're speaking about my community, my family, in a very real way. A cult," he repeated in a tone that demanded she accept. "With a member or members trained in the medical field, certainly. The days of doctors mining bodies for parts went out with catgut. We have no use for damaged organs."

She kept her eyes level on his. "I don't believe I mentioned the organ taken was damaged."

For a moment he only stared, then blinked. "You've said it came from an indigent. It was bound to be flawed. Excuse me. My wife and I should mingle."

He took the still-simpering Fawn firmly by the elbow and drew her away.

"You owe me." Roarke grabbed a flute of champagne off a tray and took one long sip. "I'm going to hear that irritating giggle in my sleep."

"She had a lot of expensive hardware." Eve considered, angling her head as she studied the glint and glitter of Fawn from across the room. "Is all that stuff she's wearing real?"

"I don't have my jeweler's loupe on me," he said dryly, "but it appears to be. And I'd estimate she's draped in, oh, roughly a quarter million or so of first-rate diamonds and sapphires. Nothing a top-flight surgeon couldn't afford," he went on, and handed her the flute. "Though he must feel a bit of a pinch having the ex-wives and various children draining some of his fees."

"Interesting. He was right up front about the case, and pretty steamed about my angle of investigation." She sipped the champagne, passed the flute back to Roarke. "It sounds to me as if he and Cagney have had a consult about it."

"That's understandable. They're friends as well as colleagues."

"Maybe Mira can give me some personal data on this group."

Roarke caught the change in rhythm of the music. "The fashion show's about to start. We'll have to mingle with Mira later. She seems to be having a very intense conversation at the moment."

Eve had seen that for herself. Cagney bent down close,

kept one hand on Mira's arm. He was, Eve noted, doing most of the talking, with a hard, focused look in his eyes that indicated what he said was both vital and unpleasant.

Mira merely shook her head, said little, then, laying a hand on his, patted it once before stepping away.

"He's upset her." The almost fierce sense of protection surprised her. "Maybe I should see what's wrong."

But then the music flashed, the crowd swirled to insure good views for the fashion display. Eve lost sight of Mira and found herself face to face with Louise.

"Dallas." Louise nodded coolly. Her hair was styled and sleek, her siren-red dress simply and beautifully cut. The diamonds in her ears didn't look like simulations. "I didn't expect to see you here."

"Same goes." *Or to see you,* Eve thought, *looking polished, perfumed, and prosperous.* "You're a long way from the clinic, Dr. Dimatto."

"You're a long way from Cop Central, Lieutenant."

"I live to socialize," Eve said so dryly that Louise's lips twitched.

"About as much as I do, I imagine. I'm Louise Dimatto." She held out a hand to Roarke. "I'm going to be consulting on a case for your wife. I believe we'll either be fast friends or hate each other before we're done."

Roarke grinned. "Should I lay bets?"

"Haven't quite figured the odds yet." She glanced over to watch the first models parade down the runway. "They always make me think of giraffes."

"Giraffes are more fun to watch," Eve commented. "Seems to me if Drake took all the bucks they sank into putting this fund-raiser together, they wouldn't need a damn fund-raiser."

"Darling, you're much too logical to understand the purpose of show and beg. The more expensive the event, the higher the donation ticket, and the heartier those involved pat each other on the back after counting the till."

"And then you add the social connection," Louise put in, favoring Roarke with a quick smile. "Those prominent in medicine making their entrance, bringing their spouses

or lovers, mingling with each other, and various pillars of
the community such as Roarke.''

Eve snorted. "Some pillar."

"I think Louise understands that anyone over a certain
financial position automatically becomes a pillar."

"And his wife attains the same status."

"Cops make lousy pillars." Eve shifted her gaze from
the display of the hot look for upcoming spring and studied Louise. "So we've established why Roarke and I are
here, but what about you? How does a doctor doing time
at a free clinic rate a ticket to a major event for Drake?"

"By being the niece of the chief of staff." Louise managed to reach through bodies and snag a flute of champagne. She used it to toast.

"You're Cagney's niece?"

"That's right."

Friends, colleagues, relatives, Eve thought. An inces-
tuous little group—and such groups tended to band together like mud balls to block outsiders. "And what are
you doing working in an armpit instead of uptown?"

"Because, Lieutenant, I do what I want. I'll see you in
the morning." She nodded to Roarke, then slipped
through the crowd.

Eve turned to her husband. "I've just taken on a consultant who's the niece of one of my suspects."

"Will you keep her?"

"For the time being," Eve murmured. "We'll see how
it shakes out."

After the last long-legged model had glided down the silver ramp and the music had subdued to a shimmer to lure
couples onto the glossy tiles of the dance floor, Eve tried
to identify what form of nutrition was disguised in the
arty structure of shape and color on her dinner plate.

Beside her, too excited to eat, Mavis bounced on her
seat. "Leonardo's designs were the aces, weren't they?
None of the others were in the same orbit. Roarke, you've
got to buy that backless-to-the-butt red number for Dallas."

"That color wouldn't suit her." Leonardo, his huge hand covering both of Mavis's, looked down at her. His gold-toned eyes shone with love and relief. He was built like a redwood and had the heart, and often the nerves, of a six-year-old approaching the first day of school.

He had indeed, as Mavis had so elegantly put it, woofed before the show.

"Now the green satin . . ." He smiled shyly over at Roarke. "I admit I had her in mind when I designed it. The color and cut are perfect for her."

"Then she'll have to have it. Won't you, Eve?"

Preoccupied with finding out if there was anything resembling meat or one of its substitutes on her plate, she merely grunted. "Is this chicken buried in here or what?"

"It's Cuisine Artiste," Roarke told her, and offered her a roll the size of a credit chip. "Where aesthetics often take priority over taste." Leaning over, he kissed her. "We'll get a pizza on the way home."

"Good idea. I should cruise around, see if I can find Mira, and if I can stir anything else up."

"I'll cruise with you." Roarke rose, pulled out her chair.

"Fine. It was a great show, Leonardo. I especially liked that green thing."

He beamed at her, then tugged her down to kiss her cheek. When she walked away, Eve heard Mavis giggle and tell Leonardo she needed a tornado to celebrate.

Tables with snowy cloths and silver candles were scattered throughout the ballroom. Six enormous chandeliers dripped out of the lofty ceiling to sprinkle muted and silver light. The wait staff moved around and through, pouring wine, removing dishes with an elegant choreography.

Generous drinks had loosened a few tongues, Eve observed. The level of sound was higher now, and the laughter louder.

Table hopping was a popular sport, and Eve noted as they wandered that most of the diners admired their food but didn't eat it.

"What was this thing, five, ten thousand a plate?" she asked Roarke.

"A bit more, actually."

"What a scam. There's Mira, heading out. Must be a pit stop because her husband's not with her. I'll go after her." She cocked her head at Roarke. "Why don't you play the crowd for me since they're loosening up some?"

"Love to. Then I want one dance, darling Eve, and pepperoni on my pizza."

She grinned and didn't worry about all the eyes watching when he kissed her. "I could go for both of those. I won't be long."

She headed directly to the bank of doors Mira had used, turned through the sumptuous foyer, and searched out the women's lounge.

Chandeliers twinkled light in the dressing area where a attendant droid in snappy black and white waited to assist or provide. The long rose-toned counter held more than a dozen individual lighted mirrors, a tidy and expansive array of decorative bottles filled with scents and creams. There were disposable brushes and combs, hair gels, sprays, and shines.

If madam had lost or forgotten her lip dye or any other enhancement, the droid would be more than happy to open the wall cabinet to provide the guest with a wide choice of the best brands in all the popular shades.

Mira sat at the end of the counter on a skirted chair. She'd switched on her mirror so the lights ringing it glowed, but she had yet to freshen her makeup.

She looked pale, Eve thought. Pale and unhappy. Feeling abruptly awkward and intrusive, she nearly backed out of the room again, but Mira caught the motion, turned, and smiled.

"Eve. I heard you were here."

"I saw you earlier." Eve walked down behind the row of chairs. "But then the fashion show started, and we got swallowed up."

"It was entertaining. There were some lovely pieces,

though I must admit Leonardo's remain unique. Is that one of his you're wearing?''

Eve glanced down at her skirts. ''Yeah. He keeps it pretty simple for me.''

''He understands you.''

''You're upset,'' Eve blurted out and had Mira's eyes widening in surprise. ''What's wrong?''

''I'm fine. A slight headache, that's all. I wanted to get out of the crowd for a bit.'' Deliberately, she shifted to the mirror and began to touch up her lips.

''I saw you earlier,'' Eve reminded her, ''talking to Cagney. Or he was talking to you. He upset you. Why?''

''This isn't interview room A,'' Mira responded, then closed her eyes in annoyance when Eve jerked back. ''I'm sorry. I'm so sorry, that was uncalled for. I'm not upset, but I am . . . disturbed. And I thought I was disguising it so well.''

''I'm a trained observer.'' Eve tried a smile. ''You never look ruffled,'' she continued. ''You just always look perfect.''

''Really?'' With a low laugh, Mira stared at her own face in the glass. She saw flaws. A woman's vanity would always pick out flaws, she mused. But how flattering and unnerving to know a woman like Eve thought her perfect. ''And I was just thinking I could use a salon treatment.''

''I wasn't talking only about how you look but your manner. It's your manner that's ruffled tonight. If it's personal, I'll butt out, but if it has anything to do with Cagney and the case, I want to know.''

''It's both. Colin is an old friend.'' Her gaze lifted, met Eve's. ''We were once more than friends.''

''Oh.'' Ridiculously embarrassed, Eve opened her bag, then realized she hadn't put anything in it but her badge and gun. She closed it again and picked up the complimentary brush.

''It was a very long time ago, before I met my husband. We remained friends, not particularly close, as years passed. People do tend to drift,'' Mira said wistfully. ''But we have a history, Eve. I didn't believe it was relevant to bring it up when you asked me to consult on the case. I still don't, professionally. But this is difficult for me on a personal level.''

"Look, if you want to back out—"

"No, I don't. And that's what I told Colin earlier. He's understandably upset by your investigation, at knowing that he and many of the surgeons he knows will be suspects until you close the case. He hoped that I would keep him informed of my findings and yours, or failing that, resign from this case.''

"He asked you to pass him confidential data?''

"Not in so many words," Mira said hastily and shifted to face Eve directly. "You have to understand, he feels responsible for the people who work for him, with him. He's in a position of authority, and that carries a weight.''

"A friend wouldn't have asked you to compromise your ethics.''

"Perhaps not, but he's under a great deal of stress. This matter will put a strain on our friendship, if not a hole through it. I'm sorry for that, I'll grieve for that. But I carry a weight as well." Then she drew a deep breath. "As primary, you have—with the information I've just given you—the right to ask me to assign another profiler on this case. I'll understand if that's what you want to do.''

Eve set the brush down, met Mira's troubled eyes levelly. "I'm going to have more data for you tomorrow. I'm hoping you can give me a profile by early next week.''

"Thank you.''

"You don't have to thank me. I want the best, and that's you." She rose quickly, unnerved when she saw tears swim into Mira's quiet eyes. "Ah, what do you know about the niece? Louise Dimatto?''

"Not a great deal." Struggling for composure, Mira recapped her lip tube. "She's always gone her own way. She's very bright, very dedicated, and very independent.''

"Can I trust her?''

Mira nearly said yes out of pure reflex, then pushed her

personal feelings aside. "I would believe so, but as I said, I don't know her very well."

"Okay. Ah, do you want me to . . . do anything here?"

The sound Mira made was between a chuckle and a sigh. Eve sounded nearly terrified the answer would be yes. "No. I think I'll just sit here for a little while, in the quiet."

"Then I better get back." Eve started out, then turned. "Mira, if it starts to turn toward him, will you be able to handle it?"

"If it turns toward him, he wouldn't be the man I thought I knew. The man I once loved. Yes, I will handle it, Eve."

But when Eve nodded and left her alone, Mira closed her eyes and let herself weep a little.

chapter ten

Instincts, Eve decided the next morning, were one thing. Facts another. A family connection between Colin Cagney and her upcoming consultant was just a little too close for comfort. So, with her hands in her pockets and her back to the window where the thick fall of snow obscured the view, she ordered her computer to run data on Louise Dimatto.

Dimatto, Louise Anne, ID# 3452-100-34FW. Born March 1, 2030, Westchester, New York, Marital status, single, No children Parents Alicia Cagney Dimatto and Mark Robert Dimatto. No siblings. Current residence, 28 Houston, unit C, New York City. Current position, general practitioner of medicine, Canal Street Clinic. Held position for two years.

Graduate of Harvard Medical School, all honors. Residency completed at Roosevelt Hospital. . . .

"Financial data," Eve ordered, and glanced over absently as Roarke walked in.

*Working. . . . Salary from Canal Street Clinic, thirty
thousand annual . . .*

Eve snorted. "She didn't buy those rocks she was
wearing on her ears with a pitiful thirty thousand a year.
That's less than I make, for Christ's sake."

*Income from trust fund, stock dividends, and interest,
approximately $268,000 annual . . .*

"That's more like it. So, with that kind of income, why
isn't she living in some fancy digs uptown?"

"A quarter million doesn't buy what it used to,"
Roarke said easily and moved over to glance at her monitor. "Who are you running, the young doctor?"

"Yeah. She'll be here in a few minutes. I have to decide whether to kick her or bring her in." Eve frowned.
"A trust fund baby with high connections at Drake, but
she puts in miserable time at a free clinic where she treats
street people for peanuts. Why?"

Cocking his head, Roarke sat on the edge of her desk.
"I know a certain cop who now has what some would
call a substantial personal income and high connections
at nearly every level of business in any area on or off
planet, yet she continues to work the streets, often putting
herself at personal risk. For peanuts." He paused a moment. "Why?"

"The money stuff, that's your deal," Eve muttered.

"No, darling, it's yours. And maybe this is hers.
Maybe, like you, this is who she is."

She considered a moment, shuffling his money and her
part of it aside—where she preferred it. "You liked her."

"On brief first impression, yes. More to the point, you
do."

"Maybe I do." She paused a moment. "Yeah, I do,
but I don't know what she'll do if the arrow points at her
uncle." She rolled her shoulders once. "I guess we'll just
have to find out. Computer, file and save all data and
disengage."

"I have the information you asked me for yesterday." Roarke slipped a disc out of his pocket, slid it into hers. "I don't know how helpful it's going to be. "I didn't see any connection between your case and NewLife. And as for Westley Friend, he didn't appear to have much of an underbelly. He comes off as a man dedicated to his family and his work."

"The more you know, the more you can cross off. I appreciate it."

"Any time, Lieutenant." Roarke took her hands, slid his up to her wrists, and tugged her closer. It gratified him to feel her pulse trip just a little faster at the contact. "Do I assume you'll be at this most of the day?"

"That's the plan. Aren't you going in to your office?"

"No, I'll be working here today. It's Saturday."

"Oh, right." The little trickle of guilt had her struggling not to squirm. "We didn't have, like plans for the weekend, did we?"

"No." His lips curved, and taking advantage of her momentary distraction, he shifted his hands to her hips. "But I could make some, for after hours."

"Yeah?" Her body bumped his, and her muscles loosened and throbbed. "What kind of plans?"

"Intimate plans." He lowered his head to catch and tease her lower lip with his teeth. "Darling Eve, where would you like to go? Or should I surprise you?"

"Your surprises are usually pretty good." Her eyes wanted to close, her bones wanted to melt. "Roarke, you're clouding my mind here."

"Why, thank you." With a low laugh, he changed angles to rub his lips over hers. "Why don't I just finish the job," he suggested and turned up the power and heat of the kiss.

When Louise stepped through the doorway with Summerset just behind her, she stopped abruptly. She supposed she could have—should have—cleared her throat or made some sound. But it was so interesting to watch that shimmer of passion, that ease of joining. And to see the edgy, somewhat abrupt Lieutenant Dallas in a private moment that proved her to be a woman with a heart and needs.

It was really lovely, she decided, the way they were framed in the window with the steady fall of snow behind them, the woman in an almost ruthlessly plain shirt and trousers with a weapon harness strapped to her side, and the man elegantly casual in black. Really lovely, she thought, that they could be so completely lost in each other. Which meant, she supposed, that marriage didn't always kill passions.

So it was Summerset who cleared his throat. "I beg your pardon. Dr. Dimatto has arrived."

Eve started to jerk back, then subsided when Roarke merely locked her against him. Whenever she tried to wiggle out of a public embrace, he made an issue of it. She fought with embarrassment, tried to seem casual. All the while, her blood was running as sweet and thick as heated syrup.

"You're prompt, doctor," she managed.

"Always, Lieutenant. Good morning, Roarke."

"Good morning." Amused at all of them, Roarke loosened his hold on Eve. "Can we offer you something? Coffee?"

"I never turn down coffee. You have an exceptional home," she added as she continued into the room.

"This place?" Eve's voice was desert dry. "It'll do until we find something bigger."

Louise laughed, set her briefcase aside. The thin light through the window caught the little gold pin on her lapel. Eve lifted a brow. "Dr. Wo had one of those on her dress last night. So did Vanderhaven."

"This." Absently, Louise lifted a hand to the pin. "Tradition. Right after the turn of the century, most medical facilities began to give a caduceus pin to doctors who'd completed their internship. I imagine a lot of them end up in a dusty drawer somewhere, but I like it."

"I'll let you get down to work." Roarke handed Louise her coffee, then glanced over at his wife. The gleam in his eye said it all. "I'll see you later, Lieutenant, and we can firm up those plans."

"Sure." Damn it, her lips were still vibrating from his. "We'll do that."

Louise waited until he'd gone through a connecting door, shut it. "I hope you won't take offense if I say that is the most beautiful man I've ever seen."

"I rarely take offense at the truth. So let's try for another. Your uncle is one of my suspects. At this time, he is on my short, and can't be eliminated. Is that going to be a problem for you?"

A line formed instantly and deeply between Louise's brows. Straight irritation, Eve decided.

"It won't be a problem because I have every confidence I'll help you eliminate him very quickly. Uncle Colin and I disagree in many areas, but he is, above all else, dedicated to insuring the quality of human life."

"That's an interesting phrase." Eve came around the desk, sat on the edge. They would have to test each other, she knew, before they could work together. "Not saving lives, maintaining them, prolonging them?"

"There are some who believe that without a level of quality, life is only pain."

"Is that your belief?"

"For me, life itself is enough, as long as suffering can be relieved."

Eve nodded, picked up her own coffee, though it had gone cold. "Most wouldn't say that Snooks, for example, was enjoying any quality of life. He was sick, he was dying, he was indigent. Ending all that for him might have been considered a mercy by some."

Louise went pale, but her eyes remained steady. "No doctor with ethics, with morals, with a belief in his oaths and his duty, would terminate a patient without consent. First do no harm. This, without question, is a promise my uncle lives by."

Eve nodded. "We'll see. I want you to take a look at the data I've accessed, then translate it for me in terms someone who didn't graduate from Harvard Medical can understand.''

Louise's brows winged up. ''You checked up on me.''

''Did you think I wouldn't?''

''No.'' Once again, Louise's face relaxed into a smile. ''I was certain you would. It's nice to be right.''

''Then let's get started.'' Eve called up the data, gestured to the chair behind the monitor, then looked over as Peabody came huffing through the door. ''You're late.''

''Subway—'' Peabody held up a hand as she struggled to catch her breath. ''Running behind. Weather sucks. Sorry.'' She took off her snow-covered coat. ''Coffee. Please. Sir.''

Eve merely jerked a thumb in the direction of the AutoChef, then answered the beep of her 'link. ''Dallas.''

''Don't you ever check your messages?'' Nadine demanded. ''I've been trying to reach you since last night.''

''I was out, now I'm in. What?''

''I'm officially requesting a one-on-one regarding the murders of Samuel Petrinsky and Erin Spindler. My information has you as primary on the first and replacement primary on the second.''

It was a game they both knew. Tele-link logs could be checked. ''The department has not yet issued a statement on either of those cases. Both are ongoing investigations.''

''Which, according to my research and sources, appear to be linked. You can say nothing and I'll go on air with what I've got, or you can do some damage control by agreeing to an interview before I break the story. Up to you, Dallas.''

She could have wiggled more, often would have. But she thought that was enough for the record. ''I'm working at home today.''

''Fine, I'll be there in twenty minutes.''

''No, no cameras in my house.'' On that she was firm. ''I'll meet you in my office at Central in an hour.''

''Make it half that. I have a deadline.''

''An hour, Nadine. Take it or leave it.'' And with that,

she cut transmission. "Peabody, you work with Dr. Dimatto. I'll be back as soon as I can."

"Traffic's ugly, Lieutenant," Peabody told her, pitifully grateful she wasn't being dragged out in it again. "The road crews haven't started clearing yet."

"Just one more adventure," Eve muttered and strode out.

She thought she'd get out clean, but the foyer monitor blinked on as she reached for her jacket. "Going somewhere, Lieutenant?"

"Jesus, Roarke, why not just knock me over the head with a blunt instrument. Keeping tabs on me?"

"As often as possible. Wear your coat if you're going out. That jacket isn't warm enough for this weather."

"I'm just going into Central for a couple of hours."

"Wear the coat," he repeated, "and the gloves in the pocket. I'm sending one of the four-wheels around."

She opened her mouth, but he'd already vanished. "Nag, nag, nag," she muttered, then nearly jolted when he swam back on-screen.

"I love you, too," he said easily, and she heard his chuckle as the image faded again.

Eyes narrowed, she fingered the jacket, considered taking a stand. But she remembered just how warm and soft the coat was. It wasn't like she was going to a murder scene, so it seemed petty not to give in, just this once. She wrapped cashmere over her ancient trousers and stepped outside into the blowing snow just as a gleaming silver vehicle rolled smoothly to the base of the steps.

It was, she thought, a honey of a ride. Powerful and sturdy as a jet-tank. She climbed up and in, amused and touched to find the heat already blowing. Roarke never missed a trick. To entertain herself, she programmed it for manual, gripped the gearshift, and shot down the drive.

It rolled over several inches of snow as if she were driving on freshly scrubbed asphalt.

Traffic was snarled and nasty. More than one vehicle was tipped sideways on the street and abandoned. She counted three fender benders in the first four blocks. She steered around them easily, automatically calling the locations of the wrecks in to Dispatch on her communicator.

Even the glide-cart vendors, who would brave almost any weather to make a buck, were taking the day off. Street corners were deserted, the sky overhead too curtained with snow for her to see or hear any air traffic.

It was, she thought, like driving through one of those old glass globes where nothing moved but the snow when it was shaken free.

Clean, she thought. It wouldn't last, but just now, the city was clean, pristine, surreal. And quiet enough to make her shudder.

She felt something very close to relief after she'd parked in the garage and walked into the noise and confusion of Cop Central.

With more than a half hour to spare before the interview, she locked the door to her office—in case Nadine rushed the mark—and contacted her commander at home.

"I apologize for interrupting your free day, Commander."

"It's yours as well, if I'm not mistaken." He glanced over his shoulder. "Get your boots on, I'll be out in just a few minutes. Grandkids," he told Eve with a quick and rare smile. "We're about to have a snow war."

"I won't keep you from it, but I thought I should inform you I've agreed to a one-on-one with Nadine Furst. She contacted me this morning at home. She's dug up some data on the Petrinsky and the Spindler cases. I thought it best to draft an official statement, answer some basic questions, than to let her go on air with speculation."

"Cooperate, but keep it as short as possible." The smile that had softened his face when he'd spoken of his grandchildren was gone, leaving it hard and blank. "We can expect other media to demand statements after she goes on air with it. What's the current status?"

"I'm working with a medical consultant on some data now. I have potential links to two other homicides, one in Chicago, one in Paris. I've contacted the primaries in each, and am waiting for data transfer. McNab is still running like crimes. My investigation points to a possible connection with several large medical facilities and at least two, if not more, medical personnel attached to them.''

"Give her as little as possible. Send me a fully updated report today, at home. We'll discuss this on Monday morning.''

"Yes, sir.''

Well, Eve thought as she leaned back from the 'link, one base covered. Now she would dance the dance with Nadine and see what reaction it caused.

She got up to unlock the door, then sat and killed the waiting time by starting the report for Whitney. When she heard the click of heels coming briskly down the hall, Eve saved the document, filed it, and blanked her screen.

"God! Could it get any worse out there?'' Nadine smoothed a hand over her camera-ready hair. "Only the insane go out in this, which makes us lunatics, Dallas.''

"Cops laugh at blizzards. Nothing stops the law.''

"Well, that explains why we passed two wrecked black and whites on the way from the station. I got an update from our meteorologist before I left. He says it's the storm of the century.''

"How many of those have we had this century now?''

Nadine laughed and began to unbutton her coat. "True enough, but he says we can expect this storm to continue right through tomorrow, with accumulations even in the city of more than two feet. This one's going to stop New York cold.''

"Great. People will be killing each other over a roll of toilet paper by afternoon.''

"You can bet I'm laying in a supply.'' She started to hang her coat on the bent hook beside Eve's, then stopped with a purr. "Oooh, cashmere. Fabulous. Is this yours? I've never seen you wear it.''

"I don't wear it on duty, which I'm officially not on today. It'd get wrecked in a heartbeat. Now, do you want to talk outerwear fashion, Nadine, or murder?''

"It's always murder first with you." But she indulged herself by giving the coat one last, long stroke before she signaled to her camera operator. "Set it up so the audience can see the snow falling. Makes a nice visual and adds to the spirit of dedication of our cop here and your dogged reporter."

She snapped open a lighted compact, checked her face, her hair. Satisfied, she sat, crossed her silky legs. "Your hair's a wreck, but I don't suppose you care."

"Let's get it done." Vaguely annoyed, Eve tunneled her fingers through her hair twice. Damn it, she'd had it dealt with before Christmas.

"Okay, we're set. I'll do the bumpers and the teases back at the station, so we'll just go right into it here. Stop scowling, Dallas, you'll frighten the viewing audience. This will roll on the noon report, but it's going to take second to the weather." And that, Nadine thought philosophically, was the breaks. She took one deep breath, closed her eyes briefly, jabbed a finger at the operator to start tape.

Then she opened her eyes, fixed a solemn smile on her face. "This is Nadine Furst, reporting from the office of Lieutenant Eve Dallas at Cop Central. Lieutenant Dallas, you are primary on a recent homicide, one that involves one of the city's homeless who was killed a few nights ago. Can you confirm that?"

"I'm primary on the matter of the death of Samuel Petrinsky, street name Snooks, who was murdered some time during the early-morning hours of January twelfth. The investigation is open and ongoing."

"There were, however, unusual circumstances in the matter of this death."

Eve looked steadily at Nadine. "There are unusual circumstances in the matter of any murder."

"That may be true. In this case, however, the victim's heart had been removed. It was not found at the scene. Will you confirm that?"

"I will confirm that the victim was found in his usual crib, and that his death occurred during what appeared to be a skilled surgical operation during which an organ was removed.''

''Do you suspect a cult?''

''That avenue of investigation is not prime, but will not be dismissed until the facts warrant it.''

''Is your investigation centering on the black market?''

''Again, that avenue will not be dismissed.''

For emphasis, Nadine leaned forward just a little, her forearm resting on her thigh. ''Your investigation has been, according to my sources, expanded to include the similar death of one Erin Spindler, who was found murdered several weeks ago in her apartment. You were not primary on that investigation. Why have you assumed that position now?''

''The possible connection between the cases is cause for both cases to be assigned one primary. This streamlines the investigation. It's simply procedure.''

''Have you, as yet, established a profile of the killer or killers?''

Here, Eve thought was the point where she would walk the shaky line between departmental policy and her own needs. ''The profile is being constructed. At this time it is believed that the perpetrator has well-trained medical skills.''

''A doctor?''

''Not all well-trained medical personnel are doctors,'' she said briefly. ''But that, too, is an avenue of our investigation. The department, and this investigator, will put all efforts into finding the killer or killers of Petrinsky and Spindler. It's my priority at this time.''

''You have leads?''

Eve waited a beat, just one beat. ''We are following any and all leads.''

Eve gave her another ten minutes, circling around and back to the information she wanted aired. There was a connection, there was medical skill, and she was focused on finding the killer.

''Good, great.'' Nadine shook her hair back, rolled her shoulders. ''I think I'll snip and edit and work that into a two-parter. I need something to compete with this damn snow." She sent her operator a warm smile. "Be a sweetheart, would you, and go on down to the van? Shoot that feed to the station. I'll be right along."

She waited until he was gone, then turned her sharp eyes to Eve. "Off the record?"

"On or off, I can't give you much more."

"You think it's a doctor, a surgeon. A very skilled one."

"What I think isn't what I know. Until I know, the case is open."

"But we're not talking cult or black market."

"Off record, no, I don't think so. No sacrifice to some bloody god, no quick profit. If money's part of it, it's a long-term investment. Do your job, Nadine, and if you find anything interesting, run it by me. I'll confirm or deny, if I can."

Fair was fair, Nadine thought. And Eve Dallas could be counted on to deal them straight. "And if I dig up something you don't have, and pass it along? What will you trade?"

Eve smiled. "You'll get the exclusive when the case breaks."

"Nice doing business with you, Dallas." She rose, tossed one look toward the blind white curtain out the window. "I hate winter," she muttered and strode out.

Eve took the next hour at Central to refine her report and transmit a copy to Whitney. Even as the transmission ended, an incoming sounded. Marie Dubois had come through.

Preferring to read through the data without distractions, she delayed her trip back home. It was after noon when she filed and saved and copied, tucking the disc into her bag.

The snow was falling faster, heavier, when she drove into it again. As a precaution, she engaged the vehicle's sensors. She sure as hell didn't want to run into a stalled vehicle because she was snow blind.

As it was, the sensors kept her from running over the

man stretched out facedown in the street and rapidly being buried in snow.

"Shit." She stopped bare inches before her wheels met his head, and shoving the door open, stumbled out to check his condition.

She was reaching for her communicator to summon a med-tech unit when he sprang up like a rocket and with one rapid backhand to the face, sent her sprawling.

Irritation came as quickly as pain. Do a damn good deed, she thought as she leaped to her feet, get punched in the face.

"You've got to be desperate, pal, to try to mug somebody in this weather. And just your luck, I'm a goddamn cop." She started to reach for her badge, then saw his hand come up. In it was a weapon very similar to the one strapped to her side.

"Lieutenant Dallas."

She knew exactly what it felt like to take a hit from a weapon like the one he held. Since it wasn't an experience she cared to repeat, she kept her hands in view.

Not a man, she realized now that she got a better look. A droid. One that had been programmed to stop her specifically.

"That's right. What's the deal?"

"I'm authorized to give you a choice."

The snow, she thought, was very likely blurring his vision as much as it was hers. She'd get an opening, by God, and bust his circuits. "What choice? And make it fast before some asshole drives along and kills us."

"Your investigation into the matter of Petrinsky and/or Spindler is to be dropped within twenty-four hours."

"Oh yeah?" She shifted her stance, cocking a hip in what would appear to be arrogance. But it brought her just a step closer. "Why would I do something like that?"

"If you do not cooperate with this request, you will be terminated, and your spouse, Roarke, will be terminated. These terminations will not be pleasant or humane. There are certain parties who have complete knowledge of the human body and will use such knowledge to make your deaths very painful. I am authorized to give you full details of the procedures.''

Going with the gut, she stumbled forward. ''Don't hurt my husband.'' She let her voice shake, watched with narrowed eyes as the droid shifted the weapon enough to hold out his free hand and stop her forward motion.

It only took an instant.

She slammed her forearm into his weapon hand, disarming him, then, trusting her boots for traction, spun into a vicious back kick. It knocked him back a foot, but not quite long enough to give her time to free her weapon.

The snow cushioned the worst of the fall when he tackled her. They fought in near silence, hampered by the snow. But she tasted blood and cursed roundly when he slipped past her guard and slammed a fist into her mouth.

An elbow to his throat had his eyes rolling back where the knee to the groin did nothing.

''Not anatomically correct, huh?'' she panted, rolling with him. ''You're cheaper without balls.'' With her teeth gritted, she managed to draw her weapon and press it hard to his throat. ''Tell me, you son of a bitch, who's so economically minded? Who the fuck programmed you?''

''I'm not authorized to give you that information.''

She shoved the weapon harder against his throat. ''This authorizes you.''

''Incorrect data,'' he said and his eyes jittered. ''I am programmed to self-destruct at this time. Ten seconds to detonation, nine . . .''

''Jesus Christ.'' She fought her way off, skidding and sliding on the snow as she tried to leap clear of the blast. She barely heard him drone ''two, one'' as she flung herself down, covered the back of her head with her hands, and braced.

The blast stung her ears, the displaced air whipped over her, and something hot flew overhead, but the thick snow muffled the worst of the explosion.

Wincing, she got to her feet and limped back to where she'd taken him down. She found blackened snow, patches of it still hissing from the flames, and scattered, twisted bits of metal and plastic.

"Damn it, damn it. Not enough left to scrape into a recycle bin." She rubbed her eyes and trudged back to her vehicle.

The back of her right hand burned, and glancing down, she noted the best part of her glove had been singed away to flesh, and the flesh was raw and red. Disgusted, and just a little dizzy, she tugged both off and flung them down in the snow.

Lucky, she decided, hissing as she pulled herself into the four-wheel. Her hair could have caught a spark and gone up. Wouldn't that have been an adventure. She called in the incident, reported the debris on the drive home. By the time she got there, the aches and bruises were singing a full chorus. She was snarling as she slammed inside.

"Lieutenant," Summerset began, then got a look at her. "What have you done? That coat is ruined. You haven't had it a month."

"He shouldn't have made me wear it, should he? Goddamn it." She yanked it off, furious to see the rips, burns, and stains. Disgusted, she dropped it on the floor and limped her way upstairs.

She wasn't a bit surprised to see Roarke coming down the upper corridor toward her. "He just couldn't wait to let you know I ruined that coat, could he?"

"He said you were hurt," Roarke said grimly. "How bad is it?"

"The other guy's in pieces that'll have to be picked up with tweezers."

He only sighed, took out a handkerchief. "Your mouth's bleeding, darling."

"It split open again when I sneered at Summerset." Ignoring the cloth, she dabbed at the blood with the back of her hand. "Sorry about the coat."

"Likely it kept certain parts of you from being ripped, so we'll consider it lucky." He pressed a kiss to her brow. "Come on. There's a doctor in the house."

"I don't care much for doctors right now."

"When have you ever?" But he led her steadily toward her office where Louise continued to work.

"More than ever, then. Nadine had just enough time to get her report on. But there wasn't enough time for somebody to see it, track me down, program the droid, and send him after me. I made somebody nervous last night, Roarke."

"Well, since that was your plan, I'd say you've had quite a successful day."

"Yeah." She sniffed. "But I lost my gloves again."

chapter eleven

Late in the afternoon, while the snow continued to fall, Eve sat alone in her office and read over Louise's simple translation of the medical data that had been gathered.

Basically, artificial organs—the process initially discovered by Friendly and his team and refined over the years—were cheap, efficient, and dependable. The transplant of human organs was not. It was necessary to find a match, to remove from a donor a healthy specimen, to preserve and transport the organ.

The building of organs from the patient's own tissues was more advantageous, as there was no risk of rejection, but was costly in time and money.

With current medical knowledge, human donors were few and far between. For the most part, healthy organs were harvested—donated or brokered—from accident victims who could not be repaired.

Science, according to Louise, was a two-sided coin. The longer we were able to preserve life, the more rare human donors became. More than 90 percent of successful transplants were artificial.

Certain conditions and diseases could be and were cured, leaving the patient with his original organs in good repair. Others, too far progressed and most usually in cases of the poor or disenfranchised, left the organ too damaged and the body too weak for these treatments. Artificial replacements were the only course of treatment.

Why take what was useless? Eve asked herself. *Why kill for it?*

She looked up as Roarke came in. "Maybe it's just another mission, after all," she began. "Just one more lunatic, this one with a highly honed skill and a personal agenda. Maybe he just wants to rid the world of those he considers beneath him and the organs are nothing more than trophies."

"There's no connection between the victims?"

"Snooks and Spindler both had connections to Canal Street, and that's it. There's no other link between them, or to hook them to the victims in Chicago and Paris. Except when you look at what they were."

She didn't need to bring up the data on Leclerk to refresh her memory. "The guy who bought it in Paris was a chemi-head, late sixties, no known next of kin. He had a flop when he could pay for it, lived on the street when he couldn't. He used a free clinic off and on, playing the system to get his social program meds when he couldn't buy a fix. You have to submit to a physical if you want the drugs. Medical records indicate he had advanced cirrhosis of the liver."

"And that's what links them."

"Liver, heart, kidneys. He's building a collection. It comes out of a health center, I'm sure of it. But whether it's Drake or Nordick or another one altogether, I don't know."

"Maybe it's not only one," Roarke suggested, and Eve nodded.

"I've thought of that. And I don't like the implications. The guy I'm looking for is highly placed. He feels protected. He is protected."

She pushed back. "He's educated, successful, and organized. He's got a reason for what he's doing, Roarke.

He was willing to kill a cop to protect it. I just can't find it.''

"Kicks?''

"I don't think so.'' She closed her eyes and brought the image of each victim into her head. "There was no glee in it. It was professional, each time. I bet he got a thrill out of it, but that wasn't the driving force. Just a happy by-product,'' she murmured.

He leaned over, tipped up her face, scanned the bruises. "It's beating you up. Literally.''

"Louise did a pretty decent job on me. She's not as annoying as most doctors.''

"You need a change of scene,'' he decided. "A distraction so you can come back to this with your mind clear on Monday. Let's go.''

"Go? Where?'' She gestured to the window. "In case you haven't noticed, we're getting dumped on.''

"So why not take advantage of it?'' He tugged her to her feet. "Let's build a snowman.''

He surprised her, constantly, but this time, she simply gaped. "You want to build a snowman?''

"Why not? I'd thought we'd fly out, spend the weekend in Mexico, but . . .'' Still holding her hand, he looked out the window and smiled. "How often do we have an opportunity like this?''

"I don't know how to build a snowman.''

"Neither do I. Let's see what we come up with.''

She did a lot of muttering, came up with alternate suggestions that included mindless sex in a warm bed, but in the end, she found herself bundled from head to foot in extreme climate gear and stepping out into the teeth of the blizzard.

"Christ, Roarke, this is crazy. You can't see five feet.''

"Fabulous, isn't it?'' Grinning, he linked his gloved hand with hers and pulled her down the snow-heaped steps.

"We'll be buried alive.''

He simply reached down, took a handful, fisted it. "Packs pretty well,'' he observed. "I never saw much snow as a boy. Dublin's for rain. We need a good base."

Bending down, he began to mound snow.

Eve watched for a moment, amazed at how intent her sophisticated husband, sleek in his black gear, scooped and packed snow.

"Is this an 'I was a deprived child' thing?"

He glanced up, one brow lifting. "Weren't we?"

She picked up a handful of snow, absently patted it onto the mound. "We've pretty well made up for it," she murmured, then frowned. "You're making it too tall. It should be wider."

He straightened, smiled, then framed her face with snow-covered hands, kissing her when she squealed. "Pitch in or back off."

She wiped the snow off her face, sniffed. "I'm going to build my own and he'll kick your snowman's butt."

"I've always admired your competitive streak."

"Yeah, well, be prepared to be amazed."

She moved off a bit and began to dig in.

She didn't consider herself artistic, so went with her strengths: muscle, determination, and endurance.

The form she worked on might have been slightly lopsided, but it was big. And when she glanced over at Roarke, she noted with glee that hers had his by a good foot.

The cold stung her cheeks, her muscles warmed with exercise, and without realizing it, she relaxed. Instead of unnerving her, the sheer silence soothed. It was like being in the center of a dream, one without sound, without color. One that lulled the mind and gave the body rest.

By the time she got to the head, she was packing and shaping with abandon. "I'm nearly done here, pal, and my guy is built like an arena ball tackle. Your pitiful attempt is doomed."

"We'll see about that." He stepped back, studied his snow sculpture with narrowed eyes, then smiled. "Yes, this works for me."

She tossed a look over her shoulder and snorted. "Better bulk him up before my guy chews him up and spits him out.''

"No, I think this is the right shape.'' He waited while Eve patted her snowman's bulging pecs, then trudged through the snow toward him.

Her eyes went to slits. "Yours has tits.''

"Yes, rather gorgeous ones.''

Stunned, Eve clamped her hands on her hips and stared. The figure was sleek and curvy, with enormous snow breasts that had been shaped into wicked points.

Roarke stroked one snowy breast lightly. "She'll lead your pumped-up slab of beef there around by the nose.''

Eve could only shake her head. "Pervert. Those boobs are way out of proportion.''

"A boy needs his dreams, darling.'' He took the snowball in the center of the shoulder blades and turned with a wolfish smile. "I was hoping you'd do that. Now that you've shed first blood . . .'' He kept his eyes on her as he scooped up snow, balled it.

She dodged left, quickly made another ball, and let it fly with the grace and speed of a major-league infielder. He caught that one on the heart, nodded an acknowledgment of her aim and speed, and went for her.

Snow flew, hard bullets, heavy cannonballs, a barrage of fire. She watched a missile explode in his face and, grinning fiercely, followed up with a trio of body blows.

He gave as good as he got, even causing her to yelp once when she took a hard hit to the side of the head, but she thought she could have taken him, would have taken him, if she hadn't started to laugh.

She couldn't stop, and it made her slow and clumsy. As she fought for breath, her arms shook, throwing off her aim. Wheezing, she held up a hand. "Truce! Cease fire.''

Snow splatted high on her chest and into her face. "I can't hear you,'' Roarke said, moving steadily forward. "Did you say, 'I surrender'?''

"No, damn it.'' She fought to snort in air, grabbed

weakly for ammo, then let out a laughing scream when he jumped her.

She went down, spilling into the thick cushion of snow with Roarke on top of her. "Maniac," she managed and concentrated on getting her breath back.

"You lose."

"Did not."

"I seem to be on top of things, Lieutenant." Aware just how tricky she could be, he clamped his hands over hers. "You're now at my mercy."

"Oh yeah? You don't scare me, tough guy." She grinned up at him. The black ski cap he'd pulled on was crusted white with snow, the glorious hair that spilled out of it wet and gleaming. "I mortally wounded you a half dozen times. You're a dead man."

"I think I have just enough life left to make you suffer." He lowered his head, nipped lightly at her jaw. "And to make you beg."

His tongue traced her lips and blurred the edges of her mind. "If you're getting ideas about starting anything out here . . ."

"What?"

"Good," she said and arched up to find his mouth with hers.

Hot and hungry from the first. With a little sound of greed, she took more. It burst through her, that wild, climbing need she'd only felt with him, for him. Trapped in the swirl of white, she gave herself to it.

"Inside." He was lost in her. No one else had taken him as deep as she could. "We need to go inside."

"Put your hands on me." Her voice was rough, her breath already ragged. "I want your hands on me."

He was tempted to rip away at the tough, thin suit, to find the flesh beneath. To sink his teeth into it. He yanked her up until they were sitting in the depression of snow, tangled and breathless.

They stared at each other a moment, both stunned at how quickly the mood had changed from playful to desperate. Then her lips curved. "Roarke?"

"Eve?"

"I think we should go in and give these snow people some privacy."

"Good idea."

"Just one thing." She moved into him, slid her arms around him, brought her mouth teasingly close. Then, snake-quick, tugged the collar of his suit out and dumped snow under it.

He was still hissing when she scrambled to her feet.

"Cheat."

"You can make me pay for it when I've got you naked."

As cold shivered down his back, he pushed himself up. "I'd be delighted."

They started in the pool, in the fluid curve where with a mere touch of the controls, the water churned and went steamy. There in the pulsing heat, he put his hands on her however he liked, driving them both from edge to edge, yanking them back, time after time just short of full release.

She was dizzy, weak, her body teetering on the brink, when he dragged her to her feet. Water cascaded from them and steamed up in clouds.

"In bed," was all he said, and he swept her up to carry her from the pool to the elevator.

"Hurry." She pressed her face against his neck, nipped her teeth into it.

Her heart was raging. She wondered that it didn't simply burst out of the cage of her ribs and fall into his hands. He already owned it. And her.

Delirious, battered with so much more than the easy lust they could spark off each other with a look, she curled into him. "I love you, Roarke."

It shot into him. Those words from her were precious and rare. They could weaken his knees, make his heart ache. He strode off the elevator, climbed up to where their bed stood centered under a sky window curtained white with snow. And fell onto the bed with her.

"Tell me again." His mouth fastened to hers, devoured, swallowed her moan. "Tell me again, while I'm touching you."

His hands streaked over her, down her, causing her flesh to tremble. She arched under him, wanting him to cover her where the heat throbbed, to pierce her there. To fill her there.

She was slick and hot where his fingers slid, and she cried out when he shoved her blissfully over the edge. But the trembling wouldn't stop, the need wouldn't fade. It built again, layer over layer, while the taste of him pulsed through her system like a drug.

"Tell me again." He drove himself into her in one violent stroke. "Damn it, tell me again. Now."

She fisted her hands in his hair, needing to anchor herself, fighting to hold on, just to hold on for one moment more. And looked into those wild blue eyes. "I love you. Always. Only. You."

Then she wrapped herself around him, and gave him the rest of her.

A weekend with Roarke, Eve thought, could smooth out the rough edges of broken glass.

The man was amazingly . . . inventive.

She'd intended to work on Sunday, but before she could roll out of bed, she was being plucked out and carried off to the holo room. The next thing she knew, she was buck naked on a simulation of Crete. It was a little difficult to complain about warm blue water, dusky hills, and baking sun, and when he implemented multifuctions and conjured up a lush, eye-popping picnic, she gave up and enjoyed herself.

New York was buried under two feet of snow. Jet ski patrols were handling any threat of looting, and medi-vac teams were scouting out the snow wrecked. All but emergency and necessary city personnel were ordered to stay home.

So why not spend the day at the beach eating fat purple grapes?

When she woke Monday morning, she was limber, clear-headed, and refueled. She kept one ear tuned to the news on the bedroom screen as she dressed. Reports were that all major streets had been cleared. Although she didn't believe that for a minute, she thought she could risk taking her own vehicle to Central.

When the 'link beeped, she finished buttoning her shirt, scooped up her coffee, and answered.

"Dallas."

Dispatch, Dallas, Lieutenant Eve. Report to Sleeper Village, Bowery. Reported homicide, Priority One. Uniforms on scene.

"Notify Peabody, Officer Delia. I'll pick her up en route. I'm on my way. Dallas out." She broke transmission, exchanged her coffee for her weapon harness. "Goddamn it. He got another one." Her eyes were flat and cold as she looked at Roarke. "He wanted it on my watch. He's made it personal."

"Watch your back, Lieutenant," Roarke ordered as she strode out. Then he shook his head. "It's always personal," he murmured.

It didn't lift her mood to see the uniforms on scene were Bowers and Trueheart. She fought her way to the curb on the streets that were lumpy and slick with snow. Then gave herself time for one long breath.

"If I look like I'm going to deck her . . ."

"Yes sir?"

"Let me," Eve snapped and pushed out of the car. Her boots sank into the snow, and she kept her eyes on Bowers as she plowed through it. The sky overhead was as hard and cold as her heart.

"Officer Bowers. Your report?"

"Subject female, undetermined age and identity." Out of the corner of her eye, Eve saw Trueheart open his mouth, then shut it again.

"We found her in her crib, as with victim Snooks.

However, there is considerable blood in this case. As I am not a medical technician, I cannot verify which piece of her was removed, if any.''

Eve scanned the area. Saw that this time there were more than a dozen faces, pale, thin, with dead eyes staring over the line of police sensors.

"Have you questioned any of these people?''

"No.''

"Do so,'' she ordered, then turned to start toward the crib that had been marked with blipping police sensors.

Bowers jerked her head at Trueheart, sending him on his way, but fell into step beside Eve. "I've already filed another complaint.''

"Officer Bowers, this is not the time or place to discuss interdepartmental business.''

"You're not going to get away with calling me at home, threatening me. You stepped way over, Dallas.''

Both baffled and irritated, Eve stopped long enough to study Bowers's face. There was anger, yes, and resentment, but there was also a sticky kind of smugness in her eyes. "Bowers, I didn't contact you at home or anywhere else. And I don't make threats.''

"I've got my 'link log as evidence.''

"Fine.'' But when Eve started forward again, Bowers grabbed her arm. Eve's hand curled into a fist, but she managed to keep it from ramming into Bowers's face. "Officer, we are on record, and you are interfering with my investigation of a reported homicide. Step back.''

"I want it on record.'' Bowers shot a glance at the lapel recorder on Peabody's uniform. Excitement was pumping through her, and the control was slipping greasily out of her hands. "I want it on record that I've gone through proper official channels to report your conduct. And that if appropriate action isn't taken by the department against you, I'll exercise my right to file suit against both you and the department.''

"So noted, Officer. Now, step back before I start exercising my rights.''

"You want to take a swing at me, don't you?'' Her

eyes glittered, her breath began to heave. "That's how your type handles things."

"Oh, yeah, I'd love to kick your arrogant ass, Bowers. But I have something a little more pressing to do at the moment. And since you refuse to follow orders, you are relieved of duty as of this moment. I want you off my crime scene."

"It's my crime scene. I was first on scene."

"You've been relieved, Officer." Eve jerked her arm free, took two steps, then swung around, teeth bared, as Bowers made another grab. "You lay hands on me again, and I'll kick your face in, then I'll have my aide place you under arrest for interfering with an investigation. We've got a personal problem here, fine and dandy. We can handle it later. You can pick the time and place. But it won't be here; it won't be now. Get the fuck off-scene, Bowers."

She waited a beat, straining to hold her own snapping temper in check. "Peabody, notify Bowers's lieutenant that she has been relieved and ordered from the scene. Request another uniform to be sent to our location to assist Officer Trueheart in crowd control."

"I go, he goes."

"Bowers, if you are not behind the sensors in thirty seconds, you will be put in restraints and charged." Not trusting herself, Eve turned away. "Peabody, escort Officer Bowers back to her vehicle."

"My pleasure, sir. Horizontal or vertical, Bowers?" she said pleasantly.

"I'm going to take her down." Bowers's voice shook with rage. "And you're going with her." Already composing her follow-up complaint, Bowers stomped through the snow.

"You all right, Dallas?"

"I'd be better if I could've pounded on her a while." Eve hissed a breath out through her teeth. "But she wasted enough of our time. Let's do our job."

She approached the crib, crouched, pulled back the tattered plastic that served as a doorway.

Blood, rivers of it, had spilled, pooled, congealed. Reaching into her field kit, Eve took out Seal-It. "Victim is female, black, age between ninety and one ten. Visible wound in abdomen appears to be cause of death. Victim has bled out. There are no apparent signs of struggle or sexual abuse."

Eve inched into the crib, ignoring the blood that stained the tips of her boots. "Notify the ME, Peabody. I need Morris. At a guess, I'd say her liver's gone. Jesus, but he wasn't worried about being neat this time. The edges of the wound are straight and clean," she added after she fixed on microgoggles, bent closer. "But there is no clamping as evidenced on other victims. No sealing to prevent bleeding."

She was still wearing her shoes, Eve noted, the hard, black slip-ons many of the city's shelters handed out to the homeless. There was a miniplayer beside the thin mattress and a full bottle of street brew.

"No robbery," she murmured and continued to work. "Time of death, calculating lowest ambient temperature is established on scene at oh two-thirty." She reached out, found an expired beggar's license.

"Victim is identified as Jilessa Brown, age ninety-eight, of no fixed address."

"Lieutenant, can you move your left shoulder? I need to give a full body shot for record."

Eve shifted to the right, eased in another inch, and felt her boot scrape something under the pool of blood. Reaching down, she closed her sealed fingers over a small object. And drew out a gold pin.

The coiled snakes of the caduceus ran with blood.

"Look what we have here," she murmured. "Peabody, on record. A gold lapel pin, catch apparently broken, was found near the victim's right hip. Pin is identified as a caduceus, a symbol of the medical profession."

She sealed it, slipped it into her bag. "He was very, very sloppy this time. Angry? Careless? Or just in a hurry?" She moved back, let the plastic fall back into place. "Let's see what Trueheart knows."

• • •

Eve wiped the blood and sealant from her hands as True-heart reported. "Mostly they called her Honey. She was well liked, kind of motherly. No one I've spoken with saw anything last night. It was rough out here, really cold. The snow finally stopped about midnight, but the winds were vicious; that's why we've got all these drifts."

"And why we'll never get any casts worth a damn." She looked at the trampled ground. "We'll find out what we can about her. Trueheart, it's up to you, but if I were in your shoes, I'd request another trainer when I got back to your station. When the dust clears some, I'm going to recommend your transfer to Central, unless you have other ideas."

"Sir. No. I'm very grateful."

"Don't be. They work your butt off at Central." She turned away. "Peabody, let's go by Canal Street before we head in. I'd like to see if Jilessa Brown was a patient there."

Louise was out in the medi-van doing on-site treatments for frostbite and exposure. Her replacement in the clinic looked young enough to have still been playing doctor in the backseat of a souped-up street buggy with the prom queen.

But he told her that Jilessa Brown was not only a patient, but a favorite at the clinic. A regular, Eve mused as she fought traffic and clogged streets on her way to Central. One who'd come in at least once a week just to sit and talk with others in the waiting room, to charm some of the lolly-tape the doctors kept in a jar for children.

She'd been, according to the doctor, a sociable woman with a sweet tooth and a mental defect that had gone un-treated during her prime. It had left her speech slurred and her mental capacity on level with an eight-year-old.

She'd been harmless. And she'd been receiving treat-ments over the last six months for cancer of the liver, advanced stage.

There had been some hope for remission, if not reversal.

Now there would be neither.

Her message light was glowing when she stepped into her office, but she ignored it and tagged Feeney.

"I've got another one."

"So I hear. Word travels."

"There was a lapel pin at the scene—it's this medical symbol. I took it by the lab, sat on Dickhead until he verified it was gold. The real thing. Can you run it for me? See if you can find out who sells them?"

"Will do. You talked to McNab?"

"Not yet." Her stomach hitched. "Why?"

He sighed, and paper rattled as he reached into his bag for his favored almonds. "London, six months ago. Funky-junkie found in his flop. He'd cooked for a few days before they found him. Kidneys were missing."

"That's what we had with Spindler, but this scene was a mess. Blood everywhere. He was either in a hurry, or he doesn't care anymore. I'll tag McNab and get the details."

"He's on his way over there. Send the pin back with him, and I'll run it."

"Thanks." Her 'link beeped incoming the minute she ended transmission. "Dallas."

"I need you in my office, Lieutenant. Now."

Bowers was all Eve could think, but nodded briskly. "Yes, Commander. On my way."

She hailed Peabody on her way out. "McNab's on his way over with details on a potential victim in London. Work with him on it. Use my office."

"Yes, sir, but—" She broke off, and decided not to be undignified and complain to her lieutenant's back. "Hell." Prepared to spend an irritating hour or so, Peabody gathered her things and hurried toward Eve's office. She wanted to get there before McNab claimed the desk.

Whitney didn't keep Eve waiting but cleared her straight through. He was at his desk, his hands folded, his eyes neutral. "Lieutenant, you had another altercation with Officer Bowers."

"Yes, sir. On record at the scene this morning." Goddamn it, Eve thought, she hated this. It was like playing tattletale with the school principal. "She became difficult and insubordinate. She laid hands on me and was ordered off scene."

He nodded. "You couldn't have handled it differently?"

Biting back a retort, Eve reached into her bag and pulled out a disc. "Sir, this is a copy of the record from the crime scene. You look at it, then tell me if I could or should have handled it differently."

"Sit down, Dallas."

"Sir, if I'm to be reprimanded for doing my job, I prefer to be reprimanded while I'm on my feet."

"I don't believe I have reprimanded you, Lieutenant." He spoke mildly, but he rose himself. "Bowers had already filed another complaint before this morning's little incident. She claims that you contacted her at home Saturday evening and threatened her with physical harm."

"Commander, I have not contacted Bowers at home or anywhere else." It was difficult, but she kept her eyes flat and her voice cool. "If and when I have threatened her—after provocation—it's been face to face, and on record."

"She's introduced a copy of a 'link log, on which the caller identifies herself as you."

Eve's eyes chilled. "My voice print is on record. I request that it be compared with the print from the 'link log."

"Good. Dallas, sit down. Please."

He watched her struggle, then sit stiffly. "I have no doubt the prints won't match. Just as I have no doubt that Bowers will continue to make trouble for you. I want to assure you that the department will handle this, and her."

"Permission to speak frankly?"

"Of course."

"She shouldn't be on the street, she shouldn't be in

uniform. She's dangerous, Commander. That's not a personal jab, it's a professional opinion.''

''And one I tend to agree with, but it's not always as simple as it should be. Which brings me to another issue. The mayor contacted me over the weekend. It appears he was contacted by Senator Brian Waylan with a request that the investigations, over which you are primary, be reassigned.''

''Who the hell is Waylan?'' Eve was on her feet again. ''What's some overfed politician have to do with my case?''

''Waylan is a staunch supporter of the American Medical Association. His son is a doctor and on staff at the Nordick Center in Chicago. It's his belief that your investigation, and the resultant media, has impinged the medical community. That it may start a panic. The AMA is concerned and willing to fund its own, private investigation into these matters.''

''I'm sure they would, as it's clear it's one of their own who's killing people. This is my case, Commander. I intend to close it.''

''It's likely that you'll get little cooperation from the medical community from this point on,'' Whitney continued. ''It's also likely that there will be some political pressure brought to bear against the department to shift the nature of the investigation.''

He indulged himself briefly with the faintest of scowls, then his face slipped back into neutral. ''I want you to close this case, Dallas, and quickly. I don't want you distracted by a personal . . . irritant,'' he decided. ''And so I'm asking you to let the department handle the Bowers situation.''

''I know my priorities.''

''Good. Until further notice, this case, and all related data, are blocked from the media. I want nothing new to leak. Any and all data relating is to be on a need-to-know basis, with full copies encoded to my attention.''

''You believe we have a leak in the department?''

''I think East Washington is much too interested in our

business. Put together a team, keep it Code Five from this point,'' he ordered, blocking any unsealed interdepart-mental reports and adding a media block. ''Put this one to bed.''

chapter twelve

"I can run a probability scan back in EDD in half the time it's going to take you to put it through this reject from the ark."

"You're not in EDD, McNab."

"You're telling me. And if you want a full run on the London victim done right, I should be doing it. I'm the E-detective."

"I'm the primary's aide. Stop breathing on me."

"You smell pretty good, She-Body."

"You're not going to have a nose to smell with in about five seconds."

Eve paused outside her office door and rapped her fists against the sides of her head. This was her team, squabbling like a couple of five-year-olds while Mom was away.

God help her.

They were glaring at each other when she stepped in. Both jerked back, shifted attention to her, and struggled to look innocent.

"Recess is over, kids. Move it into the conference room. I tagged Feeney on my way down. I want all data on all cases streamlined and cross-checked by end of shift.

We need to bag this bastard before he adds to his collection.''

After she'd turned on her heel and strode out, McNab broke into a grin. ''Man, I love working with her. You think we'll headquarter in her home office on this one? Roarke's got the best toys on the block.''

Peabody only sniffed and began to gather discs and files. ''We work where the lieutenant says we work.'' She rose, bumped into him, and felt her nerves sizzle. She stared dolefully into his cheerful green eyes. ''You're in my way, McNab.''

''I keep trying. So how's Charlie?''

She counted to ten, then replied, ''*Charles* is fine, and it's none of your business. Now move your skinny ass.'' She gained some pleasure in elbowing him aside as she stomped out.

McNab merely sighed, rubbed his sore gut. ''You sure do it for me, She-Body,'' he muttered. ''Christ knows why.''

Eve paced the conference room. She needed to put Bowers and that situation out of her mind. She was nearly there, she told herself. Just a little more cursing, a little more pacing, and she would have put Bowers in some deep, dark hole. With a few rats for company, she decided, and a single crust of moldy bread.

Yeah, that was a good image. She took two more cleansing breaths and rounded on Peabody as her aide entered. ''Death scene stills, on the board. Work up a location map, highlighting each crime scene. Victims' names referenced with appropriate city.''

''Yes, sir.''

''McNab. Give me what you've got.''

''Okay, well—''

''And keep the chatter and editorials to a minimum,'' Eve added and made Peabody snicker.

''Sir,'' he began, miffed, ''I've got your top health and research centers in the cities in question. On mainframe, disc and hard copy.'' Since the hard copy was handy, he nudged it across the desk. ''I cross-checked your short list of docs from New York. You can see there that all of them have an affiliation with at least one of the other centers. My research indicates that there are only three hundred–odd surgeons with organ plucking as a specialty who possess the skill required to have performed the procedure that killed all subject victims.''

He stopped, damn proud of his quick, no-nonsense report. ''I'm still running like crimes. The reason for the time lag stems from the filing and investigative avenues pursued in other areas.''

He just couldn't stand it anymore. He sat on the edge of the desk, crossed his slick green airboots at the ankles. ''See, it looks to me like some of the homicide guys either buried the cases because it's, like, who cares, or figured it was just another weird street crime. They gotta plug it in before IRCCA can pick it up on the first pass. Otherwise, we have to dig, which I'm doing. What I'm hitting mostly is cult and domestic stuff. I've got a lot of castrations performed in the home by irate cohabitators or spouses. Man, you wouldn't believe how many women whack a guy off permanent because he didn't keep his dick in his pants. Six new eunuchs in North Carolina in the past three months. It's like an epidemic or something.''

''That's a fascinating bit of trivia, McNab,'' Eve said dryly. ''But for now, let's stick with the internal organs.'' She jerked a thumb toward the computer. ''Narrow it down. I want one health center per city that fits.''

''You ask, it's done.''

''Feeney.'' Eve's shoulders relaxed fractionally when he strolled in, carrying his bag of nuts. ''What have you got on the pin?''

''Nothing to that one. Three locations in the city carry that design in eighteen carat. The jewelry store at the Drake Center, Tiffany's on Fifth, and DeBower's downtown.''

He juggled the bag absently, watching Peabody clip stills to the board. ''The eighteen carat runs about five grand. Most of the classier health centers run an account with Tiffany's on the pin. They buy in bulk to give to graduating interns. Gold or silver, depending on placement. Last year, Tiffany's moved seventy-one gold, ninety-six silver. Ninety-two percent of those were through direct accounts with hospitals.''

"According to Louise, most doctors have them," Eve commented. "But not all of them wear them. I saw Tia Wo wearing one, Hans Vanderhaven. And Louise," she added with a frown. "We'll have to see if we can find out who's lost one recently. Keep tabs on the three outlets. Whoever did might want a replacement."

She tucked her hands in her pockets and turned to the board. "Before we start, you need to know the commander's put a media block on us. No interviews, no comments. We're Code Five, so all data pertaining to any of these cases is now on a need-to-know basis. Files are to be encoded."

"Departmental leak?" Feeney wanted to know.

"Maybe. But there's pressure, political pressure, coming in from East Washington. Feeney, how much can you find out about Senator Waylan of Illinois without alerting him or his staff of a search?"

A slow smile brightened Feeney's rumpled face. "Oh, just about anything down to the size of his jockies."

"I'm betting on fat ass and small dick," she muttered and had McNab snorting. "Okay, here are my thoughts. He's collecting," she began, moving to the board to gesture at the stills. "For fun, for profit, because he can. I don't know. But he's systematically collecting defective organs. He removes them from the scene. In at least one case, we know there was a transfer bag, so odds are that pattern holds for all. If he's careful to preserve the organ, he has to have some place to keep them."

"A lab," Feeney said.

"It follows. Private. Maybe even in his home. How does he find them? He's tagged each one of them ahead of time. These three," Eve added, tapping a finger on stills, "were all taken out in New York and all had a connection with the Canal Street Clinic. He has access to their data. He's either associated with the clinic or he has someone on the inside passing him what he wants.''

"Could be a cop," Peabody murmured and shifted uncomfortably when all eyes turned to her. "Sir." She cleared her throat. "The beat cops and scoopers know these people. If we're concerned about a leak in the department, maybe we should consider the leak includes passing data to the killer.''

"You're right," Eve said after a moment. "It could be right at our door.''

"Bowers works the sector where two of the victims were taken out.'' McNab swiveled in his chair. "We already know she's a wild hair. I can run an all-level search and scan on her.''

"Shit.'' Uneasy, Eve paced to the window, winced against the bouncing glare of sun off snow. If she ordered the search, it would have to go through channels, be put on record. It could, and would in some quarters, smell of harassment.

"We can order it out of EDD," Feeney said, understanding. "My name goes on the request, it puts it off you.''

"I'm primary," Eve murmured. So it was duty to the job and to the dead. "The order goes out of here, with my name on it. Send it now, McNab, let's not piss around.''

"Yes, sir." He swung back to the computer.

"We're getting no cooperation from the primary in Chicago," she went on. "So we turn the heat up there. We wait for the data to come in from London." She walked back to the board, studied the faces. "But we sure as hell have enough to keep us busy in the meantime. Peabody, what do you know about politics?''

"A necessary evil that on rare occasions works without corruption, abuse, and waste." She smiled a little. "Free-Agers rarely approve of politicians, Dallas. But we're terrific at nonviolent protests.''

"Tune up your Free-Ager and take a look at the American Medical Association. See how much corruption, abuse, and waste you can find. I'm going to put a fire under that asshole at CPSD, and check with Morris to see if the autopsy's finished on Jilessa Brown.''

Back in her office, she tried Chicago first, and when she was again passed to Kimiki's E-mail, she snarled and opted to go over his head.

"Putz," she said under her breath and waited to be transferred to his shift commander.

"Lieutenant Sawyer."

"Lieutenant Dallas, NYPSD," she said briskly, measuring her man. He had a long, thin, weary face the color of tobacco, eyes of a deep gray, and a mouth thin as a stiletto from corner to corner. "I'm working on a series of homicides here that appear to link with a case out of your house."

She continued to watch his face as she detailed information, saw the faint line form between his brows. "One minute, New York."

He blanked the screen, leaving Eve drumming her fingers on the desk for three full minutes. When he came back on, his face was carefully composed. "I haven't received a request for data transfer in this matter. The case you refer to has been shifted to inactive and unsolved."

"Look, Sawyer, I talked to the new primary over a week ago. I made the request. I've got three bodies here, and my investigation points to a connection with yours. You want to dump the case, fine, but dump it here. All I'm asking is a little professional cooperation. I need that data."

"Detective Kimiki is currently on leave, New York. We get our share of dead files here in Chicago, too. I'd say your request just fell through the cracks."

"Are you going to fish it out?"

"You'll have the files within the hour. I apologize for the delay. Let me have your ID number and transfer information. I'll handle it personally."

"Thanks."

One down, Eve thought when she finished with Chicago. She caught Morris in his office.

"I'm putting it together now, Dallas. I'm only one man."

"Give me the highlights."

"She's dead."

"You're such a joker, Morris."

"Anything to brighten your day. The abdomen wound was cause of death. Wound was caused by a laser scalpel, again wielded with considerable skill. The victim was anesthetized prior to death. In this case, the wound was left unsealed, and the victim bled out. Her liver was removed. She had herself a ripe case of cancer, which had certainly affected that particular organ. She's had some treatment for it. There was some scarring that's typical with an advanced stage, but there was some nice pink tissue as well. The treatment was slowing down the progress, fighting the fight. She might, with regular and continued care, have beaten it back."

"The incision—does it match the others?"

"It's clean and it's perfect. He wasn't in a hurry when he cut. In my opinion, it's the same pair of hands. But the rest doesn't match. There wasn't any pride in this one, and she wasn't going to die. She had a good shot of living another ten years, maybe more."

"Okay. Thanks."

She sat back, closed her eyes to help all the new data shift through her mind. And opened them again to see Webster in her doorway.

"Sorry to disturb your nap."

"What do you want, Webster? You keep showing up, I'm going to have to call my advocate."

"Wouldn't be a bad idea. You got another complaint against you."

"It's bogus. Have you run the voice prints?" The temper she'd managed to lock away beat viciously for freedom. "Goddamn it, Webster, you know me. I don't make crank calls."

She pushed herself out of her chair. Until that moment, she hadn't realized just how much rage she'd been chaining down. It roared through her, ripped at her throat until, for lack of something better, she grabbed an empty coffee mug off her desk and heaved it against the wall.

Webster stood, lips pursed, nodded toward the shards. "Feel better?"

"Some, yeah," she replied.

"We'll be running the voice prints, Dallas, and I don't expect them to match. I *do* know you. You're a direct, in-the-face kind of woman. Wimpy 'link threats aren't your style. But you've got a problem with her, and don't minimize it. She's screaming about your treatment of her on the crime scene this morning."

"It's on record. You screen it, then talk to me."

"I'm going to," he said wearily. "I'm going through channels on this, step by step, because it'll work better for you. Now I see you've ordered a search and scan on her. That doesn't look good."

"It applies to a case. It's not personal. I ordered one on Trueheart, too."

"Why?"

Her eyes went flat and cool. "I can't answer that. IAB has nothing to do with my dead files, and I've been ordered to keep all data pertaining on a need-to-know. I'm Code Five per Whitney's orders."

"You're just going to make this harder on yourself."

"I'm doing my job, Webster."

"I'm doing mine, Dallas. Fucking A," he muttered, and jammed his hands in his pockets. "Bowers just went to the media."

"About me? For Christ's sake."

"It was quite a little rant. She's claiming departmental cover-up, all kinds of happy shit. Your name tends to bump ratings, and this story's going to be all over the screen by dinnertime."

"There is no story."

"You are the story," Webster corrected. "Hotshot homicide cop, the cop who took down one of the country's top politicians a year ago. The cop who married the richest son of a bitch on or off planet—who also happens to have a very shadowy past. You're ratings, Dallas, and one way or the other, the media's going to run with this."

"That's not my problem." But her throat was tight and her stomach uneasy.

"It's the department's problem. Questions are going to be asked and need to be answered. You're going to have to figure out when and how to make a statement to defuse this situation."

"Damn it, Webster, I'm in a media block. I can't talk to them because too much of it touches on my investigation."

He gave her a level look, hoping she knew it was friend to friend now. "Then let me tell you, you're in a squeeze. The voice prints will be compared, and a statement on the results will be issued. The record from the crime scene this morning will be reviewed, and a decision on your conduct and hers will be rendered. Your request for a search and scan will be put on hold pending those decisions. That's the official line I'm required to give you. Now, on a personal note, I'm telling you, get a lawyer, Dallas. Get the best fucking lawyer Roarke's money can buy, and put this away."

"I'm not using him or his money to clean up my mess."

"You've always been a stubborn bitch, Dallas. It's one of the many things I find attractive about you."

"Bite me."

"I did. It didn't take." Eyes sober again, he stepped forward. "I care about you—as a friend and a colleague. I'm warning you, she intends to take you under. And not everyone's going to hold out a hand to keep you from sinking. When you're in the position you've reached—professional and personal—there's a lot of latent jealousy simmering. This is the kind of thing that pops the lid on it."

"I'll handle it."

"Fine." He shook his head and started out. "I'll just tell you again: Watch your excellent ass."

She sat, lowered her head to her hands, and wondered what the hell to do next.

• • •

At the end of her shift, she opted to get the hell out. She took the files with her, including the data Chicago had finally transferred. But she was by God going home on time. A vicious headache kept her company on the drive.

She was snarled in northbound traffic, between Fifty-first and Fifty-second on Madison when Bowers stomped up the stairs from the subway at Delancy. She was, for Ellen Bowers, decidedly cheerful. As far as she was concerned, she'd scalded Eve Dallas's ass. Fried the bitch, she thought and very nearly skipped down the sidewalk.

It had been so gratifying to stand in front of a camera, have a reporter nod understandingly, while she detailed all the abuse she'd suffered.

Man oh man, it was about fucking time it was her face on-screen, her words being heard.

She'd wanted, oh, she'd wanted to tell them how it had all started years ago, back in the academy when Dallas had walked in and taken over. Fucking taken over. Broken all the records. Yeah, she'd broken them, all right. Broken them by giving instructors blow jobs. Probably gone down on the female supervisors, too. And anybody with any sense knew the slut had been doing Feeney and probably goddamn Whitney for years. God knew what kind of sick sex games she played with Roarke in that big, fancy house.

Her days were over, Bowers decided and treated herself by stopping into a 24/7 and springing for a quart of chocolate chunky ice cream. She'd eat the whole goddamn quart while she wrote her daily report in her private journal.

Bitch thought she could kick Ellen Bowers around and get away with it. Surprise, surprise. All that bouncing around from precinct to precinct, from assignment to assignment had finally paid off.

She had contacts. Damn right. She knew people.

She knew the right people.

This time, the destruction of Eve Dallas would be her

springboard to fame, respect, and she'd be the one sitting at a desk in Homicide.

She'd be the one with her face on the screen.

Yeah, yeah, it was about goddamn time, she thought again as black hate crawled into her belly. And when she was done grinding Dallas into dust, she was going to see to it that prick Trueheart paid for his disloyalty.

She knew damn well Dallas had let him fuck her.

That's the way it was, that's the way it worked. That's why she'd never let some slick-talking creep stick his dick into her. She knew what people thought; she knew what people said. Sure she did.

They said she was a troublemaker. They said she was a sloppy cop. They said maybe she had a little blip in the brain somewhere.

They were all assholes, every last one of them, from Tibble right on down to Trueheart.

They weren't going to slide her quietly out of the department, shake her loose of the job with half pension. She'd fucking *own* the NYPSD when she was done.

All of them were coming down, all of them, starting with Dallas.

Because it all started with Dallas.

The rage worked under her cheer. It was always there, whispering to her. But she could control it. She'd controlled it for years. Because she was smart, smarter than all of them. Every time some department asshole ordered her to take a personality test, she hushed those whispers with a careful dose of Calm-It and passed.

Maybe she needed higher doses just lately, and it was best if she mixed some Zoner in for a nice soothing cocktail, but she was still in control.

She knew how to get around the assholes and their tests and their questions. And she knew what buttons to push, you bet she did. Her finger was on the trigger now, and it was staying there.

She had an inside track—and nobody knew but her. And now she had a nice, tidy pile of untraceable credits just for doing what she'd wanted to do in the first place: going public.

Her teeth flashed in a smile as she turned the corner and headed down the dark street toward her building. She was going to be rich, famous, powerful, as she was meant to be.

And with a little help from her friend, she'd pin Dallas to the wall.

"Officer Bowers?"

"Yeah?" Eyes narrowed, she turned, peered into the dark. Her hand lowered, hovered near her stunner. "What?"

"I have a message. From your friend."

"Oh yeah?" Her hand shifted, reached up to pat her container of ice cream. "What's the message?"

"It's delicate. We need privacy."

"No problem." She stepped forward, thrilled that there might be more she could use. "Come on up."

"I'm afraid you need to come down." The droid leaped out of the dark, his eyes colorless, his face blank. He swung the metal pipe once, cracking it against the side of her head before she could suck in air to scream.

The ice cream flew, landed with a splat. Blood smeared the sidewalk as he dragged her across. Her body bounced with muffled bumps on the stairs as he pulled it through the open basement door and down.

Efficiently, he climbed up again, locked the door. He didn't need the light. He'd been programmed to see in the dark. Quickly, he stripped off the uniform, took her ID, her weapon, and bundled all, including the pipe, in the large bag he'd brought with him. It would be placed in a recycle bin he'd already chosen and sabotaged.

And there in the cold dark, with emotionless skill, he used his hands and feet to break her to pieces.

chapter thirteen

"Sloppy, half-assed work." Eve fumed as she paced Roarke's office. She had to bitch to someone, and he was there. He made sympathetic noises while he scanned an incoming fax and went over the latest progress report from one of his largest interplanetary undertakings, the Olympus Resort.

It occurred to him that the resort could use another personal visit and that his wife could use a vacation. He made a mental note to work it in around their schedules.

"Two different primaries," she continued, striding around the office. "Two different cops, and both of them fucked up the case. What are they using to train them in Chicago—old videos of the Three Boobs?"

"I think that's Stooges," Roarke murmured.

"What?"

He glanced up, focused fully on her, and smiled at the absolute baffled fury on her face. "Stooges, darling. The Three Stooges."

"What's the difference, they're still incompetent knotheads. Half the paperwork's missing. There's no documentation of witness interviews or reports, the postmortem documents are lost. They did manage to ID the victim, but nobody did a background check. Or if it was done, it's not in the file."

Roarke made some notations on the fax—a small adjustment that dealt with approximately three quarters of a million and change, and shot it off to his midtown office and his assistant's attention. "What do you have?"

"A dead guy," she snapped, "with a missing heart." She frowned as Roarke rose and walked over to select a bottle of wine from his chill box. "I can see one cop screwing up a case. I don't like it, but I can see it. But two cops screwing up the same one, it just doesn't hold. And now both of them are out of touch, so I'm going to have to do some dance with their boss tomorrow."

She had so much anger and frustration bottled up inside her. "Maybe somebody got to them. Bribed, threatened. Shit. The leak on this might not just be in the NYPSD, it might be all over the damn place."

"And your interfering senator is from the great state of Illinois, as I recall."

"Yeah." Christ, she hated politics. "I have to clear it with the commander, but I should probably dance with this Chicago boss in person."

Taking his time, Roarke poured two glasses, carried both across the room to stand in front of her. "I'll take you."

"It's cop business."

"And you're my cop." He lifted her hand, curled her fingers around the stem of the glass. "You won't go to Chicago without me, Eve. That's personal. Now, drink some wine and tell me the rest."

She could have argued, for form's sake. But it seemed like a waste of energy. "Bowers filed a couple more complaints." She ordered herself to relax her jaw and sip. "She was first on scene this morning, and she caused trouble so I relieved her of duty. It's on record, and when they review, they won't be able to fault my actions, but she's really getting in my face."

Her stomach muscles began to tighten with tension as she spoke of it, thought of it. "My contact at IAB came down to warn me she's stirring the pot, that she went to the media.''

''Darling, the world is full of assholes and morons.'' He reached up, skimmed a finger down the shallow dent in her chin. ''Most are surprisingly recognizable. She'll end up sinking herself.''

''Yeah, eventually, but Webster's worried.''

''Webster?''

''The guy I know in IAB.''

''Ah.'' Hoping to distract her a little, he cupped a hand at the back of her neck, rubbed. ''I don't believe I've heard that name before. And how well do you know him, darling?''

''We don't run into each other much anymore.''

''But there was a time . . .''

She shrugged, would have shifted, but his fingers tightened just enough to make her eyes narrow. ''It was nothing. It was a long time ago.''

''What was?''

''When we got drunk and naked and bounced around on each other,'' she said between her teeth. ''Happy?''

He chuckled, leaned in to kiss her lightly. ''I'm devastated. Now you'll have to get drunk and naked and bounce around with me to make up for it.''

It wouldn't have hurt her ego, she realized, if he'd pretended to be just a little jealous. ''I've got work.''

''Me, too.'' He set his glass aside, pulled her against him. ''You are such work, Lieutenant.''

She turned her head, told herself she was not going to enjoy the way his teeth scraped along her neck at just the perfect point. ''I'm not drunk, pal.''

''Well.'' He nipped the glass out of her hand, put it down. ''Two out of three works for me,'' he decided and pulled her to the floor.

When the blood stopped roaring in her head and she could think again, she told herself she would not let him know she'd enjoyed being ravished on the office floor.

''Well, you had your fun, ace, now get off of me.''

With a little humming sound, he burrowed against her throat. "I love the taste of you. Right here." As he nibbled, he felt her heart pick up speed again and kick against his. "More?"

"No, cut it out." Her blood was starting to buzz again. "I've got work." She shoved at him, putting some muscle behind it while she still could. There was a combination of relief and disappointment when he rolled aside.

She scrambled up, grabbed his shirt as it was closest to hand. She sent him a bland look. Christ, was all she could think, the man had such a body. "You going to lie there, naked and smug, all night?"

"I would, but we have work to do."

"We?"

"Mmm." He rose and settled for his trousers. "Your missing documents. If they ever existed, I can get them back for you."

"You can—" She stopped herself, holding up a hand. "I don't want to know how you could manage that, I really don't. But I'm going to handle this through the proper channels."

As soon as she said it, she wanted to bite her tongue. That little statement was going to make it hard to ask him to dig up data, unofficially, on the Westley Friend suicide.

"Up to you." He shrugged, picked up his wine again. "But I could probably have your data in a couple of hours."

It was tempting, too tempting. She shook her head. "I'll just plod along on my own, thanks. That's my 'link," she added, glancing back through the open connecting door to her office.

"I'll transfer it here." He moved around the desk, tapped a quick series of keys, and had his own 'link beeping. "Roarke."

"Roarke, damn it, where's Dallas?"

He kept his gaze on Nadine's image on-screen, catching the brisk shake of Eve's head. "Sorry, Nadine, she's not available right now. Can I do something for you?"

"Turn on your screen, channel 48. Shit, Roarke. You

tell her to call me with a rebuttal. I can get it on live the minute she does.''

"I'll let her know. Thanks.'' He disengaged, then looked across the room. "View screen on, channel 48.''

Instantly, the screen filled with Bowers's face and a spew of venom. "With three separate complaints filed, the department won't be able to overlook Lieutenant Dallas's corrupt or abusive behavior any longer. Her thirst for power has caused her to cross lines, to ignore regulations, to slant reports, and to misuse witnesses in order to close cases in her favor.''

"Officer Bowers, those are serious accusations.''

"Each one is fact.'' Bowers jabbed a finger toward the perfectly groomed reporter. "And each will be proven through the internal investigation already under way. I've assured the Internal Affairs Bureau that I'll be turning over all documentation in these matters. Including those that prove Eve Dallas has habitually traded sexual favors for information and for promotions within the NYPSD.''

"Why, you slut,'' Roarke said easily, and slipped a supportive arm around his wife even as his own blood began to boil. "I'll have to divorce you now.''

"It's not a joke.''

"She's a joke, Eve. A poor and pitiful one. Screen off.''

"No, screen on. I want to hear it all.''

"It's long been suspected, and will be verified, that Dallas's husband, Roarke, is involved in a variety of criminal activities. He was, in fact, a prime suspect in a murder investigation early last year. An investigation Dallas was— conveniently—in charge of. Roarke was not charged in that matter, and Dallas is now the wife of a powerful, wealthy man who uses her connections to cover his own illegal activities.''

"She's gone too far.'' Under Roarke's hand, Eve began to vibrate with rage. "She's gone too far when she brings you into it.''

His eyes were cool, much too cool, as he studied the face on-screen. "I could hardly be left out.''

"Officer Bowers, by your own admission, Lieutenant Dallas is a powerful, perhaps dangerous, woman.'' The on-air reporter couldn't keep the gleam of delight out of his eyes. "Tell me, why are you risking going public at this time with your suspicions?''

"Someone has to speak the truth.'' Bowers lifted her chin, fixed her face in sober lines and shifted slightly so that she stared directly into the camera. "The department may choose to cover up for a dirty cop, but I honor my uniform too much to be a part of it.''

"They'll hang her for this.'' Eve drew in a breath, let it out slowly. "However much sticks to me, she's just terminated her own career. They won't transfer her this time. They'll kick her.''

"Screen off,'' Roarke ordered again, then wrapped Eve in his arms. "She can't hurt you. She can, for the short term, inconvenience and irritate, but that's all. You can, if you like, sue for defamation. She crossed several steps over from freedom of speech. But . . .'' He ran his hands up and down Eve's back. "Take the advice of someone who's dodged those slings and arrows before. Let it go.'' He pressed a kiss to her forehead, to support and to soothe. "Say no more than necessary. Stay above it, and the longer you do, the quicker it'll pass.''

Closing her eyes, she let him draw her in, cradle her head on his shoulder. "I want to kill her. Just one quick snap of the neck.''

"I can have a droid made up in her likeness. You can kill it as often as you like.''

It made her laugh a little. "It couldn't hurt. Look, I'm going to try to get some work done. I can't think about her; it makes me crazy.''

"All right.'' He let her go, slipped his hands into his pockets. "Eve?''

"Yeah?'' She paused in the doorway, glanced back.

"You could see it if you looked at her closely, looked at her eyes. She's not quite sane.''

"I did look. And no. No, she's not.''

Therefore, Roarke mused as his wife closed the door

between them, Bowers was that much more dangerous. The lieutenant wouldn't approve, he thought, but it couldn't be helped. He would work in his private room that evening, on his unregistered equipment.

And any and all data on Bowers would be in his hands by morning.

It was, Eve thought as she sat in her idling vehicle and studied the crowd blocking the gate leading to the house, infuriating enough to have to dodge reporters when it was job-related, when it was on-scene or at Cop Central.

But it was beyond infuriating to have a three-deep line of reporters screaming questions at her through the iron-work of her own gate. When it was personal. When it had nothing to do with the job.

She continued to sit, watching the temperature of the crowd rise even as the ambient temperature struggled up to begin to melt the snow in steady drips. Behind her, the foolish snow people she and Roarke had built were losing weight rapidly.

She considered various options, including Roarke's casual suggestion that they implement the electric current on the gate. In her mind she visualized dozens of drooling reporters jittering with the shock and dropping helplessly to the ground with their eyes rolling back white.

But she preferred, as always, a more direct approach.

She turned on the megaphone and started forward at a slow but steady speed.

"This is private property, and I am off duty at this time. Move back from the gate. Anyone coming through the gate will be arrested, charged, and detained for trespass-ing."

They didn't budge an inch. She could see mouths open-ing and closing, as questions were shot at her like arrows. Cameras were held up, pushed forward with the lenses like eager mouths waiting to swallow her.

"Your choice," she muttered. She engaged the mech-anism for the gate, letting it swing open slowly as she approached.

Reporters hung onto the rungs or stampeded toward the opening. She just kept driving, kept mechanically repeating her warning.

It gave her some satisfaction to watch some of them scramble for cover when they realized she wasn't going to stop. She glanced balefully at those ballsy enough to grab the handle on the sides of her vehicle and pace her while shouting through the closed window.

The minute she cleared the gate, she slammed it shut, hoping to catch a few fingers in the process. Then, with a thin smile, she punched the accelerator and sent a pair of idiots tumbling clear.

The echoes of their curses were like music that kept her mood elevated all the way downtown.

She headed straight to the conference room when she arrived at Central and, grumbling when she found it empty, sat down to man the computer herself.

She had, by her calculations, an hour to work before she had to head to Drake and keep her first interview appointments.

Peabody had her doctors lined up like arcade ducks. Eve intended to knock them off one at a time before the end of the day. With any luck, she mused, any luck at all, she'd ring a few bells.

She brought up data:

Drake Center, New York
Nordick Clinic, Chicago
Sainte Joan d'Arc, France
Melcount Center, London

Four cities, she thought. *Six bodies known.*

After hammering her way through the data McNab had accessed, she narrowed her search down to these health and research centers. All had one interesting thing in common: Westley Friend had worked at, lectured at, or endorsed each of them.

"Good work, McNab," she murmured. "Excellent job. You're the key, Friend, and you're another dead man. Just who's friend were you? Computer, any personal or professional connection between Friend, Dr. Westley, and Cagney, Dr. Colin.''

Working. . . .

"Don't be in such a hurry," she said mildly. "All similar connections between subject Friend and Wo, Dr. Tia; Waverly, Dr. Michael; Vanderhaven, Dr. Hans." Enough of a list for now, she decided. "Engage."

Recalibrating . . . working. . . .

"You do that little thing," she murmured and pushed away from the desk to get a cup of coffee. She winced at the smell instantly. She'd gotten spoiled, she thought, as the sludgy brew sat nastily in the mug. There'd been a day when she'd slugged down a dozen cups of Cop Central poison without a complaint.

Now, even looking at it made her shudder.

Amused at herself, she set it aside and wished to God that Peabody would report in so she could get some decent coffee out of her office.

She was considering making a dash for it herself, when Peabody walked in, closed the door behind her.

"You're late again," Eve began. "This is a bad habit. How the hell am I supposed to . . ." She trailed off, focusing on Peabody's face. Sheet white with eyes huge and dark. "What is it?"

"Sir. Bowers—"

"Oh, fuck Bowers." Eve snatched up the miserable coffee and gulped. "I don't have time to worry about her now. We're working murder here."

"Somebody's working hers."

"What?"

"Dallas, she's dead." Peabody took a concentrated breath, in and out, to help slow the rapid thump of her heart. "Somebody beat her to death last night. They found her a couple of hours ago, in the basement of her building.

Her uniform, weapon, ID, had all been stripped and taken from the scene. They ID'd her by prints." Peabody swiped a hand over white lips. "Word is there wasn't enough left of her face to make her visually."

Very carefully, Eve set down her cup. "It's a positive ID?"

"It's her. I went down and checked after I heard it in the bullpen. Prints and DNA match. They just confirmed."

"Jesus. Jesus Christ." Staggered, Eve pressed her fingers to her eyes, tried to think.

Data is complete.... Display, vocal or hard copy?

"Save and file. God." She dropped her hands. "What have they got on it?"

"Nothing. At least nothing I could dig out. No witnesses. She lived alone, so nobody was expecting her. There was an anonymous call reporting trouble at that location. Came in about oh five-thirty. A couple of uniforms found her. That's all I know."

"Robbery? Sexual assault?"

"Dallas, I don't know. I was lucky to get this much. They're shutting it in fast. No data in, no data out."

There was a sick ball in her stomach, a slick weight rolling there she didn't quite recognize as dread. "Do you know who's primary?"

"I heard Baxter, but I don't know for sure. Can't confirm."

"Okay." She sat, tunneled her fingers through her hair. "If it's Baxter, he'll give me what data he can. Odds are, it's not connected to ours, but we can't discount it." Eve lifted her gaze again. "Beaten to death?"

"Yeah." Peabody swallowed.

She knew what it was to be attacked with fists, to be helpless to stop them. To feel that stunning agony of a bone snapping. To hear the sound of it just under your own scream. "It's a bad way," she managed. "I'm sorry for it. She was a wrong cop, but I'm sorry for it."

"Everybody's pretty shaken up."

"I don't have much time here." She pinched the bridge of her nose. "We'll tag Baxter later, see if he can fill in some details. But for now, we've got to put this aside. I've got the interviews starting in less than an hour now, and I need to be prepared."

"Dallas, you need to know . . . I heard your name come up."

"What? My name?"

"About Bowers," she began, then broke off in frustration as the 'link beeped.

"Hold on. Dallas."

"Lieutenant, I need you upstairs, immediately."

"Commander, I'm prepping for a scheduled interview session."

"Now," he said briefly and broke transmission.

"Damn it. Peabody, look through the data I just accessed, see what rings, and make a hard copy. I'll review it on the way to interview."

"Dallas—"

"Hold the gossip until I have time." She moved fast, her mind on the upcoming interviews. She wanted to wangle a tour of the center's research wing. One of the questions that had popped into her mind the night before might be answered there.

Just what did medical facilities do with damaged or diseased organs they removed? Did they study them, dispose of them, experiment on them?

This collector had to have a purpose. If that purpose somehow tied in with legal and approved medical research, it would make more sense. It would give her a handle.

Research had to be funded, didn't it? Maybe she should be following the money. She could put McNab to work tracing grants and donations.

Distracted, she walked into Whitney's office. The little ball of dread in her stomach rolled again, hard, when she saw Webster, her commander, and Chief Tibble waiting.

"Sir."

"Close the door, Lieutenant." No one sat. Whitney remained standing behind his desk. Eve had a moment to think he looked ill before Tibble stepped forward.

He was a tall man; striking, tireless, and honest. He looked at Eve now with dark eyes that remained steady and gave away nothing. "Lieutenant, I want to advise you that you're entitled to have your advocate present at this time."

"My advocate, sir?" She let herself glance at Webster, then back at her chief. "That won't be necessary, sir. If IAB has more questions for me, I'll answer them without the buffer. I'm aware there was a media broadcast last night where accusations and statements about my character and professional behavior were attacked. They are groundless. I'm confident any internal investigation would prove them to be so."

"Dallas," Webster began, then closed his mouth when Tibble pinned him with a look.

"Lieutenant, are you aware that Officer Ellen Bowers was murdered last night?"

"Yes, sir. My aide just informed me."

"I need to ask you your whereabouts last evening between eighteen-thirty and nineteen hundred hours."

She'd been a cop for eleven years and couldn't remember ever being sucker punched so effectively. Her body jerked before she could control it, her mouth went dry. She heard her own breath catch, then release.

"Chief Tibble, am I to understand I'm a suspect in the murder of Officer Bowers?"

His eyes never wavered. She couldn't read what was in them. Cop's eyes, she thought with a quick shimmer of panic. Tibble had good cop's eyes.

"The department requires verification of your whereabouts during the time in question, Lieutenant."

"Sir. Between eighteen-thirty and nineteen hundred hours, I was en route from Central to my home. I believe I logged out at eighteen-ten."

Saying nothing, Tibble walked to the window and stood with his back to the room. Dread was an ache now, which spread in the gut with tiny, scrabbling claws. "Commander, Bowers was causing me difficulties, potentially serious ones, which I handled through proper channels and through proper procedure."

"That's documented, Lieutenant, and understood." He kept his hands behind his back, linked together with frustration. "Proper procedure must be followed. An investigation into the murder of Officer Bowers is under way, and at this time, you are a suspect. It is my belief that you'll be cleared quickly and completely."

"Cleared? Of beating a fellow cop to death? Of abandoning everything I believe in and I've worked for? And why would I have done this?" Panic had a line of sweat, icy cold, snaking down her spine. "Because she tried to smear me in the department and in the media? For Christ's sake, Commander, anyone could see she was on self-destruct."

"Dallas." This time Webster stepped forward. "You threatened her with physical harm, on record. Call your advocate."

"Don't tell me to call my advocate," she snapped. "I haven't done anything but my job." Panic was growing teeth now, edgy and sharp. All she could do was fight it with temper. "You want me in interview, Webster? Fine, let's go. Right here, right now."

"Lieutenant!" Whitney whipped the word out, watched her head snap around, the fury in her eyes hot and open. "The department must conduct internal and external investigations into the matter of the death of Officer Bowers. There is no choice." He let out a long breath. "There is no choice," he repeated. "While this investigation is open and active, you are suspended from duty."

He nearly winced when he saw her eyes go from hot and alive to blank and dazed. Nearly cringed when he saw every ounce of color drain out of her face. "It is with regret, Lieutenant, great personal regret, that I ask you to turn in your weapon and your shield."

Her mind had gone dead, utterly dead, as if some elec-

trical current had been shut off. She couldn't feel her
hands, her feet, her heart. "My shield?"

"Dallas." He stepped to her, his voice gentle now, his
eyes storming with emotion. "There's no choice. You are
suspended from duty, pending the results of the internal
and external investigations in the matter of the death of
Officer Ellen Bowers. I must ask for your weapon and
your badge."

She stared into his eyes, couldn't look anywhere else.
Inside her head was a scream: dull, distant, desperate. Her
joints felt rusty as she reached down for her badge, then
over to release her weapon. Their weight in her hand
made it shake.

Putting them in Whitney's was like ripping out her own
heart.

Someone said her name, twice, but she was walking
out of the room, blind, heading toward the glide fast, her
boots clicking on scarred tile. Dizzy, she gripped the rail
until her knuckles went white.

"Dallas, goddamn it." Webster caught up to her,
grabbed her arm. "Call your advocate."

"Get your hand off me." The words were weak, shaky,
and she couldn't find the strength to pull away. "Get it
off and stay away."

"You listen to me." He dragged her clear of the glide,
pushed her against a wall. "Nobody in that room wanted
this. There's no choice. Goddamn it, you know how it
works. We clear you, you get your badge back. You take
a few days' vacation. It's going to be that simple."

"Get the fuck away from me."

"She had diaries, discs." He spoke quickly, afraid
she'd break and run. "She put down all kinds of shit
about you." He was crossing the line and didn't give a
damn. "It has to be looked into and dismissed. Somebody
beat her to pieces, Dallas, to fucking pieces. It'll be all
over the media within the hour. You're tied to her. If
you're not automatically suspended pending, it looks like
cover-up."

"Or it looks like my superiors, my department, my colleagues believe me. Don't touch me again," she warned in a voice that shook so badly he stepped back.

"I've got to go with you." He spoke flatly now, furious that his own hands weren't steady. "To see that you clear only personal items from your office, and to escort you from the building. I need to confiscate your communicator, your master and vehicle codes."

She closed her eyes, fought to hold on. "Don't talk to me."

She managed to walk. Her legs felt like rubber, but she put one in front of the other. God, she needed air. Couldn't breathe.

Dizzy, she braced a hand on the doorway of the conference room. It seemed to swim in front of her eyes, as if she was looking into water. "Peabody."

"Sir." She sprang up, stared. "Dallas?"

"They took my badge."

Feeney was across the room like a bullet from a gun. He had one hand on Webster's shirt and the other already fisted and ready. "What kind of bullshit is this? Webster, you prick bastard—"

"Feeney, you have to take the interviews." She laid a hand on his shoulder, not so much to stop him from laying into Webster, but for support. She didn't know how much longer she had before she folded. "Peabody's got . . . Peabody's got the schedule, the data."

His fingers uncurled, closed gently over hers, and felt them tremble. "What's this about?"

"I'm a suspect." It was so odd to hear the words, hear her own voice float. "In the Bowers's homicide."

"That's a fucking crock."

"I have to go."

"Wait just one damn minute."

"I have to go," she repeated. She looked at Feeney with eyes dazed with shock. "I can't stay here."

"I'll take you, Dallas. Let me take you."

She looked at Peabody, shook her head. "No. You're with Feeney now. I can't—stay here."

She bolted.

"Feeney, Jesus." Eyes swimming, Peabody turned to him. "What do we do?"

"We fix it, goddamn it, son of a bitch, we fix it. Call Roarke," he ordered and relieved some fury by kicking viciously at the desk. "Make sure he's there when she gets home."

Now she pays. Stupid bitch. Now she pays a price she'd consider higher than her own life. What will you do now, Dallas? Now that the system you've spent your life fighting for has betrayed you?

Now will you see, now that you're shivering outside, that the very system you've sweated for is meaningless? That what matters is power?

You were nothing more than a drone in a hive that collapses constantly in upon itself. Now you're less than that.

Because the power is mine, and it is legion.

Sacrifices were made, it's true. Deviations from the plan were taken. Had to be taken. Risks were weighed, and with them, perhaps a few small mistakes. Any worthy experiment accepts those minor missteps.

Because the results justify all.

I am so close, so very close. Now the focus has switched, the tide turned. The hunter is now the prey of her own kind. They will rip her to pieces as mindlessly as wolves.

It was all so simple to accomplish. A few words in a few ears, debts called in. A flawed and jealous mind used, and yes, sacrificed. And no one will mourn the detestable Bowers any more than the dregs I removed from society will be mourned.

Oh, but they will cry for justice. They will demand payment.

And Eve Dallas will pay.

She's no longer even the minor irritant she proved herself to be. With her removed, all my skills and energies can go back into my work. My work is imperative, and the glory that will spew from it, my right.

When it's done, they'll whisper my name with awe. And weep with gratitude.

chapter fourteen

Roarke stood in the cold, helpless, and waited for Eve to come home. Word had come through in the middle of his delicate negotiations with a pharmaceutical company on Tarus II. He intended to buy them out, revamp their organization, and link it with his own company based on Tarus I.

He had cut them off without hesitation the instant he'd received the transmission from Peabody. The tearful explanation from the habitually stalwart cop had shaken him. There had been only one thought: to get home, to be there.

And now to wait.

When he saw the Rapid Cab coming up the drive, he felt a hot bolt of fury lance through him.

They'd taken her vehicle. Bastards.

He wanted to race down the steps, rip open the door, to bundle her out and up and carry her away somewhere, somewhere she wouldn't hurt as he could only imagine she hurt.

But it wasn't his anger she needed now.

He came down the steps as she got out of the cab. And she stood pale as death in the hard winter light, her eyes dark, glazed, and, he thought, impossibly young. The strength, the tough edge she wore as naturally as her weapon, was gone.

She wasn't sure she could speak, that the words would push through her throat, it burned so. And the rest of her was numb. Dead.

"They took my badge." Suddenly it was real, the brutal reality of it punched like a fist. And grief gushed up, hot, bitter, to spill out of her eyes. "Roarke."

"I know." He was there, his arms hard around her, holding tight as she began to shake. "I'm sorry, Eve. I'm so sorry."

"What will I do? What will I do?" She clung, weeping, not even aware that he picked her up, carried her inside, into the warmth and up the stairs. "Oh God, God, God, they took my badge."

"We'll straighten it out. You'll get it back. I promise you." She was shaking so violently, it seemed her bones would crash together and shatter. He sat, tightened his grip. "Just hold onto me."

"Don't go away."

"No, baby, I'll stay right here."

She wept until he feared she'd be ill; then the sobs faded away, and she was limp in his arms. Like a broken doll, he thought. He ordered a soother and took her to bed. She, who would fight taking a painkiller if she were bleeding from a dozen wounds, sipped the sedative he brought to her lips without protest.

He undressed her as he would an exhausted child.

"They made me nothing again."

He looked down at her face, into eyes, hollow and heavy. "No, Eve."

"Nothing." She turned her head away, closed her eyes, and escaped.

She'd been nothing. A vessel, a victim, a child. One more statistic sucked into an overburdened, understaffed system. She'd tried to sleep then, too, in the narrow bed in the hospital ward that smelled of sickness and approaching death. Moans, weeping, the monotonous beep, beep, beep of machines, and the quiet slap of rubber soles on worn linoleum.

Pain, riding just under the surface of the drugs that dripped into her bloodstream. Like a cloud full of thunder that threatened from a distance but never quite split and spilled.

She was eight, or so they'd told her. And she was broken.

Questions, so many questions from the cops and social workers she'd been taught to fear.

"They'll throw you into a hole, little girl. A deep, dark hole."

She would wake from the twilight sleep of drugs to his voice, sly and drunk, in her ear. And she would bite back screams.

The doctor would come with his grave eyes and rough hands. He was busy, busy, busy. She could see it in his eyes, in the sharp sound of his voice when he spoke to the nurses.

He didn't have time to waste on the wards, on the poor and the pathetic who crowded them.

A pin . . . was there a gold pin on his lapel that winked in the lights? Snakes, coiled up and facing each other.

She dreamed within the dream that the snakes turned on her, leaped on her, hissing with fangs that dug into flesh and drew fresh blood.

The doctor hurt her, often, through simple hurry and carelessness. But she didn't complain. They hurt you more, she knew, if you complained.

And his eyes looked like the snakes' eyes. Hard and cruel.

"Where are your parents?"

The cops would ask her. Would sit by the bed, more patient than the doctor. They snuck her candy now and then because she was a child with lost eyes who rarely spoke and never smiled. One brought her a little stuffed dog for company. Someone stole it the same day, but she remembered the soft feel of its fur and the kind pity in the cop's eyes.

"Where is your mother?"

She would only shake her head, close her eyes.

She didn't know. Did she have a mother? There was no memory, nothing but that sly whisper in her ear that had fear jittering through her. She learned to block it out, to block it all out. Until there was no one and nothing before the narrow bed in the hospital ward.

The social worker with her bright, practiced smile that looked false and tired around the edges. *"We'll call you Eve Dallas."*

That's not who I am, she thought, but she only stared. *I'm nothing. I'm no one.*

But they called her Eve in the group homes, in the foster homes, and she learned to be Eve. She learned to fight when pushed, to stand on the line she'd drawn, to become what she needed to become. First to survive. Then with purpose. Since middle childhood, the purpose had been to earn a badge, to make a difference, to stand for those who were no one.

One day when she stood in her stiff, formal uniform, her life had been put in her hands. Her life was a shield.

"Congratulations, Dallas, Officer Eve. The New York Police and Security Department is proud to have you."

In that moment, the thrill and the duty had burned through her like light in a strong, fierce blaze that had seared away all the shadows. And finally, she'd become someone.

"I have to ask for your badge and your weapon."

She whimpered in sleep. Going to her, Roarke stroked her hair, took her hand, until she settled again.

Moving quietly, he walked to the 'link in the sitting area and called Peabody.

"Tell me what's going on here."

"She's home? She's all right?"

"She's home, and no, she's far from all right. What the hell have they done to her?"

"I'm at the Drake. Feeney's running the interviews

we'd set up, but they're running late. I've only got a minute. Bowers was murdered last night. Dallas is a suspect.''

"What kind of insanity is that?"

"It's bogus—everybody knows it—but it's procedure."

"Fuck procedure."

"Yeah." The image of his face on her screen, the cold, predatory look in those amazing eyes, had her fighting back a shudder. "Look, I don't have a lot of details. They're keeping the lid on Baxter—he's primary—but I got that Bowers had all this stuff about Dallas written down. Weird stuff. Sex and corruption, bribery, false reports.''

He glanced back at Eve when she stirred restlessly. "Is no one considering the source?"

"The source is a dead cop." She ran a hand over her face. "We'll do whatever it takes to get her back and get her back fast. Feeney's going to do a deep-level search on Bowers," she said, lowering her voice.

"Tell him that won't be necessary. He can contact me. I already have that data."

"But how—"

"Tell him to contact me, Peabody. What's Baxter's full name and rank?"

"Baxter? Detective, David. He won't talk to you, Roarke. He can't."

"I'm not interested in talking to him. Where's McNab?"

"He's back at Central, running data."

"I'll be in touch."

"Roarke wait. Tell Dallas . . . tell her whatever you think she needs to hear."

"She'll need you, Peabody." He broke transmission.

He left Eve sleeping. Information was power, he thought. He intended for her to have all the power he could gather.

"I'm sorry to keep you waiting, Detective . . ."

"Captain," Feeney said, sizing up the slickly groomed man in the Italian suit. "Captain Feeney, filling in temporarily for Lieutenant Dallas as primary. I'll be conducting the interview.''

"Oh." Waverly's expression showed mild puzzlement. "I hope the lieutenant isn't unwell."

"Dallas knows how to take care of herself. Peabody, on record."

"On record, sir."

"So official." After a slight shrug, Waverly smiled and sat behind his massive oak desk.

"That's right." Feeney read off the revised Miranda, cocked a brow. "You get that?"

"Of course. I understand my rights and obligations. I didn't think I required a lawyer for this procedure. I'm more than willing to cooperate with the police."

"Then tell me your whereabouts on the following dates and times." Referring to his notebook, Feeney read off the dates of the three murders in New York.

"I'll need to check my calendar to be sure." Waverly swiveled a sleek black box, laid his palm on top to activate it, then requested his schedule for the times in question.

Off duty and clear during first period. Off duty and clear during second period. On call and at Drake Center monitoring patient Clifford during third period.

"Relay personal schedule," Waverly requested.

No engagements scheduled during first period. Engagement with Larin Stevens, booked for overnight during second period. No engagements scheduled during third period.

"Larin, yes." He smiled again, with a twinkle. "We went to the theater, had a late supper at my home. We also shared breakfast, if you understand my meaning, Captain."

"That's Stevens," Feeney said briskly as he entered the name in his book. "You got an address?"

All warmth fled. "My assistant will provide you with it. I'd like the police connection to my personal friends kept to a minimum. It's very awkward."

"Pretty awkward for the dead, too, Doctor. We'll check out your friend and your patient. Even if they clear you for two of the periods, we've still got one more."

"A man's entitled to spend the night alone in his own bed occasionally, Captain."

"Sure is." Feeney leaned back. "So, you pop hearts and lungs out of people."

"In a manner of speaking." The smile was back, digging charming creases into his cheeks. "The Drake has some of the finest organ transplant and research facilities in the world."

"What about your connections with the Canal Street Clinic?"

Waverly raised a brow. "I don't believe I know that facility."

"It's a free clinic downtown."

"I'm not associated with any free clinics. I paid my dues there during my early years. You'll find most doctors who work or volunteer at such places are very young, very energetic, and very idealistic."

"So you stopped working on the poor. Not worth it?"

Unoffended, he folded his hands on the desk. Peeking out from under his cuff was the smooth, thin gold of a Swiss wrist unit. "Financially, no. Professionally, there's little chance for advancement in that area. I chose to use my knowledge and skill where it best suits me and leave the charity work for those who are suited to it."

"You're supposed to be the best."

"Captain, I *am* the best."

"So, tell me—in your professional opinion . . ." Feeney reached in his file, drew out copies of the crime scene stills and laid them on the highly polished surface of the desk. "Is that good work?"

"Hmm." Eyes cool, Waverly turned the photos toward him, studied them. "Very clean, excellent." He shifted his gaze briefly to Feeney. "Horrible, of course, on a human level, you understand, but you asked for a professional opinion. And mine is that the surgeon who performed here is quite brilliant. To have managed this under the circumstances, with what certainly had to be miserable conditions, is a stunning achievement.''

"Could you have done it?''

"Do I possess the skills?'' Waverly nudged the photos back toward Feeney. "Why, yes.''

"What about this one?'' He tossed the photo of the last victim on top of the others, watched Waverly glance down and frown.

"Poorly done. This is poorly done. One moment.'' He pulled open a drawer, pulled out microgoggles, and slipped them on. "Yes, yes, the incision appears to be perfect. The liver has been removed quite cleanly, but nothing was done to seal off, to maintain a clear and sterile field. Very poorly done.''

"Funny,'' Feeney said dryly, "I thought the same thing about all of them.''

"Cold son of a bitch,'' Feeney muttered later. He paused in the corridor, checked his wrist unit. "Let's find Wo, chat her up, see about getting a look at where they keep the pieces of people they pull out. Jesus, I hate these places.''

"That's what Dallas always says.''

"Keep her out of your head for now,'' he said shortly. He was working hard to keep her out of his and do the job. "If we're going to help her close this, you need to keep her troubles out of your head.''

Face grim, he strode down the corridor, then glanced over as Peabody fell into step beside him. "Make an extra copy of all data and interview discs.''

She met his gaze, read it, and for the first time during the long morning, smiled. "Yes, sir.''

"Christ, stop sirring me to death.''

Now Peabody grinned. "She used to say that, too. Now she's used to it.''

The shadows in his eyes lifted briefly. "Going to whip me into shape, too, Peabody?"

Behind his back, Peabody wiggled her brows. She didn't think it would take her much time to do just that. She fixed her face into sober lines when he knocked on Wo's door.

An hour later, Peabody was staring, horrified and fascinated, at a human heart preserved in thin blue gel.

"The facilities here," Wo was saying, "are arguably the finest in the world for organ research. It was at this facility, though it was not as expansive as it is today, that Dr. Drake discovered and refined the anticancer vaccine. This portion of the center is dedicated to the study of diseases and conditions, including aging, that adversely affect human organs. In addition, we continue to study and refine techniques for organ replacement."

The lab was as large as a heliport, Feeney decided, sectioned off here and there with thin white partitions. Dozens of people in long coats of white, pale green, or deep blue worked at stations, manning computers, compuscopes, or tools he didn't recognize.

It was quiet as a church. None of the open-air background music some large facilities employed whispered through the lab, and when he inhaled, the air tasted faintly of antiseptic. He made certain he breathed through his nose.

They stood in a section where organs were displayed in the gel-filled bottles, the labels attached to the bases.

At the near door, a security droid stood silently, in case, Feeney thought with a sneer, somebody got the sudden urge to grab a bladder and run for it.

Jesus, what a place.

"Where do you get your specimens?" Feeney asked Wo, and she turned to him with a frigid look.

"We do not remove them from live, unwilling patients. Dr. Young?"

Bradley Young was thin, tall, and obviously distracted. He turned from his work at a sheer white counter populated with scopes and monitors and compu-slides. He frowned, pinched off the magni-clip he wore perched on his nose, and focused pale gray eyes.

"Yes?"

"This is Captain Feeney and his . . . assistant," she supposed, "from the police department. Dr. Young is our chief research technician. Would you explain how we go about collecting our specimens here for research?"

"Of course." He ran a hand over his hair. It was thin, like his bones, like his face, and the color of bleached wheat. "Many of our specimens are more than thirty years old," he began. "This heart for example." He moved across the blinding white floor to the container where Peabody had been standing. "It was removed from a patient twenty-eight years ago. As you can see, there is considerable damage. The patient had suffered three serious cardiac arrests. This heart was removed and replaced with one of the first runs of the NewLife unit. He is now, at the age of eighty-nine, alive, well, and living in Bozeman, Montana."

Young smiled winningly. He considered that his finest joke. "The specimens were all either donated by patients themselves or next of kin in the event of death, or acquired through a licensed organ broker."

"You can account for all of them."

Young just stared at Feeney. "Account for?"

"You got paperwork on all of them, ID?"

"Certainly. This department is very organized. Every specimen is properly documented. Its donor or brokerage information, its date of removal, the condition at time of removal, surgeon, and team. In addition, any specimen that is studied on premises or off must be logged in and out."

"You take these things out of here?"

"On occasion, certainly." Looking baffled, he glanced at Dr. Wo, who merely waved a hand for him to continue. "Other facilities might request a specific specimen with a specific flaw for study. We have a loan and a sale policy with several other centers around the world."

Click, Feeney thought, and took out his book. "How

about these?'' he asked, and read off Eve's list.

Again, Young glanced at Wo, and again received a go-ahead signal. "Yes, those are all what we would consider sister facilities.''

"Ever been to Chicago?''

"A number of times. I don't understand.''

"Captain,'' Wo interrupted. "This is becoming tedious.''

"My job's not filled with high points,'' he said easily. "How about giving me the data on the organs you checked in here within the last six weeks.''

"I—I—that data is confidential.''

"Peabody,'' Feeney began, keeping his eyes on the suddenly nervous Young, "start warrant procedures.''

"One moment; that won't be necessary.'' Wo gestured Peabody back in a way that had Peabody's eyes narrowing. "Dr. Young, get the captain the data he requested.''

"But it's confidential material.'' His face set suddenly in stubborn lines. "I don't have clearance.''

"I'm clearing it,'' she snapped. "I'll speak with Dr. Cagney. The responsibility is mine. Get the data.''

"We appreciate your cooperation,'' Feeney told her.

She turned dark, cold eyes on him when Young left to retrieve the data. "I want you out of this lab and this center as soon as possible. You're disrupting important work.''

"Catching killers probably doesn't rate as high on your scale as poking at livers, but we all gotta earn our paycheck. You know what this is? He took the sealed pin out of his pocket, held it at eye level.

"Of course. It's a caduceus. I have one very much like it.''

"Where?''

"Where? At home, I imagine.''

"I noticed some of the docs around here wearing one. I guess you don't wear yours to work.''

"Not as a rule, no.'' But she reached up, as if out of habit, running her fingers on her unadorned lapel. "If you're done with me now, I have a great deal of work.''

"We're done, for now. But I have a couple of more interviews set for tomorrow. I'd like to see your pin, if you'd bring it in."

"My pin?"

"That's right. Someone lost one recently." He lifted the one he held a little higher. "I need to make sure it wasn't you."

She tightened her lips and walked away.

"A lot of steam in that one, Peabody. We'll take a closer look at her when we get back to Central."

"She used to be president of the AMA," Peabody remembered. "Waverly's current president. The AMA put pressure on East Washington to put pressure on the mayor to put pressure on us to kick the case."

"Wheels in wheels," Feeney murmured. "Let's get this data back and see what rolls out of them. Now, what's the deal with Vanderhaven?"

"His interview was scheduled next, but he canceled. Professional emergency." She glanced around to be certain no one was within hearing distance. "I called his office, said I was a patient, and was told the doctor had taken leave for the next ten days."

"Interesting. Sounds like he doesn't want to talk to us. Get his home address, Peabody. We'll pay a house call."

Roarke was studying data of his own. It had been child's play for him to slide into Baxter's computer and access information on Bowers's murder.

It was a pity that, as yet, there was little information to be had.

But there was plenty, of the vile and hysterical variety, to be found in Bowers's logs and diaries.

He ran a search on them, using Eve's name, and found bits and pieces stretching back for years. Comments, accusations when Eve had been promoted to detective, when she received commendations. Roarke raised both eyebrows when he read Bowers's statement that Eve had seduced Feeney in order to bag him as her trainer. And then the lurid speculation on her affair with her commander to insure she was assigned important cases.

But these, and others that popped from time to time, were mild compared with the diatribes that began on the day Bowers and Eve had clashed over the body of a sidewalk sleeper.

That obsession, Roarke mused, had festered over time until that one moment, that single twist of fate that had burst it and spilled the poison over both of them.

Now one was dead.

He looked toward the screen where he could monitor the bedroom and see his wife sleeping.

And the other broken.

Still scanning, he waved a hand at his communication screen when Summerset came on. "Not now."

"I'm sorry to disturb you, but Dr. Mira is here. She'd very much like to speak with you."

"I'll be down." He rose, studied Eve another moment. "System off," he murmured, and the equipment behind him shifted from a low hum to silence.

He stepped out of the room. The door behind him locked automatically and could only be opened with the palm and voice prints of those authorized. Only three people had ever been inside.

To save time, he used the elevator. He didn't intend to be away from Eve any longer than necessary.

"Roarke." Mira sprang up from her chair, hurried across the room to grab both of his hands. Her usual calm face showed strain around the eyes and mouth. "I only just heard. I came right over. I'm so sorry to intrude, but I had to come."

"You're never an intrusion."

She tightened her grip on his hands. "Please. Will she see me?"

"I don't know. She's sleeping." He glanced over his shoulder toward the stairs. "I gave her something. I could kill them for this." He spoke almost to himself, his voice soft and terrifyingly gentle. "For putting that look I saw on her face. I could kill them for that alone."

Because she believed him, her hands trembled a little. "Can we sit?"

"Of course. Sorry. My mind isn't on my manners."

"I hope they won't have to be with me. Roarke . . ." She sat in one of the beautifully curved chairs, leaned forward to lay her hand on his again, hoping the contact would help them both. "While others may be outraged or sympathetic or have any variety of reactions to what happened today, you and I are perhaps the only ones who fully understand what this has done to her. To her heart, her sense of self. Her identity."

"It's destroyed her." No, he realized, he couldn't sit, and rising, stalked to the window to stare out at the cold afternoon. "I've seen her face death, her own and others'. I've seen her face the misery and fears of her past and the shadows that cover pieces of it. I've seen her terrified of her own feelings. But she stood. She gathered herself and she stood up to it. And this, this departmental procedure, has destroyed her."

"She'll gather herself again, and she'll stand up to this. But not alone. She can't stand up to this alone."

He turned, faced her. The light streamed through the window behind him; the dangerous blue of his eyes made Mira think of a cold and vengeful angel ready to leap into hell.

"She never has to be alone."

"What you have with her will save her. Just as it saved you."

He angled his head, changing the slant of light and the uneasy vision she'd had of him. "That's an interesting way to put it. But you're quite right. She did save me, and I'd forgotten I was lost. I love her more than life, and I'll do whatever needs to be done."

Mira studied her hands a moment, lifted her fingers up, let them fall. "I won't ask you questions about your methods, or your . . . connections in certain areas. But I will ask if there's anything I can do to help."

"How far will discounting Bowers's accusations go toward getting Eve's badge back?"

"It will help considerably with IAB. But until the homicide investigation is closed or the suspicion against Eve is dismissed publicly and without prejudice the department walks a firm line."

"You can test her? Truth test, personality profile, probabilities."

"Yes, but she has to be willing, and she has to be ready. It's a difficult process, physically and emotionally. But that, too, would weigh on her side."

"I'll speak with her about it."

"She'll have to grieve, but don't let her grieve too long. At some point, she'll need her anger. It'll be her most important source of strength."

She rose, stepped toward him. "I've asked to be permitted to evaluate Bowers's emotional and mental state, using the records of the last several weeks, her diaries— the content and tone—interviews with associates and acquaintances. It'll take time. I have to be very thorough, very careful. Though I'm giving it priority status, I doubt I can furnish the department with a conclusion in less than two weeks."

"I could take her away," he considered.

"That might be for the best, even for a few days. But I doubt she'll go." She opened her mouth, shut it again.

"What?"

"I know her so well. I have such strong feelings for her. But I'm still a psychiatrist. I believe I know how she'll react, at least initially. I don't want you to feel as if I'm overstepping or violating her privacy by . . . analyzing."

"I know she matters to you. Tell me what to expect."

"She'll want to hide. In sleep, in silence, in solitude. She may very well lock you out."

"She won't have much luck with that."

"But she'll want to, try to, simply because you're closer to her than anyone ever has been. I'm sorry," she said and pressed her fingers to her left temple. "Could I trouble you for a little brandy?"

"Of course." Instinct had him laying a hand on her

cheek. "Dr. Mira," he said very gently, "sit down."

She felt weak and weepy. Sitting, she steadied herself, waited while Roarke took a decanter from a carved cabinet and poured her a snifter of brandy.

"Thank you." She took a small sip, let it warm her. "This suspension, the suspicion, the mark on her record is not just a matter of the job and procedure to Eve. Her identity was taken from her once before. She rebuilt it and herself. For her, this has stripped her of it again, of what and who she is. What she needs to be. The longer she closes herself down, closes herself off, the harder it will be to reach her. It may affect your marriage."

He only lifted a brow at that. "She won't have any luck with that whatsoever."

Mira gave a quiet, shaky laugh. "You're a very stubborn man. That's good." She sipped more brandy, studying him. And what she saw eased some of her own worry. "At some point, you may find yourself having to put your sympathy for her situation aside. It would be easier for you to coddle and pamper and let her drift. But I think you'll recognize the point where she'll need you to make her take the next step."

She sighed then, set the brandy aside. "I won't keep you from her any longer, but if there's anything else I can do. If she wants to see me, I'll come."

He considered her loyalty, her affection, and wondered how they weighed against her duty. He never minded playing the odds. "How long will it take for you to complete a full-level search and scan on Bowers?"

"The paperwork is being rushed through on the orders for it. It shouldn't take more than another day, perhaps two."

"I have the data now," he said simply and waited while she stared at him.

"I see." She said nothing while he helped her into her coat. "If you transfer the data to my home unit, my personal unit," she added with a glance over her shoulder. "I assume you have no trouble accessing my personal unit?"

"None whatsoever."

She laughed just a little. "How very terrifying you are. If you transfer what you have, I'll begin work on it this evening."

"I'm very grateful." He saw her off, then went back upstairs to watch over Eve.

chapter fifteen

Dreams chased her, memory bumping into memory in a chaotic race. Her first bust and the solid satisfaction of doing the job she'd trained to do. The boy who'd kissed her sloppily when she'd been fifteen and had surprised her because she'd felt no fear or shame, but a mild interest.

A drunken night with Mavis at the Blue Squirrel with so much laughter it hurt the ribs. The mutilated body of a child she'd been too late to save.

The weeping of those left behind and the screams of the dead.

The first time she'd seen Roarke, that dazzling face onscreen in her office.

Then back, always back to a cold room with a dirty red light pulsing against the window. The knife in her hand dripping with blood, and the pain shrieking so wild, so loud, she could hear nothing else. Could be nothing else.

When she woke, it was dark, and she was empty.

Her head throbbed with a dull, consistent ache that was the dregs of weeping and grief. Her body felt hollow, as if the bones had slipped away while she'd slept.

She wanted to sleep again, to just go away.

He moved through the dark, quiet as a shadow. The bed shifted slightly as he sat beside her, found her hand. "Do you want the light?"

"No." Her voice felt rusty, but she didn't bother to clear it. "No, I don't want anything. You didn't have to stay here, in the dark."

"Did you think I'd let you wake alone?" He brought her hand to his lips. "You're not alone."

She wanted to weep again, could feel the tears beating at the backs of her eyes. Hot, helpless. Useless. "Who called you?"

"Peabody. She and Feeney were here; so was Mira. McNab's called several times. And Nadine."

"I can't talk to them."

"All right. Mavis is downstairs. She won't leave, and I can't ask her to."

"What am I supposed to say to her? To anyone? God, Roarke, I'm stripped. The next time I go into Central, it'll be to interview as a murder suspect."

"I've contacted a lawyer. You've nothing to worry about there. If and when you agree to interview, it'll be here, in your own home, on your own terms. Eve."

He could see her silhouette, the way she turned away from him and stared into the dark. Gently, he cupped her face, turned it toward him. "No one you work with, no one who knows you believes you had anything to do with what happened to Bowers."

"I don't even care about that. It's nothing but form. No physical evidence, no clear motive, and the opportunity is slim. I don't care about that," she repeated and hated, hated the way her breath hitched. "They'll have a cloud but no proof, not enough for the PA, but enough to keep my badge away. Enough to keep me out."

"You've people who care about you who'll work to see that doesn't happen."

"It has happened," she said flatly. "And nothing can change it. You can't change it. I just want to sleep." She shifted away, shut her eyes. "I'm tired. Go down with Mavis, I'm better off alone now."

He ran a hand over her hair. He'd give her the night to grieve, to escape.

But when he left her alone, she opened her eyes, stared at nothing. And didn't sleep.

Getting out of bed in the morning seemed like wasted effort.

She shifted, looked up through the glass overhead. The snow was gone and the sky was the dull gray of depression. She tried to think of some reason to get up, get dressed, but could think of nothing, could feel nothing but a low, dragging fatigue.

She turned her head, and there was Roarke in the sitting area, sipping coffee and watching her.

"You've slept long enough, Eve. You can't go on hiding in here."

"It seems like a good idea right now."

"The longer it does, the more you'll lose. Get up."

She sat up, but drew her knees into her chest and rested her head on them. "I don't have anything to do, nowhere to go."

"We can go anywhere you like. I've cleared my schedule for a couple of weeks."

"You didn't have to do that." Anger struggled to surface but turned pale and listless and faded. "I don't want to go anywhere."

"Then we'll stay home. But you're not lying in bed with the covers over your head."

A bubble of resentment worked its way free. "I didn't have the covers over my head," she muttered. And what did he know? she thought. How could he know how she felt? But there was enough pride left to have her getting up, dragging on a robe.

Pleased with the small victory, he poured her coffee, topped off his own. "I've eaten," he said casually, "but I don't believe Mavis has."

"Mavis?"

"Yes, she stayed last night." He reached over, pressed

a button in the interhouse 'link. "She'll keep you company."

"No, I don't want—"

But it was too late as Mavis's face swam on-screen. "Roarke, is she awake yet—Dallas!" Her smile broke out, a little wobbly, but there, as she spotted Eve. "I'll be right there."

"I don't want to talk to anyone," Eve said furiously when the screen went blank. "Can't you understand that?"

"I understand very well." He rose, laid his hands on her shoulders. It broke his heart as he felt them droop. "You and I went through a large part of our lives without having anyone who mattered or who we mattered to. So I understand very well what it is to have someone." He leaned forward to press his lips to her brow. "To need someone. Talk to Mavis."

"I've got nothing to say." Her eyes filled again and burned.

"Then listen." He squeezed her shoulders once, then turned as the door burst open and Mavis flew in. "I'll leave you two alone," he said, but he doubted either of them heard him as Mavis was already wrapping herself around Eve and babbling.

"Those suck-faced pissheads," he heard her sob out, and he nearly smiled as he closed the door.

"Okay," Eve murmured and buried her face in Mavis's blue hair. "Okay."

"I wanted to go find Whitney and call him a suck-faced pisshead in person, but Leonardo said it was better to come straight here. I'm sorry, so sorry, so sorry." She reared back so abruptly Eve nearly went down. "What the hell's wrong with them!" Mavis demanded, throwing her arms out and sending the diaphanous pink sleeves of what might have been a nighty flapping.

"It's procedure," Eve managed.

"Well, screw that in the ass sideways. No way they're going to get away with this. I bet Roarke's already hired a platoon of hot-shit lawyers to sue their suck-faces off.

You'll own the goddamn city of New York when this is over."

"I just want my badge." And because it was Mavis, Eve dropped onto the sofa and buried her face in her hands. "I've got nothing without it, Mavis."

"You'll get it back." Shaken, Mavis sat, draped an arm around Eve's shoulders. "You always make the right thing happen, Dallas."

"I'm locked out." Weary, Eve sat back, closed her eyes. "You can't make things happen when they're happening to you."

"You made them happen for me. When you collared me all those years ago, it changed my life."

It was an effort, but Eve worked up a ghost of a smile. "Which time?"

"The first time—the other couple were just like, you know, slips. You made me wonder if I could be more than a grifter scamming marks, then you made me see I could. And last year when things were bad for me, when it looked like they were going to put me in a cage, you were there for me. You made the right things happen."

"I had the badge, I had control." Her eyes went bleak again. "I had the job."

"Well, now you've got me and you've got the iciest guy on or off planet. And that's not all. You know how many people called here last night? Roarke wanted to stay up here with you so I asked Summerset if I could, like, take the calls and stuff. They just kept coming in."

"How many from reporters wanting a story?"

Mavis sniffed, then got up to call up the menu on the AutoChef. Roarke had given her orders to see that Eve ate, and she intended to follow them. "I know how to ditch the media dogs. Let's have ice cream."

"I'm not hungry."

"You don't need to be hungry for ice cream and—oh yeah there's a God—chocolate chip cookies. Mag squared."

"Mavis—"

"You took care of me when I needed you," Mavis said

quietly. "Don't make me feel like you don't need me."

Nothing could have worked more completely. Though she sent one longing look toward the bed, to the oblivion she might find there, Eve sighed. "What kind of ice cream?"

Eve drifted through the day, like someone wandering in and out of sweeps of fog. She avoided her office and Roarke's, used a headache as an excuse to crawl away for a few hours. She took no calls, refused to discuss the situation with Roarke, and finally closed herself in the library on the pretense of choosing reading material.

She turned on the search screen so anyone monitoring would think she was browsing through, then ordered curtains closed, lights off, and curled on the couch to escape into sleep.

She dreamed of coiled snakes slithering up a gold staff that dripped with blood. And the blood slipped and slid and beaded over paper flowers tucked into a brown glass bottle.

Someone called for help in a voice thin with age.

She stepped into the dream, into a landscape blinding white with snow, wind that stung the eyes and carried the voice away. She ran through it, her boots skidding, her breath puffing out in visible waves, but there was nothing but that wall of cold white.

"Cunt cop." A hiss in the ear.

"What are you up to, little girl?" Terror in the heart.

"Why'd somebody wanna put a hole in him that way?" A question still unanswered.

Then she saw them, the doomed and the damned, frozen in the snow, their bodies twisted, their faces caught in that shocked insult of death. Their eyes staring at her, asking the question still unanswered.

Behind her, behind that white curtain, came the crack and snick of ice breaking. Of something breaking free with sneaky, whispering sounds that were like quiet laughter.

The walls of white became the walls of a hospital cor-

ridor, stretched out like a tunnel with no end in sight, the
curves slick as water. It came for her, its footsteps slow
with the wet sound of flesh on tile. With her blood roaring
in her head, she turned to face it, to fight it, reaching for
her weapon. Her hand came up empty.

"What are you up to, little girl?"

The sob ripped at her throat, the fear swallowing her
whole. So she ran, stumbling down the tunnel, her breath
whistling out in panic. She could smell his breath behind
her. Candy and whiskey.

The tunnel split, a sharp right or left. She stopped, too
confused by fear to know which way to go. The sham-
bling steps behind her had a scream bubbling in her throat.
She leaped right, plunged into silence. Fresh sweat popped
onto her skin, rolled down her face. Up ahead a light,
dim, and the shadow of shape in it still and quiet.

She ran for it. Someone to help. God, someone help
me.

When she reached the end, there was a table, and on
the table her own body. The skin white, the eyes closed.
And where her heart had been was a bloody hole.

She woke shuddering. On watery legs she got up,
lurched toward the elevator. She braced herself against the
wall as it took her down. Desperate for air, she stumbled
off, hurried outside where the cold bit blood back into her
face.

She stayed out for nearly an hour, walking off the horror of the dream, the sticky sweat, the inner shudders. A
part of her seemed to stand back, staring in righteous disgust.

*Get a hold of yourself, Dallas. You're pathetic. Where's
your spine?*

Just leave me alone, she thought miserably. *Leave me
the hell alone.* She was allowed to have feelings, wasn't
she? Weaknesses? And if she wanted to be left alone with
them, it was no one's business.

Because nobody knew, no one could understand, no
one could feel what she felt.

*You've still got your brain, don't you? Even if you have
lost your guts. Start thinking.*

"I'm tired of thinking," she muttered and stopped to
stand in the snow that was going to slush. "There's nothing to think about and nothing to do."

Hunching her shoulders, she started back toward the
house. She wanted Roarke, she realized. Wanted him to
hold her, to make it all go away. To beat the demons back
for her.

Tears were surging back, and she struggled against
them. They made her tired. All she wanted now was
Roarke and to crawl into some warm place with him and
have him tell her it was going to be all right.

She stepped inside, the old running shoes she'd put on
soaked through, her jeans wet nearly to the knees. She
hadn't stopped for a jacket before going out, and the sudden warmth had her swaying in mild shock.

Summerset watched her a moment, his lips tight, his
eyes dark with worry. Deliberately, he fixed his most arrogant expression on his face and slipped into the foyer.

"You're filthy and wet." He sniffed derisively. "And
you're tracking water all over the floor. You might show
a bit of respect for your own home."

He waited for the flash of temper, the cold flare of her
eyes, and felt the heart she didn't know he had squeeze
when she simply stared at him.

"Sorry." She looked down blankly at her feet. "I
didn't think." She laid a hand on the newel post, noticed
with a kind of distant interest that it seemed cold enough
to snap, and started up the stairs.

Unnerved, Summerset moved quickly to the communication center. "Roarke, the lieutenant has just come in
from outside. She wore no outer gear. She looks very
bad."

"Where is she?"

"She's heading up. Roarke, I insulted her and . . . she
apologized to me. Something must be done."

"It's about to be."

Roarke strode out of his office, made straight for the

bedroom. The minute he saw her, wet, white, and trembling, fury sprang up to join concern. It was time, he decided, to lead with the fury.

"What the hell do you think you're doing?"

"I just went out for a walk." She sat but couldn't quite get her frozen fingers to work well enough to peel off her wet shoes. "I needed some air."

"So you go out without a coat. Making yourself sick's next in your master plan for dealing with this."

Her mouth fell open. She'd wanted him, wanted him to comfort and soothe, and he was snapping at her, yanking off her shoes as if she were a child about to be spanked. "I just wanted some air."

"Well, you seem to have gotten it." Jesus, he thought, Jesus, her hands were like ice. He yanked back the urge to warm them himself and stood back from her. "Get in the damn shower, boil yourself as you're prone to."

Hurt swam into her eyes, but she said nothing. It only infuriated him more when she rose and walked obediently into the adjoining bath.

He closed his eyes when he heard the water running. Let her grieve, Mira had told him. Well, he'd let her grieve long enough. She'd said he'd know the moment to shake her out of it.

If not now, he told himself, *when?*

He ordered up brandy for both of them, swirled his without interest as he waited for her.

When she came out, wrapped in a robe, he was ready. "Perhaps it's time we talk about your options."

"Options?"

"What you'll do." He picked up the second snifter, put it in her hand, then sat comfortably. "With your training and experience, private security is likely the best avenue. I have a number of organizations where your talents would come in very handy."

"Private security? Working for you?"

He lifted a brow. "I can promise you, your income will be more substantial than it was, and you'll be kept very busy." He sat back, draped his arm over the back of the sofa, and appeared blissfully relaxed. "That particular option would free up your time, allow you to travel more freely. You'd be expected to accompany me on a number of business trips, so it would have a number of benefits to both of us."

"I'm not looking for a damn job, Roarke."

"No? Well, my mistake. If you've decided to retire then, we can explore other options."

"Options, for God's sake. I can't think about this."

"We could consider making a child."

The snifter jerked in her hand, brandy sloshing over the rim as she spun around. "What?"

"That got your attention," he murmured. "I imagined we'd start our family a bit farther down the road, but under the current circumstances, we could easily push it up."

She wondered why her head didn't explode. "Are you crazy? A baby? Do you mean a baby?"

"That's the conventional way to start a family."

"I can't—I don't—" She managed to catch her breath. "I don't know anything about babies, kids."

"You have a great deal of leisure time just now. You can learn. Retiring makes you a perfect candidate for professional motherhood."

"Professional—Jesus." She was certain she felt all the blood the hot water had stirred back to life in her body drain away again. "You've got to be joking."

"Not entirely." He rose, faced her. "I want a family. It doesn't have to be now, it doesn't have to be a year from now, but I want children with you. I also want my wife back."

"Private security, families." Her eyes filled and stung again. "Just how much do you want to dump on me when I'm down?"

"I expected better of you," he said coolly and had the tears drying up.

"Better? Better of me?"

"A great deal better. What have you done the last thirty-odd hours, Eve, but cry and hide and feel sorry for yourself? Where do you expect that to get you?''

"I expected you to understand." Her voice broke and nearly undid him. "To give me some support."

"To understand you crawling away, to support your self-pity." He sipped brandy again. "No, I don't think so. It gets tiring, watching you wallow in it."

It stole her breath away, the light disgust in his voice, the disinterest in his eyes. "Just leave me alone then!" She shouted it, tossed the brandy aside so that the glass bounced and rolled as the liquor soaked the carpet. "You don't know how I feel."

"No." Finally, he thought, finally here was her fury. "Why don't you tell me?"

"I'm a goddamn cop. I can't be anything else. I busted my ass at the academy because it was the answer. It was the only way I knew to make something of myself. To finally be something that wasn't another number, another name, another victim the system sucked up and struggled with. *I* did it," she said furiously. "I made me so that nothing, *nothing* that happened before had to matter."

She whirled away. There were tears again, but these were hot and potent and full of rage. "What I didn't remember, what I did, none of it could change where I was going. Being a cop, being in control, using the system that had, by God, used me all my fucking life. From the inside, with a badge, I could believe in it again. I could make it work. I could stand for something."

"Why have you stopped?"

"They stopped me!" She spun back, her hands fisted. "Eleven years, the years that matter, when I trained and I learned and I worked to make a difference somewhere. The bodies stacked up in my mind, the blood I've waded through, and the waste. I see it in my sleep, every face of the dead. But it didn't stop me, never would have stopped me, because it matters too much. Because I can look at them and know what I have to do. And I can live with everything that happened to me, even the things I don't remember."

He nodded coolly. "Then fight back, and get what you need."

"I've got nothing. Goddamn it, Roarke, can't you see? When they took my badge, they took everything I am."

"No, Eve. They didn't take what you are unless you let them. They only took your symbols. If you need them," he continued, stepping to her, "pull yourself together, stop whining, and get them back."

She jerked away from him. "Thanks for the support." Her voice cracked like ice under a pick as she turned and walked out of the room.

Driven by temper, she stormed through the house, down to the gym. She stripped off the robe, dragged on a unisuit. Her blood blazing, she activated the combat droid and beat the shit out of it.

Upstairs, Roarke sipped brandy and grinned like a fool as he watched her on a monitor. He imagined she'd replaced the droid's face with his. "Go ahead, darling," he murmured. "Pound me into dust." He winced a little when she jammed her knee hard into the droid's crotch, felt a sympathetic twinge in his own balls.

"I guess I had that coming," he decided and made a mental note to order a new combat droid. This one was toast.

It was good progress, he mused after she'd left the mangled droid on the mat, stripped off her sweat-soaked suit, and stomped into the pool house. He counted thirty strong, steady laps when Summerset hailed him.

"I'm sorry to disturb you, but a Detective Baxter is at the gate. He wishes to see Lieutenant Dallas."

"Tell him she remains unavailable. No." On impulse, Roarke shifted gears. He was more than a little tired of doing nothing himself. "Let him in, Summerset. I'll see him. I have a few words for the NYPSD. Send him to my office."

"I'll be happy to."

Baxter was doing his best not to gawk. His mood was glum, his nerves on edge, and he'd already dealt with the

wave of reporters at the gate. Beating on the windows of
an official vehicle, for Christ's sake, he thought. Where
was the respect and the good healthy fear for cops these
days?

And now he found himself being led through a fucking
palace by a stiff-assed butler type. The place was like
something out of a video. One of his favorite pastimes
had been to razz Eve about the unlimited credit well she'd
fallen into with Roarke. Now he had all this new material
and didn't have the heart to use it.

He got another eyeful when he walked into Roarke's
office. The equipment alone was enough to make his eyes
want to pop out of his head, and the setting, acres of
treated glass, miles of glossy tiles, made him feel shabby
in his off-the-rack suit and well-broken-in shoes.

Just as well, he decided. He felt pretty damn shabby all
around.

"Detective." Roarke remained seated behind the desk,
the position of power. "Your identification?"

They'd met more than once, but Baxter simply nodded
and took out his badge. Couldn't blame the guy for being
tight-assed under the circumstances, Baxter decided. "I
need to interview Dallas regarding the Bowers homicide."

"I believe you were informed yesterday that my wife
is unavailable at this time."

"Yeah, I got the message. Look, it's got to get done.
I've got a job to do here."

"Yes, you have a job." Not bothering to disguise the
threat in his eyes, Roarke got to his feet. Every movement
precise, like a wolf stalking prey. "Eve doesn't, because
your department is quick to turn on their own. How the
hell can you stand here with that badge in your hand?
You come into her home prepared to interrogate her? You
son of a bitch, I ought to make you eat that fucking badge
and send you back to Whitney on a pike."

"You've got a right to be upset," Baxter said evenly,
"but I've got an investigation going, and she's part of
it."

"Do I seem upset, Baxter?" His eyes glinted like a

sword turned edge-up in the sun as he came around the desk. "Why don't I show you, right now, what I am?" Fast as a lightning strike, Roarke's fist shot out.

Eve walked in just as Baxter went flying. She had to leap forward to get to Baxter and block his body with hers before Roarke could follow up. "Jesus, Roarke. Are you crazy? Back off, back off. Baxter?" She tapped his cheeks, waited for his eyes to roll back into their proper position. "You okay?"

"I feel like I got hit with a hammer."

"You must've slipped." She cast aside pride and put the plea in her eyes. "Let me help you up."

He shifted his gaze to Roarke, then looked back at her. "Yeah, I must've slipped. Shit." He wiggled his aching jaw and let Eve pull him up. "Dallas, I guess you know why I'm here."

"I think I can figure it out. Let's get it over with."

"You don't speak to him without your lawyers," Roarke said. "We'll contact them and get back to you, Detective, as to when it's convenient for my wife to speak with you."

"Baxter." As she spoke, she kept her eyes on Roarke. "Give us a minute here, will you?"

"Sure, yeah, no problem. I'll just, ah, wait out there."

"Thanks." She waited until the door shut. "He's just doing his job."

"Then he can do it properly, when you're suitably represented."

With a frown, she moved closer, took his hand. "Your knuckles are going to swell. Baxter's got a head like a rock."

"It was worth it. It would have been even better if you hadn't interfered."

"Then I'd be laying bail for you." Intrigued, she cocked her head. She'd seen him furious often enough to recognize it simmering in his eyes. "Less than an hour ago, you were telling me to stop whining, and now I walk in and watch you deck the primary on the investigation that's put me here. Just where the hell do you stand, Roarke?"

"With you, Eve. Always."

"Why did you kick at me like that?"

"To piss you off." He smiled a little, cupped her chin. "It worked. You're going to need some ice on your knuckles as well."

She linked her aching fingers with his. "I killed your droid."

"Yes, I know."

"I pretended it was you."

"Yes," he said again. "I know." He took her hand, curled it into a fist and brought it to his lips. "Want to hit the real thing now?"

"Maybe." She stepped to him, into him, wrapped her arms tight around him. "Thanks."

"For?"

"For knowing me well enough to understand what I needed." She closed her eyes, pressed her face to his neck. "I think I understand you well enough to know it wasn't easy for you to do."

His arms came hard around her. "I can't stand to see you hurt this way."

"I'm going to get through it. I'm not going to be less than you expect. Or less than I expect of myself. I need you with me." She let out a breath, eased back. "I'm going to let Baxter back in. Don't hit him anymore, okay?"

"Can I watch while you hit him? You know how it excites me to see you pound on someone."

"Let's see how it goes."

chapter sixteen

When Eve let Baxter back into the room, he gave Roarke a long, wary look. "I figure I'd've done the same," was all he said, then turned to Eve. "I've got something to say before we go on record."

"Okay." She stuck her hands in her pockets, nodded. "Go ahead."

"This bites."

Her lips twitched, her shoulders relaxed. He looked a great deal more uncomfortable and unhappy than she felt. "Yeah, it does. So let's get it over with."

"You call your lawyer?"

"No." She shifted her gaze to Roarke's. "He's my rep for this little party."

"Oh fine." On a sigh, Baxter rubbed his aching jaw. "If he hits me again, I expect you to take him down." He pulled out his recorder, then just held it gripped in his hand. Misery was all over his face. "Damn it. We go back some way, you know, Dallas."

"Yeah, I know. Just do the job, Baxter. It'll be easier all around."

"Nothing easy about it," he muttered, then switched the recorder on, set it on the desk. He read off the time and date data, the revised Miranda. "You know the drill, right?"

"I know my rights and obligations." Because her legs were a little weak, she sat. It was different, she thought dully, so very different to be on this side of the line. "I want to make a statement. Then you can go for the details."

It was like a report, Eve told herself. Like any of the hundreds of reports she'd written and filed over the years.

Routine.

She would think of it that way, had to think of it that way to keep that icy ball out of her gut. Facts to be recorded. Observations to be made.

But her voice wasn't quite steady as she began. "When I responded to the scene of the Petrinksy homicide, I didn't remember Officer Ellen Bowers. Subsequently, I learned we had done some time at the academy together. I don't remember any encounters, conversations, or interactions with her before the meeting at the crime scene. Her work on-scene was inefficient, her attitude poor. As superior officer and primary on-scene, I reprimanded her for both problems. This incident is on record."

"We have Peabody's on-scene records. They're being evaluated," Baxter said.

The ball of ice tried to form, but she willed it away. And this time, her voice was stronger. "Bowers's trainee," Eve continued, "Officer Trueheart, proved to be observant and to know the residents of the area in question. I requested his assistance in interviewing a witness who was known to him, and his assistance proved helpful. This action on my part was not a personal decision but a professional one. Shortly thereafter, Officer Bowers filed a complaint against me, citing abusive language and other technical infractions. The complaint was answered."

"Those files and reports are also under evaluation." Baxter's voice was neutral, but his eyes signaled her to keep going. Get out her facts, tell her story clearly.

"Officer Bowers was again first on when I reported to the scene in the matter of Jilessa Brown. That incident is also on record and shows Bowers's insubordinant and un-professional behavior. Her accusation that I contacted her with threatening remarks will be proved groundless when voice prints are examined. And her subsequent complaint has no base. She was an irritant to me, nothing more.''

She wished she had water, just one quick sip, but didn't want to stop. ''At the time she was killed, I was en route from Central to this location. As I understand it, this time frame gives me little opportunity to have sought Bowers out and to have killed her in the manner determined to have caused her death. My log records can be checked to verify, and I will, if required, submit to truth testing and evaluation so as to aid your investigation and the closing of this case.''

Baxter looked at Eve and nodded. ''You're sure as hell making my job easier.''

''I want my life back.'' *My badge,* she thought, but didn't say it. Couldn't. ''I'll do what I have to do to get it.''

''We've got to answer motive here. Ah . . .'' His gaze shifted briefly, warily, to Roarke. He couldn't say he cared for—or trusted—the cold, blue stare that answered him. ''Bowers's logs and diaries make certain accusations regarding you and certain members of the NYPSD. Ah . . . trading sex for professional gain.''

''Have you ever known me to trade sex for anything, Baxter?'' Her tone was dry, faintly amused. She worked fiercely to make it so. ''I've managed to resist all your offers over the years.''

His color rose. ''Come on, Dallas.'' He cleared his throat when Roarke dipped his hands in his pockets and rocked back and forth on his heels. ''You know all that's just the usual bull.''

''Yeah, I know that.'' He was often a pain in the ass, she thought—not without some affection. He was also a good cop and a decent man. ''And this is unusual bull. Straight out, then. I have never offered, traded, or engaged in any sexual behavior in order to receive special treatment in training or on the job. I earned my badge, and when I wore it . . . I respected it.''

''You'll get it back.''

''We both know there's no guarantee of that.'' Misery came back, swirled in her eyes as they met his. ''But my chances are better if you find out who killed her and why. So you've got my cooperation.''

''Okay. You say you didn't remember Bowers from the academy, yet she details a number of incidents about you in various logs over nearly twelve years. Logically, there must have been some contact between you.''

''None that I'm aware of. I can't explain it, logically or otherwise.''

''She claims knowledge of your misrepresentation of evidence, of mishandling of witnesses, of falsifying reports in order to close cases and enhance your record.''

''Those are groundless accusations. I would demand to see proof.'' Temper began to inch up, washing healthy color back into her face and a steely gleam into her eyes. ''She could have written any damn thing—that she had a flaming affair with Roarke, had six of his children, and raised golden retrievers in Connecticut. Where's the proof, Baxter?'' She leaned forward, misery replaced by insult. ''I can't do anything but deny, deny, deny. I can't even face her, because somebody took her out. She can't be officially interviewed, sanctioned, or reprimanded. Is anybody asking why she was murdered and my butt left swinging when I was investigating a series of deaths certain high levels didn't want investigated?''

He opened his mouth, shut it again. ''I can't discuss departmental business with you, Dallas. You know that.''

''No, you can't discuss shit with me, but I can speculate.'' She pushed out of the chair and began to pace. ''Taking my badge doesn't mean they took my goddamn brain. If somebody wanted to cause me trouble, they didn't have to look far. Bowers fell right into their laps. Push her obsession, or whatever the hell it was she had for me, twist her up with it, then take her out in a brutal manner so the finger can point in my direction. I'm not

only off the case, I'm out. I'm out," she repeated.
"There's a new investigation, and the department's in the
middle of a media frenzy screaming corruption, sex, and
scandal that can't help but bog down the works and give
whoever's slicing out parts of people time to cover more
tracks."

She whirled back to him. "You want to close your
case, Baxter, then look at the one I had to leave behind
and find the link. There's a goddamn link, and Bowers
was nothing more than a handy tool, easily disposed of.
She meant nothing to me," she said, and for the first time,
there was some pity in her voice. "She meant less to
whoever had her killed. I was the target."

"The investigation is ongoing," Baxter reminded her.
"Feeney's got your load."

"Yeah." Considering, she nodded slowly. "They mis-
calculated there."

The rest was form, and they both knew it. Standard
questions with standard responses. She agreed to make
herself available for truth testing the following afternoon.
When Baxter left, she put the unpleasantness of that upcoming event out of her mind.

"You handled that very well," Roarke commented.

"He went easy on me. His heart wasn't in it."

"Perhaps I should have apologized for punching him."
Roarke smiled. "But my heart wouldn't have been in it."

She laughed a little. "He's a good cop. I need good
cops right now." And thinking of them, she engaged the
'link and put a transmission through to Peabody's personal porta-link.

"Dallas." Peabody's square face glowed with relief,
then immediately a cloud of concern and guilt darkened
her eyes. "You okay?"

"I've been better. Does your schedule allow for a meal
today, Peabody?"

"A meal?"

"That's right. This is a personal call on your personal
unit." Eve spoke carefully, trusting Peabody to read between the lines. "And a request, if time and inclination

permit, for you to join me at home for a meal. You're free to bring a couple of dates. If you can't fit this in, I understand.''

Barely three seconds passed. ''It so happens I'm hungry right now. I'll just round up my dates. We'll be there in less than an hour.''

''It'll be good to see you.''

''Same goes,'' Peabody murmured and broke transmission.

After a moment's hesitation, Eve turned to Roarke. ''I need data, as much as I can get, on Bowers: her personal info, all job records, and reports. I need to access Baxter's case files and bring up all he has so far on her murder. I need the ME's findings, the sweepers' reports, any and all interview records pertaining.''

While Roarke watched, she strode around the room. ''They wiped my case log at Central and here. I want that data back, and whatever Feeney's gathered since I got kicked. I don't want to ask him to copy it to me. He would, and I'm already going to ask him for more than I have a right to. I need everything I can dig on Westley Friend's suicide and who his closest associates were at the time of his death.''

''It so happens I already have that information, or most of it, for you.'' Roarke grinned at her when she turned around and stared at him. ''Welcome back, Lieutenant.'' He held out a hand to her. ''You've been missed.''

''It's good to be back.'' She went to him, took his hand. ''Roarke, however this turns out, the department may consider it more efficient damage control to . . . they may not reinstate me.''

His eyes on hers, he brushed his fingers through her hair, rubbed them firm and steady over the tension at the base of her neck. ''That would be their very great loss.''

''Whatever happens, I have to do this. I have to finish what I started. I can't walk away from the faces I see in my sleep. I can't turn my back on the job that saved me. If, after it's done, it's still over for me . . .''

''Don't think that way.''

"I have to prepare for it." Her eyes were dark and steady, but he could see fear riding in them. "I want you to know I'll get through it. I won't fall apart on you again."

"Eve." He cupped her face in his hands. "We'll make this right. Trust me."

"I am trusting you. For God's sake, Roarke, I'm going rogue. And I'm taking you with me."

He laid his lips firmly on hers. "I wouldn't have it any other way."

"You'll probably enjoy the hell out of this," she muttered. "Okay, we'd better get started. Can you do something to the computer in my office to confuse CompuGuard?"

"Is that a rhetorical question?" With a laugh, he slid an arm around her waist and started toward the connecting doors.

It took him under ten minutes. She tried not to be impressed, but the simple fact was, it baffled her just how quickly those clever fingers of his could seduce electronics and make them hum.

"You're clean and clear," he told her.

"You're sure CompuGuard won't click to it when I run NYPSD data on here?"

"If you're going to insult me, I'll just go play with my own toys and leave you alone."

"Don't be so sensitive. I could do a lot of time in a cage for this, you know."

"I'd visit you every week."

"Yeah, from the cage next door." When he only grinned at that, she shifted close. "How do I access the data?" she began, only to have him slap her hand away before she could touch the keyboard.

"Please, you're such an amateur." He danced his fingers over the keyboard. The machine hummed cooperatively, lights blinking. When a husky female computer-animated voice announced, "Transfer complete," Eve raised her eyebrows.

"What happened to the default voice on this?"

"If I'm going to be working on this unit, I get to pick who talks to me."

"You're awfully simple at times, Roarke. Now, get out of my chair. I've got work to do before they get here."

"You're welcome," he said just a bit testily, but before he could rise, she grabbed his shirt, yanked, and crushed her mouth to his in a long, hard kiss.

"Thanks."

"You're very welcome." He patted her butt as they shifted positions. "Coffee, Lieutenant?"

"A couple of gallons would be a good start." She managed a smile. "Computer, print out stills of all crime scene photos, all pertaining files. On-screen, autopsy results on Bowers, Officer Ellen."

Working . . .

"Yeah," Eve said under her breath. "We're working."

Within thirty minutes, she had hard copies of specific data tucked in a drawer and had scanned reports to bring herself up to date. She was ready when Feeney arrived with Peabody and McNab.

"I've got one thing to say," Feeney began before Eve could speak. "We're not letting it go down this way. I've said my piece to Whitney, official and personal."

"Feeney—"

"Just shut up." His usually rumpled face was tight with anger, his voice clipped. When he jabbed his finger at a chair, Eve sat automatically without even the thought of protesting. "I trained you, goddamn it, and I got a right to say what I've got to say about one of mine. You let them kick you around this way, I'll fucking kick you harder. You got a raw deal, no question. Now it's time to get your own back. If you haven't filed legal protest papers, I want to know why the hell not."

Her brow knit. "I didn't think of it."

"What? Your brain go on holiday?" He stabbed a finger at Roarke. "What the hell's the matter with you, with all your fancy lawyers and your pile of credits? You gone soft in the head, too?"

"The papers have been drawn up and are waiting for her signature, now that she's finished . . ." He shot Eve a bland smile. "Whining."

"Bite me," she suggested, "both of you."

"I told you to shut up," Feeney reminded her. "Get them in before the end of the day," he told Roarke. "Some wheels run slow. I've got my written statement, as former trainer, former partner, to add to it. Nadine's multipart feature's going to generate a lot of nice heat on top of it."

"What feature?" Eve demanded and earned a scowl from Feeney.

"Been too busy whining to watch any screen? She's put together interviews with survivors of victims from cases you closed. It's powerful stuff. One of the strongest came from Jamie Lingstrom. He talks about how his grandfather called you a right cop, one of the best, and how you put your life on the line to bring down the bastard who killed his sister. Kid was on my doorstep last night giving me grief for letting them take your badge."

Stunned, baffled, she only stared. "There was nothing you could do."

"Try telling that to a young boy who wants to be a cop, who believes the system should work. Maybe you'd like to tell him why you're sitting on your butt in this fortress doing nothing about it."

"Jesus, Captain." McNab mumbled it and fought back a wince when Feeney pinned him with a look.

"I didn't ask for comments, Detective. Didn't I teach you anything?" he demanded of Eve.

"You taught me everything." She got to her feet. "You're not usually so good at the bad cop routine, Feeney. You must've saved it up, because it's damn effective. But you wasted it. I'd already decided to stop doing nothing."

"About damn time." He pulled a bag of nuts out of his pockets, dug in. "So, what angle are you playing?"

"All of them. You need to know I intend to pursue the investigation, both on the case that was turned over to you, and the Bowers homicide. It's not a reflection on any of you, or on Baxter, but I can't sit on my hands anymore."

"About damn time," he said again. "Let me bring you up to date."

"No." She said it sharply, moving forward. "I'm not having that, Feeney. I'm not putting your badge at risk."

"It's my badge."

"I didn't ask Peabody to get all of you here so you could leak data on the investigation. I asked you to come so I could let you know what I'm doing. That's bad enough. Until the department is satisfied, I'm a murder suspect. I believe the Bowers case is connected to the one you're investigating. You need everything I've got. Not just what's in the reports, but what's in my head."

"You think I don't know your head?" Feeney snorted, crunched a nut. "I guess not since you haven't clicked to what's in mine. Get this, Dallas. I'm primary on this case. I make the decisions. As far as I'm concerned, you're key, and if you've finished twiddling your thumbs, let's get to work. Either of you got a problem with that?" he asked Peabody and McNab and received a unified "No, sir."

"You're outranked and outvoted, Dallas. Now, somebody get me some damn coffee. I'm not doing this briefing dry."

"I don't need the briefing." Eve stated. "I've got all the data."

Feeney quirked his brow at Roarke. "Well, surprise, surprise. I still want the coffee."

"I'll get it." Barely restraining herself from dancing, Peabody headed for the kitchen.

"I heard something about food," McNab commented.

"Get your own." With a sniff, Peabody disappeared into the adjoining room.

"Boy's got his mind on his stomach half the time," Feeney muttered, then grinned like a proud papa. "Never had to worry about that with you. Where do you want to start?''

"You're primary.''

"Hell I am.'' He said it comfortably and sat. "You draft in this fancy Irishman?'' he added, jerking his head in Roarke's direction.

"He comes with the package.''

Satisfied, Feeney smiled. "It's a damn good package.''

It came back to routine. She set up a board, posted the stills of the dead. On the other half she had Peabody tack stills of suspects, while she and Feeney dissected the transcripts of every interview.

She leaned forward, studying the videos of the organ wing, the research lab, and its rows of samples. "Did you cross-check these? All samples accounted for?''

"Right down the line,'' Feeney agreed. "Privately donated, brokered, or accessed through public channels.''

"What do you get out of their data reports? How do they use the samples?''

"It's thick going,'' Feeney admitted. "Seems to be straight research and study on disease and aging. It's a lot of medical mumbo.''

Yeah, she thought, and the mumbo was heavy going. "What do you think about using Louise Dimatto?''

"It's touchy,'' Feeney admitted. "We got the connection to Cagney and to the Canal Street Clinic, but all her background checks come through clean. And she cut through the muck of it when you used her.''

"I'd risk it. I don't know if she'll find anything dicey. They're organized, smart, and careful. But she'll save you time. McNab, I want you to dig in and see what series of droids Drake uses for security, then find me what manufacturers do self-destruct programs. Explosions, not shutdowns or circuit melts.''

"I can tell you that.'' He shoveled noodles into his mouth. "The last part, I mean. Private manufacture of explosives for self-destruct's illegal. It's a straight government and military deal. They used to use them for espionage droids, or antiterrorism events. Supposedly, that device was discontinued about five years ago, but nobody really believes it.''

"Because it's not true." Roarke leaned back in his chair, selected a cigarette, lighted it. "We manufacture that device for a number of governments, including the United States. As it's what you might call a one-shot deal, it's fairly profitable. Replacement units are in continual demand.''

"No private concerns?"

He acted shocked. "That, Lieutenant, would be illegal. No,'' he added, and blew out smoke. "None. And as far as I know, no other manufacturer sells under the counter privately.''

"Well, that nudges East Washington in a little tighter.'' She wondered what Nadine Furst could do if leaked the connection. Rising, she walked to the board, studied once again the picture of what had been left of Bowers.

"This looks, on the surface, like overkill. A frenzy, crime of passion. But if you look deeper and go over the autopsy report carefully, it's clear it was systematic. The killing blow came first, outside the building. A blunt instrument, long, thick and heavy, struck once, precisely on the left side of the face and head. ME confirms that this caused death. Not instantaneous, but within five minutes, and the victim would not have regained consciousness.''

"So why not leave her there and walk away?" Peabody put in.

"Exactly. Job was done. The rest was staging. Drag her inside, take her ID. She was quickly identified through prints as every cop's are on file, then her uniform and ID are found a couple of blocks away in a broken recycle unit. Planted, by my guess. But it would appear, on the surface, that taking her uniform and identification was a ploy to slow or prevent her identification.''

"You're too smart to have done that if you'd whiffed her,'' Peabody put in, then flushed when Eve gave her a hard stare. "I just meant Detective Baxter would cop to that conclusion quick enough.''

"Right. Just more staging,'' Eve went on. "Virtually

every bone in her body was broken, her fingers crushed, her face battered beyond visual recognition. While it was structured to appear that it was a vicious, mindless attack, it was precise. Programmed," she said turning back.

"A droid." Feeney nodded. "Fits."

"There was no other human element. The sweepers and crime scene team didn't find any blood but hers, no skin cells, no hair, nothing. You can't use your fists like that and not split or bruise your own skin. Whoever ordered this missed that step—or knew they wouldn't need it to get me out on a technical. They're not cops, but it's likely they own some."

Peabody's eyes popped wide. "Rosswell."

"It's a good leap." Eve nodded in approval. "He knew Bowers, worked out of the same house. He's connected to the other investigation, and he either bungled it or he's covering. Either way, he's earned a closer look. He's got a gambling problem," she added. "Let's find out how he stands financially just now."

"That would be a pleasure. Funny," Feeney considered. "He was at Central this morning. I hear Webster had him in for a chat about Bowers. He made himself pretty vocal around the Homicide bullpen from what I hear. Had some stuff to say about you. Cartright knocked him on his ass."

"Did she?" Eve beamed. "I always liked Cartright."

"Yeah, she's a right one. Caught him full in his fat gut with her elbow, knocked him flat, and then she gives him a big smile and says, 'Oops.' "

"Darling, we really must send her some flowers."

Eve slanted Roarke a glance. "That's inappropriate. Peabody, you're on Rosswell. McNab, find me some connection between East Washington and the Drake to explain the droid. Feeney, you'll contact Louise, see if she can find anything off in the organ records."

"There are likely other records."

This time Eve turned fully to Roarke. "What do you mean?"

"I mean that if, indeed, there are illegal activities of a

medical nature going on at the Drake, it's highly likely there are careful records of it somewhere. They wouldn't be on the facility's mainframe but buried on another unit.''

''How the hell do we find it?''

''I believe I can help you there. But, unless you have a specific target, it will take some time to go through this entire list of suspects.''

''I'm not going to ask how you'll do it,'' Feeney decided. ''But start with Tia Wo and Hans Vanderhaven. Wo was supposed to meet me today with her gold pin, and she never showed. Vanderhaven's taken an unscheduled leave. All we can get at this point is he's in Europe. Peabody and I were about to track both of them down when you called, Dallas.''

''If the pin found on-scene belongs to either of them, they'll try to replace it.''

''Got that covered,'' McNab assured her. ''I'm linked into all the sources in the city for that particular piece. Already doing a search on other sources in Europe if that's where the other doc flew. We'll have a record of every sale made.''

''Good coverage.''

''We'd better get started.'' Feeney rose, looked at Eve. ''What're you going to be doing while we're busting our butts?''

''Taking a quick trip. I'll be back tomorrow. Baxter's setting up a truth testing and evaluation with Mira.''

''You could put that off. We get a break, you could be clear without it in a few days.''

The faint smile she'd worked up faded. ''I'll never be clear without it.''

''You stick with level one. They can't make you go higher.''

She kept her eyes on his. ''I'll never be clear unless I go the route. You know that, Feeney.''

''Goddamn it.''

''I can handle it.'' Aware that Roarke had gotten to his

feet, she sent Feeney a warning look. "It's just routine, and Mira's the best handler there is."

"Yeah." But there was a sick feeling in his gut as he turned to grab up his coat. "Let's ride, people. We'll be in touch, Dallas. You can tag any of us, any time, on our personals."

"As soon as I know something."

"Sir." Peabody stopped in front of Eve, shifted her feet. "Hell," she muttered and grabbed Eve into a fierce hug.

"Peabody, this isn't the time to get sloppy. You're embarrassing yourself."

"If Rosswell's connected, I'm going to fry his ass."

In a quick jerk, Eve hugged back and released. "That's the spirit. Get the hell out of here. I've got places to go."

"Nobody gave me a hug," McNab complained as they headed out and made Eve snort out a laugh.

"Well." Fighting to steady her emotions, she turned back to Roarke. "Looks like we've got a plan."

His eyes fixed on her face, he came toward her. "I didn't realize there were levels of this testing process."

"Sure. It's no big deal."

"Feeney seemed to think otherwise."

"Feeney's a worrier," she said with a shrug, but when she started to turn away, Roarke took her arm.

"How bad is it?"

"It's not a cruise on airskates, okay? And I can handle it. I can't think about it now, Roarke, it'll mess up my head. Just how quick can that spiffy transpo of yours get us to Chicago?"

Tomorrow, he decided, they would damn well deal with it. But for now, he gave her the smile he knew she needed. "Just how quick can you pack?"

chapter seventeen

The sun was already dipping down in the western sky, sending shadows to droop over Chicago's jagged skyline. She saw the last glints of it shimmer and bounce off the lake.

Should she remember the lake? she wondered.

Had she been born there, or had she just passed through to spend a few nights in that cold room with the broken window? If she could stand in that same room now, how would she feel? What images would dance through her head? Would she have the courage to turn and face them?

"You're not a child now." Roarke slipped a hand over hers as the transport began its gentle descent into the Chicago Air and Space Complex. "You're not alone now, and you're not helpless now."

She continued to concentrate on breathing evenly, in and out. "It's not always comfortable to realize you can see what goes on in my head."

"It's not always easy to read your head, or your heart. And I don't care for it when they're troubled and you try to hide it from me."

"I'm not trying to hide it. I'm trying to deal with it." Because the descent always made her stomach jitter, she turned away from the view port. "I didn't come here on some personal oddessy, Roarke. I came here to gather data on a case. That's priority."

"It doesn't stop you from wondering."

"No." She looked down at their joined hands. There was so much that should have separated them, she thought. How was it nothing did? Nothing could. "When you went back to Ireland last fall, you had issues, personal issues to deal with, to face or resolve. You didn't let them get in the way of what had to be done."

"I remember my yesterdays all too clearly. Ghosts are easier to fight when you know their shape." Linking their fingers, he brought hers to his lips in a gesture that never failed to stir her. "You never asked me where I went the day I went off alone."

"No, because I saw when you came back you'd stopped grieving so much."

His lips curved against her knuckles. "So, you read my head and heart fairly well, yourself. I went back to where I lived as a boy, back to the alley where they found my father dead, and some thought I'd put the knife in him. I lived with the regret that it hadn't been my hand that ended him."

"It's not a thing to regret," she said quietly as the transport touched down with barely a whisper.

"There we part ways, Lieutenant." His voice, so beautiful with that Irish lilt, was cold and final. "But I stood there, in that stinking alley, smelling the smells of my youth, feeling that same burn in the blood, the fire in the belly. And I realized, standing there, that some of what I'd been was still inside me and always will be. But there was more." Now his voice warmed again, like whiskey in candlelight. "I'd made myself different. Other, you could say. I'd made myself other, and it was you who's made me more."

He smiled again as blank surprise filled her eyes. "What I have with you, darling Eve, I never thought to have with anyone. Never thought to want it or need it. So I realized as I stood there in an alley where he must have beaten me black a dozen times or more, where he'd laid drunk and finally dead, that what mattered about what had come before was that it had led me to where I was. That he hadn't won, after all. He'd never won a bloody thing from me.''

He flipped the catch on her safety harness, then his own, while she said nothing. ''When I walked away through the rain, I knew you'd be there. You have to know that whenever you decide to look into your own, whatever you find, when you walk away from it, I'll be there.''

Emotions swirled inside her, filling her to bursting. ''I don't know how I managed to get through a day before you.''

It was his turn to look surprised. He drew her to her feet. ''Ah, every once in a while you manage to say the perfect thing. Steady now?''

''Yeah, and I'm staying that way.''

Because power clears paths and money waxes them smooth, they were through the jammed shuttle terminal in minutes and out to the private valet area where he had a car waiting.

She took one look at the sleek silver torpedo shape with its elaborate and streamlined two-seater cockpit and scowled. ''Couldn't you have booked something a little less conspicuous?''

''I don't see why we should be inconvenienced. Besides,'' he added as they climbed in, ''this thing drives like a fucking rocket.'' So saying, he engaged the engine, hit the accelerator, and blasted out of the lot.

''Jesus, Jesus, Jesus, slow down! You maniac.'' She struggled into her harness as he laughed. ''The airport cops will tag your ass before we clear the first gate.''

''Have to catch me first,'' he said cheerfully. He punched a control, sent them into a screaming vertical lift that had her mixing curses and prayers. ''You can open your eyes now, darling, we're clear of airport traffic.''

Her stomach was still somewhere around her ankles. ''Why do you do things like that?''

"Because it's fun. Now, why don't you program in the address of this retired cop you want to talk to, and we'll see which is the best route."

She opened one eye, saw they were horizontal again and zipping smoothly along a six-lane thruway. Still scowling, she started to search the glossy dash for the destination and map feature.

"It's voice controlled, Eve. Just engage the computer and give it your destination of choice."

"I knew that," she snapped. "I was just looking. I want to have a clear picture of the place where we're going to die when you crash this toy and kill us dead."

"The Stargrazer 5000X is loaded with safety and life support systems," he said mildly. "As I helped design it, I'm fully aware of all of them."

"Yeah, that just figures. Engage computer."

Computer engaged. How may I assist you?

As it was the same husky female voice he'd installed in her home unit, Eve felt obliged to give him a baleful stare. "Who the hell is this?"

"You don't recognize it, do you?"

"Should I?"

"It's you, darling. After sex."

"Get out."

He laughed again, a quick rumble of amusement. "Get the directions, Lieutenant, before we end up in Michigan."

"That isn't my voice," she muttered, but began to worry about it as she read off the address.

A holographic map shimmered into place on the windscreen, the most direct route blinking in red.

"Isn't that handy?" Roarke commented. "This is our exit."

The sudden sharp turn at ninety miles an hour had Eve jerking back in the seat. She would hurt him later, she promised herself as he careened down the ramp. Hurt him really, really bad.

If they lived long enough.

Wilson McRae lived in a tidy white house in a line of other tidy white houses, all centered on thumb-sized lawns. Each driveway was a glossy black, and though the grass was winter withered, it was trimmed neatly and un-cluttered.

The road ran straight as a ruler with young maple trees planted every twelve feet.

"It's like something out of a horror video," Eve commented.

"Darling, you're such an urbanite."

"No, really. There was this one where aliens invade, you know, undercover and all, and they'd—what do you call it—zombiedized the people. So they all dressed alike and walked alike. Ate the same stuff at the same time of day."

Her gaze shifted from house to house suspiciously while Roarke looked on in amusement. "They're kind of like . . . hives, you know? Don't you expect to see all these doors open at exactly the same moment and have people who look exactly the same way walk out of these exactly the same houses?"

He sat back in the snazzy car and studied her. "Eve, you're scaring me."

"See?" She laughed as she climbed out her side. "Creepy place, if you ask me. I bet you don't even know you're being zombiedized when it's happening."

"Probably not. You go first."

She snickered and didn't feel the least foolish to have her hand linked with his as they started up the perfectly straight walkway to the white door. "I got the personal background on him. Nothing jars. Eight years married, one kid and another on the way. House is mortgaged and well within their financial scope. I couldn't find any sudden influx of income to indicate he'd been paid off."

"You're banking that he's straight."

"I've got to hope he is and can give me a handle. I don't have any authority," she added. "He doesn't have to talk to me. I can't check in with the local cops, I can't use any cop-to-cop pressure."

"Try charm," Roarke suggested.

"You're the one with the charm."

"True. Try anyway."

"How's this?" She smiled winningly.

"You're scaring me again."

"Smart-ass," she muttered and when she rang the bell and heard the echo of three cheery chimes, rolled her eyes. "Man, I would self-terminate before I lived in a place like this. I bet all their furniture matches, and they've got cute little cows or something sitting around the kitchen."

"Kittens. Fifty says it's kittens."

"Bet. Cows are sillier. It's going to be cows." She tried the smile, slightly less winning, when the door opened. A pretty woman leading with her hugely pregnant belly answered.

"Hello. Can I help you?"

"I hope so. We'd like to speak with Wilson McRae."

"Oh, he's down in his workshop. Can I tell him what this is about?"

"We've come from New York." Now that she was here, facing big, curious brown eyes, Eve wasn't sure how to begin. "It's in reference to one of your husband's cases, before he retired from the force."

"Oh." Her dark eyes clouded. "You're cops? Come in, I'm sorry. Will so rarely sees any of his associates anymore. I think he misses them terribly. If you don't mind waiting in the living room? I'll go down and get him."

"She didn't ask to see ID." Eve shook her head as she wandered the living room. "A cop's wife, and she lets strangers into the house. What's wrong with people?"

"They should be shot for being so trusting."

She sent him a slanted look. "This from the guy with enough security to keep alien invaders out of his house."

"You're awfully hung up on aliens today."

"It's this place." Restless, she moved her shoulders. "Didn't I tell you? Everything matches." She poked a finger into the tidy cushion of the blue and white sofa that matched the blue and white chair that matched the white curtains and blue rug.

"I imagine it's a comfort to some people." He cocked his head as he studied her. She needed a quick round with her hairdresser, and though she was in desperate need of new boots, he knew she wouldn't even consider it. She looked long, lean, edgy, and just a little dangerous pacing around the solid suburban room. "You, on the other hand, would go mad here."

She jingled the loose credits in her pockets. "Oh yeah. What about you?"

"I'd make a break for it in about two hours." He reached up to skim his finger down her chin. "But I'd take you with me, darling."

She grinned at him. "I guess that means we match. That doesn't bother me."

She turned when she heard voices. She didn't have to see Wilson McRae to understand he wasn't terribly pleased to have company. He came in just ahead of his now frazzled looking wife with his mouth set in a dissatisfied frown, his eyes wary.

All cop, Eve decided on the spot. He was sizing them up, scanning for threat or weapon and braced to defend.

She judged him at just under six feet, a well-built one eighty. His light brown hair was cut ruthlessly short over a square, sturdy face. Shades darker than his hair, his eyes stayed cool as they skimmed from her to Roarke and back.

"My wife didn't get your names."

"Eve Dallas." She didn't offer her hand. "This is Roarke."

"Roarke?" It piped out of the woman just before color flooded her face. "I thought I recognized you. I've seen you on-screen dozens of times. Oh, please, sit down."

"Karen." With one quiet word he had her subsiding, in obvious distress and puzzlement. "You a cop?" he asked Roarke.

"No, indeed not." He laid a hand on Eve's shoulder. "She's the cop."

"Out of New York," Eve continued. "I need some of your time. A case I've been working on crosses one you had before you retired."

"That's the operative word." She caught resentment mixed in the wariness in his tone. "I'm *retired.*"

"Yeah." She kept her eyes steady and level on him. "Just recently, someone's been wanting to see me retire. One way or the other. Could be a . . . medical thing."

His eyes flickered, his mouth tightened. Before he could speak, Roarke stepped forward and aimed a charming smile at Karen. "Ms. McRae, I wonder if I could trouble you for some coffee? My wife and I drove straight in from the airport."

"Oh, of course. I'm so sorry." Her hands fluttered up from their resting place on her belly to her throat. "I'll make some right away."

"Why don't I help you?" With a smile in place that could have melted a woman's heart at fifty paces, he put a gentle hand on the small of her back. "We'll let our respective spouses talk shop. You have a lovely home."

"Thank you. Will and I have been putting it together for nearly two years now."

As their voices faded, Will never took his eyes off Eve's. "I'm not going to be able to help you."

"You don't know what I want or what I need. Yet. I can't show you ID, McRae, because they took my badge a few days ago." She watched his eyes narrow. "They found a way to get me out, off the case, so I figure I was getting close to something. Or they just didn't like the heat. And I figure they found a way to get you out and have that asshole Kimiki take over the investigation."

Will snorted, and some of the wariness faded. "Kimiki can barely find his own dick with both hands."

"Yeah, I got that. I'm a good cop, McRae, and their mistake this time was another good cop's got the case now. We've got three bodies in New York with parts missing. You had one here, same MO. There's another in

Paris, one in London. We're still running like crimes.''

"I can't help you, Dallas."

"What'd they use on you?"

"I've got a family." He said it, low and fierce. "A wife, a five-year-old son, a baby on the way. Nothing happens to them. Nothing. You get that?"

"Yeah." She got something else, too. Fear that wasn't for himself. Frustration at being helpless against it. "Nobody knows I'm here, and nobody's going to know. I'm on my own in this, and I'm not letting go."

He walked past her to the window, smoothed the pretty white curtains. "You got kids?"

"No."

"My boy, he's spending a couple of days with Karen's mother. She's due any day. The kid's amazing. Beautiful." He turned, gestured with a jerk of his head to a framed holoprint on the end table.

Obligingly, Eve moved over, lifted it, and studied the cheerfully grinning face. Big brown eyes, dusty blond hair, and dimples. Kids mostly looked the same to her. Cute, innocent, and unfathomable. But she knew the response expected of her. "He's a beaut, all right."

"They said they'd do him first."

Eve's fingers tightened on the frame before she set it carefully down again. "They contacted you?"

"Set a fucking droid on me. Caught me by surprise, knocked me around some. I don't give a shit about that." He whirled back. "Told him to tell his keeper to go to hell. I did the job, Dallas. Then the droid explains just what'll happen to my family, my little boy, my wife, the baby she's carrying. Scared me bloodless. So I figure I'll send them away, do the job, get these bastards. Then I get pictures in the mail, pictures of Karen and Will, coming out of a toy store, the market, playing in the yard at my mother's, where I sent them. And one of that fucking droid holding Will. Holding him," he said in a voice pitched low but vibrating with vicious fury. "He had his hands on my son. Message that came with it said the next time they'd cut out his heart. He's five years old."

He sat, buried his head in his hands. "Sometimes the badge can't come first."

She understood love now, and the terror it could bring to you. "Did you tell your boss?"

"I didn't tell anybody. It's been eating at me for months." He sat, continued to lean over, while his fingers kept raking through his close-cropped hair. "I'm working private security at night, playing down in that idiot workshop half the day making birdhouses. I'm going crazy here."

Eve sat beside him, leaned in. "Help me get them. Help me put them away where they can't touch your family."

"I can't ever go back to the job." He lowered his hands. "I can't ever pick up a badge again. And I can't be sure just how far they can reach out."

"Nothing you tell me goes in a report, official or otherwise. Tell me about the droid; give me a line here."

"Hell." He rubbed his eyes. For weeks he'd lived with doing nothing, with backing down, with the fear. "Six two, two ten. Caucasian, brown and brown. Sharp features. Top-line model. Combat trained."

"I met his brother," she said with a thin smile. "What buttons were you pushing when the threats started?"

"I'd shaken out some slime from the black market, but it wasn't going anywhere. Nothing I'd run on the victim turned up anything that made it look like a personal hit. I went in circles awhile, but I kept coming back to how it was done. So goddamn neat, right?"

"Yeah, very neat and tidy."

"There's a free clinic a few blocks from the crime scene. The victim had been in there a few times. I interviewed the rotation doctors, ran them. It looked like a dead end, too. But it didn't feel like one," he added, relaxing a little when Eve nodded.

"I started circling out, hitting other med centers, cross-checking surgeons. I started scratching at the Nordic Clinic, and the next thing I know, the boss calls me in and says that fathead Waylan's making noises about harassment, entrapment, Christ knows what, and demanding that we show some respect for the medical community. Shit.''

"Waylan. He cropped up on my watch, too.''

"Damn embarrassment to the state,'' Will began. "Karen's the one who gets into politics. Don't get her started on Waylan.'' For the first time, he grinned, and his face looked abruptly younger. "In this house, we hate him. Anyhow, I figured there was something there, too. What the hell does he care—except he's got relatives in the AMA. I'm starting to check it out, then I'm blind-sided, flat on my back, and the goddamn droid's got a laser at my throat.''

He sighed, rose to pace. "I was going to tell my boss, put it in the report, but on my next shift, I get called upstairs. Commander tells me that there's more com-plaints about the tone of my investigation. I'm not getting support from the brass; instead, they're warning me to watch my step, don't step on the wrong toes. Ease back, it was only scum that got taken out, anyway. Don't hassle nice people. Rich, powerful people,'' McRae said, turning back. "Pissed me off. That's when I decided to send my family away and dig in deeper. Until I got the pictures, then I folded. Faced with the same choice, I'd do the same thing again.''

"I'm not going to beat you up over it, Will. I don't have what you have to risk. The way I look at it, you took it as far as you could, for as long as you could.''

"I gave up my badge.'' His voice cracked, and she watched him suck it in. "They took yours.''

He needed something, she thought, and worked up a smile for him. "We got fucked either way, didn't we.''

"Yeah. We got fucked royal, Dallas.''

"I'm going to ask you to give me anything you can, and maybe we can return the favor. Did you copy any of your files?''

"No. But I remember a lot of it. I've been going over the details in my head for months. I've written some of it down for myself.'' He glanced over his shoulder as he heard his wife's voice. "Karen doesn't know anything about this. I don't want her upset."

"Give me the name of somebody you put away who's been sprung."

"Drury. Simon Drury."

"I'm here about Drury." She glanced over, lifted a brow as Roarke strolled in carrying a tray loaded with cups, plates. Coffee and cookies, she mused, then struggled with a scowl as she noted the cream pitcher in the shape of a cheerful white kitten.

The man never lost a damn bet.

"Looks great." She helped herself to a cookie, mildly fascinated by the way Karen had to maneuver her body, shift her spectacular belly in order to sit down. How, Eve wondered, did a woman function on any level hauling all that bulk around?

Noting where Eve's gaze had focused, Karen smiled and stroked a hand over the mound. "I'm due today."

Eve choked on the cookie. If Karen had whipped out a laser on full and blasted it in her direction, she'd have felt less panic. "Today? Like now?"

"Well, not this minute, apparently." Laughing, Karen sent Roarke an adoring look as he served her tea. Quite obviously, they'd bonded between cookies and kittens. "But I don't think she's going to wait much longer."

"I guess you'll be glad to—you know—get it out of there."

"I can't wait to meet her—hold her. But I love being pregnant."

"Why?"

She laughed again at Eve's obvious puzzlement, then shared a tender look with her husband. "Making a miracle."

"Well." Since that dried up her pregnancy conversation, Eve turned back to Will. "We don't want to take up any more of your time. I appreciate the help. If you could get me any of your old notes on Drury, I'd be grateful."

"I can dig them out." He rose, paused by his wife to lay a hand over hers, linking them over their child.

• • •

At Eve's request, Roarke drove aimlessly while she filled him in on her conversation with Wilson McRae.

"Do you blame him?"

She shook her head. "Everyone has their own, what do you call it, Achilles' heel. They found his and put the pressure on. Guy's got a kid, another on the way, a pretty little wife in a pretty little house. They knew just where to jam him."

"She's a teacher." Roarke cruised the freeway under the flood of safety lights and kept the speed steady. "She's been working on-screen for the last six months and plans to continue that way for at least another year or two. But she misses the personal contact with her students. She's a very sweet woman who's worried about her husband."

"How much does she know?"

"Not all, but more, I believe, than he thinks. Will he go back when you close the case?"

Not *if,* she noted, but *when.* It bolstered the heart to have someone with so much faith in her. More faith, she realized, than she had in herself just now. "No. He'll never get past giving it up. They stole that from him. And sometimes you never get back everything."

She closed her eyes a moment. "Will you drive downtown? I need to look. I need to see if I remember."

"There's no need to take on more now, Eve."

"Sometimes you never get rid of everything, either. I need to look."

Another city, she thought, with some of its old stone and brick desperately preserved, and so much of it crumbled to dust to make room for sleek steel and quick prefab.

There would be snazzy restaurants and clubs, slick hotels and glittering shops in the areas where the power board wanted the tourists, and their I'm-on-vacation money, to congregate. And there would be sex joints, dives, scarred units, and alley filth in others where only the doomed and the foolish gathered.

It was there Roarke drove the gleaming silver car

through the narrow streets, where the lights pumped in hard colors and promised all the darker delights. Street LCs shivered on corners and hoped for a trick to take them out of the wind. Dealers prowled, angling for a mark, ready to do business at discounted rates because the cold kept all but the desperately addicted inside.

Sidewalk sleepers huddled inside their cribs, drank their brew, and waited for morning.

"Stop here," she murmured it, squinting at a corner building with bricks pitted and laced with graffiti. The lower windows were barred and blocked with wood. It called itself Hotel South Side in a sign that blinked jerkily in watery blue.

She got out, staring up at the windows. Some were cracked, all were blackened with cheap privacy screens. "Too much the same," she said quietly. "All these places are too much the same. I don't know."

"Do you want to go in?"

"I don't know." As she dragged a hand over her face, through her hair, a lanky man with icy eyes moved out of the shadows.

"Looking for action? Need a boost? You got some jingles, I got what you need. Prime Zeus, Ecstasy, Zoner. Mix or match."

Eve flicked him a glance. "Back off, creep, or I'll pop your eyes out of your head and make you eat them."

"Hey, bitch, you're on my turf, you get some manners." He'd already tagged the car, and figured his marks as stupid, rich tourists. He flipped out his pocket blade, grinning as he tipped the killing point. "Let's have the wallets and jewelry and all that good shit. We'll call it even."

She took a second to debate whether to kick his teeth in or restrain him for the beat cop. A second was all Roarke needed. With her mouth pursed, Eve watched his fist flash out, a fast flurry of movement that had the knife skittering down the sidewalk. She didn't have time to blink before he had the dealer by the throat two inches off the ground.

"I believe you called my wife a bitch."

The only response was a wheezing gag as the man struggled like a landed trout. Merely shaking her head, Eve strolled over, scooped up the knife, folded the blade back in place.

"Now," Roarke continued in a mild, amazingly pleasant voice, "if *I* pop your eyes out, I get to eat them. If I still see you, say, five seconds after I toss your pitiful ass aside, I'm going to have a hell of an appetite."

He bared his teeth in a grin, heaved. The dealer hit the sidewalk with a rattle of bones, scrambled up, and took off in a limping sprint.

"Now." Fastidiously, Roarke dusted off his hands. "Where were we?"

"I liked the part about you eating his eyes. I'll have to use that one." She slipped the knife into her pocket, kept her hand over it. "Let's go in."

There was a single yellow light in the lobby, and a single burly droid behind the smeared security glass. He eyed them balefully, jerked a thumb at the rate sign.

For a dollar a minute, you got a room with a bed. For two, you got the additional amenity of a toilet.

"Third floor," Eve said briefly. "East corner."

"You get the room I give you."

"Third floor," she said again. "East corner."

His gaze lowered to the hundred dollar credit Roarke flipped into the tray. "Don't mean a shit to me." He reached behind, took a key code from a rack. His fingers snagged the credit, then tossed down the key. "Fifty minutes. You go over, you pay double."

Eve took the key for 3C, relieved to see her hand was still steady. They took the stairs.

It wasn't familiar, yet it was painfully familiar. Narrow steps, dirty walls, thin sounds of sex and misery seeping through them. Cold, from the wind battering the brick and glass, reached down and froze the bones.

She said nothing as she slipped the key into the slot, pushed the door open.

The air was bitter and stale, with echoes of sweat and

sex. The sheets on the bed shoved into the corner were stained with both and the rusty shadows of old blood.

With the breath strangling in her throat, she stepped inside. Roarke closed the door behind them, waited.

A single window, cracked. But so many were. The old floor, slanted and scarred. But she'd seen hundreds like it. Her legs trembled as she made herself walk across it, stand at that window and stare out.

How many times, she wondered, had she stood at windows in filthy little rooms and imagined herself leaping out, letting her body fall, feeling it smash and break on the street below? What had held her back, time after time, made her face the next day and the next?

How many times had she heard the door open and prayed to a God she didn't understand to help her. To spare her. To save her.

"I don't know if this is the room. There were so many rooms. But it was one like it. It's not so different from the last room, in Dallas. Where I killed him. But I was younger here. That's all I know for sure. I get a faded image of myself in my head. And of him. His hands around my throat."

Absently, she reached up, soothed the memory of the ache. "Over my mouth. The shock of him pushing himself inside me. Not knowing, not knowing at first, what that meant. Except pain. Then you know what it means. You know you can't stop it. And as much as it hurts when he beats you, you hope when you hear the door open that's all he'll do. Sometimes it is."

Eyes closed now, she rested her brow on the cracked glass. "I thought maybe I'd remember something from before. Before it all started. I had to come from somewhere. Some woman had to carry me inside her the way Karen's carrying her goddamn miracle. For God's sake, how could she leave me with him?"

He turned her, wrapped his arms around her, drew her in. "She might not have had a choice."

Eve swallowed back the grief and the rage, and finally the questions. "You always have a choice." She stepped back, but kept her hands on his shoulders. "None of this matters now. Let's go home."

chapter eighteen

There wasn't any point in pretending to unwind. Nor was there any point in thinking about what she had to face the next day. Work was the answer. Before she could tell Roarke her intentions, he was making arrangements to have a meal sent up to his private office.

"It makes more sense to use that equipment," he said simply. "It's faster, more efficient, and more thoroughly cloaked." He arched a brow. "That's what you want, isn't it?"

"Yeah. I want to tag Feeney first," she began as they started upstairs. "Fill him in on my conversation with McRae."

"I'll input the disc he gave you while you're doing that, do a quick cross-reference."

"You're almost as good as Peabody."

He stopped at the door, grabbed her up in a steaming kiss. "You can't get that from Peabody."

"I could if I wanted." But it made her grin as he uncoded the locks. "But I like you better for sex."

"I'm relieved to hear it. Use the minilink. It's fully jammed and untraceable."

"What's one more com-tech violation?" she muttered.

"That's what I always say." He sat behind the console, slid into the U, and got to work.

"Feeney, Dallas. I'm back from Chicago."

"I was just about to tag you. We got a hit on the lapel pin."

"When?"

"Just came in. Gold caduceus purchased less than one hour ago at Tiffany's, charged to the account of Dr. Tia Wo. I'm picking Peabody up for a little overtime. We're going to go have a chat with the doctor."

"Good. Great." Everything inside her yearned to be there at the sticking point. "You track Vanderhaven?"

"He's skipping around Europe. He's not landing. You ask me, he's running."

"He can't run forever. I'm about to run some data I got from a source in Chicago. I'll see what else we can find on her. Anything looks like weight, I'll pass it through Peabody's personal."

"We'll fill you in when we're done. I've got to get moving here."

"Good luck."

He was already gone. She stared for a moment at the black screen, then shoved away from the console. "Goddamn it."

She hissed, balled her fists, then snarled when the AutoChef beeped to signal meal delivery. "It's a pisser all right," Roarke murmured.

"It's stupid. The point is to close the case, not to be the one to snap the locks on it."

"The hell it isn't."

She looked at him, shrugged violently, then strode across the room to get the food. "Well, I've just got to get over it." She grabbed a plate, dropped it noisily on a table. "I *will* get over it. When this is done, I might just let you pay me a maxibus load of money to refine your security. The hell with them."

He left the computer doing its scan and rose to pour wine. "Mmm-hmm," was his only comment.

"Why the hell should I bust my ass the way I do? Work

with equipment that's not fit for the recycling heap, play politics, take orders, log in eighteen-hour days, to have them spit in my face.''

"It's a puzzle all right. Have some wine."

"Yeah." She took the glass, gulped down a healthy swallow of six-hundred-dollar-a-bottle wine like tap water, and continued to prowl. "I don't need their stinking regulations and procedures. Why the hell should I spend my life walking through blood and shit? Fuck all of them. Is there any more of this?" she demanded, gesturing with her empty glass.

If she meant to get drunk, he decided, he could hardly blame her. But she'd blame herself. "Why don't we have a little food to go with it?"

"I'm not hungry." She spun around. The gleam that came into her eyes was a flash, dangerous and dark. She was on him in one leap, fast and rough, with her hands dragging at his hair and her mouth brutal.

"That seems hungry enough to me." He murmured it, his hands skimming down her to soothe. "We'll eat later." So saying, he jabbed a mechanism and had the bed sliding out of the wall seconds before they fell onto it.

"No, not that way." She strained, bucking under him as his mouth shifted to her throat to nibble. She reared up, sank her teeth into his shoulder, tore at his shirt. "This way."

The hot stream of lust flooded through him, clawed at his throat and loins. In one rough move, he caged her wrists in his hand and yanked her arms over her head.

Even as she struggled for freedom, he crushed his mouth to hers, devouring, taking greedy swallows of her ragged breaths until they turned to moans.

"Let go of my hands."

"You want to use, but you'll take what I give you now." He leaned back, his eyes wildly blue and burning into hers. "And you won't think of anything but what I'm doing to you." With his free hand, he opened the buttons of her shirt, one at a time, letting his fingertip graze flesh as he moved from one to the next, as he exposed her. "If you're afraid, tell me to stop." His hand cupped her breast, covered, molded. Possessed.

"I'm not afraid of you." But she trembled, nonetheless, her breath catching as he circled his thumb, light, whisper light, over her nipple until it seemed every nerve in her body was centered just there. "I want to touch you."

"You need to be pleasured." He dipped his head, licked delicately at her nipple. "You need to go where I can take you. I want you naked." He flipped open the button of her jeans, slid his hand down, scraped his nails lightly over her so that she arched against him helplessly. Quivered. "I want you writhing." He lowered his head, took the sensitized point of her breast gently in his teeth, bit down with an exquisite control that sent her heart hammering against that marvelous mouth. "And later . . . screaming," he said and sent her stumbling over the edge with teeth and fingers.

Flames burst in her body, seared her mind clean as glass. There was nothing but the feel of his hands and mouth on her, the violent glory of being driven slowly, thoroughly, then brutally to peak again and again while her trapped hands flexed helplessly, then finally went limp.

There was nothing he couldn't take from her. Nothing she wouldn't give. The sensation of his skin sliding and slipping over hers made her breath catch, her heart stutter.

He dazed her, delighted and destroyed her.

He knew there was nothing, nothing more arousing than the surrender of a strong woman, that melted-bone yielding of a tough body. He took, tender and patient until he felt her float, heard her sigh. Then, ruthless and greedy, so that she shuddered and moaned. The arrow point of purpose now was to pleasure her. To make that long, limber body pulse and glow. To feed it as he fed on it.

He dragged her clothes aside, spread her wide. And feasted.

Her breath sobbed out, became his name repeated mindlessly, again and again, as she came in a long, hot gush. Her hands, free now, clutched and clawed at the sheets, at his hair, his shoulders. The desire to taste him was a desperate ache. The blood burned in her head, hammered her heart toward pain.

She reared up, bowed back as his mouth began to travel up her, scraping teeth against her hip, sliding tongue along her torso. Then she was rolling with him, her fingers digging into damp flesh, scraping viciously along the muscled ridge of his shoulders, her mouth wild and willful as it found his.

With one hard thrust, he was deep inside her, with each violent plunge, he seemed to go deeper, stroking into her fast and fierce. Still, the thirst couldn't be slaked.

Once again her body bowed, forming a bridge with muscles quivering from strain and pleasure. His fingers dug into her hips, his eyes were slits of wicked blue that never left her face.

Her body gleamed with sweat. Her head thrown back in full abandon as she absorbed each violent stroke. He watched it build one last time, felt the power of it swarming into her, into him, that surge of outrageous energy, the one shivering stab of fear that came when control was about to snap.

"Scream." He panted it out with the madness of her swallowing him whole. "Scream now."

And when she did, he went blind and emptied himself into her.

He'd bruised her. He could see the marks of his own fingers on her skin as she lay facedown on the rumpled bed. Her skin had a surprising delicacy she was never aware of and that he forgot at times. There was such toughness under it.

When he started to draw the sheet over her, she stirred. "No, I'm not sleeping."

"Why don't you?"

She shifted, balled the pillow under her head. "I did want to use you."

He sat beside her, sighed heavily. "Now I feel so cheap."

She turned her head to look at him, nearly managed a smile. "I guess it's okay, since you got off on it."

"You're such a romantic, Eve." He gave her a playful swat on the butt and rose. "Do you want to eat in bed or while you work?"

He glanced back from the AutoChef, intending on heating up their meal. Seeing her studying him with narrowed eyes, he lifted a brow. "Again?"

"I don't think about sex every time I look at you." She scooped back her hair and wondered idly if she had any clothes left that could still be worn. "Even if you are naked and built and just finished fucking my brains out. Where are my pants?"

"I have no idea. Then what were you thinking?"

"About sex," she said easily, and, finding her jeans inside out and tangled, tried to unknot them. "Philosophically."

"Really." He left the plates warming and came back to search out his own trousers, making do with only them as she'd already confiscated his shirt. "And what is your philosophical opinion of sex?"

"It really works." She hitched on her jeans. "Let's eat."

She plowed her way through a rare steak and delicate new potatoes while she studied the data on-screen. "The first thing we have are connections. Cagney and Friend in the same class at Harvard Medical. Vanderhaven and Friend consulting at the center in London sixteen years ago, at the Paris center four years ago." She chewed, swallowed, cut more beef. "Wo and Friend serving on the same board and working the same surgical floor at Nordick in '55, then her continuing to be affiliated with that clinic to the present. Waverly and Friend both officers of the AMA. And Friend regularly consulting at the Drake where Waverly is attached, and has been attached for nearly a decade."

"And," Roarke continued, topping off their wine-glasses, "you can follow the pattern deeper and connect the dots. Every one of them meshes in some manner with another. Links to links. I imagine you can expand and find the same incestual type of relationship in the European centers.''

"I'm going to have McNab do the match, but yeah, we'll find other names.'' The wine was cool and dry and perfect for her mood. "Now, we have Tia Wo, who does regular consults at Nordick. McRae was checking public transpo to see if she'd traveled to Chicago on or around the date of his murder. He didn't find anything but that doesn't mean it isn't there.''

"I'm ahead of you,'' Roarke told her and ordered up new data. "No records of private or public transportation tickets in her name, but that wouldn't include the mass shuttle that goes back and forth hourly between the two cities. You just need credit tokens. I have her schedule at Drake showing she had rounds on the afternoon of that date. Should have been finished by four o'clock. I'm pulling up her office log now.''

"I won't be able to use it. I mean, Feeney won't be able to use that data. He'll need a warrant.''

"I don't. Her security's rather pathetic,'' Roarke added as he finessed controls. "A five-year-old hacker with a toy scanner could break this. On-screen,'' he ordered.

"Okay, rounds until four, office consult four-thirty. Logged out at five, and has a six o'clock dinner with Waverly and Cagney. Feeney can check to see if she kept that appointment, but even if she did, it would give her time. She didn't have anything the next day until eight-thirty A.M., and that's a lab consult with Bradley Young. What do we know about him?''

"What would you like to know? Computer, all available data on Young, Dr. Bradley.''

Eve pushed away from her plate and rose while the computer worked. "Dinner with Cagney and Waverly. Cagney put pressure on Mira to shuffle the case back or drop it. Waverly just struck me wrong. There's more than one person involved in this deal. Could be the three of them. They have a dinner meeting, discuss the when and how. One or all of them head over to Chicago, do the job, come back. Then Wo transports the sample to Young in the lab.''

''It's as good a theory as any. What you need is to find the buried records. We'll work on that.''

''Vanderhaven rabbits to Europe rather than face a routine interview. So . . . how many of them?'' Eve murmured. ''And when did it start? Why did it start? What's the motive? That's the hang-up here. What's the point? One rogue doctor who'd gone over the edge would be one thing. That's not what we've got. We've got a team, a group, and that group has ties to East Washington, maybe to the NYPSD. Weasels, anyway, in my department, maybe others. In health clinics. Somebody passing data. I need the why to find the who.''

''Organs, human. No real money in them today. If not for profit,'' Roarke mused, ''then for power.''

''What kind of power can you get from stealing flawed organs out of street people?''

''A power trip,'' he said with a shrug. ''I can, therefore I do. But if not for power, then for glory.''

''Glory? Where's the glory?'' Impatient, she began to prowl again. ''They're useless. Diseased, dying, defective. Where's the glory factor?'' Before he could speak, she held up a hand, eyes going to slits in concentration. ''Wait, wait. What if they're not useless. If someone's figured out something that can be done with them.''

''Or to them,'' Roarke suggested.

''To them.'' She turned back to him. ''Every bit of data I've scanned says that all research points to the impracticality or impossibility of reconstruction or repair of seriously damaged organs. Artificial are cheap, efficient, and outlast the body. The major facilities we're dealing with haven't funded research in that area in years. Since Friend developed his implants.''

''A better mousetrap,'' Roarke suggested. ''Someone's always looking for better, quicker, cheaper, fancier. The one who invents it,'' he added gesturing with his wine. ''Gets the glory—and the profit.''

"How much do you make annually on the NewLife line?"

"I'll have to check. One minute." He shifted in his chair, called up another unit, and ordered a financial spread. "Hmmm, gross or net?"

"I don't know. Net, I guess."

"Just over three billion annually."

"Billion? Billion? Jesus, Roarke, how much money do you have?"

He glanced back at her, amused. "Oh, somewhat more than that, although this particular three billion isn't my personal take. One does have to feed the company, you know."

"Forget I asked, it just makes me nervous." She waved her hand and paced. "Okay, you take in three billion every year on the manufacture of the implants. When Friend developed it, he got plenty of glory. Tons of media, hype, awards, funding, whatever it is these guys get off on. He got it in truckloads. And he got a cut of the pie, too. It's his—what did you call it?—mousetrap. So . . ."

She trailed off, working it out in her head while Roarke watched her. It was, he thought, a delight to see her gears meshing. Oddly arousing, he mused, sipping his wine, and decided he would have to seduce her, in an entirely different manner, when they were finished for the night.

"So somebody, or a group of them, hits on a new technique, a new angle, using flawed organs. They've found, or nearly found, a way to buff them up and pop them back in. But where do you get them? You can't use the property of health clinics. It's tagged, logged, assigned. Donors and brokers would object to their body parts being used for something other than they've signed for. Big problems, bad press. Plus there are probably federal restrictions."

She stopped, shook her head. "So you kill for them? You murder people so you can experiment? It's a hell of a stretch."

"Is it?" Roarke toasted her. "Look at history. Those in power have habitually found nasty uses for those without it. And often, all too often, they claim it's for the greater good. You could have a group of highly skilled, educated, intelligent people who've decided they know what's best for humanity. Nothing, in my opinion, is more dangerous.''

"And Bowers?"

"Casualties in the war on disease, in the quest for longevity. The quality of life for the many over the destruction of life for the few."

"If that's why," she said slowly, "the answer's in the lab. I'll need to find a way into Drake."

"I should be able to bring Drake to you, right here."

"That's a start." She blew out a breath, took her seat again. "Let's take a closer look at Young."

"Geek," Roarke said a few moments later when they scanned the data.

"What?"

"You really are behind on your retro-slang, Eve. What we have here is your classic techno-geek—what McNab might be without his charm, his affection for the ladies, and his interesting fashion sense."

"Oh, like most EDD guys. Got it. They'd rather spend time with a motherboard than breathe regular. Thirty-six, single, lives with his mother."

"Classic geekdom," Roarke explained. "Educationally, he excelled, except in social areas. President of the compu-tech club in high school."

"That would be a geek club."

"That would be correct. Ran the E-society and newsletter in college—Princeton—where he graduated at the tender age of fourteen."

"Genius geek."

"Precisely. He added the med-lab and found another niche. I employ hordes of his type. They're invaluable. Happily laboring to develop those new mousetraps. I'd say if Mira did a profile here, she would find him a socially stunted, massively intelligent introvert with sexual phobias, an acute arrogance level, and an inherent predilection for taking orders from authority figures even though he considers them inferior.''

"Female authority figures should play in. He lives with his mommy. He works for Wo. Ties in. He's been employed at Drake for eight years, heads the research lab on organs. He's not a surgeon,'' she mused. "He's a lab rat.''

"And likely doesn't interact well with people. He's more comfortable with machines and samples.''

"Let's run the dates on all the murders, find out where he was.''

"I'll have to dip into his logs for that. Give me a minute.''

He began to work, paused, frowned a little. "Well, well, he's a bit more security-conscious than our Dr. Wo. We have some layers here to get through.'' He swiveled the chair, slid out a keyboard, and began to work manually. "Interesting. It's a lot of cover for a schedule log. What have we here?'' His brow creased as he studied what looked to Eve to be random symbols on the monitor. "Clever boy,'' Roarke murmured. "He's got himself a fail-safe device. Sneaky bastard.''

"You can't get through it.''

"It's tricky.''

She angled her head. "Well, if you're going to let some geek beat your ass, I guess I need another partner.''

He sat back, eyes narrowed, and looked, she thought, amazingly sexy sitting bare-chested at the controls with a scowl on his magnificent face. "What is that expression you're so fond of? Ah yes, *bite me*. Now, stop breathing down my neck and get me some coffee. This is going to take some time.''

Snorting out a laugh, Eve strolled to the AutoChef. At his seat, Roarke rolled his shoulders, pushed up metaphorical sleeves, and began to wage his little war with the keyboard.

Eve drank two cups of coffee while his turned stone cold and sat untouched. His curses, delivered in a low, vicious voice, became steadily more inventive. And, she observed with some fascination, more Irish.

"Bloody buggering hell, where did he get this?" Frustration shimmered in his eyes as he pounded out a new combination of keys. "Oh no, you slippery bastard, there's a trap there. I can see that well enough. He's good. Aye, damn good; but I've nearly got him. Fuck me!" He shoved back, snarled at the monitor.

Eve opened her mouth, then thinking better of it, shut it again and got another cup of coffee. It was so rare to see him . . . out of sorts, she decided.

Toying with another angle, she took a chair across the room and used the 'link to contact Louise. She was greeted by a slurred "Dr. Dimatto" and a fuzzed video.

"It's Dallas, I've got a job for you."

"Do you know what the hell time it is?"

"No. I need you to check the records on the main system at your clinic. Any and all incoming and outgoing transmissions to this list of clinics. Paying attention?"

"I hate you, Dallas."

"Uh-huh. The Drake, Nordick in Chicago—are you getting this?"

The video cleared, showing an image of a rumpled, heavy-eyed Louise. "I worked a double today, did a medi-van run. I have the morning shift. So you'll excuse me for telling you to go to hell."

"Don't cut me off. I need this data."

"Last I heard, you were off the case. It's one thing for me to agree to a consult with a cop and another to pass confidential data to a civilian."

The word *civilian* stung a great deal more than Eve expected it to. "People are still dead, whether I have a badge or not."

"And if the new investigator asks for my help, I'll cooperate, within the limits of the law. If I do what you want me to do and get caught, I could lose the clinic."

Eve balled her fists, struggling with frustration. "Your clinic's an armpit," she tossed back. "How much would it take to rip it into the twenty-first century?"

"Half a million, minimum, and when I manage to break

the limits on my trust fund, it'll get it. So to repeat myself, you go to hell.''

"Just hold on a minute. One damn minute, okay?" She shifted the unit to mute. "Roarke?" She called out again, testily, when he ignored her, and she received an annoyed grunt in response. "I need a half a million dollars for a bribe.''

"Well, tap your account, there's plenty there. Don't talk to me until I get this fucker.''

"My account?" she repeated, but only hissed at his back, afraid Louise would disconnect and refuse another transmission. "I'll have a half million transferred anywhere you want, the minute the data's accessed for me.''

"I beg your pardon?''

"You want the money for the clinic, you get me the data I need. Here's the list of health centers." She tossed them up, gratified to see Louise shove herself up and grab a memo book.

"If you're stringing me, Dallas—''

"I don't lie. Get the data, don't get caught, and get it to me. We'll arrange for a transfer of funds. So don't string me, Louise. Do we have a deal or not?''

"Damn, you play tough. I'll get the data and be in touch when I can. You've just saved hundreds of lives.''

"That's your job. I save the dead." She broke transmission just as Roarke let out one pithy "Ha! I'm in.'' He wiggled his fingers to loosen them, picked up his coffee, and sipped. "Jesus, are you trying to poison me?''

"I put that there an hour ago. And what the hell do you mean dip into my own account, there's plenty there?''

"Plenty of what? Oh." He rose to stretch his shoulders and replace his stale coffee. "You have a personal account that's been open for months. Don't you ever look at your finances?''

"I have—had—a cop's salary, which means I have no finances. My personal account has about two hundred dollars in it, since Christmas wiped out the rest.''

"That would be your professional account. You have

your salary automatically transferred. I thought you meant your personal account.''

"I've only got one account.''

Patiently, he sipped his coffee, rotated his neck. He decided he wanted a session in the whirlpool. "No, you have two accounts with the one I opened for you last summer. Do you want to see this log?''

"One damn minute.'' She slapped a hand on his bare chest. "You opened it for me? What the hell did you do that for?''

"Because we got married. It seemed logical, even normal.''

"Just how much seemed logical, even normal to you?''

He ran his tongue around his teeth. She was, he knew well, a woman with a temper and what he often thought as a screwed sense of pride. "I believe, if memory serves, the account was seeded with five million—though that's certainly increased due to interest and dividends.''

"You—What is *wrong* with you?'' She didn't punch. He'd been prepared to block a fist. Instead, she all but skewered her finger through his chest.

"Jesus. You need a manicure.''

"Five million dollars.'' She threw her hands up in the air, arms flapping in frustration. "What do I want with five million dollars? Damn it all to hell and back again, Roarke. I don't want your money. I don't need your money.''

"You just asked me for half a million,'' he pointed out with a charming smile that only widened when she let out a thin scream of frustration. Then he said, "Okay. Marital spat or murder investigation? You choose.''

She closed her eyes, struggled to remember her priorities. "We're going to deal with this later,'' she warned him. "We are really going to deal with this later.''

"I'll look forward to it. For now, aren't you interested in the fact that our favorite geek happened to be visiting certain pertinent cities on certain pertinent dates?''

"What?'' She whirled to stare at the screen. "Oh God, it's right there. Right there. Chicago, Paris, London. Right in his goddamn log. I've got one of them. Son of a bitch, when I get him into interview, he'll roll over on the rest quick enough. I'll fry his sorry ass and then . . .''

She trailed off, stepped back, felt Roarke's hands come down on her shoulders to rub. ''I forgot for a minute. Stupid.''

''Don't.'' He lowered his lips to the top of her head.

''No, I'm okay. I'm okay with it.'' *Had to be,* she ordered herself. ''I just have to figure out how to get this to Feeney without compromising him or the case. We can copy it to disc, drop the disc in an overnight mail drop. We need it to go through departmental channels to reach him. Need it documented. He can run it then, and he can use an anonymous tip to get a warrant to seize the logs and to bring him into interview. It'll take the best part of a day that way, but it won't screw up the case or put him in a bind.''

''Then that's what we'll do. It's falling into place, Eve. You'll have what you need soon, and all of this will be behind you.''

''Yeah.'' The case, she thought, and very likely her badge.

chapter nineteen

Eve convinced herself she was completely prepared when she walked into Mira's office. She would do what needed to be done, then move on. And she knew, very well, that the results of what she did and what was done to her over the next few hours would weigh heavily in the department's decision. Her suspension could be lifted. Or suspension could lead to dismissal.

Mira went directly to her, took Eve's arms in her hands. "I'm so terribly sorry."

"You didn't do anything."

"No, I didn't. I wish I could have." She could feel the tension, snapping tight, in the muscles she gripped. "Eve, you're not required to submit to these tests and procedures until you're fully ready."

"I want it done."

With a nod, Mira stepped back. "I understand that. Sit down first. We'll talk."

Nerves danced up her spine, were ruthlessly shaken off. Nerves, Eve knew, would only add to the trauma. "Dr. Mira, I'm not here for tea and conversation. The sooner it's over, the sooner I know where I stand."

"Then consider it part of the procedure." Mira's voice

was uncharacteristically sharp as she gestured to a chair. She wanted to soothe, and would be required to distress. "Sit down, Eve. I have all your data here," she began when Eve shrugged and dropped into a chair. Arrogantly, Mira thought. That was good. A little arrogance would help get Eve through what was to come. "I'm required to verify that you understand what you've agreed to."

"I know the drill."

"You're submitting to personality evaluation, violent tendency ratio, and a truth test. These procedures include virtual reality simulations, chemical injections, and brain scans. I will personally conduct or supervise all procedures. I'll be there with you, Eve."

"You don't carry this weight, Mira. It's not on you."

"If you're here because an associate arranged or had a part in the circumstances that brought you to this point, put you in this position, I carry some of the weight."

Eve's eyes sharpened. "Your profile indicates an associate?"

"I can't discuss my profiling with you." Mira picked up a disc from her desk, tapped a finger against it while her gaze remained steady on Eve's. "I can't tell you what data and conclusions are on this copy of my reports. A copy of reports already filed to all appropriate parties." She tossed it carelessly back on the desk. "I need to check the equipment in the next room. Wait here a moment."

Well, Eve thought when the door closed, *that invitation was clear enough. What the hell,* she decided and nipped the disc off the desk, stuffed it into the back pocket of her jeans.

She wanted to pace, wanted to find a way to keep herself loose before she snapped. But she forced herself to sit again, to wait, to blank her mind.

They wanted you to think, she reminded herself. To worry and to sweat. The more you did, the more open and vulnerable you were to everything that was beyond that door.

They would, she thought, use their equipment, their

scans, their injections, to strip your control and dig into your mind. Your fears.

The less you took in with you, the less they had to exploit.

Mira opened the door again. She didn't come back into the room, didn't so much as glance at the desk, but nodded at Eve. "We're ready to start."

Saying nothing, Eve rose and followed Mira down one of the corridors that formed the maze of Testing. This one was in pale green, the color of hospitals. Others would be glassed with techs and machines lurking behind them like smoke.

From this point, every gesture, expression, and word and every thought would be documented, evaluated, analyzed.

"This Level One procedure should take no more than two hours," Mira began. Eve stopped short, grabbed her arm.

"Level One?"

"Yes, that's all you're required to take."

"I need Level Three."

"That's not necessary; it's not recommended. The risks and side effects of Level Three are too extreme for these circumstances. Level One is recommended."

"My badge is riding on this." Her fingers wanted to tremble. She wouldn't allow it. "We both know it. Just like we both know passing Level One is no guarantee of getting it back."

"Positive results and my recommendation will weigh very heavily in your favor."

"Not heavily enough. Level Three, Mira. It's my right to demand it."

"Damn it, Eve. Level Three is for suspected mental defectives, extreme violent tendencies, murderers, mutilators, deviants."

Eve drew in a long breath. "Have I been cleared of any suspicion regarding the murder of Officer Ellen Bowers?"

"You're not a prime suspect, nor is the investigation pointing in your direction."

"But I'm not clear, and I intend to be." Eve drew a breath in, let it out. "Level Three. It's my right."

"You're making this harder than it has to be."

Eve surprised them both by smiling. "It can't be. It already bites."

They passed through a set of clear, reinforced doors. She had no weapon to be surrendered here. The computer politely requested she enter the door on the left and remove all articles of clothing, all jewelry.

Mira saw Eve close her fingers protectively over her wedding ring. And her heart broke a little. "I'm sorry. You can't wear it during the scans. Would you like me to keep it for you?"

"They've only taken your symbols."

She heard Roarke's voice in her head as she tugged off his ring. "Thanks." She moved into the room, closed the door. Mechanically, she removed her clothes, keeping her face impassive for the techs and machines who were monitoring her even now.

She despised being naked in front of strangers. Hated the vulnerability and lack of control.

She refused to think.

The light blinked over the opposing door, and another automated voice told her to step through for the physical exam.

She went in, stood on the center mark, stared straight ahead while the lights blinked and hummed and her body was checked for flaws.

The physical was quick, painless. When she was cleared, she tugged on the blue jumpsuit provided, followed the directions into the adjoining room for the brain scan.

She lay flat on the padded bench, ignoring the faces behind the glass walls, letting her eyes drift closed as the helmet was lowered onto her head.

Just what game would they play? she wondered, brac-

ing herself as the bench glided silently up until she was
sitting.

The VR session plunged her into the dark, disorienting
her so that she gripped the sides of the bench to keep her
balance.

She was attacked from behind. Huge hands shot out of
the dark, hauled her off her feet, and tossed her high. She
hit the hard floor of what she saw now was an alley,
skidded on something slimy. Her bones jarred, her skin
burned as it was scraped away. She sprang up fast, one
hand reaching for her weapon.

Before she could free it from its holster, he was charging. She pivoted, breath grunting out, as she spun into a
back kick to catch him center body.

"Police, you stupid son of a bitch. Freeze."

She crouched, her weapon in both hands, prepared to
shoot out a stunning blast, when the program shoved her
into brilliant sunlight. Her weapon was still out, her finger
twitching on the trigger. But now it pointed at a woman
holding a screaming child.

Heart pistoning in her chest, she jerked the weapon up.
She could hear her own ragged pants as she lowered it.

They were on a rooftop. The sun was blinding, the heat
enormous. And the woman stood swaying on a narrow
ledge. She looked at Eve with eyes that seemed already
dead. And the child struggled and shrieked.

"Don't come any closer."

"Okay. Look, look, I'm putting it away. Watch."
Keeping her movement slow, Eve holstered her weapon.
"I just want to talk to you. What's your name?"

"You can't stop me."

"No, I can't." Where the hell was her backup? Where
was the jumper team, the shrinks? Name of God. "What's
the kid's name?"

"I can't take care of him anymore. I'm tired."

"He's scared." Sweat rolled down her back as she
eased a step closer. It was brutally hot, heat bouncing off
the sticky tar of the roof in shimmering waves. "And he's

hot. So are you. Why don't we go back there in the shade for a minute?''

"He cries all the damn time. All night. I never get any sleep. I can't stand it.''

"Maybe you should give him to me. He's heavy. What's his name?''

"Pete.'' Sweat poured off the woman's face, had her short, dark hair sticking in ringlets to her cheeks. "He's sick. We're both sick, so what's the point?''

The child was screaming, one shrieking wail after another. The sound of it sliced her head, her heart. "I know some people who can help.''

"You're just a fucking cop. You can't do shit.''

"If you jump, nobody can. Jesus, it's hot out here. Let's go inside, figure this out.''

The woman let out a weary sigh. "Go to hell.''

Eve made the leap, caught the boy around the waist as the woman leaned forward. His screams were like razors scraping over her brain as she made one desperate grab. She hooked the woman under the armpit, dug in desperately while her muscles trembled and threatened to rip. The toes of her boots slapped hard into the wall of the ledge to keep the weight from sending them all to the sidewalk below.

"Hold on. Goddamn it.'' Sweat poured into her eyes, stinging, blinding while she struggled for better purchase. The boy was wiggling like a wet fish. "Grab onto me!'' she shouted as the woman stared up at her with eyes already empty.

"Sometimes you're better off dead. You should know, Dallas.'' The woman smiled as she said Eve's name. And she laughed as Eve's grip began to slip.

Then she was in another alley, shivering, curled into a ball of pain and numb shock.

And she was a child, battered and broken, without a name, without a past.

They were using her own memories now, sliding them in from her early data records. She hated them for it, hated them with a rage that simmered nastily under a slick coat of panic.

An alley in Dallas, a young girl with a bloody face, a broken arm, and nowhere to run.

Goddamn you. Damn all of you. She's not part of this. She wanted to scream it, to fight her way clear of the influence and images being poured into her brain and crash through the glass wall.

Her pulse began to race, her rage began to rise. And with barely a blink, the program shifted her to the streets of lower Manhattan, on a frigid night. Bowers stood in front of her, leering.

"You stupid bitch, I'll bury you in complaints. Everyone's going to know what you are. Nothing but a whore who fucked her way up the ranks."

"You've got a real problem, Bowers. Maybe after I finish writing you up for insubordination, threatening a superior officer, and being a general asshole, the department will find its balls and kick you clear."

"We'll see who they kick." Bowers shoved hard, taking Eve back two steps.

The fury was there, right there, shooting out of her heart, trembling in her fingertips. "Don't put your hands on me."

"What the hell are you going to do about it? Nobody's here but you and me. You think you can come down on my turf and make threats."

"I'm not threatening you, I'm telling you. Keep your hands off me, keep out of my face, out of my business, or you'll pay for it."

"I'm going to ruin you. I'm going to strip you bare and expose you, and there's not a damn thing you can do to stop me."

"Yeah. Oh yeah, there is."

Eve found the metal pipe in her hand. Felt her fingers curl tightly around it, her muscles bunch and brace to swing. More annoyed than surprised, she tossed it aside, leaned in, and grabbed Bowers by the front of her uniform coat. "Put your hands on me again, and I'll knock you on your fat ass. File all the complaints you want, my rep will hold. But I promise you, I'll see you out of that uniform and off the streets before I'm done. You're a fucking disgrace.''

She released her in disgust, started to walk away. Out of the corner of her eye, she caught a blur of movement. She ducked, spun, and felt the pipe whistle by her head and ruffle her hair.

"I was wrong," she said in a voice gone dangerously cold. "You're not a fucking disgrace. You're just crazy."

Bowers bared her teeth as she swung the pipe again. Eve leaped out of reach, then went in hard. She caught a glancing blow on the shoulder, used the pain and the momentum to push her body into Bowers. They went down in a tangled heap.

Her hand closed over the pipe again, wrenched, twisted, and once again heaved it aside. She had her weapon out, her eyes glittering, as she used it to jerk up Bowers's chin.

"And you're finished." Breath ragged, she shoved Bowers over, yanked her arms behind her back, and fumbled in her pocket for restraints. "You're under arrest for assault with a deadly, you piss-faced, brainless bitch."

Even as she started to smile, she found herself in the dark again, straddling a bloody mess. Her hands thickly coated with gore.

Shock, horror, and a bright, silver fear slammed into her as she scrambled back. "Jesus. Jesus Christ, no. I didn't do this. I couldn't do this."

When she covered her face with her bloody hands, Mira closed her eyes. "That's enough. End program." Sick at heart, she watched Eve's body twitch as the session ended. And as the helmet was removed, their eyes met through the glass.

"This phase of Testing is complete. Please exit through the marked door. I'll meet you inside."

Her knees buckled when she pushed off the inclined bench, but she locked them straight, took a minute to even her breathing, and walked into the next area.

Another padded bench, a chair, a long table where instruments were already neatly lined. More machines, monitors. Blank white walls.

Mira entered. "You're entitled to a thirty-minute rest break. I suggest you take it."

"Get it done."

"Sit down, Eve."

She sat on the bench, doing her best to put the last session out of her mind, to prepare for the next.

Mira took the chair, folded her hands in her lap. "I have children I love," she began, causing a line of puzzlement to dig between Eve's brows. "I have friends who are vital to me and acquaintances and colleagues I admire and respect." Mira let out one shallow breath. "I have all those feelings for you." She leaned forward, put her hand over Eve's and squeezed hard.

"If you were my daughter, if I had any authority over you, I would not permit you to submit to Level Three on this phase. I'm asking you, as a friend, to reconsider."

Eve stared down at Mira's hand. "I'm sorry this is difficult for you."

"Oh God, Eve!" Mira sprang up, turned away, and struggled to bring her whirling emotions under control. "This is a very invasive procedure. You'll be helpless, unable to defend yourself, physically, mentally, emotionally. If you fight it, as will be instinctive for you, it will put a strain on your heart. I can counter this reaction, and will."

She turned back, already knowing it was useless. "The combination of drugs and scans I'll have to use for this level will certainly make you ill. You'll have nausea, headaches, fatigue, disorientation, dizziness, possibly a temporary loss of muscle control."

"Sounds like a hell of a party. Look, you know I'm not going to change my mind. You've been inside it often enough to know how it works. So what's the point in scaring the shit out of both of us? Just do it."

Resigned, Mira crossed to the table, picked up a pressure syringe she'd loaded herself. "Lie back, try to relax."

"Sure, maybe I'll take a little nap while I'm at it." She lay back, stared at the cool blue light in the ceiling. "What's that for?"

"Just focus on it. Just look at the light, look through the light, imagine yourself inside it, in all that cool, soft blue. This won't hurt. I need to unfasten the top of your jumpsuit."

"Is that why you have blue chairs in your office? So people can sink into the blue?"

"It's like water." Mira worked quickly, gently, baring Eve's shoulder, her arm. "You can slide right into the water. A little pressure now," she murmured as she injected the first drug. "It's just a calmer."

"I hate chemicals."

"I know. Breathe normally. I'm going to hook up the scanners, the monitors. There won't be any discomfort."

"I'm not worried about it. Do you have my ring?" Already her head felt light, her tongue thick. "Can I have my ring back?"

"I have it. As soon as we're done here, I'll give it back to you." With the skill of long practice, Mira attached the scanners to Eve's temples, her wrists, her heart. "I have it safe. Relax, Eve. Let the blue surround you."

She was already floating, one drifting part of her mind wondering why Mira had made such a big deal out of it. It was just a painless, foolish ride.

With a cautious eye, Mira studied the monitors. Heart rate, blood pressure, brain waves, all physical stats normal. For now. She glanced down, seeing Eve's eyes were closed, her face relaxed, her body limp. She indulged herself, brushing a hand over Eve's cheek; then, after hooking restraints to her wrists and ankles, she picked up the second syringe.

"Can you hear me, Eve?"

"Mmm. Yeah. Feel fine."

"Do you trust me?"

"Yeah."

"Then remember I'm here with you. Count back from one hundred for me. Slowly."

"Hundred, ninety-nine, ninety-eight, ninety-seven." As the second drug swam into her blood, her pulse jittered, her breathing hitched. "Ninety-six. God!" Her body arched, limbs jerking against the restraints as the shock rocked her system.

"No, don't fight. Breathe. Listen to my voice. Breathe, Eve. Don't fight."

There were thousands of hot, hungry bugs crawling over her skin, under it. Someone was choking her, and the hands were like jagged ice. Her heart fought to break out of her chest with vicious hammer blows. Terror, red and ripe, blinded her as her eyes sprang open and she realized she was restrained.

"Don't tie me down. Jesus, don't."

"I have to. You could hurt yourself. But I'm here. Feel my hand." She squeezed it over the tight ball of Eve's fist. "I'm right here. Slow, deep breaths, Eve. Listen to my voice. Slow, deep breaths. Lieutenant Dallas." She snapped it out when Eve continued to gasp and struggle. "I gave you an order. Cease struggling, breathe normally."

Eve gulped in air, whooshed it out. Her arms shuddered but stopped straining.

"Look at the light," Mira continued, adjusting the dosage, watching the monitors. "Listen to my voice. You don't need to hear anything but my voice. I'm right here. You know who I am?"

"Mira. Dr. Mira. It hurts."

"Only for a moment more. Your system needs to adjust. Take long, slow breaths. Watch the light. Long, slow breaths." She repeated the same directions, over and over in a quiet monotone until she saw the monitors level, watched Eve's face go lax again.

"You're relaxed now, and all you hear is my voice. Do you still have pain?"

"No, I don't feel anything."

"Tell me your name."

"Dallas, Lieutenant Eve."

"Date of birth."

"I don't know."

"Place of birth."

"I don't know."

"City of residence?"

"New York."

"Marital status."

"Married. Roarke."

"Place of employment."

"NYPSD. Cop Central. No . . ." The monitors began to blip, indicating agitation, confusion. "I was. I'm suspended. They took my badge. I'm cold now."

"It'll pass." But Mira leaned back and ordered the temperature of the room to increase five degrees. For the next several minutes, Mira asked simple, inane questions to establish normal blood pressure, the pattern of brain waves, respiration, heart rate.

"Was your suspension from duty warranted?"

"It was procedure. While under investigation, I can't serve."

"Was it warranted?"

Eve's brow creased in confusion. "It was procedure," she repeated.

"You're a cop down to your bones," Mira muttered.

"Yes."

The simple answer nearly made Mira smile. "You have used maximum force in the line of duty, answer yes or no."

"Yes."

Tricky ground now, Mira thought. She knew that once, a young, terrified girl had killed. "Have you ever, other than to protect yourself or another, taken a life?"

The image flashed. The horrid room, the pools of blood, the knife gored to the hilt and dripping with red. Pain, so brutal the memory of it struck like lightning, made her whimper. "I had to. I had to."

The voice was a child's and had Mira moving quickly. "Eve, stay here, and answer the question yes or no. Answer yes or no, Lieutenant, have you ever, other than to protect yourself or another, taken a life?"

"No." The word came out on an explosion of breath. "No, no, no. He's hurting me. He won't stop."

"Don't go there. Listen to my voice, look at the light. You are not to go anywhere unless I tell you. Do you understand?"

"It's always there."

She'd been afraid of just this. "It's not there now. No one is here but me. What is my name?"

"He's coming back." She began to shake, to struggle. "He's drunk, but not too drunk."

"Lieutenant Dallas, this is an official procedure sanctioned by the NYPSD. You are under suspension, but have not been terminated from service. You are obliged to follow the rules of this procedure. Do you understand your obligations?"

"Yes. Yes. God, I don't want to be here."

"What is my name?"

"Mira. Oh Christ. Mira, Dr. Charlotte."

Stay with me, Mira thought. *Stay right here with me.* "What was the nature of the case you were investigating when suspended from service?"

"Homicide." The shuddering stopped, and the data on the monitors began to level. "Multiple."

"Were you acquainted with an Officer Ellen Bowers?"

"Yes. She and her trainee were first on-scene at two of the homicides. Victims Petrinksy and Spindler."

"You had altercations with Bowers?"

"Yes."

"Relate your view of those altercations."

More images slid in and out of her brain. She lived it as she recited it. The heat, the punch of hate that had annoyed and baffled, the cold words, the vicious ones.

"You were aware that Bowers filed complaints against you."

"Yes."

"Was there validity to these complaints?"

"I used profanity when dealing with her." Even weighed down with drugs, she sneered. It lifted Mira's troubled heart. "It's a technical breach of regulations."

If she hadn't been sick with worry, Mira might have laughed. "Did you threaten this officer with physical harm?"

"I'm not sure. I might have said I'd kick her ass if she kept screwing up. I thought it, anyway."

"In her logs, she has stated that you exchanged sexual favors for advancement in the department. Is that true?"

"No."

"Have you ever had a sexual relationship or encounter with Commander Whitney?"

"No."

"Have you ever had a sexual relationship or encounter with Captain Feeney?"

"Jesus. No. I don't go around fucking my friends."

"Have you ever accepted a bribe?"

"No."

"Have you ever falsified a report?"

"No."

"Did you physically attack Officer Ellen Bowers?"

"No."

"Did you cause her death?"

"I don't know."

Mira jerked back, shaken. "Did you kill Officer Ellen Bowers?"

"No."

"How might you have caused her death?"

"Someone used her to get me off, to get me out. They wanted me. She was easier."

"You believe that a person or persons currently unknown killed Bowers in order to remove you from the investigation you were pursuing?"

"Yes."

"How does that make you responsible for her death?"

"Because I had a badge. Because it was my case. Because I let it be personal instead of seeing how they could use her. That puts her on my head."

Mira sighed, adjusted the dose again. "Focus on the light, Eve. We're nearly done."

• • •

Roarke paced the waiting area outside Mira's office. What the hell was taking so long? He should have known Eve was conning him when she'd said it wouldn't take more than a couple of hours. It was no big deal. Just as he'd known when he realized she'd gotten out of the house without telling him that morning that she hadn't wanted him here.

Well, he was here, by God. She'd just have to deal with it.

Four hours, he thought with another glance at his wrist unit. How the devil could some tests and questions take four hours? He should have pressed her, pushed her into explaining exactly what would be done.

He knew something about Testing, the basic process a cop went through whenever maximum force was employed. It wasn't pleasant, but she'd gotten through it before. He understood the elemental strain of Level One, and the additional burden of truth testing.

It was again, unpleasant, very often left the subject a little shaky for a few hours.

She'd get through that as well.

Why the hell weren't they done with her?

His head came up, and his eyes went to pools of ice when Whitney walked in.

"Roarke. I'd hoped she'd be finished by now."

"She doesn't need to see you here when she is. You've done more than enough already, Commander."

Whitney's eyes went blank, and the shadows under them were deep. "We all follow orders, Roarke, and procedure. Without them, there's no order."

"Why don't I tell you what I think of your procedure?" he began, stepping forward with blood in his eye.

The door opened. He turned quickly, an arrow of shock piercing his heart when he saw her.

She was pale as death. Her eyes seemed to be carved deep into the skull, the irises like gold glass, the pupils huge. Mira had a supporting arm around her, and still she swayed.

"You're not ready to get up. Your system needs more time."

"I want out of here." She would have shaken Mira off, but was seriously afraid she'd pitch forward onto her face. She saw Roarke first, felt twin surges of frustration and relief. "What are you doing here? I told you not to come."

"Shut the hell up." There was only one emotion pumping through him, and it was all fury. He was across the room in three quick strides, and pulling her away from Mira. "What the hell did you do to her?"

"What she was supposed to do." Eve made the effort to stand on her own feet, though it had the nausea swimming back, the clammy sweat popping out. She would not be sick again, she promised herself. She'd already been violently ill twice and would *not* be sick again.

"She needs to lie down." Mira's face was nearly as pale as Eve's, and every line of strain showed. "Her system hasn't had time to recover. Please convince her to come back and lie down so I can monitor her vitals."

"I have to get out of here." Eve looked straight into Roarke's eyes. "I can't stay here."

"All right. We're going."

She let herself lean against him until she saw Whitney. Then it was instinct as much as pride that had her forcing her aching body to attention. "Sir."

"Dallas. I regret the necessity of this procedure. Dr. Mira needs to keep you under observation until she's satisfied you're well enough to leave."

"With respect, Commander, I'm free to go where the hell I want."

"Jack." Mira linked her fingers together, felt useless. "She took Level Three."

His eyes flashed, shifted back to Eve's face. "Level Three was not necessary. Damn it, it was not necessary."

"You took my badge," Eve said quietly. "It was necessary." She forced herself straight again, praying Roarke would understand she needed to walk out under her own power. She made it to the door before the trembling started again, but she shook her head fiercely when he turned.

"No, don't, don't carry me. God, leave me something here."

"All right, just hold on." He hooked an arm around her waist, took most of her weight. Bypassing the glide, he walked her to the elevator. "What's Level Three?"

"Bad." Her head was pounding brutally. "Really bad. Don't hassle me. It was the only way."

"For you," he murmured, drawing her into the crowded elevator when the doors whisked open.

Her vision grayed at the edges. Voices from the people who jammed in with them drifted, echoed, and fell away like waves in an ocean. She lost her bearings, and herself, only dimly aware of movement, of Roarke's voice close to her ear telling her they were nearly there.

"Okay, okay." The gray spread, closed in as he guided her to the visitor's parking area. "Mira said how this was just one of the side effects. No big deal."

"What's one of the side effects?"

"Shit, Roarke. Sorry. I'm gonna pass out."

She never heard him curse as he swung her into his arms.

chapter twenty

She was out, unconscious or asleep, for four hours. She didn't remember getting home, being put to bed. Fortunately for all parties, she didn't remember Roarke calling in Summerset, or the butler using his medical training to examine her and prescribe rest.

When she woke, the headache remained, but the sickness and the shakes had passed.

"You can take a blocker."

Still dim, she blinked her vision clear and stared at the little blue pill Roarke held out. "What?"

"There's been enough time since your treatment for you to take a blocker. Swallow."

"Not more drugs, Roarke, I—"

It was as far as she got before he squeezed her jaw, popped the pill in her mouth. "Swallow."

Scowling, she did so, more out of reflex than obedience. "I'm okay. I'm fine."

"Sure you are. Let's go dancing."

She squirmed into a sitting position and dearly hoped her head would stay in its proper place on her shoulders. "Did anyone see me go down?"

"No." The hand on her jaw gentled. "Your kick-ass rep is intact."

"That's something, anyway. Man, I'm starving."

"Not surprising. Mira said you'd probably lost everything you'd eaten in the last twenty-four hours. I called her," he added when she frowned at him. "I wanted to know what had been done."

She saw the anger in his eyes, and the worry. Instinctively, she lifted a hand to his cheek, stroked. "Are you going to give me grief about it?"

"No. You couldn't have done anything else."

Now she smiled, let her head rest on his shoulder. "I was pissed off when I saw you there, mostly because I was glad you were there."

"How long will you have to wait for the results?"

"A day, maybe two. I can't think about it. I've got enough to keep me busy until . . . Shit, where are my clothes? My jeans? There's a disc in the pocket."

"This?" He picked up one he'd set on the table beside the bed.

"Yeah. Mira let me steal it out of her office. It's the profile. I need to read it." She tossed the covers back. "Feeney's got the disc we sent him by now. He should have picked up Wo or be on his way to. If he's already interviewed Wo, Peabody might be able to slip me some data on how it went."

She was already up, pulling on clothes. She was still very pale, with shadows like bruises under her eyes. He imagined the headache was beginning to dull from agony to simple misery.

And there was no stopping her.

"Your office or mine?"

"Mine," she said as she rummaged through a drawer and found one of her stash of candy bars. "Hey!" He snatched it out of her hand, jerked it out of reach as she made a grab.

"After dinner."

"You're so strict." Because her mouth was set for

chocolate, she tried a soft-eyed smile. "I've been sick. You're supposed to pamper me."

"You hate it when I do that."

"I'm sort of getting used to it," she said as he pulled her from the room.

"No candy before dinner. We're having chicken soup," he decided. "The ageless cure for everything. Since you're feeling so much better," he continued as they turned into her office, "you can get it while I bring up Mira's profile."

She wanted to be cranky about it. After all, her head was achy, her stomach raw, her system still slightly off. Any other time, she thought as she sulked in the kitchen, he'd have annoyed the hell out of her by keeping her in bed, guarding her like a damn watchdog. But when she'd actually, maybe, appreciate just a little hovering, he was giving her kitchen duty. And if she complained, damn him, he'd smirk at her.

So she was stuck, she admitted, as she took a steaming bowl of impossibly fragrant soup out of the AutoChef. And the first spoonful slid down her throat like glory, hit her abused stomach, and nearly made her whimper in gratitude. She ate another, ignoring the cat who'd homed in on the scent and was wrapping himself around her ankles like a furred ribbon.

Before she could stop herself, she'd eaten the entire bowl. Her head was clear, her system humming competently, and her mood wonderfully lifted. Licking the spoon, she eyed the cat.

"Why is he always right?"

"Just a little talent of mine," Roarke said from the doorway. And, damn it, he did smirk. He crossed to her, tapped a finger on her cheek. "Your color's back, Lieutenant, and from the looks of you, the headache's gone and your appetite's just fine."

He glanced down at the empty bowl. "And where's mine?"

Roarke wasn't the only one who could smirk. She set the empty bowl down, snatched the full one out of the

AutoChef, and dug into that. "I don't know. Maybe the cat ate it."

He only laughed, bent down, and scooped up the loudly complaining cat. "Well, pal, since she's so greedy, I guess we're on our own. He programmed the AutoChef himself while Eve stood where she was, lazily spooning up soup.

"Where's my candy bar?"

"I don't know." He took out one bowl, set it on the floor where the cat all but leaped into it. "Maybe the cat ate it." He took out his own bowl, picked up a spoon, and strolled out.

"You've got a great ass, ace," she commented when she followed him in. "Now, get it out of my chair."

He grinned at her. "Why don't you come sit in my lap."

"I don't have time for your perverted games." Because he didn't appear to be moving, she rolled a chair over beside his and studied the monitor. "You have to skim through the shrink talk," she told Roarke. "All the fifty-credit words. Mature, controlled, intelligent, organized."

"That's nothing you didn't know."

"No, but her profiles are gold in court, and they confirm the direction of the investigation. God complex. High level of medical knowledge and surgical skill. Probably duality of nature. Healer/destroyer." Eve frowned at that, leaning forward as she scrolled down the text.

In breaking his oath to do no harm, he has put himself above the tenets of his profession. He is certainly, or was certainly, a doctor. With the level of skill shown in these murders, it is probable that he is currently practicing his art, saving lives, improving the qualities of lives in his patients on a daily basis. He is healer.

However, in taking lives, disregarding the rights of the people he has killed, he has removed himself from the responsibilities of his art. He is destroyer. There is no remorse, no hesitation. He is, I believe, fully aware of his actions. He has justified them in some way that

*will be connected to medicine. He chooses the sick, the
old, the dying. They are not lives to him, but vessels.
The care he takes when removing the samples indicates
it is the work itself, the samples themselves, that are of
importance. The vessels are no more vital than a test
tube in a laboratory. Easily disposed of and replaced.*

Still frowning, Eve leaned back. "Two natures."

"Your own Jekyll and Hyde. The doctor with a mission," Roarke went on, "and the evil inside him that
overpowered and destroyed."

"Destroyed who?"

"The damned, the innocent. And in the end, himself."

"Good." Her eyes were coldly fierce. "The end part.
Two natures," she said again. "Not split personality.
That's not what she's saying."

"No, two sides of the coin. The dark and the light. We
all have it."

"Don't get philosophical on me." She pushed away,
needing to move while her mind worked.

"But in the end, that's what we're dealing with. His
philosophy. Or hers. He takes, because he can, because
he needs, because he wants. From his view, the vessels,
for lack of a better word, are unimportant, medically."

She turned back. "Then we're back to the organs themselves. Their use. And the glory. Reconstruction, rejuve-
nation, healing of what's considered by current science to
be beyond healing. What else could it be? He's found a
way, or believes he can find a way, to take a dying part
and give it life."

"Dr. Frankenstein. Another mad, flawed genius who
was destroyed by his own mind. If we move into that area,
he's not just a surgeon, but a scientist, a researcher. A
seeker."

"And a politician. Damn, I need to know more about
Friend, and I need to know what Feeney got out of his
interview with Wo."

"Why didn't you say so? Do you want hard copy or
full video/audio transcript?"

She stopped pacing as if she'd run into a wall. "You can't do that. You can't get into interview files."

He sighed lustily. "I don't know why I tolerate your constant insults. It would, however, be simpler if you got the file number and time and date stamp, but I can work without it."

"God. I don't want to know how you do it. And I don't believe I'm going to stand here and let you do it."

"Ends and means, darling. It's all just ends and means."

"I'm getting coffee," she muttered.

"Tea. Your system's had enough insults for one day. And I'll have a cup myself. The data on Friend's suicide will be up on the wall screen."

She walked to the kitchen window, away, back again. What was she doing? she asked herself. How far over the line would she go?

As far as it took, she decided, and even as she turned to the 'link, it beeped.

"Dallas."

"Got to make it fast." Peabody's face was set, her voice brisk. "Louise Dimatto was attacked at the clinic early this morning. We didn't get the data until a few minutes ago. She's at the Drake. I don't have details yet, but she's critical."

"I'm on my way."

"Dallas. Wo's at the Drake, too. Attempted self-termination is the current data. They don't think she's going to make it."

"Damn it. Did you get her into interview?"

"No. I'm sorry. And Vanderhaven's still loose. We picked up Young. He's in holding until we can get to him."

"I'm on my way."

"They won't let you see Wo or Louise."

"I'm coming in," Eve said shortly, and broke transmission.

.   .   .

She got as far as the nurses' station in Intensive Care before she was blocked.

"Dimatto, Louise. Room and condition."

The nurse eyed her. "Are you family?"

"No."

"I'm sorry. I can only give that information to immediate family and authorized personnel."

Eve reached down out of habit, then curled her fingers into a frustrated fist when she remembered she had no badge to slap on the counter. "Wo, Doctor Tia. Same questions."

"Same answers."

Eve took a deep breath, prepared to launch the dozen vile and frustrated curses dancing on the tongue, when Roarke stepped forward smoothly. "Nurse Simmons. Dr. Wo and I are on the board of this facility. I wonder if you could page her attending and ask him to speak with me. The name's Roarke."

Her eyes popped wide, her color rose. "Roarke. Yes, sir. Right away. The waiting area is just to your left. I'll page Dr. Waverly immediately."

"Page Officer Peabody while you're at it," Eve demanded and was met with a baleful look.

"I don't have time—"

"If you'd be so kind," Roarke interrupted, and Eve thought resentfully that he should bottle the charm oozing out of his pores for the less fortunate, "we'd very much like to speak with Officer Peabody. My wife . . ." He laid a hand on Eve's vibrating shoulder. "Both of us are quite anxious."

"Oh." The nurse gave Eve a considering stare, obviously stunned to realize the disheveled woman was Roarke's wife. "Certainly. I'll take care of it for you."

"Why didn't you ask her to kiss your feet while you were at it?" Eve muttered.

"I thought you were in a hurry."

The waiting room was empty but for a view screen tuned to the latest comedy series. Eve ignored it and the coffeepot that likely held the first cousin to mud.

"I bribed her into that hospital bed, Roarke. I used your money to do it so she'd get me data I couldn't get myself."

"If that's true, she made her own choice as we all do. And the one who's responsible for her being in that bed is the one who attacked her."

"She'd have done anything to whip that clinic into shape." Eve covered her eyes with the tips of her fingers, pressed hard. "It's what mattered most to her. I used her on a hunch to close a case that isn't even mine anymore. If she dies, I have to live with knowing that."

"I can't tell you you're wrong, but I'll tell you again: You didn't put her here. If you keep thinking that way, you'll go soft." He nodded when she dropped her hands back to her sides. "You're too close to finishing what you started to go soft. Shake it off, Eve, and do what you do best. Find the answers."

"Do those answers have anything to do with why my niece is in a coma?" Face haggard and grim, Cagney stepped into the room. "What are you doing here?" he demanded. "You involved Louise in business that was none of hers, put her in jeopardy for your own ends. Now, I suspect while doing work for you, she was viciously attacked and is fighting for her life."

"What's her condition?" Eve demanded.

"You have no authority here. As far as I'm concerned, you're a murderer, a corrupt cop, and a deviant. Whatever your reporter friends try to do to spin the public view, I know you for what you are."

"Cagney." Roarke's voice was soft as Irish mist. "You're overwrought and have my sympathy, but mind your step here."

"He can say what he likes." Eve stepped deliberately between them. "And so can I. I admire Louise for her purpose and her spine. She threw your fancy position in your rich-man's center right back in your face and went her own way. I'll accept whatever part I have in her being here now. Can you?"

"She had no business in that place." His handsome,

pampered face was ravaged, his eyes sunk deep into shadows. "With her mind, her talent, her background. No business wasting her gifts on the scum people like you scrape off the streets night after night."

"The kind of scum that can be harvested for whatever parts might be useful, then disposed of?"

His eyes burned into hers. "The kind that would try to kill a beautiful young woman for the credits in her pocket, for the drugs she used to try to keep their pitiful lives going. The kind I imagine you sprang from. Both of you."

"I thought, to a doctor, all life was sacred."

"So it is." Waverly strode in, his lab coat swirling. "Colin, you're not yourself. Go get some rest. We're doing everything that can be done."

"I'll go stay with her."

"Not now." Waverly put his hand on Cagney's arm, and his eyes were filled with sympathy. "Take a break in the lounge at least. I promise I'll page you if there's any change. She'll need you when she wakes up."

"Yes, you're right. Yes." He lifted an unsteady hand to his temple. "My sister and her husband— I sent them back, to my home. I should go be with them for a while."

"That's the right thing to do. I'll call you."

"Yes, thank you. I know she's in the best of hands."

Waverly walked him to the door, murmured something, then watched him leave before turning back. "He's very shaken. No amount of medical experience prepares you when it's one of your own."

"How bad was it?" Eve asked.

"Her skull was fractured. There was considerable hemorrhaging, swelling. The surgery went quite well, all in all. We're scanning her at regular intervals for brain damage. We can't be sure yet, but we're hopeful."

"Has she regained consciousness?"

"No."

"Can you tell us what happened?"

"You'll have to get those details from the police. I can only give you her medical data, and I shouldn't be doing that. You'll have to excuse me. We're monitoring her very closely.''

"Dr. Wo?"

His already-weary face seemed to sink into itself. "We lost Tia moments ago. I came to tell Colin, but didn't have the heart to add to his burden. I hope you'll show him some consideration.''

"I need to see her records," Eve muttered when she was alone with Roarke. "How did she die, what did she take or do? Who found her and when? Damn it, I don't even know who pulled her case.''

"Find a source.''

"How the hell can I—" She broke off. "Hell, give me your porta-link.''

He handed it to her and smiled. "Say hello to Nadine for me. I'll see if they'll page Peabody again.''

"Such a smart guy," she muttered and tagged Nadine at Channel 75.

"Dallas, for God's sake, you've been dodging me for days. What's going on? Are you okay? Those stupid bastards! Did you see my feature? We're flooded with calls on it.''

"I don't have time for questions. I need data. Contact whoever you bribe at the ME's office and get me everything you can on Tia Wo, self-termination. She'll be coming in within the hour. I need method, time of death, who found her and called it in, who's handling the case, attending physician. Everything.''

"I don't hear from you for days, then you want everything. And who says I bribe anybody?" She sniffed, looked insulted. "Bribing public officials is illegal.''

"I'm not a cop at the moment, remember? The sooner the better, Nadine. And wait, can you dig any dirt on Senator Brian Waylan, Illinois?''

"You want to know if I can dig any dirt on a U.S. senator?" She gave a low, rumbling laugh. "You want a truckload or a tanker?''

"Whatever there is—emphasis on his stand on artificial organs. You can get me at home or on Roarke's porta.''

"I don't happen to have Roarke's private numbers. Even I have my limits."

"Have Summerset patch you in. Thanks."

"Wait, Dallas, are you okay? I want to—"

"Sorry, no time." She broke transmission and rushed to the doorway just as Peabody strode down the corridor. "Where the hell have you been? I had you paged twice."

"We're just a little busy. Feeney sent me down to check on Wo, who kicked about fifteen minutes ago. Her current cohabitant was there and got hysterical. It took me and two orderlies to hold her down so they could sedate her."

"I thought she lived alone."

"Turned out she had a lover, kept it quiet. She got home and found Wo in bed pumped full of barbs."

"When?"

"I guess it's been a couple hours. We got word after we came in on Louise. Cartright hooked the suspicious death, but it looks like straight self-termination. I have to risk this coffee."

She crossed to the counter, sniffed the pot, gagged a little, but poured a cup anyway. "She didn't show for interview," Peabody continued. "Feeney and I went to her place, got a warrant for entry. She wasn't there. We looked for her here and came up empty. We had a couple of confirmations that she'd been in her office and the organ wing. We picked up Young and he lawyered up before you could swallow spit. We're holding him for formal in the morning, but he could dance on bail for the night. We were heading back to Wo's when we got word on Louise, so we came in, got her status."

She gulped down coffee and shuddered. "So, how was your day?"

"It sucked. What can you give me on Louise?"

Peabody glanced at her wrist unit, then looked over before Eve could control the wince. "Sorry. Damn, Dallas."

"Don't worry about it. You're on duty and pressed for time."

"I'm supposed to be having a fancy French dinner followed by what I figured might be some fancy sex." She tried a smile. "But there you go. Louise got hit at the clinic. Blow to the head. Fractured right wrist indicates defensive wound. We figure she saw whoever bashed her. They used the desk 'link."

"Christ, that took some muscle."

"Yeah, and they did a number on her with it. She was in her office. Whoever did it left her there. There's a small drug cabinet in there, for samples. It was broken open and rifled. It happened between three and four this afternoon. She was off shift at three, logged her last patient at three-ten. A doctor on the next rotation found her just after four. They called it in and started work on her there."

"What's your take on her chances?"

"It's a damn good center. Some of the equipment looks like it should be at NASA II. She's had a fleet of doctors in and out of her room. We've got a uniform on the door twenty-four/seven." She finished off the coffee. "I heard the nurses saying that she's young and strong. Her heart and lungs are prime. The brain scans haven't shown anything to worry about yet. But you can tell they want her to come out of it. The longer she stays under, the more worried they look."

"I have to ask you to call me if there's any change. I need to know."

"You don't have to ask. I should get back."

"Yeah. Tell Feeney I'm working on a couple of angles. I'll pass along anything that looks worthwhile."

"Will do." She started out, hesitated. "I think you should know: Word is the commander's been dogging the chief. He's taken some pokes at IAB, and he's breathing down Baxter's neck to close off on Bowers. He's been over to the one-six-two to do some digging on her on his own. Basically, he's busting his ass to get you reinstated."

Unsure how to feel, she simply stared. "I appreciate you telling me."

"One more thing: Rosswell's personal account showed regular deposits over the last two months of ten thousand a pop. All E-transfers.'' Her lips curved when Eve's eyes narrowed and gleamed. ''He's dirty. Feeney's already sicced Webster on him.''

''Times in nicely with Spindler's murder. Nice work.''

Roarke waited until she was alone before he came back in. He found her sitting on the arm of a sofa, staring down at her hands. ''You've had a long day, Lieutenant.''

''Yeah.'' She rubbed her hands on her knees, shook off the mood, then looked at him. ''I was thinking about topping it off with something special.''

''Is that so?''

''How about a little nighttime B and E?''

His grin flashed. ''Darling. I thought you'd never ask.''

chapter twenty-one

"I'm driving."

Roarke's hand paused as it reached for the car door, and his brow winged up. "It's my car."

"It's my deal."

They studied each other a minute, crowded together at the driver's side door. "Why are you driving?"

"Because." Vaguely embarrassed, she dug her hands in her pockets. "Don't smirk."

"I'll try to resist. Why?"

"Because," she said again, "I drive when I'm on a case, so if I drive, it'll feel like—it'll feel official instead of criminal."

"I see. Well, that makes perfect sense. You drive."

She started to climb in while he circled around to the passenger side. "Are you smirking behind my back?"

"Yes, of course." He sat, stretched out his legs. "Now, to make it really official, I should have a uniform. I'll go that far, but I refuse to wear those amazingly ugly cop shoes."

"You're a real joker," she muttered and jerked the car into reverse, did a quick, squealing spin, and shot out of the garage.

"Too bad this vehicle doesn't have a siren. But we can pretend nothing works on it, so you'll feel official."

"Keep it up. Just keep it up."

"Maybe I'll call you sir. Could be sexy." He smiled blandly when she glared at him. "Okay, I'm done. How do you want to play this?"

"I want to get into the clinic, search for the data I sent Louise in for, and anything else interesting, then get out. Without getting caught by some beat droid. I figure with your light and sticky fingers, it should be a walk."

"Thank you, darling."

"That's sir to you, ace."

She streamed through the smoke of a corner glida grill and headed south. "I can't believe I'm doing this. I must be crazy. I must have lost my mind. I keep crossing lines."

"Think of it this way. The lines keep moving. You're just keeping up."

"I continue keeping up this way, I'll end up wearing security bracelets. I used to go by the book. I believe in the book. Now I just rewrite the pages."

"Either that or go back to bed and pull the covers over your head."

"Yeah, well . . . we make choices. I've made mine."

She found a second-level spot four blocks north of the Canal Street Clinic and tucked the car between a sky scooter and a dented utility truck. If anyone bothered to look, she mused, Roarke's elegant two-seater would stick out like a swan among toads, but it wasn't against the law to drive a hot-looking car in this sector.

"I don't want to park any closer. This thing has anti-theft and antivandalism features, right?"

"Naturally. Engage all security," he ordered as they climbed out. "One more thing. He reached in his pocket. "Your clutch piece . . . sir."

"What the hell are you doing with this?" She snatched it from him.

"Giving it to you."

"You're not authorized to carry and neither am I." She

hissed out a breath as he met that information with another smirk. "Just shut up," she muttered and jammed the weapon into her back pocket.

"When we get home," he began as they walked down to street level, "you can . . . reprimand me."

"Keep your mind off sex."

"Why? It's so happy there." He laid a casual hand on her shoulder as they moved briskly down the block. The few doorway lurkers faded back, intimidated either by the steely look in Eve's eyes or the warning glint in Roarke's.

"The place is a dump," she told him. "No palm plate, no camera. But the locks are decent. They've got to meet code because of the drugs. They'll be standard Security Reds, maybe with timers. Antitheft alarms. Cartright caught the scene here, and she's a straight cop. There'll be a seal. I don't have my master anymore."

"You have better." He gave her shoulder a quick rub. "You have me."

"Yeah." She tossed him a look, saw in that fabulous face the glint that told her he was enjoying himself. "Seems like."

"I could teach you how to get through locks."

It was tempting, much too tempting. God, she missed the weight of her weapon, her badge. "I'll just keep a lookout for beat droids and other nuisances. If you trip the alarm, we just walk away."

"Please. I haven't tripped an alarm since I was ten." Insulted, he turned to the door of the clinic while Eve cruised the block.

She made two passes, lost in her own thoughts. One event, she decided, had built on another. An old resentment from academy days, a dead sleeper, a conspiracy of death, and here she was, stripped of her badge and playing lookout while the man she'd married coolly broke into a building.

How the hell was she going to get back? How could she get back, if she didn't get started? She turned, ready to tell him to stop. And he stood, watching her, his eyes calm and blue, with the door open at his back.

"In or out, Lieutenant?"

"Fuck it." She strode past him and went inside.

He locked up behind them, turned on the narrow beam of a penlight. "Where's the office?"

"Through the back. This door works on a release from inside."

"Hold this." He passed her the light, gestured for her to aim it at the lock. Crouching, he gave it a quick scan. "I haven't seen one of these in years. Your friend Louise was very optimistic with her half million bid."

He took out what appeared to be a pen, unscrewed it, then flicked a finger over the tip of the long, thin wire he exposed.

She'd known him nearly a year, had been as intimate with him as one person could be with another, and he still managed to surprise her. "You carry burglary tools around with you all the time?"

"Well." Eyes narrowed, he slid the wire into the slot. "You just never know, do you? There she is, hang on." He finessed, turning his head to hear the seductive click of tumblers. There was a quiet buzz as locks disengaged. "After you, Lieutenant."

"You're slick." She breezed through, leading with the light. "There's no window," she continued. "We can use the room lights. It's a manual." She switched it on, blinked to adjust.

A quick scan showed her the sweepers had done their work, left behind their usual mess. The crime scene team's touch was evident in the sticky layer coating every surface.

"They've already lifted prints, swept for fibers, hair, blood, and fluids. Won't help much. God knows how many of the staff are in and out of this room in any given day. They've got their evidence bagged and tagged, but I don't want to touch or disturb anything that doesn't need to be."

"What you want's on the computer."

"Yeah, or on a disc, if Louise had already found it. You start on the machine. I'll do the discs."

When Roarke sat, making quick work of the pass-lock feature, Eve went through the discs filed on the shelf, flipping through them by the corners. Each was labeled with a patient's name. Spindler's was missing.

Frowning, she moved to the next file, scanning through. These appeared to be records of diseases, conditions, injuries. Straight medical shit, she thought, then stopped, eyes narrowing as she read.

The label said simply The Dallas Syndrome.

"I knew she was a smart-ass." Eve plucked out the disc. "Damn smart. Got it."

"I haven't finished playing."

"Just run this," she began, then stopped to yank Roarke's porta-link out of her pocket. "Block video. Dallas."

"Lieutenant, Peabody. Louise is awake; she asked for you. We're going to get you in, but it's got to be fast."

"I'm there."

"Come up the east-side stairs. I'll get you through. Step on it."

"Close it up." Eve jammed the 'link back in her pocket. "We've got to move."

"Already done. This time, I drive."

It was just as well, Eve thought as she bared her teeth and hung on. She had a rep for being nerveless and occasionally reckless behind the wheel, but compared with Roarke, she was a suburban matron manning a car pool.

She did no more than hiss when he screamed into a parking slot in the center's garage. Saving her breath, she shoved out and pounded up the east-side stairs.

Faithful as a spaniel, Peabody yanked the door open. "Waverly's going to be back with her in a few minutes. Just give me time to bump the uniform off the door and take over for him. Feeney's already inside, but she won't talk to anyone but you."

"What's her prognosis?"

"I don't know yet. They're not talking." She looked up at Roarke. "I can't let you in."

"I'll wait."

"I'll be quick," Peabody promised. "Watch for it."

She strode away, squaring her shoulders back to add authority. Eve moved smoothly to the end of the corridor, shifted slightly to bring Louise's door into view.

She saw Peabody glance at her wrist unit, shrug, then jerk her thumb to indicate she'd take over duty while the uniform took a break. He didn't hesitate. Sprung, he hurried down the hallway toward food, coffee, and a chair.

"I won't be long," Eve promised. She made the dash, slipped through the door Peabody opened.

The room was larger than she'd expected, and the light was dim. Feeney nodded and flipped the shield on the wide window, closing off the view from outside.

Louise was propped in the hospital bed, the bandages wrapped around her head no whiter than her cheeks. Scanners and IVs ran from her to machines and monitors that hummed and beeped and blinked with lights.

She stirred as Eve approached the bed and opened eyes that were deeply bruised and blurry. A smile ghosted around her mouth.

"I sure as hell earned that half million."

"I'm sorry." Eve wrapped her fingers around the bed guard.

"*You're* sorry." With a weak laugh, Louise lifted her right hand. The wrist was cased in a clear stabilizer. "Next time, *you* get *your* head bashed in, and *I'll* be sorry."

"Deal."

"I got the data. I put it on a disc. It's—"

"I've got it." Feeling helpless, Eve leaned over, laid her hand over Louise's uninjured one. "Don't worry."

"You've got it? What the hell did you need me for?"

"Insurance."

Louise sighed, closed her eyes. "I don't know how much good it'll do you. I think it goes deep. Scary. Christ, they gave me primo drugs here, I'm about to go flying."

"Tell me who hurt you. You saw them."

"Yeah. So stupid. I was pissed. Put the disc away for safe keeping, then figured I'd handle it myself. Confront the enemy on my turf. Fading out here, Dallas.''

"Tell me who hurt you, Louise."

"I called her in, let it rip. Next thing . . . caught me off guard. Never thought . . . Jan. Faithful nurse. Go get the bitch for me, Dallas. I can't kick her ass until I can stand up.''

"I'll get her for you."

"Get all the bastards," she mumbled, then drifted off.

"She was coherent," Eve said to Feeney, hardly aware she still held Louise's hand. "She wouldn't have been that coherent if there was brain damage."

"I'd say the lady has a hard head. Jan?" He took out his memo pad. "Nurse at the clinic? I'll pick her up."

Eve slid her hand away, shoved it into her pocket as she battled impotence. "Will you let me know?"

His eyes met hers over Louise. "First thing."

"Good. Great. I'd better get out before I'm tagged." She stopped with her hand on the door. "Feeney?"

"Yeah."

"Peabody's a good cop."

"That she is."

"If I don't get back, ask Cartright to take her."

His throat closed, so he swallowed hard. "You'll be back, Dallas."

She turned, met his eyes again. "If I don't get back," she said evenly, "ask Cartright to take her. Peabody wants Homicide, she wants to make detective. Cartright can bring her along. Just do that for me."

"Yeah." His shoulders slumped. "Yeah, okay. God-damn it," he muttered when she'd slipped out the door. "Goddamn it."

Roarke gave her the silence he thought she needed on the drive home. He was certain, in her mind, she was riding with Feeney and Peabody, standing beside the door of Jan's apartment, issuing the standard police order and warning.

And because she'd need to, kicking in the door.

"You could use some sleep," he said when they were

home and inside. "But I imagine you need to work."

"I've got to do this."

"I know." The hurt was back in her eyes, the weariness back in her face. "I've got to do this." He drew her into his arms, held her.

"I'm okay." But she wallowed in him, for just a moment. "I can deal with whatever happens as long as we close this one out. I couldn't accept whatever I'll have to accept if we don't put this one away."

"You will." He stroked a hand over her hair. "We will."

"And if I start to sulk again, just slap me around."

"I do so enjoy beating my wife." He closed his hand over hers and started upstairs. "Best to use the unregistered equipment. I've had a unit working on searching for buried records at the lab. We may have hit."

"I've got the disc Louise made. I didn't give it to Feeney." She waited while he uncoded the door. "He didn't ask for it."

"You've chosen your friends well. Ah, hard at work." He glanced at the console, smiling slowly as he scanned the readouts from his scan of the lab at the Drake. "And it appears we've found something. Some interesting megabites of unregistered, unaccounted-for data. I'll need to work on this. He'll have covered this well, as he did his own log, but I know how his mind travels now."

"Can you run this on the side?" She handed him the disc. When he popped it into a secondary unit, then sat down at the main controls, she frowned. "Pop the Friend information on one of the screens. And I guess you want coffee?"

"Actually, I'd rather a brandy. Thanks."

She rolled her eyes and went to retrieve it. "You know, if you'd bring in some droids instead of leaving everything to that tight-assed snot Summerset—"

"You're moving perilously close to sulking."

She clamped her mouth shut, poured brandy, ordered coffee for herself, and sat down to work with her back to him.

She studied the data on Westley Friend's death first. There had been no suicide note. According to his family and closest friends, he had been depressed, distracted, edgy during the days before his death. They had assumed it was due to the stress of his work, the lecture tours, the media and advertising schedule he kept to endorse NewLife products.

He'd been found dead in his office in the Nordick Clinic, at his desk, with the pressure syringe on the floor beside him.

Barbs, she mused, eyes narrowed. The same method as Wo.

There were no coincidences, she told herself. But there were patterns. There were routines.

At the time of his death, she read, he had been heading a team of prominent doctors and researchers involved in a classified project.

She noted with grim satisfaction that Cagney's, Wo's, and Vanderhaven's names were listed as top team members.

Patterns, she thought again. *Conspiracies.*

Just what was your secret project, Friend, and why did it kill you?

"It goes deep," Eve murmured. "It goes long, and they're all in it."

She turned back to Roarke. "Hard to find a killer when they come in bulk. How many of them have a part in this or knew and turned a blind eye? Close ranks." She shook her head. "And it doesn't end with doctors. We're going to find cops, politicians, executives, investors."

"I'm sure you're right. It won't help you, Eve, to take it personally."

"There's no other way to take it." She leaned back on the desk. "Run Louise's disc, will you?"

Louise's voice slid out. "Dallas, looks like you owe me five hundred K. I can't say I'm positive what—"

"Mute that, would you?" Roarke picked up his brandy and worked the keyboard one-handed. "It's distracting."

Eve gritted her teeth, hit mute. *This taking orders crap,*

she decided, *had to stop.* The sudden thought flashed that they might reinstate her but bust her down to detective or uniform. She barely resisted lowering her head to the console and screaming.

She took a deep breath, then another. Then focused on the monitor.

I can't say I'm positive what it all means, but I have some theories, and don't like any of them. You'll see from the records that follow that regular calls have gone out from the main 'link here at the clinic to the Drake. While we might contact some department there on occasion for a consult, there are too many, too often, and all from the main 'link. Rotation doctors use this office 'link. Only nurses and clerical staff use the main regularly. There are also calls to the Nordick in Chicago. Unless we had a patient who had used that facility and whose records would be there, we would have little reason to contact an out-of-state. Possibly, in rare cases, to reach a specialist. This same principle applies to the centers in London and Paris. You'll find only a few calls there.

I've checked, and the contact numbers for each facility are the organ wings. I've also checked the logs here for who was on duty when these calls were made. There's only one staff member whose schedule fits the time frame. I'm going to have a little chat with her after I file this. I can't think of an explanation she can come up with that'll satisfy me, but I'm going to give her a chance before I call the cops.

I assume, when I do, I'm to keep your name out of it. How about a bonus? We won't call it blackmail. Ha ha.

Get these murdering bastards, Dallas.
Louise.

"Didn't I tell you just to get the data?" Eve mumbled. "What the hell were you thinking, hotshot?"

She glanced at her wrist unit, calculated that even now

Feeney and Peabody would be hauling Jan's butt into interview. She thought she would cheerfully give up a decade of her life to be inside that room and in charge.

No sulking, she reminded herself and began to scan the 'link logs when the one beside her beeped.

"Dallas." She frowned as she saw Feeney's face. "You get Jan into interview already?"

"No."

"You've picked her up?"

"More or less. She's about to be bagged and tagged. We found her in her apartment, dead and still fresh. Whoever took her out did it fast and neat. Single blow to the head. Prelim time puts it less than thirty minutes before we got to her door."

"Hell." Eve closed her eyes a minute, shifted her thoughts. "That puts it under that same amount of time after Louise regained consciousness. Defensive wound indicated she'd seen her attacker and could identify."

"Somebody didn't want Jan to talk." Feeney pursed his lips, nodded. "Follows."

"That puts it back at the Drake, Feeney. Wo's out. We need to find out where the other doctors on the short list were in that hour period. You've got the security discs and logs from Jan's building."

"Peabody's confiscating right now."

"He wouldn't have done it himself. He's not stupid. You're going to find a droid, six two, two ten, Caucasian, brown and brown. But somebody had to activate and program."

"Droid." Feeney nodded. "McNab hit something interesting when he scanned for data on the self-destruct units. Senator Waylan headed the subcommittee that studied their military uses."

"I have a feeling he won't be running for another term." She rubbed her fingers over her eyes. "Check the logs for security droids at the Drake. Wake up McNab. He could run a systems check on them if you can get a warrant for it. Even if the program was wiped, he'd find the lag time. When you've . . ."

She trailed off, snapping back. "Sorry," she said in a careful voice. "Just thinking out loud."

"You think good, kid. Always have. Keep going."

"I was going to say that in some of the research I've done, I found that Westley Friend's self-termination used the same method as Dr. Wo, and they were both—along with some of our other cast of characters—involved in some classified project at the time of his death. It seems a little too neat. Someone might want to suggest to Morris that he consider that dose was forcibly administered."

"It was her pin found on scene."

"Yeah, and it was the only mistake in this whole business. That's a little too neat, too."

"Smelling goat, are you, Dallas? Scapegoat?"

"Yeah, that's what I'm smelling. Be interesting to find out how much she knew. If I had access to her personal logs . . ."

"I think I'll just wake up McNab, keep the boy busy awhile. You stand by."

"I'm not going anywhere."

When the transmission ended, she picked up her coffee and got up to prowl. It had to go back to Friend, she decided. Revolutionary new implant that made certain hot areas of organ research obsolete. Meaning end of funding, end of glory for those heavily involved in those areas.

"What if a group of doctors or interested parties continued and restarted research on a covert level?" She turned to Roarke, grimaced when she noted he was manning the keyboard. "Sorry."

"It's all right. I've got his pattern now. It's nearly routine from here." He glanced up, pleased to see her focused, restless, edgy. That, he thought, was his cop. "What's your theory?"

"It's not one rogue doctor," she began. "Look at this little operation. I can't do this out on my own. I've got you, with your questionable skills. Feeney, Peabody, and McNab, sliding under regs and procedure to feed me data. I enlisted a doctor on the side. I've even got Nadine running research. It's too big for one cop—and a cop working outside the system—to handle alone. You need contacts, fillers, assistants, experts. There's a team, Roarke. He's got a team. We know he had the nurse. My best guess is she fed him data on patients, the kind that use the clinic or make use of the medi-van service. Sleepers, LCs, dealers, chemi-heads. Dregs,'' she concluded. ''Vessels.''

''She contacted someone with possible donors, let's say.'' Roarke nodded. ''Every business needs a good inside track. And this appears to be a business.''

''She passed data straight to the labs. Her contact with the outside centers could have, likely was, for verification of a hit. She'd be what you'd call middle management, I guess.''

''Close enough.''

''I bet we find she has a nice nest egg stashed. They'd pay well. We know their lab man had to be Young. Every business needs a geek, right?''

''Can't run one otherwise.''

''The Drake's enormous, and our geek was pretty much in charge of the organ wing. He'd know just where to stash outside samples. And he had a medical license. He'd be the likely candidate to assist the surgeon, to bag the sample, to transport it back to the lab. That's two.''

She crossed to the AutoChef, getting more coffee. ''Wo. Politics and administration. A skilled surgeon who enjoyed power. Former president of the AMA. She knew how to play the game. She'd have high connections. But obviously, she was also considered dispensable. Maybe she had a conscience, maybe she was getting nervous, or maybe they just sacrificed her to throw the investigation off the scent. It worked for Friend,'' she mused. ''He wouldn't have been pleased, do you think, if he'd discovered this rogue research conspiracy. It would have cut into his profits, his glory. There go the lecture fees, the big banquets in his honor, the media hype.''

''Only if what they're doing, or hope to do, works.''

''Yeah. They're willing to kill to make it work, so why not take out the competition? It used to be organ building.

Louise sort of explained it in the initial report she did for me. They took tissue from a damaged or defective organ and built a new one in the lab. Grew them in molds so the tissue'd take the right shape. That solved the rejection problem. You used the patient's own tissue so the body'd accept it and tick along. But it takes time. You just don't grow yourself a new, happy heart overnight.''

She walked back to the console, eased a hip on the edge, and watched him work as she talked it out. ''They do that kind of thing in vitro. You got like nine months to deal there. You can grow the bad part back or repair it.

''Then Friend comes along,'' she continued. ''Building and brokering organs has been the thing. It's tough to grow them for anyone over—I forget—like ninety because of the timing and the age of the tissue. Takes weeks to grow a new bladder and you've got to do molding and layering and stuff. A lot of work, a lot of money to order one up. But Friend comes up with this artificial material that the body accepts. It's cheap, it's durable, and it can be molded to order. Mass-produced. Applause, applause, let's all live forever.''

He glanced up at that, had to grin. ''Don't you want to?''

''Not with a bunch of interchangeable spare parts. But anyhow, he gets carried through the streets, the crowd roars and throws buckets of money and adulation at him. And the guys doing organ building and reconstruction research are shoved right out into the cold. Who wants to hang around peeing in a diaper while their new bladder's growing in some lab when they can pop into surgery, get a new, improved one, and be peeing like a champ inside a week?''

''Agreed. And that manufacturing arm of Roarke Industries thanks the full bladders everywhere. But since everyone's happy this way, what good will this little group of mad scientists prove by continuing their work?''

''You keep your own,'' she said simply. ''Medically,

it's probably some major miracle—regeneration—like the Frankenstein guy. Here's this half-dead, messed-up heart. Not gonna tick much longer. But what if it can be fixed, completely, like new? You got the part you were born with, not some piece of foreign matter. The Conservative party, which includes Senator Waylan, would dance in the street. Plenty of them have artificial tickers, but they like to stomp around every few years and talk about how it's against the rules of God and humankind to prolong life by artificial means.''

"Darling, you've been reading the papers. I'm so impressed.''

"Kiss my ass.'' And it felt good to grin. "I'm betting when Nadine gets in touch, she'll tell me Waylan stands against artificial life aids. You know, the 'if God didn't give it to you, it's immoral' line.''

"NewLife routinely deals with protests from natural-life groups. I imagine we'll find the senator supports their stand.''

"Yeah, and if he can make a few bucks running interference for a group who promises a new medical and natural miracle, so to speak, so much the better. It would have to be a quick procedure. It couldn't be risky to the patient,'' she went on. "They'd never outdo the implant unless what they do is as convenient and as successful. Business,'' she said again. "Profit. Glory. Votes.''

"Agreed, again. I'd say they've been working with animal organs up until recently. They must have reached a level of success with that.''

"Then they moved up the evolutionary scale. Kept low on it from their viewpoint. Scum, as Cagney put it.''

"I'm in,'' he said mildly and had her blinking.

"In what? *In?* What've you got? Let me see.''

Even as she dashed around the console, he ordered data on-screen. When he pulled her neatly onto his lap, she was too distracted for even a token protest.

"Neat as a pin,'' she murmured. "Names, dates, procedures, results. Jesus Christ, Roarke, they're all there.''

*Jasper Mott, October 15, 2058, heart sample success-
fully removed. Evaluation concurred with previous diagnosis. Organ severely damaged, enlarged. Estimated
period until termination, one year.*
   Logged as donor organ K-489.
   Regeneration procedure begun October 16.

She bypassed the rest, focused on her case, her first
victim, Snooks.

*Samuel M. Petrinsky, January 12, 2059, heart sample
successfully removed. Evaluation concurred with previous diagnosis. Organ severely damaged, arteries brittle and clogged, cancer cells stage two. Sample
enlarged, estimated period until termination, three
months.*
   Logged as brokered organ S-351.
   Regeneration procedure begun January 13.

She skimmed down the rest, out of her depth with the
medical jargon. But the last line was easily understood.

*Procedure unsuccessful. Sample terminated and dis-
posed of, January 15.*

"They stole three months of his life, then failed and
tossed his heart away."
"Look at the last one, Eve."
She noted the name—Jilessa Brown—the date, the
sample removed.

*January 25. Preliminary regeneration successful. Stage
two begun. Sample responding to injection and stimuli.
Noticeable regrowth of healthy cells. Stage three begun
January 26. Naked eye exam shows pinkening of tissue.
Sample fully regenerated within thirty-six hours of first
injection. All scans and evaluations conclude sample is*

healthy. No indication of disease. Aging process suc-
cessfully reversed. Organ fully functional.

"Well." Eve drew a deep breath. "Applause, applause.
Now let's fry their asses."

I have done it. Through skill and patience and power,
through a judicious use of fine minds and greedy hearts,
I have succeeded. Life, essentially endless, is within my
reach.

It remains only to repeat the process again, continue the
documentation.

My heart trembles, but my hands are steady. They are
ever steady. I can look at them and see how perfect they
are. Elegant, strong, like works of art carved by divine
hands. I've held beating hearts in these hands, have
slipped them delicately into the human body to repair, to
improve, to prolong life.

Now, finally, I have conquered death.

Some of those fine minds will have regrets, will ask
questions, will even doubt the steps that had to be taken
now that the goal has been reached. I will not. Great
strides often crush even the innocent under the heel.

If lives were lost, we will consider them martyrs to the
greater good. Nothing more, nothing less.

Some of those greedy hearts will wheedle and whine,
will demand more and calculate how to gain it. Let them.
There will be enough for even the most avaricious among
them.

And there will be some who will debate the meaning
of what I've done, the means by which it was accom-
plished, and the use of the process. In the end, they'll
shove and elbow their way in line, desperate for what I
can give them.

And pay whatever is asked.

Within a year, my name will be on the lips of kings
and presidents. Glory, fame, wealth, power. They are at
my fingertips. What fate once stole from me I have

snatched back tenfold. Grand health centers, cathedrals to the art of medicine, will be built for me in every city, in every country on this planet, and everywhere man races to beat death.

Humanity will cannonize me. The saint of their survival.

God is dead, and I am His replacement.

chapter twenty-two

How to do it was problematic. She could copy the data and send it to Feeney along the same route she had the other information. He'd have it in hand the next day. It would be enough for a warrant, for search and seizure, to drag high-level staff members into interview.

It was a way, a completely unsatisfying way.

She could go to the Drake Center herself, punch her way into the lab, record the data, the samples, pound on high-level staff members until they spilled their guts.

It was not the way, but it would have been very satisfying.

She tapped the disc she'd copied on her palm. "Feeney will close it within forty-eight hours, once he has this. It may take longer to round up everyone involved on at least two continents. But it'll stop."

"We'll put it in overnight now." He laid his hands on her shoulders, massaged the tension and fatigue. "I know it's hard not being there at the end of it. You can comfort yourself knowing there wouldn't be an end in a couple of days unless you'd found the answers. You're a hell of a cop, Eve."

"I was."

"Are. Your test results and Mira's evaluation will put you back where you belong. On the other side of the line." He leaned down, kissed her. "I'll miss you."

It made her smile. "You manage to wiggle in, whichever side of the line I'm on. Let's get this data on its way. Then we'll watch the cleanup on-screen in a day or two, like normal citizens."

"Wear your coat this time."

"My coat's trash," she reminded him as they came down the stairs.

"You have another." He opened a door, took out a long sweep of bronze cashmere. "It's too cold for your jacket."

Eyeing him, she fingered the sleeve. "What, do you have some droids in a room somewhere manufacturing these?"

"In a manner of speaking. Gloves in the pocket," he reminded her and shrugged on his own coat.

She had to admit, it was nice to be wrapped in something warm and soft against the bitter air. "Once we dump this data, let's come back, get naked, and crawl all over each other."

"Sounds like a plan."

"And tomorrow, you go back to work and stop hovering."

"I don't believe I've been hovering. I believe I've been playing Nick to your Nora, and quite well."

"Nick who?"

"Charles, darling. We're going to have to spend time educating you in the entertainment value of classic early–twentieth-century cinema."

"I don't know where you find time for that stuff. It must be because you don't sleep like a regular human being. You're out there piling up billions and buying small worlds and—which reminds me, we need to discuss this idiotic idea of yours about stuffing money in some account for me. I want you to take it back."

"All five million plus, or less the half million you're donating to the Canal Street Clinic?"

"Don't get smart with me, pal. I married you for your body, not your bucks."

"Darling Eve, that's so touching. And all the while I thought it was my coffee connection."

Love could swamp her at the oddest times, she realized. "That didn't hurt. Tomorrow, you do whatever it is you do to zap it back out and close it down. And next time you . . . Louise. Oh Christ. Head to the Drake! Head there now! Damn it, how did this slip by us?"

He punched up speed, clipped the curb at the corner. "You think they'll go after her?"

"They took out Jan. They can't let Louise talk." Ignoring jams and privacy, she used the car 'link and tagged Feeney on his communicator.

"Get to the Drake," she told him. "Get to Louise. I'm on my way, ETA five minutes. They'll go for her, Feeney. They've got to go for her. She had data."

"We'll head out. She's under guard, Dallas."

"It won't matter. The uniform won't question a doctor. Contact him, Feeney, tell him not to let anyone in that room."

"Confirmed. Our ETA fifteen minutes."

"We'll be there in two," Roarke promised her as he flew across town. "Waverly?"

"Current president of AMA, chief of surgery, organ specialist, board member. Affiliated with several top-level centers worldwide." She slapped a hand on the dash to keep her balance when he swung into the garage. "Cagney—he's her uncle, but he's chief of staff, chairman, and one of the most respected surgeons in the country. Hans Vanderhaven, international connections. God knows where he is right now. If not them, there are others who can walk right in and get to her without anyone blinking twice. There must be a dozen ways to off a patient, then cover the tracks."

She sprang out of the car, raced for the elevator. "They don't know she's talked to me. She's smart enough to keep that to herself, maybe to play dumb if anybody tries to pump her. But they might have gotten something out of Jan before they killed her. They've got to know by now she has data on the calls, asked questions, made accusations."

She watched the numbers light above the door, willed them to hurry.

"They'd wait until the floor was quiet, until the change of shifts, most likely."

"We won't be too late," she promised herself, and sprang out of the elevator the moment the doors opened.

"Miss!" A nurse came scrambling around the desk as Eve rushed by. "Miss, you're required to check in at the desk. You're not authorized." Racing after them, she dragged out her beeper and called security.

"Where's the uniform assigned to this door?" Eve demanded, shoving and finding the door itself secured.

"I don't know." Grim-faced, the nurse moved over to block them from the door. "This is a family or authorized personnel only area."

"Unlock this door."

"I will not. I've called security. The patient in this room is not to be disturbed as per doctor's orders. I'll have to ask you to leave."

"Go ahead and ask." Rearing back, Eve broke the door open with two vicious kicks. Her clutch piece seemed to leap into her hand as she ran through. "Oh God, goddamn."

The bed was empty.

The nurse sputtered when Eve whirled on her, grabbed her by the collar of her pale peach uniform smock. "Where's Louise?"

"I—I don't know. She's supposed to be here. She was logged out as not to disturb when I came on shift twenty minutes ago."

"Eve. Here's your uniform."

Roarke was crouched on the other side of the bed, testing the unconscious cop's pulse. "He's alive, sedated heavily I'd say."

"Which doctor logged her as not to be disturbed?"

"Her attending. Dr. Waverly."

"Do something for that uniform," she ordered the nurse. "Cops will be here in ten minutes. I want you to order this building sealed, all exits."

"I don't have the authority."

"Do it!" Eve repeated. She spun on her heel. "Organ wing, best guess. We'll have to separate when we get there. We can't cover the whole wing in time unless we do."

"We'll find her." They hit the elevator together. He pried open the plate, flipped some controls. "We're now straight express. Brace yourself."

She didn't even have the breath to curse. The speed pressed her into the corner, made her eyes tear and her heart thunder. She had a moment to pray he'd remembered to engage the brakes when they jerked to a stop that had her stumbling hard into him.

"Some ride. Here, take my piece."

"Thanks, Lieutenant, but I have my own." His face was cold and set as he drew out a sleek nine-millimeter. A weapon, like all handguns, that had been banned decades earlier.

"Shit," was all she had time to say.

"I'll go east, you take the west side."

"Don't fire that weapon unless—" she began, but he was out and gone.

She got her bearings and moved down the corridor, sweeping with her weapon as she came to a turn or a door. She fought the urge to rush. Each new area had to be carefully searched before she moved to the next.

She gazed up to the cameras scanning. It would be a miracle, she knew, if she came across her objective without being expected. And she knew she was being led when doors that should have been locked gave way as she approached.

"Okay, you son of a bitch," she whispered. "You want a one-on-one? So do I."

She made another turn, faced double doors fashioned of heavy, opaque glass. There was a palm plate, a cornea scanner, timed locks. A computerized voice activated as she stepped forward.

Warning. This is a secured area. Authorized Level Five personnel only. Hazardous biological material contained within. Warning. Anticontamination suits required. No entry without authorization.

The doors slid smoothly open.

"I guess I've just been authorized."

"Your tenacity is admirable, Lieutenant. Please, come in."

Waverly had removed his lab coat. He was dressed as if for an elegant evening engagement in a perfectly cut dark suit with a silk tie. His gold caduceus glinted in the bright lights.

He smiled charmingly and held a pressure syringe against the pulse in Louise's throat. Eve's heart bumped once, hard against her ribs. Then she saw the gentle rise and fall of Louise's breasts.

Still breathing, she thought, and she intended to keep it that way.

"You got sloppy in the end, Doc."

"I don't think so. Just a few loose ends needing to be tied off and snipped. I suggest you put down your weapon, Lieutenant, unless you want me to administer this very fast-acting, very lethal medication to our young friend here."

"Is that the same stuff you used on Friend and Wo?"

"As it happens, Hans treated Tia. But, yes. It's painless and efficient. The drug of choice for discriminating self-terminators. She'll be dead in less than three minutes. Now, put down your weapon."

"You kill her, you've got no shield."

"You won't let me kill her." He smiled again. "You can't. A woman who risks her life for dead derelicts will swallow her pride for the life of an innocent. I've made quite a study of you in the past couple of weeks, Lieutenant—or should I say *former* Lieutenant Dallas."

"You saw to that, too." She would count on her wits now, Eve thought, as she laid the gun on the counter beside her. And on Roarke.

"You made that simple, all in all. Or Bowers did. Close doors and secure," he ordered, and she heard them snick together at her back, locking her in. Locking backup out.

"Did she work with you?"

"Only indirectly. Move away from your weapon, slowly, to the left. Very good. You have a good mind, and we won't be disturbed in here for some time. I'm happy to cooperate and fill in the blanks for you. It seems only fair, under the circumstances."

To brag, she realized. He needed to brag. Arrogance, God complex. "I don't have too many blanks yet to fill. But I'm interested in how you roped Bowers in."

"She walked into it. Or you did. She turned out to be a handy tool to get rid of you, since threats didn't do the job, and bribery seemed absurd, considering both your record and your financial situation. You cost this area of the Drake a very expensive security droid."

"Well, you've got more."

"Several. One is even now dealing with your husband." The flash in her eyes delighted him. "Ah, that concerns you, I see. I've never been a believer in true love, but the two of you do make a lovely couple. Did."

Roarke was armed, she reminded herself. And he was good. "Roarke isn't easy to deal with."

"He doesn't trouble me overmuch." The arrogance seeped through as Waverly shrugged. "Now, the two of you together were an irritant, but . . well, you were asking about Bowers. It simply fell into place. She was a paranoid violent tendency that slipped through the system and ended up in uniform. There are others, you know."

"It happens."

"Every day. You being assigned to the investigation on—what was his name?"

"Petrinsky. Snooks."

"Yes, yes, that's right. Rosswell was supposed to be

assigned to that matter, but there was some slipup in dispatch.''

"How long have you owned him?"

"Oh, only a few months. If all had gone according to plan, the entire business would have been filed and forgotten.''

"Who've you got in the ME's department?"

"Just a midlevel clerk with an affection for pharmaceuticals.'' He smiled slowly, winningly. "It's a simple matter to find the right person with the right weakness.''

"You killed Snooks for nothing. You failed with him.''

"A disappointment to us. His heart didn't respond. But there must be failures in any serious search for progress, just as there are obstacles to be overcome. You've been quite an obstacle. It was clear very quickly that you'd dig hard and deep and uncomfortably close. We had this problem in Chicago, but we handled it quite easily. You weren't so quickly dispatched, so it took other means. A little cooperation from Rosswell, a bit of ruffling of Bowers's feathers, false data planted, then, of course, we arranged for both of you to meet on another murder scene. She reacted very much as predicted, and while you were admirably controlled, it was enough.''

"So you had her killed, knowing procedure would require my suspension and an investigation.''

"It seemed that had solved our little problem, and with Senator Waylan putting pressure on the mayor, we'd have time to finish. We were so very close to complete success.''

"Organ regeneration.''

"Exactly.'' He all but beamed at her. "You have filled in blanks. I told the others you would.''

"Yeah, I've filled them. Friend screwed up your cushy circle with his artificial implants, knocked away your funding.'' She hooked her thumbs in her pockets, moved a little closer. "You'd have been pretty young then, maybe just getting your toehold. Must've pissed you off.''

"Oh, it did. It took me years to establish myself enough to gather the resources, the team, the equipment to com-

petently continue the work we'd been doing when Friend
destroyed it. I hadn't quite reached the brass ring of prominence when he and some colleagues began experimenting
with melding live tissue with the artificial material. But
Tia, she believed in me, in my passions. She kept me well
informed."

"Did she help you kill him?"

"No, that I did unassisted. Friend had gotten wind of
my interests, experiments. Didn't care for them. He intended to use his influence to cancel my funding—pitiful
as it was—to research the regeneration of animal organs.
I canceled him and his little project first."

"But then you had to go under," she said easing forward with her eyes steady on his. "You planned to move
to human organs eventually, so you covered your tracks."

"And covered them well. Enlisted some of the very
best hands and minds in the medical field. And all's well
that ends well. Watch your step."

She stopped at the foot of the gurney, laid a hand casually on the guard. "You know they've got Young. He'll
roll over on you."

"He'd die first." Waverly chuckled. "The man is ob-
sessed with this project. He sees his name shining in medical journals for the ages. He believes I'm a god. He
would bite through the artery in his own wrist before he'd
betray me."

"Maybe. I guess you couldn't count on that kind of
loyalty from Wo."

"No. She was always a risk, always on the outskirts of
the project. A skilled doctor but a fairly unstable woman.
She began to balk when she discovered our human samples had been . . . appropriated without permission."

"She didn't expect you to kill people."

"They're hardly people."

"And the others?"

"In this arena? Hans believes as I do. Colin?" He
moved an elegant shoulder. "He prefers to wear blinders,
to pretend not to know the full extent of the project. There

are more, of course. An undertaking of this magnitude requires a large if select team.''

"Did you send the droid after Jan?"

"You've found her already." He shook his head in admiration, and his hair gleamed like gold under the bright lab lights. "My, that was quick. Of course. She was one of those loose ends."

"And what will Cagney say when you tell him Louise was another loose end?"

"He won't know. It's very simple, if you know how, to dispose of a body in a health center. The crematorium is efficient and never closed. What happened to her will remain a mystery."

In an absent gesture, Waverly stroked a hand over Louise's hair. Eve wanted to taste his blood for that alone.

"It will likely break him," Waverly considered. "I'm sorry for it. Very sorry to have to sacrifice two fine minds, two excellent doctors, but progress, great progress, requires heavy sacrifice."

"He'll know."

"Oh, on some level, certainly. And he'll deny. He does his best work in denial. But he will consider himself responsible. Guilty, I suppose, by omission. He is certainly aware that experiments and research are being conducted in this and other facilities, without official sanction. He tends to look the other way easily, to call out his loyalty to the club. One doctor does not turn on another."

"But you do."

"My loyalty is to the project."

"What do you hope to gain?"

"Is that the blank you can't fill? My God, we have done it." Now his eyes sparkled, emerald green and full of power. "We can rejuvenate a human organ. Within one day, a dying heart can be treated and brought back to health. Not just health, but strength, youth, vigor." Excitement had his voice rising, deepening. "Better in some cases than it was before it was damaged. It can be all but reanimated, and that, I believe, is possible with a bit more study."

"Bring the dead to life?"

"The stuff of fiction, you're thinking. So were trans-plants once, cornea replacement, in vitro repair. This can and will be done, and very soon. We're nearly ready to go public with our discovery. A serum that, when injected directly into the damaged organ through a simple surgical procedure, will regenerate the cells, will eradicate any dis-ease. A patient will be ambulatory within hours, and will walk out, cured, in under forty-eight. With his own heart or lungs or kidneys, not some artificial mold."

He leaned toward her, eyes gleaming. "You still don't understand the scope. It can be done over and over again, to every organ. And from there, it's a small step to mus-cle, to bone, to tissue. With this beginning, we'll draw in more funding than we can possibly use to complete the work. Within two years, we will be able to remake a hu-man being, using his own body. Life expectancy can and will double. Perhaps more. Death will essentially become obsolete."

"It's never obsolete, Waverly. Not as long as there are people like you. Who will you choose to remake?" she demanded. "There's not enough room, not enough re-sources for everybody to live forever." She watched his smile turn cagey. "It'll come down to money then, and selection."

"Who needs more aging whores or sidewalk sleepers? We have Waylan in our pocket, and he'll push his influ-ence in East Washington. The politicians will jump right on this. We've found a way to clean up the streets over the next generation, to employ a kind of natural selection, survival of the fittest."

"Of your selection, your choice."

"And why not? Who better to decide than those who've held human hearts in their hands, slid into the brain and gut? Who understands better?"

"That's the mission," she said quietly. "To create and mold and select."

"Admit it, Dallas, the world would be a better place without the dregs that weigh it down."

"You're right. We just have a different definition of dregs."

She shoved the gurney hard to the right and leaped over it.

Roarke crouched at the secured door. His entire world had become that single control panel. There was a raw bruise on his cheekbone, a jagged gash in his shoulder.

The security droid was minus his left arm and head, but it had taken entirely too much time.

He forced his mind to stay focused, his vision to remain clear, and his hands steady. He never flinched when he heard footsteps pounding down the corridor behind him. He could recognize the slap of cheap cop shoes a mile off.

"Jesus, Roarke, was that droid your work?"

"She's in there." He didn't glance back at Feeney, but continued to search for the next bypass. "I know it. Give me room, don't get in my light."

Peabody cleared her throat as the computer warning sounded again. "If you're wrong—"

"I'm not wrong."

She rammed her fist into his face and relished the sting of knuckles meeting flesh. Something ripped as she tackled him and sent them crashing onto the floor.

He wasn't soft, and he was desperate. She tasted her own blood, felt her bones jar, saw one quick burst of stars when her head cracked against the wheels of the gurney.

She didn't use the pain, she didn't need it. She used her rage. Half blind with it, she straddled him, slamming her elbow into his windpipe. He gagged, strained for air. And she twisted the syringe he'd nearly pumped into her side out of his hand.

Wheezing, eyes huge, he went still as she tipped it against his throat. "Scared, you bastard? Different on the other end, isn't it? Move the wrong way, and you're dead. What did you say? Within three minutes? I'll just sit here and watch you die, like you watched all those people die."

"Don't." It was a rusty croak. "I'm choking. Can't get air."

"I could put you out of your misery." She smiled as his eyes wheeled in his head. "But it's just too damn easy. You want to live forever, Waverly? You can live forever in a fucking cage."

She started to climb off him, sighed once. "I just have to," she muttered, and rammed one short-armed jab into his face.

She was just pulling herself to her feet when the doors swung open. "Well." She swiped the back of her hand across her swollen mouth. "The gang's all here." Cautiously, she turned the syringe upside down. "You might want to seal this, Peabody, poison precautions, it's lethal. Hey, Roarke, you're bleeding."

He stepped to her, gently wiped her lip with his thumb. "You, too."

"Good thing we're in a health center, huh? Ruined that fancy coat."

Now he grinned. "You, too."

"Told ya. Feeney, you can interview me when you clean up this mess. Somebody ought to take a look at Louise. He must have sedated her. She slept through this whole thing. And pick up Rosswell, would you? Waverly rolled over on him."

"It'll be a pleasure. Anybody else?"

"Cagney and Vanderhaven, who happen to be in the city, according to Dr. Death here. There'll be more, here and there." She glanced back where Waverly lay unconscious. "He'll give it up. He's got no balls at all." She picked up her clutch piece, stuck it in her back pocket. "We're going home."

"Good work, Dallas."

For a moment, her eyes were absolutely bleak, then she grinned, shrugged. "Yeah. What the hell." Sliding her arm around Roarke, she walked away.

"Peabody."

"Captain?"

"Get Commander Whitney out of bed."

"Sir?"

"Tell him Captain Feeney respectfully requests his administrative ass on-scene here as soon as possible."

Peabody cleared her throat. "Is it okay if I rephrase that slightly?"

"Just get him here." With that, Feeney walked over to take a look at Dallas's good work.

She was dead asleep when the 'link beeped. For perhaps the first time in her life, she simply rolled over and ignored it. When Roarke shook her shoulder, she just grunted and yanked the cover over her head.

"I'm sleeping here."

"You just had a call from Whitney. He wants you in his office at Central in an hour."

"Shit. That can't be good." Resigned, she pushed the covers back, sat up. "The test results and evaluation can't be in yet. It's too early. Goddamn it, Roarke. I'm busted."

"Let's go in and find out."

She shook her head, dragged herself out of bed. "This isn't for you."

"You aren't going in alone. Pull yourself together, Eve."

She bit down on the despair, rolled back her shoulders, and looked at him. He was already in a business suit, his hair shining and sleek. The bruise on his cheekbone had nearly faded away with treatment, but the shadow of it added just a hint of the dangerous.

"How come you already are?"

"Because staying in bed half the morning unless sex is involved is a waste of time. Since you didn't appear to be cooperative in that area, I started my day with coffee instead. Stop stalling and go take your shower."

"Okay, fine, great." She stalked into the bathroom so they could worry in different rooms.

She refused breakfast. He didn't press. But as he drove

downtown, she reached for his hand. He held it until he'd parked at Central and turned to her.

"Eve." He cupped her face, relieved that though she was pale, she didn't tremble. "Remember who you are."

"I'm working on it. I'll be all right. You can wait here."

"Not a chance."

"Okay." She took a bracing breath. "Let's do it."

They rode in silence. As cops piled off and on the elevator from floor to floor, gazes flickered toward her, then away. There was nothing to be said, and no way to say it.

Her stomach rolled as she stepped off, but her legs were steady as she approached the outer office of the commander.

The door was open. Whitney stood behind his desk and gestured her inside. His gaze shifted briefly to Roarke.

"Sit down, Dallas."

"I'll stand, sir."

They weren't alone in the room. As before, Tibble stood at the window. Others sat silently: Feeney with his morose face, Peabody with her lips clamped tight, Webster eyeing Roarke specutively. Before Whitney could speak again, Mira hurried in.

"I'm terribly sorry to be late. I was with a patient." She took a seat beside Peabody, folded her hands.

Whitney nodded, then opened the center drawer of his desk. He took out her badge, her weapon, laid them in the center. Her gaze lowered to them, lingered, then lifted without expression.

"Lieutenant Webster."

"Sir." He rose. "The Internal Affairs Bureau finds no cause for sanction or reprimand or for further investigation into the conduct of Lieutenant Dallas."

"Thank you, Lieutenant. Detective Baxter is in the field, but his investigative report on the homicide of Officer Ellen Bowers has been written and filed. The case has been closed, and Lieutenant Dallas is cleared of any suspicion or involvement in that matter. This confirms your evaluation, Dr. Mira.''

''Yes, it does. The test results and evaluation clear the lieutenant in all areas and confirm her aptitude for her position. My reports have been entered into the subject's file.''

''So noted,'' Whitney said and turned back to Eve. She hadn't moved, hadn't blinked. ''The New York Police and Security Department offers its apologies to one of its finest for an injustice done to her. I add my own personal apology to it. Procedure is necessary, but it is not always equitable.''

Tibble stepped forward. ''The suspension is lifted and will be expunged from your record. You will not be penalized in any way for the enforced time away from the job. The department will issue a statement to the media detailing what facts are deemed pertinent and necessary. Commander?''

''Sir.'' Whitney's face remained passive as he picked up her badge, her weapon, held them out. Emotion sparked in his eyes when she simply stared at them. ''Lieutenant Dallas, this department and myself would suffer a great loss if you refuse these.''

She remembered to breathe and lifted her gaze, met his, then reached out and took what was hers. Across the room, Peabody sniffled audibly.

''Lieutenant.'' Whitney offered his hand across the desk. A rare grin broke out on his face when she clasped it. ''You're on duty.''

''Yes, sir.'' She turned, looked straight at Roarke. ''Just let me get rid of this civilian.'' Watching him, she tucked away her badge, shrugged into her harness. ''Can I see you outside a minute?''

''Absolutely.''

He sent the sniffling Peabody a wink and walked out after his wife. The minute they were out of view, he spun her around, kissed her lavishly. ''It's nice to see you again, Lieutenant.''

"Oh God." Her breath hitched in and out. "I've got to get out of here without . . . you know."

"Yes." He wiped a tear off her lashes. "I know."

"You have to go or I'll fall apart. But maybe you could be around later, so I could."

"Get to work." He tapped a finger on her chin. "You've been loafing long enough."

She grinned, swiped the back of her unsteady hand inelegantly under her nose as he walked away. "Hey, Roarke?"

"Yes, Lieutenant?"

She laughed, rushed at him, leaped, and gave him a hard, smacking kiss. "See you."

"You certainly will." He flashed her one last devastating grin before the elevator doors closed him in.

"Lieutenant Dallas, sir." Peabody snapped to attention, a dopey grin on her face when Eve turned around. "I didn't want to interrupt, but I'm ordered to return your communicator." She dashed forward, shoved it into Eve's hand, and bounced her up and down in a hug. "Hot damn!"

"Let's maintain a little dignity here, Peabody."

"Okay. Can we go out later to celebrate and get drunk and stupid?"

Eve pursed her lips in thought as they headed for the glide. "Got plans tonight," she said thinking of that last flashing grin of Roarke's, "but tomorrow works for me."

"Frigid. So look, Feeney said I should tell you we've still got some details to wrap up to close this case good and tight. International connections, the East Washington angle, a full sweep of staff at the Drake, coordinating cooperative investigations with CPSD."

"It'll take some time, but we'll clean it up. Vanderhaven?"

"Still at large." She sent Eve a sidelong look. "Waverly's out of the health center. He's cleared to be interviewed any time, and he's already singing out names hoping for leniency. We figure he'll spit out Vanderhaven's hole. Feeney figured you'd want to take the interview.''

"He figured right." Eve hopped off the glide, changed directions. "Let's go kick some ass, Peabody."

"I love when you say that. Sir."

If you enjoyed *Conspiracy in Death*
you won't want to miss J. D. Robb's newest
novel of romantic suspense . . .

LOYALTY IN DEATH

Here is a special excerpt from this
provocative new novel coming soon from
The Berkley Publishing Group . . .

Death is impartial. From the rich and privileged leading their glossy lives in silver towers over the city to the poor and desperate cking out survival on the streets and in the alleys below those minor palaces, death shows no bias.

On this particular night, a beggar died unnoticed under a bench in Greenpeace Park. A history professor fell bloodied, his throat slashed three feet from his front door for the twelve credits in his pocket. A woman choked out one last scream as she crumpled under her lover's pounding fists.

And not yet done, death circled its bony finger, then jabbed it gleefully between the eyes of one J. Clarence Branson, the fifty-year-old co-president of Branson Tools and Toys.

He'd been rich, single and successful, a jolly man with reason to be as co-owner of a major interplanetary corporation. A second son, and the third generation of Bransons to provide the world and its satellites with implements and amusements, he'd lived lavishly.

And had died the same way.

J. Clarence's heart had been skewered with one of his own multi-power porta drills by his steely-eyed mistress, who'd bolted him to the wall with it, reported the incident to the police, then had calmly sat sipping claret until the first officers arrived on scene.

She continued to sip her drink, settled cozily in a high-backed chair in front of a computer-generated fire while Lieutenant Eve Dallas examined the body.

"He's absolutely dead," she coolly informed Eve. Her name was Lisbeth Cooke, and she made her living as an advertising executive in her deceased lover's company. She was forty, sleekly attractive and very good at her job. "The Branson 8000 is an excellent product—designed to satisfy both the professional and the hobbyist. It's very powerful and accurate."

"Uh-huh." Eve scanned the victim's face. Pampered and handsome, even though death had etched a look of stunned and sorrowful surprise on his face. Blood soaked through the breast of his blue velvet dressing gown and puddled glossily on the floor. "Sure did the job here. Read Ms. Cooke her rights, Peabody."

While her aide attended to the matter, Eve verified time and cause of death for the record. Even with the voluntary confession, the business of murder would follow routine. The weapon would be taken into evidence, the body transported and autopsied, the scene secured.

Gesturing to the crime scene team to take over, Eve crossed the royal red carpet, sat across from Lisbeth in front of the chirpy fire that blew out lush heat and light. She said nothing for a moment, waiting several beats to see what reaction she might get from the fashionable brunette with fresh blood splattered somehow gaily on her yellow silk jumpsuit.

She got nothing but a politely inquiring stare. "So . . . you want to tell me about it?"

"He was cheating on me," Lisbeth said flatly. "I killed him."

Eve studied the steady green eyes, saw anger but no shock or remorse. "Did you argue?"

"We had a few words." Lisbeth lifted her claret to full lips painted the same rich tone as the wine. "Most of them mine. J. C. was weak-minded.'' She shrugged her shoulders and silk rustled. ''I accepted that, even found it endearing in many ways. But we had an arrangement. I gave him three years of my life.''

Now she leaned forward, eyes snapping with the temper behind the chill. ''Three years, during which time I could have pursued other interests, other arrangements, other relationships. But I was faithful. He was not.''

She drew in a breath, leaned back again, very nearly smiled. ''Now he's dead.''

''Yeah, we got that part.'' Eve heard the ugly suck and scrape as the team struggled to remove the long steel spike from flesh and bone. ''Did you bring the drill with you, Ms. Cooke, with the intention of using it as a weapon?''

''No, it's J. C.'s. He putters occasionally. He must have been puttering,'' she mused with a casual glance toward the body the crime scene team was now removing from the wall in a ghastly ballet of movements. ''I saw it there, on the table, and thought, well, that's just perfect, isn't it? So I picked it up, flicked it on. And used it.''

It didn't get much simpler, Eve mused, and rose. ''Ms. Cooke, these officers will take you down to Cop Central. I'll have some more questions for you.''

Obligingly, Lisbeth swallowed the last of the claret, then set the glass aside. ''I'll just get my coat.''

Peabody shook her head as Lisbeth tossed a full-length black mink over her bloody silks and swept out between two uniforms with all the panache of a woman heading out to the next heady social engagement.

''Man, it takes all kinds. She drills the guy, then hands us the case on a platter.''

Eve shrugged into her leather jacket, picked up her field kit. Thoughtfully, she used solvent to clean the blood and Seal-It from her hands. The sweepers would finish up, then secure the scene. ''We'll never get her on Murder One. That's just what it was, but I'll lay odds it's pleaded down to Manslaughter within forty-eight hours.''

''Manslaughter?'' Genuinely shocked, Peabody gaped at Eve as they stepped into the tiled elevator for the trip down to the lobby level. "Come on, Dallas. No way."

"Here's the way." Eve looked into Peabody's dark, earnest eyes, studied her square, no-nonsense face under its bowl cut hair and police issue hat. And was nearly sorry to cut into that unswerving belief in the system. "If the drill proves out to be the victim's, she didn't bring a weapon with her. That cuts down on premeditation. Pride's got her now, and a good dose of mad, but after a few hours in a cell—if not before—survival instinct will kick in and she'll lawyer up. She's smart so she'll lawyer smart."

"Yeah, but we've got intent. We've got malice. She just made a statement for the record."

That was the book. As much as Eve believed in the book she knew the pages often became blurred. "And she doesn't have to renege on it, just embellish it. They argued. She was devastated, upset. Maybe he threatened her. In a moment of passion—or possibly fear—she grabbed the drill."

Eve stepped off the elevator, crossed the wide lobby with its pink marble columns and glossy ornamental trees. "Temporary diminished capacity," she continued. "Possibly an argument for self-defense, though it's bullshit. But Branson was about six two, two-twenty, and she's five four, maybe one-fifteen. They could make that work. Then, in shock, she contacts the police immediately. She doesn't attempt to run or to deny what she did. She takes responsibility—which would earn points with a jury if it comes down to it. The PA knows that, so he'll plead it down."

"That really bites."

"She'll do time," Eve said as they stepped outside into a cold as bitter as the scorned lover now in custody. "She'll lose her job, spend a hefty chunk of credits on her lawyer. You take what you can get."

Peabody glanced over at the morgue wagon. "This one should be so easy."

"Lots of times the easy ones have the most angles." Eve smiled a little as she opened the door of her vehicle.

"Cheer up, Peabody. We'll close the case and she won't walk. Sometimes that's as good as it gets."

"It wasn't like she loved him." At Eve's arched brow, Peabody shrugged. "You could tell. She was just pissed because he'd screwed around on her."

"Yeah, so she screwed him—literally. So remember, loyalty counts." The car 'link beeped just as she started the engine. "Dallas."

"Hey, Dallas, hey. It's Ratso."

Eve looked at the ferret-face and beady blue eyes on screen. "I'd never have guessed."

He gave the wheezy inhale that passed for a laugh. "Yeah, right. Yeah. So listen, Dallas, I got something for you. How 'bout you meet me and we'll deal. Okay? Right?"

"I'm heading into Central. I've got business. And my shift's over ten minutes ago, so—"

"I got something for you. Good data. Worth something."

"Yeah, that's what you always say. Don't waste my time, Ratso."

"It's good shit." The blue eyes skittered like marbles in his skinny face. "I can be at The Brew in ten."

"I'll give you five minutes, Ratso. Practice being coherent."

She broke the connection, swung away from the curb and headed downtown.

"I remember him from your files," Peabody commented. "One of your weasels."

"Yeah, and he just did ninety days on a D & D. I got the indecent exposure tossed. Ratso likes to flaunt his personality when he's piss-faced. He's harmless," Eve added. "Mostly full of wind, but every now and again he comes up with some solid data. The Brew's on the way, and Cooke can hold for a bit. Run the serial number on the murder weapon. Let's verify if it belonged to the victim. Then find the next of kin. I'll notify them once Cooke's booked."

The night was clear and cold with a stiff wind snapping

down the urban canyons and chasing most of the foot traffic indoors. The glide-cart vendors held out, shivering in the steam and stink of grilling soydogs, hoping for a few hungry souls hearty enough to brave February's teeth.

The winter of 2059 had been brutally cold, and profits were down.

They left the swank Upper East Side neighborhood with its clear, unbroken sidewalks and uniformed doormen and headed south and west where the streets went narrow and noisy, and the natives moved fast, their eyes on the ground and their fists over their wallets.

Smashed against curbs, the remnants of the last snowfall was soot-gray and ugly. Nasty patches of ice still slicked sidewalks and lay in wait for the unwary. Overhead, a billboard swam with a warm blue sea hemmed by sugar-white sand. The busty blonde frolicking in the waves wore little more than a tan and invited New York to come to the islands and play.

Eve was surprised some winter-crazed commuter hadn't rammed her between those golden, jiggling tits with his sky-scooter.

She entertained herself with thoughts of a couple of days in Roarke's island getaway. Sun, sand and sex, she mused as she negotiated bad-tempered evening traffic. Her husband would be happy to provide all three, and she was nearly ready to suggest it. Another week or two maybe, she decided. After she cleared up some paperwork, finished some court appearances, tied a couple of dangling loose ends.

And, she admitted, felt a little more secure about being away from the job.

She'd lost her badge, and had nearly lost her way too recently for the sting to have faded. Now that she had both back, she wasn't quite ready to set duty aside for a quick bout of indulgence.

By the time she found a parking space on the second level street ramp near The Brew, Peabody had the requested data. "According to the serial numbers, the murder weapon belonged to the victim."

"Then we start off with Murder in the Second," Eve said as they trooped down to the street. "The PA won't waste time trying to prove premeditation."

"But you think she went there to kill him."

"Oh yeah." Eve crossed the sidewalk toward the murky lights of an animated beer mug with dingy foam sliding down the sides.

The Brew specialized in cheap drinks and stale beer nuts. Its clientele ran to grifters down on their luck, low-level office drones and the cut-rate licensed companions who hunted them, and a smatter of hustlers with nothing left to hustle.

The air was stale and over-heated, conversation scattered and secret. Through the smeared light, several gazes slid to Eve, then quickly away.

Even without Peabody's uniform beside her, she whispered cop. They would have recognized it in the way she stood—the long, rangy body alert, the clear brown eyes steady, focused and flat as they took in faces and details.

Only the uninitiated would have seen just a woman with short, somewhat choppily cut brown hair, a lean face with sharp angles and a shallow dent in the chin. Most who patronized The Brew had been around and could smell cop at a dead run in the opposite direction.

She spotted Ratso, his pointy rodent face nearly inside the mug as he sucked back beer. As she walked toward his table, she heard a few chairs scrape shyly away, saw more than one pair of shoulders hunch defensively.

Everyone's guilty of something, she thought, and sent Ratso a fierce bare-toothed smile. "This joint doesn't change, Ratso, and neither do you."

He offered her his wheezy laugh, but his gaze had danced nervously over Peabody's spit-and-polish uniform. "You didn't hafta bring backup, Dallas. Jeez, Dallas, I thought we was pals."

"My pals bathe regular." She jerked her head toward a chair for Peabody, then sat herself. "She's mine," Eve said simply.

"Yeah, I heard you got you a pup to train." He tried

a smile, exposing his distaste for dental hygiene, but Peabody met it with a cool stare. "She's okay, yeah, she's okay since she's yours. I'm yours, too, right, Dallas? Right?"

"Aren't I the lucky one." When the waitress started over, Eve merely flicked her a glance that had her changing directions and leaving them alone. "What have you got for me, Ratso?"

"I got good shit, and I can get more." His unfortunate face split into a grin Eve imagined he thought cagey. "If I had some working credit."

"I don't pay on account. On account of I might not see your ugly face for another six months."

He wheezed again, slurped up beer and sent her a hopeful look out of his tiny, watery eyes. "I deal square with you, Dallas."

"So, start dealing."

"Okay, okay." He leaned forward, curving his skinny little body over what was left in his mug. Eve could see a perfect round circle of scalp, naked as a baby's butt at the crown of his head. It was almost endearing, and certainly more attractive than the greasy strings of paste-colored hair that hung from it. "You know The Fixer, right? Right?"

"Sure." She leaned back a little, not so much to relax but to escape the puffs of her weasel's very distasteful breath. "He still around? Christ, he must be a hundred and fifty."

"Nah, nah, wasn't that old. Ninety-couple maybe, and spry. You bet The Fixer was spry." Ratso nodded enthusiastically and sent those greasy strings bobbing. "Took care of himself. Ate healthy, got regular sex from one of the girls on Avenue B. Said sex kept the mind and body tuned up, you know."

"Tell me about it," Peabody muttered and earned a mild glare from Eve.

"You're giving me past tense here."

Ratso blinked at her. "Huh?"

"Did something happen to The Fixer?"

"Yeah, but wait. I'm getting ahead of things." He dug his skinny fingers into the shallow bowl of sad-looking nuts. Chomped on them with what was left of his teeth as he looked at the ceiling, and pulled his easily scattered thoughts back into line. "About a month ago, I got some . . . I had me a view-screen unit, needed a little work."

Eve's eyebrows lifted under her fringe of bangs. "To cool it off," she said mildly.

He wheezed, slurped. "See, it got sorta dropped, and I took it into Fixer so's he could diddle with it. I mean, the guy's a genius, right? Nothing he can't make work like brand fucking new."

"And it's so clever the way he can change serial numbers."

"Yeah, well." Ratso's smile was nearly sweet. "We got to talking, and The Fixer, he knows how I'm always looking for a little pick-up work. He says how he's got this job going. Big one. Really flush. They got him building timers and remotes and little bugs and shit. Done up some boomers, too."

"He told you he was putting together explosives?"

"Well, we was sorta pals, so yeah, he was telling me. Said how they heard he used to do that kind of shit when he was in the army. And they was paying heavy credits."

"Who was paying?"

"I don't know. Don't think he did either. Said how a couple guys would come to his place, give him a list of stuff and some credits. He'd build the shit, you know? Then he'd call this number they give him, leave a message. Just supposed to say like the products are ready, and the two guys would come back, pick the stuff up and give him the rest of the money."

"What did he figure they wanted with the stuff?"

Ratso lifted his bony shoulders then looked pitifully into his empty mug. Knowing the routine, Eve lifted a finger, turned it down toward Ratso's glass. He brightened immediately.

"Thanks, Dallas. Thanks. Get dry, you know? Get dry talking."

"Then get to the point, Ratso, while you still have some spit in your mouth."

He beamed as the waitress came over to slop urine-colored liquid in his mug. "Okay, okay. So he says how he figures maybe these guys are looking to shake down a bank or jewelry store or something. He's working on some bypass unit for them, and he's clued in that the timers and remotes sets off the boomers he's got going for them. Says maybe they'll want a little guy who knows his way under the street. He'll maybe put in a word for me."

"What are friends for?"

"Yeah, that's it. Then I get a call from him a couple weeks later. He's really wired up, you know? Tells me the deal isn't what he figured. That it's bad shit. Real bad shit. He ain't making any sense. Never heard old Fixer like that. He was real scared. Said something about Arlington, and how he needed to go under awhile. Could he flop with me until he figured out what to do next? So I said sure, hey sure, come on over. But he never did."

"Maybe he went under somewhere else?"

"Yeah, he went under. They fished him outta the river a couple days ago. Jersey side."

"I'm sorry to hear that."

"Yeah." Ratso brooded into his beer. "He was okay, you know? Word I got is somebody cut his tongue right outta his head." He lifted his tiny eyes, fixed them mournfully on Eve. "What kinda person does that shit?"

"It's bad business, Ratso. Bad people. It's not my case," she added. "I can take a look at the file, but there's not a lot I can do."

"They offed him 'cause he figured out what they was gonna do, right? Right?"

"Yeah, I'd say that follows."

"So you gotta figure out what they're gonna do, right? You figure it out, Dallas, then you stop them and take them down for doing The Fixer like that. You're a murder cop, and they murdered him."

"It's not as simple as that. It's not my case," she said

again. "If they fished him out in New Jersey it's not even my damn city. The cops working it aren't likely to take kindly to me horning in on their investigation."

"How much you figure most cops gonna bother with somebody like Fixer?"

She nearly sighed. "There are plenty of cops who'll bother. Plenty who'll work their butt off trying to close the case, Ratso."

"You'll work harder." He said it simply, almost child-like faith in his eyes. And Eve felt her conscience stir restlessly. "And I can find out shit for you. If Fixer talked to me some, he coulda maybe talked to somebody else. He didn't scare easy, you know. He come through the Urban Wars. But he was plenty scared when he called me that night. They didn't do him that way 'cause they was gonna take out a bank."

"Maybe not." But she knew there were some who would gut a tourist for a wrist unit and a pair of air boots. "I'll look into it. I can't promise any more than that. You find out anything that adds to this, you get in touch."

"Yeah, okay. Right." He grinned at her. "You'll find out who did Fixer that way. The other cops, they didn't know about the shit he was into, right? Right? So that's good data I give you."

"Yeah, good enough, Ratso." She rose, dug credits out of her pocket and laid them on the table.

"You want me to run down the file on this floater?" Peabody asked when they stepped back outside.

"Yeah. Tomorrow's soon enough." As they climbed back up to her vehicle, Eve dug her hands into her pockets. "Do a run on Arlington, too. See what buildings, streets, citizens, businesses, that kind of thing have that name. If we find anything we can turn it over to the investigating officer."

"This Fixer, did he weasel for anybody?"

"No." Eve slid behind the wheel. "He hated cops." For a moment, she frowned, drummed her fingers. "Ratso's got a brain the size of a soybean, but he's got Fixer down. He didn't scare easy, and he was greedy.

Kept that shop of his open seven days a week, worked it solo. Rumor was he had his old army-issue blaster under the counter, and a hunting knife. Used to brag he could fillet a man as quick and easy as he could a trout.''

''Sounds like a real fun guy.''

''He was tough and sour and would sooner piss in a cop's eye than look at one. If he wanted out of this deal he was in, it had to be way over the top. Nothing much would've put this old man off.''

''What's that I hear?'' Cocking her head, Peabody cupped a hand at her ear. ''Oh, that must be the sound of you getting sucked in.''

Eve hit the street with a bit more bounce than necessary. ''Shut up, Peabody.''

J. D. Robb is the pseudonym for #1 *New York Times* bestselling author Nora Roberts. Nora Roberts is the first writer to be inducted into the Romance Writers of America Hall of Fame. The author of such novels as *The Reef, Homeport, Inner Harbor,* and *Holiday in Death,* she lives in Maryland.